For Gillie

Praise for Julia Crouch:

'An amalg[...]sion!' Sam Hayes

Julia Crouch is the author of three other internationally published novels: *Cuckoo*, *Every Vow You Break* and *Tarnished*. Before becoming a writer she was a theatre director/playwright and then a graphic/website designer. She lives in Brighton with her husband and three children.

Also by Julia Crouch and available from Headline

Cuckoo
Every Vow You Break
Tarnished

THE LONG FALL

JULIA CROUCH

headline

First published in Great Britain in 2014 by
HEADLINE PUBLISHING GROUP

First published in paperback in 2014 by
HEADLINE PUBLISHING GROUP

1

Cataloguing in Publication Data is available from the British Library

B format ISBN 978 1 4722 0723 4

Typeset in Sabon by Avon DataSet Ltd, Bidford-on-Avon, Warwickshire

Printed and bound in Great Britain by Clays Lts, St Ives plc

Headline's policy is to use papers that are natural, renewable and
recyclable products and made from wood grown in sustainable forests.
The logging and manufacturing processes are expected to conform to the
environmental regulations of the country of origin.

HEADLINE PUBLISHING GROUP
An Hachette UK Company
338 Euston Road
London NW1 3BH

www.headline.co.uk
www.hachette.co.uk

Acknowledgements

Thanks to:

Brian Kellett for information on A&E procedures; Jonathan Ford for brilliant answers to my questions about hedge fund management; Eva Nella and Gabriella Triantafyllis for Greek translations and advice on Athens landmarks; Eri Voulgaraki and everyone at the wonderful Pyrgos Villas, Agios Kirikos, Ikaria, where I stayed on my research trip; Owen and Eva (again) for finding the island for me in the first place; Marya Hornbacher, whose honest memoir *Wasted* helped me understand anorexia; Harvard Student Agencies, whose *Let's Go Europe 1980* was invaluable both then and now; my agent, Simon Trewin at WME, who talks great plot; Ali Hope, my editor at Headline, whose constant encouragement and incisive comments really kicked me into shape – and Emily Kitchin, who I know had a hand in it all as well; my first readers: Tim and Nel, who put up with my hovering and hand-wringing, and finally Joey, who sometimes has to fend for himself while his mum is wrangling in the writing shed.

Anything I have got wrong is my own fault. And, as well as taking a few liberties with the island's geography, I also made up the sculpture in the airport in Ikaria.

Never regret thy fall,
O Icarus of the fearless flight
For the greatest tragedy of them all
Is never to feel the burning light.

Oscar Wilde

FISHERMAN

15 August 1980. Ikaria, Greece.

There were two truly unforgettable days in the life of Giorgos Moraitis. This was the first. The other he wasn't to know for another thirty-three years.

It had been a good morning's fishing, and he had stayed out much longer than usual, racing over the pitching, rolling Meltemi-whipped waves, the wind pushing his little boat far, far out, until his island home was just a line of darker blue on the horizon.

He had a good catch. Mostly *barbounia*, which would please his mother – she could get a good price for them, grilled over charcoal, for the feast of the *Panagia*. He planned to stop by the eastern beach, too, and drop off a couple of fish for the Americans. He liked the tiny girl, the thin one with the pale face and blue eyes. He hoped he would see her again up in the village. But it was hopeless, of course. The tall boy was in love with her. He could see that.

He, Giorgos, didn't stand a chance.

He sighed. He would love to get away from the island, to see the world, meet a girl. The rare presence of foreigners made him long for it even more. But when would he ever get a chance to do that? All his life was duty.

He weighed anchor and started the long, zigzagging journey back to the shore, tacking into the strong offshore wind and using the big cliff above the beach as his navigation point. As he sailed, he thought about the girl and how he could possibly win her away from the tall American. He imagined how her tiny body would feel in his strong, brown, sailor's arms.

As he drew closer, the island began to form into distinct colours and shapes. He changed and changed direction over the spumy waves until he was near enough to make out the gold and blue dome of his village church against the green of the mountainside. It was then that his eye was caught by a movement up on the big cliff.

Holding his hands up to his brow to shield his eyes from the sun, he made out three figures. He couldn't see clearly – they were just dots, like ants, on the big rocks – but he thought it must be the Americans. No villager would be fool enough to be up on the cliff in the midday sun in the howling wind. They seemed to be dancing – playing some sort of game? It was strange to watch. A strange thing to be doing.

Then he realised that what he was watching was very far from a dance. One of the figures rammed into another. The third came in and shoved the first, who staggered towards the edge of the cliff.

Everything seemed to freeze for a second – Giorgos, the sea and the wind included – as the first figure hung, suspended. Then, with a rush, all came back to life, and the figure tumbled through the air to land with a crack that Giorgos swore he could hear, far out as he was on the roaring water. The two remaining figures stood motionless at the cliff edge, then one turned and ran away from the scene, streaming down the grassy top until it was out of sight. A few minutes later, the other followed. All that was left was the cliff, its sharp, high drop, and a tiny fallen speck down on the shore below.

Giorgos changed his tack and angled the prow of his boat towards where the body lay.

PART ONE

BEFORE AND AFTER

EMMA

20 July 1980, 10 a.m. English Channel between Dover and Calais. Ferry.

So, Emma James: the new you begins! You've worked for this. Well done.

<u>List 1</u>
What you'll be leaving behind:
A small town in the north of England.
The whole north of England, in fact.
Clammy attentions suffered as only child of ageing parents.
Stupid Ripon boys (good bloody riddance).
Thatcher's Britain (at least for a short while) with all its mealy minded Me, Me, Me
(and good bloody riddance, too).

<u>List 2</u>
What you have to look forward to:
A new, glamorous life as a grown-up at Cambridge.
Books.

Intelligent discussion.
Writing.
A life as a writer!
Lovers.
Parties.

List 3
The in-between bit:
First time abroad.
First long time alone.
£300 in traveller's cheques.
One month InterRailing around Europe.
Seeing art.
Meeting interesting people.
Cheap alcohol.
Defining yourself away from all the crap in List 1.
Writing every day.
Total freedom.
Total freedom.
Total freedom.
Filling up (at least) the two notebooks you've brought with you.
This being the first.

Yeah!

KATE

2013

The African sun outlines the golden halo of her hair.

The two little girls – whose names she didn't know at the time, but who she had since been told were Mariam and Bintu – smile up at her as she reads to them, the white of their teeth somehow reflecting light at her so that even she could see why she had been described as radiant. She has her right arm round Bintu and the tripartite curlicues of that damn tattoo, visible on the inner part, between wrist and elbow, seem to echo the arrangement of the image's three subjects.

Objectively speaking, it was a beautiful picture. Iconic. Extremely useful. International Charity Image 2013, no less. But Kate felt uncomfortable about the whole thing. She hadn't asked to be the Face of Kindness.

Whatever, though. It had happened, and Sophie the PR consultant said it was wonderful.

So that was why she was sitting there, smiling and nodding, her sweat clogging thick studio make-up, watching her own 'iconic image' on the studio monitor as *Hello UK!* Anchorwoman Sally Marshall reeled off her introduction and Camera Two pointed at her face like a gun.

She squirmed and tried to keep her nails away from her teeth.

The floor manager counted down from ten, silently flicking her fingers for the last five, four, three, two, one, and . . .

As Sally Marshall turned to her interviewee and beamed, she shifted her arm to increase the valley of her cleavage. Was this, Kate found herself wondering, intentional? A weapon in the quest for ratings? Kate was glad she had decided at the last minute to slip a camisole under the V of her own dress. Not that she had much going on down there to worry about, but still.

'Kate Barratt, welcome.'

'Good morning, Sally,' she said, as brightly as she could manage.

Two days earlier, when her nerves had almost led Kate to cancel the interview, Sophie PR emailed her a bulleted briefing list: *Golden Rules for Addressing the Media*. The first was *Always greet your interviewer by name, if possible.*

'That's a *beautiful* image,' Sally Marshall said. 'Tell us the story behind it.'

Kate told her about the girls' school that Martha's Wish had just opened in an impoverished West African country – the charity's thirtieth such project. She reeled off the impressive statistics she had learned by heart: how many girls currently received schooling in that country, the changes the Martha's Wish programme would make to that statistic, and the projected resulting shift in the fortunes of women – and therefore of the whole country – in ten years' time.

'And tell us about the little girls in the photograph,' Sally said, her smile bright, her eyes studiedly concerned.

Kate told the fictional but plausible story Sophie had worked up with her a couple of days ago.

'Well. Mariam and Bintu are both six years old. Were it not for Martha's Wish building our school in their village, they would not have access to education. Mariam says she wants to be a doctor, and Bintu a lawyer. With their schooling guaranteed at least till the age of sixteen, these dreams are no longer unattainable.'

'And I believe the photographer just caught you unawares as you read to them?'

Kate nodded. At least that was wholly true. 'Steve Mitchell documented our field trip last year.'

'That's the top American *Vogue* fashion photographer Steve Mitchell?'

'Um, yes. He donated his time to us.' Kate felt herself reddening as she tried to pick up the thread of her interrupted story. 'And – and this photo was just one in a series which we used for our annual report and website.'

'And it's caused quite a stir, hasn't it?'

'Yes,' Kate said and, for a moment, there was a pause. She had broken Sophie's second Golden Rule: *Don't give one-word answers*. But she didn't want to sound as if she were trumpeting.

'What happened?' Sally leaned forward and smiled, attempting to raise her Botox-thwarted eyebrows.

Kate had no choice: she had to go for it. 'Well, it was picked up by social media, where it became the most shared worldwide image of the year. And now it's won International Charity Image 2013 . . .'

'Which is why you're here today!'

'More than that,' Kate said, keen to move on from what she considered to be a point of vanity, 'the recognition has done wonders for Martha's Wish. Donations have soared compared to last year, and we're planning to dramatically increase our activity—'

She stopped mid-sentence, appalled to see her own talking head replaced on the monitor by a film of her and Mark in their finery stepping out of a taxi and onto a red carpet leading up to a Mayfair hotel. How on earth had the TV people got hold of that?

'Now,' Sally said over the film, 'this is you and your husband, the hedge fund manager Mark Barratt at a Martha's Wish gala dinner last year.'

She made it sound as if all they ever did was hold gala dinners. Kate watched herself on the film, tiny and tense beside the formal solidity of Mark, who led her through the door of the hotel with his habitual air of being in a hurry to get the thing over and done with. The gala dinner had been Sophie PR's idea, and, like the African photograph, it had raised a great deal of money.

'And I understand that you and Mark give a major annual donation to the charity,' Sally went on, as the film cut to an ageing rock star, renowned for his humanitarian work, stepping from a limousine onto the same carpet. Sophie had managed to get him on board because she did yoga in Primrose Hill with his new wife.

'We do,' Kate said, glad that her visible discomfort at all this flaunting was not on camera.

'Whaddaya know?' Sally said, winking into Camera One as she replaced the gala dinner on the broadcast monitor. 'A banker with a heart!'

Kate winced.

'And tell me,' Sally said, turning again to face Kate, her voice serious once more, 'what's the story behind Martha's Wish? That's an interesting name.'

Kate's eyes flicked to the monitor to check that her thick pancake of foundation hid the flush that had spread to her cheeks. She thought she had made it quite clear when the producer had visited her while they were trowelling it on in hair and make-up that she didn't want to talk about this.

And now they had sprung it on her on live national breakfast TV.

Fighting the urge to run away, she closed her eyes and breathed. She tried to keep it factual.

'Martha was our daughter. She loved reading, and one of her favourite books was called *Children of the World*, in which children from different countries talk about their lives. She was shocked that in some parts of the world girls weren't expected to go to school. She said that when she grew up, she wanted to make sure that every girl in the world had a school place.'

She stopped and swallowed. The damn tears were stabbing at her eyes. It was no doubt TV gold, but she hadn't asked to be part of it. The studio felt hot, stifling, and she was aware of the sour smell of something electrical near to burning point.

Sally nodded sympathetically and reached across the vast red studio sofa, placing a hand on her knee.

'But you lost poor Martha, didn't you, Kate?' she said, her eyes glistening like a crocodile's.

Kate slipped her hand inside her tailored jacket pocket and rubbed the pebble she had found long ago at *Gwel an Mor*, the beachside house she and Mark owned in Cornwall. It was a holey stone, supposed to ward off evil spirits, and she carried it with her always, in case of emergencies.

With enormous self-control she nodded, remembering Sophie's third Golden Rule: *If you argue or appear flinty, you will only harm your cause.* Flinty was an understatement, though. At that moment, Kate felt murderous.

'Martha died of an inoperable brain tumour. She was eight.'

13

'I'm so sorry,' Sally said, as if it were somehow her own personal tragedy.

When she set up the charity, Kate had still been unmoored by Martha's death. If she hadn't been, she might have thought it through and called it something else. Mark had even suggested as much at the time. But she had wanted her girl to live on forever, and the charity's promise of lasting goodness was an enormous comfort.

And back then, how was she, the grieving mother, to predict the moment when she would be called upon to explain? Or how she would feel about doing so? There was a brief outline of the story on the Martha's Wish website. That should be enough for the world.

But no. It seemed like every last drop of pathos had to be wrung from her.

She told herself she had to do it, because of the girls like Mariam and Bintu who, without her dancing on a wire for them, would face that potently life-shortening combination of being poor, illiterate and having too many children, too young.

It wasn't really too much to ask, given all that, was it? She needed to put herself aside. She should feel churlish for having allowed Sally's questioning to stir up such rage.

'It's beautiful,' Sally went on, 'that Martha lives on.'

Kate nodded, blinking, examining her red, raw hands. It was. It was beautiful.

'Let's have another look at the photograph,' Sally said, and, on the monitor, the image of the two of them on the studio sofa was replaced by that of Kate and the two girls.

'The Face of Kindness,' Sally cooed.

The picture was one of the rare shots of Kate that did her justice. In it, she looked at least a decade younger than her fifty years, and the golden light that surrounded her softened the sharp edges she knew she possessed after a lifetime of being too thin. Her beauty, which she had often heard about but never believed, was plain for all to see in this shot. There was nothing to suggest that she was anything other than a kind, wonderful, warm and loving person.

Of course, the image had its detractors, keen to troll anonymously on countless websites. Her paleness next to the black girls was a symbol of white Western imperialism, some said: of a certain patronising philanthropy. But, she would have argued, had she been able to see her opponents face to face, what alternatives were there? She put surplus wealth to good purpose, and the photograph had galvanised that process.

If that's what it took, then so be it. Amendments had to be made.

And with that thought, her stomach contracted.

Had she lived, Martha would be fifteen. And Kate would have given anything in the world – she would have gone out to West Africa and knocked all the schools they had built down – to have her back.

That was also part of what she understood to be her sharp edges.

But it was only a small piece of the story. There was something far, far worse: Kate knew that she was utterly responsible for the death of her daughter. Through what she had done, she had brought it on them all.

EMMA

23 July 1980, 1 a.m. Somewhere south of Paris. Train.

So much for writing every day . . . Oops!!! If you want to be a proper writer, Emma, you should at least make the effort on this, your big adventure.

Just to note, so I don't forget:

Great time in Paris – Louvre, Notre Dame (including the amazing Sainte-Chapelle with its stained glass), The Orangerie, Jeu de Paume and Musée Rodin. Lived on crêpes bought in the street, and cheap wine – 3F50 a bottle!

Let's Go Europe says sleeping in Paris is a waste of time and money. But I need my zzzzz, so stayed in a crowded hostel full of the first Americans I have ever come across not in a film. Met up with a group of girls from Washington State (which is different from Washington D.C. Whaaat?), who told me about when Mount St Helen's erupted in May. One of them (Lori) talked about her dad driving them all away from their home as fast as he could, with the windscreen wipers going, washing off all the ash.

Most evenings I tripped around with the American gals 'riding the Metro', as they put it. Smells funny, the Metro, like perfume, cake and sewage all mixed up. And you can buy sweets and stuff from these machines they have on the platforms.

We 'hung out' outside the Centre Georges Pompidou, smoking, drinking wine, talking, eating baguettes and Camembert. Must have put on about half a stone while I was with them. I'm bloated with all the bread I've been allowing myself to eat. Must take care. Must eat more healthily/less.

Met a band from Brighton. They were busking on the concourse there and made loads of money. Said I'd get in touch once I got back!

How cool is that? Nothing like that happens in Ripon.

Read *Tess of the D'Urbervilles* in my down time. Poor girl.

Anyway, heading south now, where I hope it's a bit warmer.

Must sleep.

23 July 1980, 1 p.m. Marseille. Restaurant on the Quai de Rive Neuve.

I'm going to try to be more descriptive with this. Paris bit was too brief. So:

This morning I stepped off the train at Gare St Charles and into the hot, herby air. It's a different world to Paris. My preconceptions of this city – from reading about it in *Let's Go* – didn't do it justice. I saw it as a dirty urban sprawl, possibly quite Arabic in influence. In fact, it feels more how I'd imagine Italy to be, although it's quite clean compared to English cities. And, despite the *Mistral*, which shoots along the alleyways blowing dust into your eyes, the light here is sparkling. You can see why the Impressionists all came down to the South.

Oh, I've got to record the old woman sitting next to me on the train. She was incredibly well dressed in what looked like a Chanel suit. Her face was caked in powder and she was drenched in some sophisticated perfume. I was practising my French on her, telling her about my university plans, and she seemed to be very *gentille*, very *sympa*.

But then, as we pass through the suburbs of Marseille, past a forest of tower blocks, she purses her bright red lips and says – as if she has some sour taste in her mouth – 'That's where *les Arabes* live.' She then goes on to tell me that *les Arabes* are parasites in France and that they should all go back to Algeria with their primitive habits!

I watch her as she's talking and I realise that under all that finery and paint I'm looking at an ugly animal.

Luckily we only had another ten minutes before we hit the station, or I would have moved seats. I've never seen such hate in anyone. Never.

Picked up a map from the tourist office at the station and headed off with rucksack to the youth hostel. *Let's Go* said it's about an hour's walk, but I must have got lost, because it took me nearly two . . .

It's a beautiful, big old chateau with a cavernous living and dining area that must have once been a ballroom, but which now echoes to the sound of Jimi Hendrix being played very loudly by Hans, the German bum who is the warden. He wears nothing but a pair of tight little shorts and ends each sentence with 'for example'. Don't know how much of him I'll be able to take.

There doesn't seem to be anyone else staying there except a group of very jolly German boys I passed on my way out who I suppose are a bit older than me, so it looks like I've got the girls' dorm all to myself! It's like having a massive, very cheap (four francs a night) hotel room. A real treat after being crammed into the place in Paris.

Dumped my stuff and headed off down to town. Hans drew me a map showing me how to get to the bus stop. I've walked so much that my poor old feet didn't want to make the journey all the way back into town. Blisters on my blisters, etc.

Got off the bus at the top of La Canabière – or, as the old sailors used to call it, the Can o'Beer (thanks, *Let's Go*) – and strolled down to the port.

There're loads of leery old men around, and they make these little clicking sounds as I go past. I'm beginning to find it quite annoying, worse than builders' wolf whistles back home.

Then when I was wandering through the old town (*Le Panier*, a warren of little narrow alleyways and tiny shops), a man jostled past me and took a left just up ahead of me. As I passed the turning, I glanced down it and saw that he was just around the corner, leering at me, with his hand working away at his very stiff, very exposed, willy!!!!

I was so shocked, I laughed out loud. Don't think that was the reaction he was hoping for . . .

What was he thinking? That I'd be turned on? Or scared? To be honest, I just think he was pathetic. He was at least as old as my dad. It's disgusting.

Anyway, thankfully, a group of older women were coming up the alley towards me, hauling baskets full of vegetables and talking in thick accents that I couldn't make head nor tail of, despite my French A level. At the sound of their voices, the man scuttled away.

Must make sure to keep on busier streets in future.

It's annoying, though. If I were a boy, that wouldn't have happened, would it?

Anyway, apart from the wanker, Marseille is amazing. I'm writing this sitting in a great little bar on the waterfront, smoking roll-ups and drinking a beer. So long as I concentrate on writing this, I don't get interrupted.

Perhaps some of the FOUR men who have tried to talk to me since I sat here were just being genuinely friendly. If so, I'm missing out: it would be nice to talk to someone. But I can't help suspecting they were all slimeballs.

So how do I meet people? Where are the young women? The only ones I see are with other people and don't seem at all interested in meeting me. So perhaps I should go up to a boy and say hello. I have to remember that the whole point of travelling on my own like this is to be open to new people, new experiences. I made the decision to come here, and I am going to make it work, whatever happens.

But it's scary. If I do go up to someone, what if he thinks I'm trying it on?

Again, can't help thinking it would be different if I were a boy. Think of John Steinbeck, Jack Kerouac, the Durrells. Does the fact that I'm a girl stand in the way of having those sorts of adventures?

Rang home today. Yes. I am a little bit homesick. Never thought I'd miss my parents – couldn't wait to get away from them.

But anyone I meet now is just part of a sea of passing faces: people passing me by. We travellers – and I think I can call myself that now – are blasé about saying goodbye. We do it every day to people and to places. I doubt, e.g., if I'll ever see those girls from Washington State again. Shouldn't imagine also that I'll ever sit in this spot again in my entire life.

It's strange: life's a collection of experiences; the end of each one is a little death.

Sigh. That's depressing. Wonder if I'm really cut out for travelling on my own? Still, it's only for a month.

Tan's coming on. Freckles all over my nose. Halfway through *The Bostonians*. A bit long-winded.

Going to have bouillabaisse later – the local fish soup, with a sort of chilli mayonnaise on the top. Sounds interesting – a far cry from Mum's shepherd's pie-type English grub.

I'm discovering the world, and the world's discovering me! I'm going to take great care to try different sorts of food and eat well and healthily and regularly. I feel fat right now, but I have to remember what Doc Norman said: six stone, even for someone as short-arse as me, is underweight by normal standards.

I know she's right, but, really, who wants normal standards?

KATE

2013

'You were seriously good, though,' Mark said as he and Kate sat in the restaurant, a glass of champagne each, waiting for Tilly who was, as usual, running late. 'If I hadn't known you'd be uncomfortable I'd hardly have guessed.'

'Though you are somewhat biased.'

Mark held up his hands. 'Not a bit of it.'

Dinner out was in honour of Kate's TV appearance that morning. She would far rather have gone home and either cooked something or got a takeaway: once out in a day was more than enough, as far as she was concerned. But, wanting to treat her, Mark had booked a restaurant that was close enough to his office for him to be able to cycle back for a late call he had with some challenging American clients.

On the plus side, she said to herself as she got ready to go out, it would be a treat to see him on a weekday evening. He had always worked late, but in the past year or so, it had become rare for him to get home before midnight. She didn't mind. Being on call at the helm of capitalism was, after all, how he made all their money. It was why they could live their lives in the way they chose, why she could give much of her spare time – and a chunk of their spare cash – to Martha's Wish.

No. She never, ever complained about his work. Martha aside – and, admittedly, that was quite a sizeable aside – she was aware that she could only count her blessings. Considering.

She sat back and cast an eye around the room. If a restaurant could be a person, this one would be Mark. Tucked away in Bankside behind the Tate Modern, it was one of his favourite places for bringing clients. The ambience was exactly him – expensively understated, shades of taupe, clean lines, not too much of anything. Jil Sander as opposed to Versace.

It had taken Kate a long time to pick up these codes from him, but now she had it as if she had been born to it. She knew which artists to admire, the right designers to wear. Even though she used it only rarely, she had the perfect car – an Audi cabriolet. Her clothes were simply, beautifully cut, her jewellery – most of which had been bought for her by Mark – was pared-down, clean-lined and surprisingly expensive for such simple-looking stuff.

It hadn't always been like this. Along with her accent, her buying habits had been quite consciously modified.

'Oysters?' Mark asked. 'While we wait for madam to turn up?'

Kate nodded. She had even brought herself to enjoy what she used to think tasted of nothing but ozone-infused snot. Of course, the fact that they contained virtually no calories helped.

The waiter placed a platter of ice, West Mersea rock oysters, Tabasco and shallot vinegar on their table and they scooped and sipped. Piano music – Kate identified it as Glenn Gould playing Bach Partitas – played at an almost subliminal level and the lighting was low, but not too low.

She glanced at their fellow diners, who blended almost imperceptibly with the decor, tinting the generous space between tables with the murmur of smiled conversation. The kind of place where wealthy married couples ate, this wasn't where one would bring one's lover. Or one's adversary, come to that. Nor, Kate thought as she watched Tilly dash across the floor to join them, should one really bring one's daughter. Completely changing the energy in the room, Tilly looked entirely out of place, all holey matt black tights, Doc Martens, tartan ski jacket and striped minidress.

'Jeez, I'm sorry.' She flopped onto the empty chair at their table. 'Tyrone spilled this massive cake on the floor and I couldn't let him clean it up on his own.'

'So I see.' Mark licked his thumb, reached over and wiped a blob of crusted, dried-on icing from her cheek. It was a curiously maternal gesture. But then, for a hard-working hedge fund manager, when it came to his daughter he could be a curiously maternal man.

'Oh fuck. Have I been going around all day with stuff on my face?' Tilly draped the back of her hand across her forehead and leaned away in a dramatic fashion. 'The shame.'

While there was no perceptible change in the attitudes of their fellow diners, it was clear that Tilly had been noticed.

She really was too vibrant for the place.

'Hey, guess what?' Tilly abruptly leaned forward, and wiggled her elbows onto the table. 'The famous vegan soap star Sally Peters had mystery meat pasty *again* today.'

'No,' Kate said in mock shock.

In her gap year, Tilly was working at the National Theatre staff canteen, serving, as she put it, 'chips to the people with the jobs I want'. As well as free theatre tickets and cheap meals, the other perk of her job was keeping abreast of the eating habits of the stars. Only the day before she had told Kate of a famous film star, renowned for her slender beauty, who consumed only bacon butties and full-fat cola.

Mark poured Tilly a glass of champagne. 'Here's to your mother,' he said. 'For a great performance on *Hello UK!*'

'We all watched it just before breakfast service,' Tilly said, raising her glass then knocking back the whole lot in one. 'Tyrone and Maria clapped after you'd done. Maria crossed herself and said, "Your mudda is a saint".'

'I'm hardly that.'

'"She look like de angel of de lord!"' Tilly waved her hands in the air, continuing her impression of Maria, who hailed from one of the West African countries where Martha's Wish built schools, and whose continuous Christian pronouncements were a great source of amusement to all the other canteen staff. '"Praise de lord for your angel mudda",' Tilly went on.

'Self-censorship, Tills,' Mark said sternly, his eyes pointedly flicking to their most immediate neighbours, who were clearly earwigging what was going on. Although Kate was sure that Tilly wasn't consciously displaying casual racism – it was just an accurate impersonation of an extreme character in her life – to an outsider it would look just like that.

Feeling her old friend shame stalking around her, Kate tried a couple of deep breaths. Her heart rate was up and she needed to seize control before it got out of hand.

'Well, here's to you, Mum, anyhow, and to Martha's Wish.' Tilly reached over for the champagne bottle and refilled her glass.

'It's all good for Martha's Wish, that's for sure,' Kate said.

'Amen to that.' Mark polished off the last oyster. 'Now, having kept us waiting for nearly half an hour, can you decide what you're going to have, Tilly? I don't know about you, but

I'm starving, oysters are hardly filling, and I have precisely one hour in which to eat.'

Tilly fell silent and stared at the menu, twirling a blond curl around her finger, her eyes lowered behind mascara-smudged lashes. She was so present, so assured, so alive. She so reminded Kate of herself at eighteen, sometimes frighteningly so.

Finally, Tilly looked up. 'I'll have the steak frites with Roquefort sauce.'

Kate smiled. The one major difference between her daughter and her younger self was that Tilly had grown up with such a robust appetite. A source of great pride, this was one less box for her to tick on the guilt list she lugged around in her heart.

The waiter took their orders, then brought the Barolo Mark had picked out, pouring while the family sat in silence. After he left, Kate sat back and took in the moment. They were all there, the people she loved. She didn't need to do her habitual family head count. The evidence was in front of her. Those who remained were all safe, all well, all accounted for.

'I've got an announcement to make,' Tilly said, and both Mark and Kate looked at her with raised eyebrows. When she had their full attention, she went on, 'I've finally decided what I'm going to do with all the vast reserves of cash I've stockpiled from the chips job.'

Even though they were able to hand Tilly money whenever she needed it, Kate and Mark saw it as vital that their privileged daughter learned its value. They had sent her to a very good private girls' day school – state schools in South London being, in Mark's view, out of the question – but Kate considered it an important part of her education to realise that there were other, less lucky people in the world. It was because of this that she had taken her along on the West African field trip that resulted in the Face of Kindness photograph. And, for the past two

Christmases, Tilly had arranged, off her own bat, to help serve dinners at a homeless shelter.

In October, she was going to Bristol University to read drama. Mark had wanted her to do English at his old college at Oxford, whereas she had been set on drama school. The final plan was a compromise that had taken Kate a lot of work to broker between the two of them. Until she went up to university, the deal was that Tilly could live at home in Battersea for free, but any extras would have to be saved up for from her earnings. Rather impressively, she had applied herself to putting aside every spare penny. The last time Kate had asked, she had stashed over two thousand pounds.

'So then, what's it to be?' Kate said, bracing herself.

'I'm going travelling.'

It was as Kate had feared. 'What?'

'I'm orf to Greece,' she said, her arms out as if she were taking a bow at the Royal Shakespeare Company.

Kate gasped. '*What?*'

'I'm going to Greece,' Tilly said again, frowning at her mother's extreme reaction. 'And then I'll slowly work my way back up north.'

'But *why?*' Kate said, and Tilly looked at her as if she were mad.

The waiter arrived and seemed to take an age to put their plates down in front of them.

'What on earth do you want to go travelling for?' Kate said as soon as he had left. Suddenly her goat's cheese soufflé didn't look as appetising as it had on the menu, and her damn heart was racing again, knocking against her ribcage, almost deafening her. She reached in her pocket and touched the stone with the hole in it.

'Where do I start? OK. I want to see more of the world. It's not like you've exactly treated me to the most exotic holidays. Cornwall, Cornwall and Cornwall.'

'And New York and West Africa,' Mark said. 'You're in danger of sounding a bit spoiled.'

Tilly snorted. 'Come on, Dad. A family visit and a Martha's Wish field trip. Don't really count as holidays, do they? Thanks to you being always busy at work and Mum's issues with planes, I was the least travelled girl in my class.'

'*Touché*,' Mark said, holding up his hands.

'Why to *Greece* of all places?' Kate said.

'I want to visit the birthplace of The Drama,' Tilly said, oblivious to the well-disguised unravelling of her mother next to her. 'I want to see the skene, the parados, the Orchestra. And, um, let's see.' She counted the reasons off on her fingers, which Kate noticed were almost as chapped and raw-looking as her own and wondered if she was provided with washing-up gloves at work. 'Cradle of civilisation? Sandy beaches? Beautiful countryside? Warm and welcoming people? Blue, blue, blue, blue sea?'

'Greece *is* jolly nice, Kate,' Mark said. 'And Tilly's a big, sensible girl now. We've got to let her go one day.'

It was all right for him. His experience of the country was utterly benign, consisting solely of two weeks in Corfu as a fifteen-year-old, staying with a school friend whose family owned a vast estate on the north-east shore. He remembered it as *My Family and Other Animals* with gorgeous Italian girls thrown in.

But for Kate it was the most inauspicious place in the world. A place that had pulled her towards it along a path of misery, and then completely derailed her life. She didn't want her daughter to go travelling, and, call her superstitious, but she certainly didn't want her anywhere near Greece. It would be tempting fate.

Kate realised she was stroking the side of her nose, the place that she knew could often end up raw and red if she didn't watch what she was doing.

'It's very different these days, as you well know,' she told Mark, forcing her hand down and trying a more reasoned tactic. 'I saw this documentary. Athens is seething with feral dogs and drug addicts. There are riots; people set fire to themselves in front of the parliament building. It's a desperate place.'

'Don't believe everything you read in the papers,' Tilly said. 'And in any case, that's just Athens, Mum.' She rolled her eyes. She was used, after all, to having an overprotective mother, and had learned through the years to bear this burden of the surviving sibling with good humour. 'You remember Ilona, the Greek girl from school, right? She's working front of house at the National at the moment and she says it's nowhere near as bad as they make out on the news, even in Athens. And it's great on the islands – people are so glad to see tourists, and everything's super cheap, so I'll be able to stay a really long time.'

'Tuck in, Kate,' Mark said. He and Tilly had made good headway with their meals, but Kate had yet to start her food.

She looked at her plate, fork poised but stilled.

'Look, if you're worried about Tilly in Athens,' Mark said, glancing at something that had flashed up on his iPhone, 'I'll make sure she stays somewhere nice, in a safer part of town.'

Tilly shook her head, making her skull-shaped earrings clatter as she did so. 'Thanks, Dad. But I've already booked a hostel online. I'm doing this on my own.'

'Already booked?' Kate said. Her voice squeaked. To try to disguise her panic, she slipped a tiny piece of the soufflé between her lips. The salty, rich taste nearly made her gag.

Tilly turned to face her. 'Mum. Calm down. It's all sorted. I'm flying out on the tenth of April.'

'But that's two weeks' time! Why didn't you tell me earlier?'

'Two and a half. And I didn't tell you because I knew you'd kick off like this. Look: it's been a shit spring so far. I want to find some sunshine. I'll be staying a week in Athens, then I'll travel around and play it by ear.'

'How long will you be gone?'

'I'm aiming to be back in September.'

'You can't last six months on two thousand pounds!' Kate said, her voice rising another octave.

'Chill pill, Mum! I'll just have to earn some money while I'm out there then, won't I? I'll pick up some bar work or pick tomatoes or something.'

'And take the jobs from Greek people who really need them?' Kate said. She looked to Mark, who was busy keying something into his iPhone, chewing his lip. He had a lot of American clients, so evenings tended to be very busy. He was not available, at any rate, to give her any kind of support.

'It might not be Greece, though. I'm planning to wend my way back up through Europe as the weather gets warmer. Croatia, Italy, France.'

'France!' Kate's hand went to her chest.

'Yes, France. Heading west to Marseille and then up.'

Speechless, Kate cut her soufflé into tiny pieces.

'I don't know what your problem is, Kate,' Mark said, finally surfacing from his screen. 'At least it's only Europe. At least she's not heading off to bloody Cambodia or Ghana or something.'

'I'd hoped that if you had to go away, you'd go and stay with Uncle Julian in Brooklyn again,' Kate said to Tilly. 'He was looking forward to taking you to all the Broadway shows.'

She glanced at Mark, whose lips had almost imperceptibly pursed at the mention of his brother. Like many men raised in boarding schools, he had enormous difficulty with the notion of homosexuality, connecting it only with the abuse that had been meted out to him by the older boys. His opera singer brother's coming out was therefore a source of submerged personal conflict for him. It had been far simpler for their father – he had simply cut Julian out of his life and will.

'Muuum,' Tilly said, sighing, her good nature nearly exhausted. 'Two grand is hardly going to last me ten minutes in New York. And really, I want to have adventures on my own, not go and stay with my dad's nice cosy brother.'

'On your own?' Kate said, dropping her fork. Despite the comfortable ambient temperature of the restaurant, she could feel a sweat breaking out at the base of her spine. 'You're going *on your own?*'

'People do travel on their own, you know. I've thought it all through. I'm going to be like Orwell, or Laurie Lee, or Hemingway or Byron – stepping out there to meet the world. If you're on your own, you're freer, more open to new experience.'

'But they're all men, Tills,' Kate said, reaching out to grasp her daughter's hand, to give her one of the few pieces of wisdom she had picked up on her own travels that she dared share with her. 'It's different for men.'

'Mother!' Tilly tried to defuse the tension building between them by putting her other hand to her chest like a character in a Restoration drama. 'I'm shocked to hear that coming from a woman of the twenty-first century!'

'And those men were writing a long time ago. It's a much more dangerous world these days.'

'Yep, we haven't got the Somme, the Napoleonic Wars, the Spanish Civil War . . .'

'You know what I mean.' Kate wiped her free hand across her forehead. The conversation was making her feel quite dizzy – as if everything were spiralling out of her control, like when Martha was ill, or before, when—

She shook her head to dispel the thought.

'But you've hardly been anywhere on your own, darling,' she said, holding her daughter's hand as if she were a balloon in danger of floating away. She tried to sound reasonable. 'Not outside London.'

Mark looked up again from his iPhone. 'All the more reason for her to give it a go.'

Kate looked at him aghast. He should be taking her side, shouldn't he? Did he *want* Tilly to go away?

'Yes. And I'm eighteen now,' Tilly chipped in. 'I could join the army now if I wanted.'

'But you don't want to do that, right?' Kate said quickly.

Tilly and Mark looked at each other, then burst into laughter.

'Look,' Tilly said, when she and her father had finally regained their composure. She touched Kate's shoulder, as if she were the mother appeasing the daughter. 'Didn't you want to have adventures when you were my age?'

Feeling bones tense beneath her fingers, Tilly instantly withdrew her hand and put it over her mouth. 'Sorry,' she said, as the air around their table seemed to drop in temperature.

Kate narrowed her eyes at her. 'I didn't have the luxury,' she said, quietly. 'Did I?'

'Sorry,' Tilly said again, closing her eyes.

'Excuse me.' Aware that she might be going to pass out, Kate bent to pick up her handbag.

'Are you all right?' Mark asked, touching her arm as she shakily got up.

She breathed out then smiled at him as if she were steady as a rock. 'I'm fine. I just need the loo.'

She hurried across the dining room and got down the stairs to the toilets as quickly as she could manage without creating a stir.

And when she was there, she knelt over the toilet, stuck her finger down her throat and allowed herself the comfort of throwing up all the very little she had eaten.

EMMA

Today is the worst day of my life.

Something worse than anything I ever thought would happen to me has happened.

To me. The bright girl with the brilliant future.

To me. The fucking stupid girl.

I'm on my own in the youth hostel girls' dorm. The laughter of Hans the warden and the German boys in the big hall downstairs jumbles with the Jimi Hendrix, echoing up the stone stairs and travelling down the corridors to tangle in my ears.

They bought wine and cooked up some *moules* and invited me to eat with them.

But I can't.

I don't know what to do.

I don't know what to do.

I don't know what to do.

I can't believe it really.

To make sure it actually happened, I'm going to write it all down, even though it's going to hurt, every detail I can remember.

* * *

33

So, after my late lunch and a stretch out on the beach, I get the bus back up from town and take the pretty, grassy footpath that runs from the bus stop to the youth hostel, between the high stone wall of the old chateau and the high metal-fenced boundary of another large property. It's quiet, late afternoon, still light. The wind has dropped and the sky sings with blue.

I'm happy.

I was happy.

A thickset man is up about a hundred yards ahead of me, walking in the same direction. I think nothing of it. I only even frown slightly when he reaches the end of the path, turns and starts walking back towards me.

I think perhaps he's forgotten something. As he gets closer, I notice he's got sunglasses on and this red cotton scarf tied around the lower part of his face, like a cowboy. I look away, keep moving. But I wrap the strap of my day bag around my hand, ready to swipe if I need to.

Even then I think I'm being stupid. I still have the chance to turn and run, but I don't do it.

You see, I thought at the time that it would have been insulting. I had to give him the benefit of the doubt. Just because he was a thickset man with a scarf over his face didn't necessarily mean he was going to be a danger to me.

But.

Just as I'm moving over to the side of the narrow lane to make space for him to pass, he grabs me. He's strong, and at least three times my size. I try to swing at him with my bag, but he just catches it in his big fist. He looks at me, his eyes full of hate.

Why *hate*?

But it chills me, tells me I'm in trouble.

Please, I say in French. Please.

Putain, he says.

He seizes my shoulders and forces me to the ground. I try to push him away, but he's too much for me.

He shoves me against the bottom of the drystone wall, pulls up my top and rips away my underwear.

It was so easy to get at me. I was wearing my jeans skirt and a vest top.

But it was hot. What was I supposed to wear?

Please, I say again. I'm a virgin. *Je suis vierge*.

I am.

I was.

There wasn't a boy worth it in Ripon.

And now look what's gone and happened.

What a waste.

He jams his hand over my mouth, forcing my head back over a stone. Just a little push further and he'll break my neck. Then, with a great shove, so *quickly*, he breaks into me and, just for a second, it feels as if my soul is forced out of my body.

It's fast, brutal, short.

It hurts so much. In every possible way.

I try to imagine I'm somewhere else. Still on the town beach I lay on after lunch, drinking in the sunshine. I strain to hear the kiss of the waves on the shore, instead of the slapping of his fat belly against my bare chest while he humps and grunts and shoves, one arm supporting his upper body on my ribs while the other pins my hands above my head, nearly snapping my bones.

* * *

The worst is the smell of him. Even after the shower I took when I got back here, it still sticks in my nostrils – old wine, Gauloises, stale sweat like old garlic. Something of fish.

Then, somewhere – oh hope! – I hear a siren. A police car, I think, come to save me. It's getting closer.

It puts him off. Swearing, he pulls his filthy dick out of me, then suddenly, shockingly, brings his knee up sharply between my legs. I think I scream, but all that comes out is a hiss of exhaled shock. Then, standing over me, he quickly kicks me hard in my stomach. Just to cap off the pain and the insult and the humiliation.

Putain.

He pulls off his scarf and spits on my face, big glob of hot, rancid gob.

The siren is so loud, for a moment that's all there is. But then it moves away, it's going past the end of the alley. It's not stopping, it's off to save someone else, somewhere else.

This is it, then, I think. I'm not saved. He'll kill me now.

Or worse.

I lie still, eyes shut, prepared to die.

But nothing happens.

Like a bad dream, he's gone.

I wait there as long as it takes for my soul and my body to find each other again. Squashed into the angle between the wall and the foot-path, I watch the sun filter through the waving grasses above me. A line of poetry repeats over and over in my brain like some sort of madness, *Glory be to God for dappled things* – Gerard Manley Hopkins, 'Pied Beauty'. I learned it off by heart for my A Level.

I don't know how long I stayed there, but at some point I was finally able to pick myself up. I pulled out my scarf and wrapped it round my shoulders to cover the grazes and cuts and gouges in my flesh. Somehow, I got myself back to the youth hostel, where Hans the warden and the German boys greeted me as if nothing had happened, because, of course, for them that was how it was.

I managed to smile and say a few inane words while I picked up my rucksack from the luggage store. I excused myself, saying I didn't feel too well, that I thought I'd eaten some bad fish at lunch. Perhaps it was because the light's poor in the big hall, but they didn't notice my knees and legs, which were cut and bloody. It saved me some awkward questions, anyway.

I scrubbed at myself under the scalding shower until I was raw. I wanted to sluice him away, wash him down the squatting toilet at the end of the cubicle, which, disgustingly, serves as a drain for the shower.

But still I feel dirty.

I don't think I'll ever be rid of him.

It hurts so much everywhere. After my shower I looked between my legs with my make-up mirror, angling it so it caught the light. I've never done that before, so I've nothing to go on, but I look as sore as I feel.

A right bloody mess.

Soiled.

How dare he do this to me?

The worst thing, though, is that I let it happen to me.

I was stupid.

I'm a young woman on her own and I take a little footpath shortcut when I could have walked the long way round on the safe main road.

I was moronic to be wearing just a little skirt and a vest top, even though it's one of the hottest days of an early summer heat wave.

I was an idiot not to turn back when I saw him walking towards me from the other end of the alleyway.

It's all my fault.

I don't know what to do.

KATE

2013

'Want to watch TV with me?' Kate called up to Tilly's bedroom from the kitchen as a kind of a peace offering. But there was no reply.

Mark had returned to his office and his American clients, promising to be back by midnight. Mother and daughter endured a tense taxi ride back from the restaurant, Tilly making no effort to conceal her frustration with what Kate knew looked like an irrational and clinging objection to her travel plans.

If only she could tell her daughter what had happened to her: how Greece had turned what was – because of France – already a terrible episode in her life into a complete, all-consuming nightmare.

She tried to tell herself that her fears were completely irrational, that the same things weren't going to happen to Tilly. That, precisely because they *had* happened to her, like lightning striking twice they were statistically less likely to happen to her daughter.

But it didn't wash.

* * *

38

Trying not to enjoy the comforting emptiness that followed a good vomit, Kate opened a bottle of red, poured herself a large glass, and called upstairs again. But Tilly probably couldn't hear her above the music she was playing, which was clearly audible two floors away.

She was a strange bird, Kate thought, preferring Greece to New York, liking Sondheim instead of whatever it was other young people listened to. Not like Kate had been, back when she was a teenager, troubling her elderly parents at all hours with the Clash, the Police, and The Damned.

She could picture Tilly now, lying on her big, red, velvet sledge of a bed, reading and letting the music swirl around her. Even if she wasn't going to come down, it was good to know she was so close.

She picked up the bottle and glass, padded across the surgically clean glossy white floor of the vast, open-plan living space and turned on the TV, aiming to find something easy and mindless to take her brain away from what she had already tagged Tilly's Bombshell.

The whole business reminded Kate of when, shortly after Martha had been taken away from them, Tilly had gone crazy over animals and started begging for a cat. It seemed that the more Kate argued that her own allergies rendered owning anything other than a hamster out of the question, the more her daughter claimed she needed one. In the same way Tilly had chosen, of all the nations in the world, the three places which, were allergies to countries a possibility, would have made her mother very ill indeed.

France and Italy would make breathing difficult, but, bad as they were, they were mere staging posts on the way to anaphylactic-shock-inducing Greece, scene of the most terrible thing Kate had ever done.

If only she could tell Tilly. But it was out of the question.

As the TV came to life, Kate was confronted by the reverse of the brain massage she was seeking: that damn Face of Kindness image, this time framing an item on *Newsnight* about girls and schooling in West Africa. No doubt this was Sophie's work, to 'keep up the momentum'.

Kate passed her hand over her eyes. She had consented to do only one TV interview to coincide with the photo winning the prize. Initially, she had felt guilty about her reticence to parade herself everywhere, but relief now far outweighed all that.

Nevertheless, something niggled inside her: a sense of things falling out of her control. She had never intended to become what the newsreader was describing on the voiceover to the image as the *founder* and *figurehead* of Martha's Wish. She had only ever wanted to balance out the bad she had done in the world with a little good, working behind the scenes and turning the awful (Martha's death) into the wonderful (schools for girls). But Sophie said she was needed to add personality to the brand.

'Like Bob Geldof and Band Aid,' she had said.

After a discussion about the merits or otherwise of the photograph – including a coruscating contribution from a professor at the School of Oriental and African Studies, a striking young woman with beaded plaits tied up in a Kente cloth, who accused Kate of being little else than a twenty-first-century imperial invader – the programme moved on to an item about a polar bear in a provincial zoo who was displaying bipolar disorder symptoms. Kate flicked off the volume, stretched out on the vast sofa, hugged a cushion to herself, and settled back for the next item: footage of bloody riots in one of the West African countries where Martha's Wish was building schools for girls.

She watched a young man being pushed over, his head being stamped on by a soldier who couldn't have been much older than fourteen. The camera lingered, for just one second, on the blood pooling around the man on the ground's hair, then it jolted up again to rejoin the fray.

The world was such a dangerous place. Couldn't Tilly just be satisfied with staying in her velvet room with her books and her Sondheim?

Kate closed her eyes.

EMMA

26 July 1980, 1 p.m. Somewhere between Marseille and Nice. Train.

I've escaped.

I'm done with France.

It's been three days and I haven't felt like writing. So, along with my body and brain, that bastard's fucked that up for me as well.

I'm not going to let him win, though. So here are my words.

Thought seriously about going home and forgetting all about this travelling on my own bollocks. But I can't. Not after all the talking I did, all the arguing with Mum and Dad that I'd be safe, and I could look after myself and all of that, all of the telling of my plans to people at school and watching their astonished faces when I said I was going on my own . . .

I've only been away six days, and look what's happened.

I couldn't do it. I couldn't go back and face all the questions and the told you so's.

No. Going back now would be admitting defeat on every level.

I'M NOT GOING TO LET HIM WIN.

* * *

In fact, now I'm on the move I feel I can almost actually breathe again.

So yah boo sucks, attacker.

Perhaps I can even use it all later? When I'm a proper writer.

Spun out the sickness story at the Marseille youth hostel. I hardly moved – partly because every part of me hurt, partly because not a bit of me wanted to. The German boys brought me some bread and soup, but I couldn't face eating.

Some Dutch girls arrived yesterday and took over my dormitory. They talked too loudly around me, asking me questions, laughing.

I could see them making faces at each other about me. I don't blame them. All they got from me were grunts and monosyllables. I only wanted to sleep, but they were making it impossible. So, this morning, I packed my rucksack, drew my strength around myself and set off for the train station.

I stuck to main roads, and kept my wits about me. Kept on thinking I saw him, of course. Twice I had to cross the road because I thought a man was following me. I could feel eyes slide over me, read their minds, smell their thoughts.

I felt naked, even in my jeans and T-shirt. And my blondeness marked me out. Along with the fact that I'm small and only eighteen, it made me an easy target.

So as I walked I got an idea. When poor Tess of the D'Urbervilles is cast out by Angel Clare and wandering the countryside looking for work, she gets round the problem of creepy men by putting on an old dress, tying a handkerchief round her face and snipping her eyebrows off. So, instead of attacking her, the next passing slimeball jeers and calls her a 'mommet of a maid'.

Like Tess, I could deal with that.

It was a plan.

Dipped into a supermarket and bought some dark brown hair dye.

A little further along the road to the station, I stopped at a clothes shop with shirts and cotton skirts pegged up outside, slapping in the wind. There, in among all the glitter and purple and leopard print was the perfect garment: an oversized black T-shirt dress that would come halfway down my calves.

Twenty francs, it cost. A whole day's budget, but it was worth it.

Had a couple of hours to kill at the railway station before my train to Milan. *Let's Go* says there's a shower in the ladies' toilets. So, for two further francs, I was able to put my new look together.

I'm in there a long time – the dye takes forty minutes to set. At one point the suspicious, beady-eyed old lady on duty bangs loudly on the door and asks if *tout va bien avec Mademoiselle*.

'*Oui, oui,*' I say, trying to sound as carefree as possible.

It's the first time I've showered since the night it happened, and there's a full-length mirror in the cubicle. I'm shocked by my bruises – an odd, blue stain starts around my navel and blooms up to my ribs and down to my hip bones. That's where he kicked me.

Then, turning round, I see the scratches, grazes and more bruises where I'd been shoved up against the flinty wall. I'm particularly raw where my pelvis meets the skin of my back. That's what makes it so uncomfortable to sit, or lie down.

It'll get better, though.

I'll get better.

So, finally, I rinse the dye off and look at a new, dark brown-haired me. Then, without really thinking what I'm doing, I get my nail scissors and start chopping at my hair, sticking my fingers into it, pulling it away and cutting it all about two inches away from my scalp.

The old lady bang-bangs on the door again.

'*Mademoiselle?*'

'*Presque fini, madame,*' I say. '*Juste dix minutes.*'

I suppose she was worried I was committing suicide or something. Well, I wouldn't do that. Wouldn't give him the satisfaction.

I hear her harrumphing away back to her station.

When I finish, I look at myself in the mirror. I've given myself Sid Vicious hair. I look like some sort of punk. I look like a stranger.

It's good.

I put on my new T-shirt shroud and wind my red and white PLO scarf around my head – like Tess's handkerchief. Decide against getting rid of my eyebrows, though.

Scoop up my shorn hair and stuff it in the supermarket carrier along with the dye box, and try (unsuccessfully) to clean the brown dye stains off the tiles (Madame can't have been too pleased when she saw them). Then I bundle out and politely thank her before scarpering into the bustling railway station where, thankfully, my train's waiting at the platform.

It feels good having hair like this, like I'm not trying to please anyone. With sunglasses, I'm almost completely hidden. I'm also so odd-looking, people have been giving me a wide berth. It's like a security blanket.

Walked down the train corridor until I found a compartment with a woman in it. Even better than that, she's a nun! Perhaps she thinks I look so weird that she doesn't dare answer my questions, but she doesn't seem to speak French or English. So I'm hoping she's an Italian nun. If she is, and if she's travelling to Italy, I'm sticking with her.

Nothing can happen to me with a nun in my carriage, surely?

26 July 1980, 4 p.m. Italy. Train.

Screw you, France.

Just done the final train change at Ventimiglia. I've stuck by my nun through both. We've managed to communicate a little through sign language and she's offered me some chocolate (which I refused), but mostly she just sits with her eyes closed, fingering her rosary and muttering to herself, unaware that she's guarding me.

It must be great to be a nun. Such a simple life.

Under her disapproving gaze, I've had two beers from the buffet car. Again blowing my daily budget, but I like the muzziness it threads around me. Before I had the beer, I felt like I had ants crawling around the base of my neck. Now I don't. The magic of alcohol.

Tried to read, but can't concentrate. Though I can write now. I feel like writing and writing, writing it all out. What's that about?

I'm always thinking of what I should have said or done after something difficult happens. I play it over in my mind, with me being bolder, firmer, stronger than I was at the time. Speaking up for myself.

So this is what I think:

I was stupid to let the thing happen to me in the first place – I should have read the signs, pre-empted the attack, turned and run, not been so naïve in the first place to think that I could just travel around on my own and not be attacked.

I was even stupider in the way I dealt with it afterwards. I should have got the group of nice German boys to go and find my attacker. I should have told the police, so he wouldn't do it again to some other poor girl.

I know all this now – though at the time I was in shock. All I wanted to do was hide in my bed.

I'm still numb now. I couldn't tell anyone about it. I couldn't. Wonder if I ever will? I just want to hold the awfulness inside myself until it dissolves.

But if I'd gone to the police, and if they'd believed me – which is doubtful – it would've meant having to give up on my big adventure. It would all have gone public, Mum and Dad would have found out – and I couldn't bear that – and the story could even have followed me to Cambridge.

'Oh, Emma James? She's the girl who got raped in France.'

No, thank you.

I'm not going to let him make me suffer any more than he has already.

I'm going to call him The French Shit. It feels useful to define him in some way. It might stop me thinking every man's going to hurt me.

Got to stop thinking about this. It's like each time I think about it, it happens all over again.

Mind fucks.

26 July 1980, 10 p.m. Milan. Pensione Lulli.

Arrived in the early evening, just before it got dark. Said goodbye to my nun. Another little death. Bones aching from bruises and sitting so long on trains.

To save money after an expensive couple of days, toyed with the idea of staying put in the station for the night. But the whole place was full of sketchy men, all – despite my new look – leering at me. Decided not to risk it.

Sat at a café, rolled a cig, ordered a beer and looked at *Let's Go*. Thought about camping, since I've lugged the tent here in my rucksack. But the campsite's miles away, and I don't really think I'm ever going to be able to sleep soundly with just a thin bit of canvas between me and the world. Not any more.

The creeps are really determined here. While I was flicking through my guidebook, two men sat at the spare chair at my table (not at the same time, thank God) and tried to talk to me. I ignored both of them and tried to appear to be absorbed in reading. The first gave up quickly, but the second seemed to be insulted that I wasn't bowled over by his charm. He stuck his face between me and my page and rattled off some nasty-sounding Italian. His breath stank of brandy.

I hated the anger in him. It reminded me too much of The French Shit. I wanted to stand up and scream at him or take my book and bat him out of my sight, hurt him. Instead, my cheeks burning, I just angled my body away from him. Thankfully, there were a lot of people around, so nothing too awful could have happened. Eventually he gave up, and, after one final slurred round of swearing, he left.

But I was chilled by his attitude.

And no one stepped in to help me.

Unable to sit there any longer, I paid for my beer then found a little shop where I bought a bottle of red wine and a packet of Drum. At the last minute I picked up two oranges as a gesture towards nutrition.

Ignoring *Let's Go*'s warning that while they might be cheap, they were also bleak (I was beyond caring: I just wanted to sleep) I went for one of the seedy little hotels lining the streets around the station. The barely alive crone at the desk charged me a thousand lire for a small single (sounds a lot, but it's only about seventy pence). So here I am, smoking and drinking and scribbling in a grubby little room with a sick-makingly filthy toilet across the corridor and paper-thin walls, through which I can hear the thumps, grunts and groans of a couple having sex.

It sounds better than my own experience, but only just.

When I got here, there was a pubic hair on my bed pillow, which I removed with a bit of tissue. A cockroach still squats at the top of the wall above me. I hope he doesn't jump. It's one in the morning and people are still thundering up and down the corridor, talking loudly, laughing and shouting. I'm cold and alone.

But at least there's a lock on the door. And at least I'm a bit drunk.

Still can't read anything but *Let's Go*. Wish I could.

KATE

2013

'Kate.'

She opened her eyes to see Mark looking down at her. He was home at last from his call with his American clients. She squinted at her watch. It was one in the morning.

'Oops. Must've dropped off.'

'Well, that's unusual,' Mark said, raising an eyebrow. It wasn't, of course, and he knew it. 'Drink? Or have you had enough?'

'Cup of chamomile would be nice.'

Mark crossed over to the kitchen and put the kettle on, crashing around in the cupboard for a mug. She could tell by the set of his shoulders – immaculately straight in his sharp dark blue suit – that he was tense, irked about something.

'How were the Americans?' she asked, sitting up slowly. She adjusted her hair, which she knew would be sticking out at angles, then she arranged the cushion – which she had still been hugging when she fell asleep – neatly behind her, hiding her glass underneath the sofa. Mark hated coming home to disorder. She wasn't a great fan of it herself.

'Not great.' Mark poured himself a generous measure of single malt. 'The Corbetti Fund is looking decidedly dodgy. Dallas is not happy.'

'Oh no.'

Kate had no idea what Mark did at work, other than invest for clients, using his innate charm and an extraordinary ability to work money. Even when she had been his secretary at the big investment bank before they married and he left to set up his hedge fund, she never really understood what all the financial stuff was about, or why it was so important. Her role had been to deal with the soft side – arranging meetings, making sure Mark knew the names of clients' children and wives, that sort of thing. Although she knew she had the intellect to grasp the bigger picture, she entirely lacked the motivation.

But she liked to show him that she was on his side.

Mark set her tea on the low table in front of her, and almost fell back onto the sofa, bringing with him the vetiver notes of the scent he had specially made for him by an Italian count in his Florentine perfumery.

She moved round to face him, watching as he cradled his glass, warming the whisky with the palms of his hands. He had dark circles under his eyes and his skin, tanned from a recent skiing trip – with clients, of course, Mark never did just pure recreation – looked sallow in the pool of light from the lamp hanging just above them.

'Poor you.' Kate picked up her mug and took a sip of tea. Its grassy cleanliness chased away the stale taste of wine that had set in her mouth and furred up the back of her teeth.

'Tomorrow's another day.' Mark ran his fingers through his short, silver hair, which she knew felt like velvet, and leaned back into the sofa, a little apart from her.

She reached out and threaded her fingers through his. He

held her hand tightly, as if she were somehow grounding him, when, in fact, the normal dynamic in their twenty-five-year marriage was the reverse. She felt grateful that he occasionally let the balance swing like that.

'It's been a good day for you, though,' he said.

Kate nodded. 'Great for Martha's Wish.'

Mark was nothing if not supportive of the charity. He had been delighted when, a year after Martha's death, Kate had told him about her plans. She suspected he was even rather relieved. He had seen how bad things had got for her when there was too much silence.

'It'll be cathartic for you,' he had said.

He didn't know the half of it, though.

His theory was that Kate blamed herself for Martha's death. She had put the fact that her youngest daughter was falling over a lot down to her having grown so quickly that she didn't know where she ended and the world began. By the time she got round to taking Martha to the doctor, the tumour was inoperable and the cancer had spread to her lungs, kidneys, liver.

And yes, she did take on the guilt for that. But what he didn't know was the deeper, karmic, sins-of-the-mother reasoning that Kate applied to Martha's death. Because of the unthinkable thing she had done before she even met Mark, it had, in her view, been entirely inevitable. She had no right whatsoever to a happy motherhood.

So the chance to do good through the charity went far beyond Mark's notion of catharsis. It was an atonement. Partial, but enough – Kate hoped – to buy the continuing health and happiness of her remaining daughter.

Mark had even provided her with twenty thousand pounds to seed the project. This was a symbolic gesture because he had always said the generous sums of money flowing from his business into the household were as much hers as his. Every account they owned was in joint names, and from there Kate was charged with the financial management, siphoning cash off into savings accounts and other schemes, paying bills and doing all the purchasing for the running of the household. She had no idea what proportion of his earnings he kept to reinvest in his own business, but she knew it was so vast that it made the sum he entrusted to her mere pocket money in his eyes: not worth bothering about at all. As far as she knew, he had never even glanced at one of their personal bank statements.

But, even so, Kate found Mark's financial vote of confidence in Martha's Wish very welcome – a sort of permission. So she got the website and logo professionally designed and employed a manager to come in and set the ball rolling in an office that Mark had persuaded one of his key investors to provide by way of a tax break.

This benevolence was just one of the ways he cared for her. It was his thing: Mark looked after Kate. He was her protector. She was certain that her tiny, youthful waifishness and consciously constructed helplessness was what drew him to her in the first place, and she had held on to all of that except the youthful part.

'I didn't much care for being on the television, though,' Kate said, squeezing his hand. She didn't like the idea of her day outshining his.

'I couldn't tell.'

She nudged his arm. 'You just want a high-profile charity wife like your New York chums, don't you?'

He smiled.

'Making your stint at the helm of capitalism more palatable for the public.' She put her arms together to force a cleavage and assumed an overly concerned stare. '"Whaddaya know, a banker with a heart."' It was a passable imitation of Sally Marshall.

He looked round at her and smiled, trying, a little unconvincingly, to be a sport.

He seemed so weary tonight. She leaned over and kissed his cheek which, underneath the day's-end stubble, was still firm at fifty-four. In the past couple of years he had graduated smoothly from handsome devil to silver fox. He'd told her that recently a matron in Miami airport had insisted he was George Clooney; she wouldn't take no for an answer.

But even in all this goodness, in the past year or so she had begun to sense that he was holding something back, as if, all the time he was with her, he was silently counting in his head.

She put these doubts down to her constant conviction that she did not deserve a single piece of the good fortune her marriage to him had brought her.

It was almost as if she was expecting it all to come to an end.

She laid her head on his chest, wishing that she could read the Morse code of his heartbeat. Hooking the index finger of her free hand, she surreptitiously rubbed the knuckle against the tip of her nose, knowing she was reddening it further.

There was always make-up, though. Concealer.

His arm moved around her shoulders, and he brought his hand to rest on her breast.

'Let's go to bed,' he said, his voice hoarse with whisky and something else.

EMMA

27 July 1980, early hours. Milan. Pensione Lulli.

OK, at about three in the morning – I'm not sure exactly, because I forgot to wind up my watch – I'm woken by people hammering on my door, shouting for someone called Maria. About three different voices, all male, all Italian, laughing and cooing at first, trying to coax this Maria out of what they suppose is her room.

Which is, in fact, my room.

I don't dare say anything in my young, lone, female voice. I just lie there, heart thudding, praying for them to go away.

Perhaps learning to sound like a man would be a useful project.

My silence gets to them. Thinking Maria's playing hard to get, they raise their voices and rattle the door so much the key falls out onto the tiled floor. Scared they might be able to somehow reach it through the gap at the bottom of the door, I tiptoe across the room to pick it up. But because I've drunk all the wine, because the room's dark, and because I forgot that when I get up and move, my bruises and aching muscles really, really hurt, I stumble into a wooden chair. Hearing the screech as it shunts across the floor, the men outside shout more, banging on the door so much I'm sure it's going to cave in.

I fish my Swiss Army penknife out of my rucksack and open it. I've never used a knife before, of course, and I don't know what I would do if I had to, so, in a panic, I have a practice with one of my oranges.

While the men keep banging, I stab and stab at the orange until it's a pulp. I use my sheet to wipe the sticky juice from my hands, then crouch on this hard, musty bed, gripping my knife, ready to spring when the door finally gives way.

I'm fierce now. I won't ever let myself be attacked again.

A woman's voice echoes into the corridor from one of the other rooms: '*Basta!*' She follows up with a torrent of something that sounds like a major Italian bollocking. The male voices die down, dropping to whispers.

Then there's nothing.

I've no idea what happened. Did they go away? Or were they still there, just waiting outside my room until, thinking they had gone, I went outside to meet my doom?

I lay there in the new silence, trying to still my beating heart and unclench my jaw. But I couldn't. I didn't get another wink of sleep.

And now it's morning, and I'm desperate for a pee, but I daren't go out into the corridor to the toilet. For all I know, those men are still there, waiting for me.

Should I just leave Italy? Mum told me to be careful here – she had her bottom pinched in Rome, on her one trip abroad. If those men last night and the dodgy types I saw yesterday in the station are anything to go by, she's got a point.

Still, not quite as bad (so far) as the France experience.

But if I go now, I'm going to miss out on Leonardo's *Last Supper* here in Milan. And Florence, too. I've ached to go there: the Uffizi, the San Marco Fra Angelicos, Michelangelo's *David*. One of my main reasons for being here is to see them in the flesh. I've written essays about them for art history, for fuck's sake.

Am I going to take the risk, though?

I don't think I can face these big, strange, noisy cities.

Not on my own, at any rate.

All the noise, and the people. I need silence. A bit of peace.

Is it me? Do I attract this sort of trouble?

27 July 1980, 2 p.m. Milan. Central Station bar.

When the midday heat made it seem as if the hotel-room walls were moving in on me, I decided it was time to make a move. My bag packed, I listened at the door for a long time until I was sure there was no one there. Then, with my penknife at the ready, I looked out into the corridor.

Of course, there was nothing there but a couple of dust-balls and something that looked like a piece of dried-up animal shit, but which could also have been a large dead insect.

After an argument with the old bag at the desk – I'd originally booked in for three nights, and she seemed to want paying for all of them, which there was no way I was doing – I managed to check out.

Italy has not been a good time.

Not as bad as France, but it could have been even worse if it hadn't been for that woman shouting at the men in the corridor.

I'm shaking now, just thinking about it.

Crossed the road back to the railway station. Seemed so much friendlier in daylight, but Milan's already lost me.

Dizzy from no food – I've got one surviving orange, but my heart just isn't in it – I've set myself up in this bar. I'm nearly floating from emptiness, but it feels quite good. I'm edgy, more alive, like I'm in control of at least one thing. I've got a half-litre of beer in front of me and now I'm sitting with this notebook and *Let's Go*, trying to work out what to do.

- Stay in Italy?
- Leave?
- Where to?
- Athens? (*Let's Go* says Greece is safer for women)
- Or head north where the men are better behaved?
- Berlin? I'd like to go to Berlin. But I want to lie on a beach again, like my beach of escape in my head when The French Shit was on me.
- There are no beaches in Berlin.

So Greece it is, then. Athens. Stay in the city as long as I can bear it, a couple of days seeing the sights to get at least some culture, then fuck off and find a lovely island with no tourists and just some sweet locals who will welcome me for what I am. Not as it seems to be here and in Marseille as a CUNT ON LEGS.

I'm shocked. Never in a million years would I have thought that being a girl on your own would be so difficult. Perhaps it was going to a girls' grammar school, where our (women) teachers told us that we were equal to boys in every way. I thought the whole world was like that, that the feminism Miss Higgs banged on about in English had nothing to do with me, because the world had changed, and we've got Patti Smith and Poly Styrene and old Thatch is running the country with her handbag.

But I was wrong.

Shudder.

KATE

Kate and Mark lay on their enormous white bed, the full moon silvering their bodies through the glass atrium some thirty feet above them. He was asleep, she wasn't.

For the first time in over two months, he had wanted her. Perhaps it had been the stress at work that had kept him at bay.

He undressed her and laid her back on the pillows and performed what she had led him to believe were all the right moves, until she went through the motions of the orgasm she had not once ever experienced from another person.

He was a considerate lover, though. Only after she had duped him did he allow himself his own release. And then, as usual, he fell instantly asleep. Coming was better than Temazepam, he once said.

She wouldn't know. Her post-coital mood was more one of lying on her back, touching her bones, turning some thoughts over, stopping others from penetrating her consciousness, until she relented and took a pill.

* * *

'I'm not happy about Tilly going travelling,' she found herself saying out loud.

'Hmmm?' Mark stirred.

'I'm not happy about Tilly going away.'

Mark lifted his head, a slight frown crossing his face. 'I thought we'd covered all that in the restaurant?' He tried to conceal it, but she could hear a tetchiness in his voice.

Kate sighed, swung her legs out of bed and fetched a fresh cotton nightdress from her dressing room. Unlike Mark, who never wore pyjamas, she preferred not to sleep naked.

'I know what your problem is,' he said as she rejoined him.

For a second she wobbled. She lay next to him and drew the duvet over herself.

Did he?

Did he really?

She turned her head to look at him. He was such a beautiful man. Beautiful, but inscrutable.

'I know it's hard for you,' he said, turning his face to her, catching her eye. 'Your only child fleeing the nest.'

She's not my only child, Kate screamed in her head.

Mark had a policy of not referring to Martha any more. It was as if to him the name was nothing more than part of the title of the charity.

'But Tilly's a sensible girl,' he went on. 'And you've got to allow her to spread her wings.'

'I know all that.' Kate sighed. She couldn't possibly explain what really lay behind her reluctance. Not to Mark, not any more. The time for that – if there ever had been one – had passed long ago. And anyway, the kernel of her objection to the travelling plan – especially the Greek bit – was so illogical that, even if he knew all the shocking facts of it, he would still be hard-pressed to understand it.

She didn't have a leg to stand on.

'Look. We'll tell her that it's not going to be all about lying on beaches and drinking retsina. She's got to get to know the country as well, visit some ancient sites, get a sense of the history and culture.'

'Oh, she's already set on that. Didn't you hear her in the restaurant?'

'So what's the problem? You could even nip out and visit her at some point, perhaps on an island. Get an authentic Greek experience. Bit of sun, sand and blue sea. Kick back your heels a little.' He propped himself up on his elbow and looked at her. 'Kate?'

Without realising it, she had curled up into a small ball.

'What is it?' he asked. 'Is it the thought of flying? You could have more hypnotism like you did for Africa.'

'It's not that. It's nothing.' She forced herself to breathe, her eyes tight shut against him.

'For God's sake, Kate. You've got to let her grow up some time.'

'Yes.' Her voice was tinier even than she felt.

'And you've got to sort yourself out, too.'

Not this again. Kate wished she could stick her fingers in her ears.

'Get out, get in touch with some friends,' Mark went on. 'Or you're going to be awfully sad and alone when she's gone. And that's too much of a burden to place on Tilly's shoulders.'

'I know.'

'And mine.'

'Yes.'

He lay down, facing away from her.

'Mark?' she said, reaching out to touch him.

'Look, love. I need to sleep. I've got to be in for a six a.m. conference call with Tokyo.'

'Sorry.'

Eventually, his breathing became slow and even, and the tell-tale gentle snore started at the back of his throat. Kate watched the moon-etched shadows of the atrium edge across the sweep of white-carpeted bedroom floor, marking the passage of her sleepless night, and the thoughts she tried to keep at bay seeped in, until she was inundated.

EMMA

31 July 1980, 3 p.m. Athens. OTE office, Patission St.

I've been here for ages, waiting for the phone-office people to place a reverse charge call to my parents. The room is cavernous, brown with dust and stinky with stale sweat. It's hot, hot, hot and I feel so weak I can hardly hold my pen.

My body still aches and I'm sweating into the cuts and grazes from when The French Shit pushed me up against that wall. Also, I now have about a million mosquito bites and a good few of them are sore and infected.

I've been here for half an hour already, holding a ticket with 347 on it. Every now and then, a board clicks to a new set of numbers, but they don't seem to be in any sort of order. Mine hasn't come up yet – unless I've missed it. Like everything else here, the system is chaotic. The fact that, even with English, French and a little German, I don't even understand the basic roots of the language doesn't help, nor that the alphabet is all over the place. Ps for Rs, indeed.

It was a LONG train ride to get here. Two days and two-and-a-bit nights in the corner of a crowded eight-seater compartment on the slowest train in the universe, which seemed to stop at every village on the way. Yugoslavia is one endless, big, dusty, hot country and, from the look of the people getting on and off the train, it's extremely poor. With my bruises, bites and blisters and the way I'm feeling increasingly spaced-out, subtracted from the world around me, it was a surreal and uncomfortable ride.

At least I could read again. I've given up on Henry James, though. I don't think I'll ever return to *The Bostonians* – not just because it is a bit of a slog, but also because I'll always associate it with The French Shit. So I read *The Tin Drum* (weird book) and then Thomas Mann. I'd rather read about death in Venice than tempt fate and run the risk of experiencing it with a visit. But it was disappointing. I know it's supposed to be beautiful and about Dionysus and Apollo and all that, but I can't view it as anything but the story of an old creep now.

That's how I view the world now. A place full of old creeps.

Ugh.

I suppose one good thing is that, as I haven't had periods now for two years, there's no danger of me being pregnant. Can you imagine the horror?

Yesterday I stood in the corridor outside my compartment and hung my head out of the train window to watch Athens approach like a slate-grey cloud shimmering in the hazy plain. There's a heatwave at the moment – it's been the hottest July ever recorded, according to the guy at the desk in the Peta Inn, where I'm staying on the roof for about twenty-five pence a night.

The pollution here is frightening – you can literally see the yellowy haze as you walk along the pavement, and every street seems to be choked with cars, engines revving, horns blasting. I've been here just one night, and already my skin's coated with a grimy layer of dust.

The upside of looking like a filthy old tramp is that with the dirt, the black shroud dress thing (which I've worn for days now) and my Sid Vicious hair, I've only had a few 'tsk tsks' from a couple of men. Most seem happy to ignore me and carry on drinking beer, flinging their worry beads around and staring at passers-by.

But, horrors, I thought I saw The French Shit today. A man walking ahead of me could have been him. He, too, suddenly stopped, turned and walked back towards me. I felt a sharp shock, prickling pins and needles all over my face. My feet wanted to run away, my hands wanted to attack him, to claw the flesh from his face.

The violence I feel towards him shocks me.

But I was on a crowded street and nothing happened. And anyway, of course, it wasn't him. I'm thousands of miles away from him. All this man wanted was to go into the *kafeneion* I had just passed.

I've got to pull myself together. I can't let him get the better of me like this.

It doesn't feel like Europe here. It's more like how I imagine Asia might be. The men seem to be more polite, less like they think they can do whatever they like with you. And today I saw a ferocious old woman telling off a group of noisy young men. Looks like they're kept in order here.

My bed is a grey-stained mattress on the top of a metal bunk bed crammed with ten others out on the roof of the hostel. If I wanted, I could reach out and hold the hand of the boy sleeping in the bunk next to mine (I don't want, though). He's called Mick, and he's an acid-casualty Australian of about twenty-five, whose beard and hair cover his entire face. But he's quite nice. I don't think he's a threat. Even so, because it's a mixed dorm, I keep my Swiss Army knife open and ready under my day bag, which I use as a pillow.

I was tempted to up the nightly fee to fifty pence and take a bed in a room downstairs (which would still be mixed), but the guy at the desk – Dimitri – said it was better on the roof – cooler and more airy. And it never rains, he says. I can believe that. Everything is parched here, and filthy. Piss just dries to stinky stains on the pavement. Dog turds look like they might crumble.

And it *is* cooler up here at night. But as soon as the sun is up – which is about six in the morning – you start sweating; by seven it's impossible to stay in your sleeping bag any more. And there's nowhere to go to cool down, or even to get any air.

Shit. So, after two hours, my call got placed. But there was no bloody answer. My parents were out. Where the fuck did they go? They never go out.

I need to talk to them. Not to tell them – just to hear their voices. Don't they know that?

Emma James: all alone in a big, scary world.

KATE

2013

'Hiya,' Tilly said, coming up behind Kate, who was hovering on the threshold of Martha's bedroom, deciding what she was going to say.

With her own space too full of her own mess – jumbled piles of clean and dirty clothes, used cotton-wool balls, bathwater-crinkled magazines – Tilly had been using her sister's bed to sort out her packing for her fast-encroaching trip. Despite her more sensible conscious mind telling her not to be so stupid, Kate couldn't bat away the gut reaction that this was a desecration of her dead daughter's room.

But it was something of a consolation to see that Tilly had adopted her own method of packing: laying all one might need neatly on a bed, then gradually editing. Although Kate rarely went abroad – a fear of flying meant that the African field trip for Martha's Wish was the only time she had done so in decades – she always used the technique to pack for Mark's business trips. Had she any women friends, she would have hesitated to admit it in front of them, but she took enormous pleasure in getting his beautiful shirts pressed into tissue for travel, making sure his Italian leather washbag was well-stocked, ensuring he had the right number of clean socks and underwear, with an extra pair of each just for luck.

That, and looking after the house and the family were the least she could do, given the second stab at life he had unwittingly granted her.

Even so, irritation at Tilly thrummed inside her, curdling the non-fat yoghurt that had been her lunch. Seeing her dead daughter's space taken over like that – even by her living offspring – hit her in the stomach like a woodcutter's axe. Particularly because, laid out on the bed like some photograph of a soldier's kit in an army recruitment booklet, were the tools Tilly was amassing for what – again, despite her rational self – Kate couldn't help seeing as her defection.

Tilly would know all this, of course, so when she came up behind her mother in the doorway, she tried to win her round with a remorselessly bouncing enthusiasm.

'Look,' she said, steering Kate into the room that recently, on separate occasions, both she and Mark had respectively accused her of preserving in aspic and amber.

Kate's shoulders stiffened. There had always been an un-spoken rule that nothing must be touched here, that the books that Martha had alphabetised in their shelves would remain untouched except for their quarterly dusting, that the drawers would retain their neatly folded and arranged contents, that the pink sheepskin throw would remain smoothed down on the bed where she died under home hospice care.

It had been eight years now, and of course Kate had found a place for her loss, had housed it so that she could carry on living. But still sometimes, like a deeply lodged piece of shrapnel shifting and tearing flesh, the unbearable fact of it would come back to visit her.

Kate saw the preservation of this room as a sticking plaster for those moments. It proved to her that her youngest daughter had existed, that she had been a force in this world.

Little Martha had been the tidy one; the one who took after Kate in that respect – although Kate had never been entirely sure which of her own personality traits were inherent and which she had adopted as a means of survival.

'It's not as if we need the space,' she had once argued to Mark when he broached the subject of, as he put it, 'repurposing' Martha's bedroom.

'It could be a yoga room for you,' he said.

'But I've got the mezzanine. And it's on the girls' floor.'

'Well, a living room, then, for Tills.'

'I don't want her living in a different room to us.'

He had looked exasperated. But he would never win.

So, as Kate surveyed the piles of going-away gear on the bed, she wondered if Tilly's rule-flouting might even be a tactic, agreed between father and daughter. Some sort of cod-therapeutic strategy to force her past what they saw as her tardy inability to surrender the room to the present.

But Kate thought she had done very well, considering, what with the charity and everything. Wasn't she entitled to this one indulgence, this shrine to her daughter?

Tilly brushed brightly past her and threw her a slim, olive-green package from the bed. 'One point five kilos,' she said. 'Fast and easy to pitch, with exceptional wind-resistance should I get caught up in the Meltemi or the Mistral.'

Meltemi. Mistral.

Kate turned the tiny tent over in her hand, marvelling despite herself at its lightness. 'You've thought of everything.'

'And look at this.' Tilly tossed over what Kate took to be a pouched-up cagoule. 'Ultra-compact sleeping bag.'

Kate gave it a squeeze. 'Very nice. Tents and sleeping bags used to take up half a rucksack.'

'Like you'd know,' Tilly snorted, rolling her eyes.

'What does that mean?'

'You "didn't have the luxury" of going off backpacking, did you?'

Kate looked at her daughter, who had just – knowingly, perhaps – tested the limit of her sense of humour. She didn't know how to react. Should she upbraid her privileged daughter for mocking her unlucky upbringing story where her parents were taken in a car crash when she was seventeen, leaving her to fend for herself?

But, seeing Tilly stand there, looking as if she wished she could unsay what she had just let out, Kate didn't have the heart.

And could she *really* tell her daughter off for poking fun at something she thought was true but which, in fact, was a dog-old lie?

No.

'What's this?' Kate said instead, picking up a packet of pills from the bed. The writing was too small for her to read without her glasses.

Pills and Greece. The idea – or memory, rather – gave her a dun feeling in the pit of her stomach. This whole bloody business was stirring up sediment she thought she had packed down many years ago.

'Water purifier tablets,' Tilly said.

'Will you need them in Greece?' Kate asked. 'Surely they have mains water everywhere now?'

'I'm planning on straying off the beaten track, though.'

Kate tried to stem the image this added to those already swirling inside her. 'Not too far, though, I hope,' she said, smiling thinly. She put the tablets down and picked up a Swiss Army penknife, feeling its familiar weight in her hand.

'I had one of these, once.'

'That's for the corkscrew, only, of course,' Tilly said. 'But there's also a screwdriver, and the blade will be useful for cutting up tomatoes and stuff.'

'While you stroll along some deserted mountain path, off the beaten track.'

'That'll be me.' Tilly smiled and took Kate's hand. 'I'm going to find the real Greece that most travellers don't ever get to see. An authentic way of life that's disappearing in Europe.'

Kate put the penknife back with the other gear on Martha's bed. She looked at her daughter – so clear, so determined, so sensible compared to how she herself had been.

She shook her head and smiled. 'Just take care, Tills, won't you?'

Tilly leaped forward and hugged her so forcefully that she nearly knocked her over.

'I knew you'd come round, Mum!'

Kate rested her head on her daughter's shoulder and closed her eyes, breathing in her scent of clean washing, and apple shampoo, and all things good.

Of course Tilly would be fine. It was absurd to think otherwise.

EMMA

1 August 1980, 2 a.m. Athens. Peta Inn roof.

At last things are beginning to look up!

Went to a bar tonight with Ena, this girl from the bunk below me. She's about twenty, and Australian too, like poor drug-addled Mick on the bunk to my right. She's a bit of a hippy, although she said she thought my Sid Vicious hair's pretty cool. Amazingly, she's been here for two whole weeks (don't know how anyone could bear that), so she knows the ropes. The only place she says you can escape the heat is the National Gardens, where you can spend the hot midday hours under the trees. But if you fall asleep, the guards come and wake you by prodding you with a stick.

She also told me that you can buy speed and Valium at the chemists here, and that you can't buy Rizlas because they grow tobacco in Greece and apparently people would just raid the fields and roll their own if they had papers.

I'm not sure if I believe that – I reckon it's more to do with discouraging dope smoking – *Let's Go* says that if you get caught with cannabis in Greece you are in really big trouble. Not that I'm in any danger of that. It just makes me fall asleep. It's a stupid person's drug. But speed, now then, that's a different matter! I'm a speed queen, not a dope fiend.

Before I left home, I even thought about bringing a couple of baggies of sulphate with me to keep me going, but I didn't fancy getting caught at customs. Poor old Mum was so amazed that I could stay up all night doing my A Level revision! And it helped me get through those awful, boring Ripon parties with the vomiting boys and the crying girls.

Stop writing about that now, Em! All that life is dead to you. You've only got your brilliant future to look forward to.

You have to remember that. ALL the bad stuff is in the past: Dull Ripon, The French Shit, all that. Don't dwell.

Back to the good stuff: Ena!!!

She's told me not to buy Marlboro when I run out of papers, because they're too expensive. What I need to get is Karelia, which are twenty drachs a packet: crazy cheap. She gave me one of hers and it was rough, like smoking sandpaper, but I could get used to it, I suppose.

After our third Amstel, she held out her hand and slipped me four little pills. Valium, she said. Mixed with the alcohol 'it really kicks the buzz up'.

Sounded good to me.

So, here it is for the record: If you drink three bottles of Amstel, take four Valium, then chase it down with another bottle, then yes, your buzz is kicked. It's like being really, really stoned – the silly part of being drunk is heightened, but you also feel chilled and slowed down somehow. Like you just don't care.

(You have to get it right, though, Ena says. A little too much of either pills or booze and you end up dead.)

Not caring is good for me right now. It's also a pretty effective method of pain control. My bruises and cuts and the dull ache between my legs are but whispers of their former selves.

Me and Ena stayed at the bar talking on and on until it closed.

She's a reader too, and we riffed on Hermann Hesse and Emily Brontë and D.H. Lawrence. I can't remember what, really. I was pretty wrecked by the time we left.

A creepy man came up to us and said, 'Hello, baby,' to Ena. She just told him to fuck right off out of her face. I'm going to do that next time!

Although I was tempted, I didn't mention Marseille and The French Shit. I'm not going to shout out about how I am a victim, how I let all that happen to me. It's not a good image to put out to someone when you first meet them. It's too heavy. And I don't want to keep on reliving it.

I'm holding out great hopes for Ena. I told her about how I was searching for authenticity – for a world unspoiled by tourism and travellers and pollution. She says it's out there, that I should go out to the islands, that I just have to keep on travelling till I find it.

I could have kissed her, you know? As she talked, I kept looking at her mouth, which is beautiful – lopsided and funny, a little loose around the words. I wondered if perhaps I could ever fancy a girl. Boys might be out of the question now. If I think of a penis, it's that one particular penis, the penis of horror.

No. A boy would freak me out.

But no one has touched me, even casually, since The French Shit. Perhaps if I got a *tender* touch from someone – Ena, say – then might that cancel out some of the hurt?

I'm going to see if she'll travel with me for a bit. I'd feel safe with her. She must be ten inches taller than me, she's quite muscular and she doesn't take any shit. Again, when some creep hissed at us when we were walking (or rather, staggering) back to Peta Inn, she just launched into him with a load of Australian swearing. She hasn't got any of the qualms I have about offending people. And

73

she lives so happily in her skin. I wish I were more like her.

So yes, the Valium and beer has made me feel really good. Oddly, though – because I thought Valium was some sort of tranquilliser – I'm finding it difficult to sleep. So I'm making the most of it by writing this by torchlight. Ena's out cold, though. I can hear her snoring underneath me. It's a sweet sound, like a little snuffling pig.

I wonder if I'm in love with her?

She says I have to try the speed too – you just go into the chemist and ask for slimming pills ('though you may have to tell them they're for a friend,' she said, laughing and flicking my bony shoulder). I'm going to give it a go tomorrow.

We'll get really wasted!!!

KATE

Kate had nine days before Tilly's departure.

She sat in the kitchen trying to eat blueberries for breakfast and thinking about what it meant to her. She still had deep-rooted, ridiculous misgivings. Despite an hour of yoga on the mezzanine above the bedroom she shared with Mark, she hadn't been able to breathe away the tightening in her belly. All she had managed were five berries, individually chewed, washed down with a cup of peppermint tea.

About four calories.

She glanced up at the photograph she and Mark had commissioned years ago from Steve Mitchell – the photographer who had more recently made her the Face of Kindness. It hung, huge on the wall, equal to any of the other contemporary artworks that filled their home.

She rarely looked at it. There was no need: she knew it off by heart. It was the shape of her family, set against a white studio background. She was wearing the long swirling Pucci dress she had practically lived in that summer; Mark stood at her side, handsome as ever, his hair only slightly threaded with

75

the silver that had since taken over. Holding her hand was Tilly – a chubby little seven-year-old girl in a Liberty lawn dress. Scampering beside her, a little apart, her knees bent and slightly blurred as if she were about to jump, was Martha – a piece of thistledown, ready to blow away.

The tumour must have already been growing in her brain, but no one knew it at the time.

They were so happy then.

It was because of this that she had never listened to Mark's oft-voiced suggestion that it might be helpful for her to have it taken down. In fact, she would fight to the death to defend her right to keep it up there.

She drained her cup of the last drop of tea.

When Tilly was born – conceived after a determined and difficult couple of years' work with an expensive private nutritional therapist – Kate had secretly called her Tilly Purpose. Her arrival shooed away all her existential doubts. Well, nearly all. She could hardly believe that she had been permitted such joy. Then, when Martha came along, she felt, for the first time ever, that she was complete. She even forgot to feel undeserving for a short while.

The short while that Martha lived.

Now Tilly was growing and going. Kate knew it was inevitable – healthy even – but she would soon be rattling around the house with no one to clear up after, no one to chat to late at night over a cup of tea or a glass of wine.

No more purpose? She shook away the thought.

As places to feel like a loose ball bearing went, this house wasn't too bad, with its tall ceilings, clean, white surfaces and – apart from the girls' floor – minimal furnishing. Mark and Kate had bought the place – the lion's share of a converted primary school – off-plan just after Tilly was born, when, even so close to the river, Battersea was still a relatively daring choice for people like them.

Kate had worked closely with the developers to upgrade the finish to her exact specification, and it was glorious. She loved the views from its vast, tall windows. The light and space and familiarity of her home were great correctives for the dark cloud that sometimes hung over her.

She put the uneaten blueberries in the fridge, placed her cup in the dishwasher, wiped down all the kitchen surfaces with bleach and performed her ritual daily wash of the kitchen and living-area floor.

After that, she washed and dried her hands and applied the rich, unperfumed hand cream that went a small way to counter-acting the effect of her daily use of harsh cleaning products. It had never seemed right, somehow, to seek to protect her skin with rubber gloves.

Then it was on to the rest of her tasks. It was Monday and therefore Martha's Wish blog day. Writing her weekly missive would help her anchor her loose ends.

On her way up the wide stone steps to her turret office, she hesitated at the girls' level, her fingers itching as they had since she had first seen Tilly's stuff in Martha's room. But she held herself back from venturing down the corridor, because, had she done so, she might not have been able to resist pulling it all out and dumping it on Tilly's bed, and that would look like she was going mad. So she turned away, continuing up, up, past the floor where she and Mark had their view and their glass atrium and their sauna and her yoga mezzanine and their twin walk-in dressing rooms. On the landing outside their bedroom door was the piece of wall where she had marked two sets of ascending heights – red for Tilly and blue for Martha. When she'd had the hallways and main living areas repainted three years ago, she made the decorators leave this strip of wall. She always touched the highest blue mark – which only reached her hip – as she passed.

And so the stairs continued to spiral more narrowly upstairs to her eyrie office, which, like a lighthouse, had the best view from the entire house. Standing sentinel on the window sills were fifty or so cacti, which she had collected over the years since Mark had bought her one to celebrate her first pregnancy – because, he said, she had turned prickly. Cut flowers made her sad as they died, but her cacti would keep going for decades – some might even outlive her. Mark's gift had started a family tradition that saw the girls 'buying' new additions for her every birthday and Christmas. Tilly still continued to do so.

Kate had no idea if she even liked cacti, but she would never have the heart to get rid of them. Besides, she thought, as she gave each one its weekly drop of water, they would give her something to look after when Tilly was gone. And, like her own personal guards, they made her feel safer as she sat at her desk with the whole of London laid out in front of her.

She switched on her computer. Her plan was to write about progress on the new school the charity had just opened in Mali. She hadn't actually gone there, because, the fact of flying aside, the political situation was far too dangerous – the Foreign Office were advising against all travel to the whole country. But the charity employed local field-workers who reported back with photographs, film, and work by the students. It was then up to Kate to collate everything and put her report together in first person plural.

While she made no specific assertions, this, combined with her picture at the top of the blog – which was called *Kate Reports* – implied that she was much more frequently out visiting the schools and pupils than the one time she had actually done so.

It was essential, Sophie PR insisted, that Kate was seen to be actively engaged on the ground. And, so long as it got results, Kate thought, why the hell not? And she enjoyed the work. She really did. In a way, she had finally realised her childhood ambition of becoming a writer, blending facts into a kind of fiction far more purposeful than the novels that had been her original ambition.

While she was waiting for her email to roll in, she Googled 'Face of Kindness' and clicked on the images tab. She shook her head in wonderment as she scrolled down the wall of pictures. Apart from two shots of Mother Teresa and one of a kitten patting a yellow fluffy duckling's head, every single result was her, Mariam and Bintu. The source websites ranged from blogs in Australia, Japan and the US to CNN and other worldwide mainstream media.

Sophie was a genius. The image had truly captured the zeitgeist.

When she was sixteen, Kate had believed she was going to amount to something one day. She always thought she had somewhat blown that dream, but perhaps, finally, it was coming true. Having spent her adult life trying to keep her head down, now here she was, her face on every server on the entire world wide web.

Perhaps, then, thirty-three years was long enough to hide away.

She switched back to her email. The messages were still arriving on her public address – the one on the website that anyone could use to contact her. Her usual routine was to scan them personally, before forwarding the lot to Patience at the office, who answered them pretending to be Kate. From the number rolling in that morning – well into the hundreds – poor Patience was going to have to live up to her name today.

Kate dealt first with her private, work email address. There were a couple of last-minute photos from a field worker called Charles in Mali, and an excited note from Patience reporting on a considerable upswing in donations, thanks to the Face of Kindness picture.

This was all good.

Feeling quite chipper about it all, she wrote a happy note back to Patience, suggesting a team meal to celebrate – at her own expense, of course – then she downloaded the new photos from Charles to the blog folder on her computer.

The public emails had finally stopped coming in, so she started scanning through them. Generally, she received an interesting mixture at that address. Most were appreciative and enthusiastic, but there was a small proportion that were critical, accusing her perhaps of being an agent of Western cultural oppression, or asking whether she had fully assuaged her rich bitch conscience yet, and why didn't she just give away all of her filthy money to the poor of the world instead of flaunting herself for sinful pride and glory.

Some of these came from members of the radical Muslim factions fighting in several of the countries the charity worked in, who didn't want girls to receive education. These she could dismiss as medieval. Others were from naively political white boys and girls who, in addition to hating their parents, also despised the police and the banks and the rich. And, of course, there were the nutters, whose recent messages ranged from harmless but lengthy elucidations of personal problems they thought the Face of Kindness might possibly solve, to downright creepy details of exactly where they'd like to put, or what they'd like to put in, that Kind Face. This last sort made Kate feel sick, sullied, and she binned and deleted each one she came across. She didn't want poor Patience – who was only a few years older than Tilly – to have to witness the filth lurking in some people's minds. Also, a tiny part of her felt somehow responsible – dirty, even – for being the fuel for such fantasies.

Old habits die hard.

But there were few such emails today. It was mostly encouraging stuff, including one extremely useful story from a woman from one of the target countries. Thanks to an education supplied by another charity years ago, she had managed to haul herself out of poverty and go on to become a doctor. She now worked to ensure that fewer women met the same premature end as her own mother had by dying in childbirth.

Kate flagged this for Patience, then carried on scrolling through the two hundred or so remaining messages.

But at the hundred-and-fifty-second, she stopped. Her fingers lifted from the mouse and her heart felt as if it had displaced itself into her larynx.

The title of the email that stalled her was *Message for Emma*. Emma.

But surely it must be a mistake? A mis-addressed email? Some sort of spam? She certainly didn't recognise the sender's name, a Mrs C. McCormack. Almost involuntarily, her trembling index finger tapped the mouse and the message popped up, filling her screen.

I need to speak to you urgently,

it said.

I'll be upstairs in the New Oxford Street Starbucks opposite Tottenham Court Road subway at midday on Thursday.

I have news. I am desperate. You have to be there. Something terrible has happened.

And there, at the bottom, the sender had signed off using her real name.

A name Kate knew only too well. A name she had thought she would never hear again.

It was impossible. She had been so careful.

Her wobbling legs carried her down the winding stairs, right into the kitchen where she pulled a bottle of vodka from the freezer and poured herself a large shot. She had worked hard at appearing clean and good. Really hard. But the sight of that name made her feel as if someone had injected her with filth.

Tasting the berries she had managed to eat for breakfast, she knocked back the vodka to keep them inside, then poured herself another. And another. Fortified by alcohol, she climbed shakily back up to her office and approached her computer as if there was a dangerous animal crouching behind its screen.

Perhaps she had misread the email?

Perhaps it said something entirely different?

But no.

It said what it said, and it was from whom it was from.

She moved the email to the trash, then instantly pulled it back into her inbox. Every part of her wanted to ignore it and get on with the life she had built precisely to exclude its sender and everything she represented.

But she couldn't.

Beattie had news.

Kate placed her forehead on her desk.

That blog post would not get written today.

EMMA

1 August 1980, 2 p.m. Athens. The Milk Bar.

This is the shittest thing.

So Ena was still fast asleep when I woke sweating in the sun with a hangover from hell. I left her a note and went out to try to call Mum and Dad again. I knew they'd be waiting for my call – it's been twelve days since I've been gone. I also felt, fool that I am, that at last I had some good things to tell them – about finding a friend and all that.

After a three-hour wait, I finally got through to them. It was soooo good to hear their voices. They don't understand what I'm doing – I'm not sure if I do myself, actually – but they're just so excited to hear from me. They weren't expecting me to be in Greece yet. What happened to Italy? Dad asked. I couldn't tell him the truth, of course. I made up something about a train strike. He seemed to swallow it.

I sounded like I was having fun, they said.

I did. I really believed I was when I called them. I really thought my luck had changed.

Now, trying to take it in as I sit here in The Milk Bar, I realise I just want to go back to our cosy little house and have Mum's shepherd's pie and feel a bit chilly and cuddle up with them in front of the fire, and go out on the hills with Patch and Dad, and go fishing and feel the mist on my face.

I said I'd call them in two days' time, but perhaps I'll go back early instead.

Perhaps I'll just head home tomorrow.

I stopped on the way back from the phone place to buy some pills. The first chemist's shop refused to serve me. He said he couldn't understand me, but that was bullshit. But the second didn't seem to give a toss, and sold me Valium and 'slimming pills' while gawping at my breasts.

The final part of the day's budget went on a litre-bottle of really rough-looking red wine – grand total about fifty pence.

I took my shopping back to the Peta Inn to find Ena, excited about the day and night we were going to have. Climbing the four flights of stone steps to get to the roof nearly made me pass out. My heart was thumping in my chest, and my vision was swimmy. No food for, what, six days? Apart from beer, I suppose. That's a sort of food, isn't it? Enough calories, anyway.

I wove through the sea of heat-shimmery metal bunk beds to where Ena and I slept. I thought she might be there on the lower bunk, shading herself from the sun. I thought she would be waiting for me.

But there was no Ena. Her bed was stripped of her sleeping bag. Her book – she was reading *The Women's Room*, which she said she'd lend me when she'd finished – wasn't there, nor was the jumble of clothes and flip-flops and scarves she had stashed under her bed.

Had someone stolen all her stuff? And, if so, where was she?

Even though the place is full of strung-out travellers and druggies, Dimitri the owner says that thefts are very rare so long as everyone carries their valuables with them and stashes their rucksacks and camping gear in the baggage store, which only he's got the key for. It's also his way of making sure no one does a runner – he's supposed to keep our passports, but he doesn't have everyone's because he's overcrowded and the tourist police sometimes do checks. Ena said most of the hostel owners do that. 'It's why,' she told me, 'it's so easy to just disappear here. Athens just swallows people up.'

Remembering this, I started to get worried for her.

I checked my own bed – everything was just how I'd left it when I got up.

I looked around. Apart from two sleeping Dutch hippies who'd arrived noisily in the middle of the night, the place was deserted. The sun had just left its highest point of the day, so anyone sensible would have gone looking for shade in the National Gardens, or a bar.

From the street below, I heard a girl's laughter echoing up the sides of the building. Thinking it could be Ena, I rushed to the parapet – a wall about four feet high at the edge of the roof. There's this story about how, two years ago, a girl either fell or jumped off it and died. I thought about her as I looked down. It's a hell of a drop.

On the street below, a group of girls and boys about my age were walking right down the middle of the road, weaving in and out of the mopeds and small open delivery trucks that buzz around all day with their loads of watermelons and beer and sacks of beans. I leaned over the parapet to get a better look. One of the girls – the one who was laughing the loudest – had the same hair and walk as Ena. I nearly called out, but then she looked round to say something to the boy behind her and I saw that it wasn't her at all.

For safekeeping, I stuffed the wine down the bottom of my sleeping bag. Then I headed downstairs to look for her. The communal kitchen was empty, except for the resident mangy old dog dozing under the table.

I went to the reception desk where Dimitri was sitting, smoking and counting money, a bottle of Coke at his side.

'Yeah?' he says.

'Have you seen Ena?' I ask him.

'Ena?'

'The tall Australian girl on the roof.'

'She go,' he says, scratching the back of his neck. His skin glistens with grease and sweat.

'Go?'

He moves his head down to one side and slightly closes his eyes – which seems to be the Greek way of saying yes. 'Israel,' he says. 'Kibbutz.'

'When?'

'This morning.' He shrugs and goes back to his counting.

Ena has gone. Ena has left me.

I don't know why I'm taking it so badly. I suppose it's because I was making plans for us. I'm so stupid. I get so carried away. She didn't owe me anything.

So why do I feel so betrayed?

SHE COULD AT LEAST HAVE SAID GOODBYE.

The reception area's in the entrance to the hostel, which must have been quite a grand house once. It's the coolest place in the whole building, with its high ceilings, stone floors and shuttered windows. But even so, when Dimitri told me about Ena going to Israel, the heat closed in on me. I steadied myself against the wall, trying to use the cold marble to short fuse the faint I could feel coming on.

I needed to eat.

When I felt a bit less wobbly, I came here, the bar we were in last night. I've got a beer, a new pack of Karelia and some chips, which are too greasy and burn my mouth, but I'm on my third portion, forcing them down.

There's a tall, skinny boy sitting at one of the tables and I just looked up and caught him watching me. He smiled and looked away. He's got long, dark, curly hair and weird blue eyes. I reckon he's probably English, or American. He doesn't look like a creep, but you never know.

He can fuck right off, then.

Goodbye, Ena. Getting it all out like this is helpful. It's like I'm writing her out of my life.

1 August 1980, a bit later. Athens. Peta Inn roof.

I've just found something.

I'm up on the roof again. The Dutch hippies have disappeared, so I'm all alone now.

When I got back, after I had thrown up all those chips – they came up like thick yellow slugs – I climbed up onto my bunk bed. The metal of the frame was almost too hot to touch, so I held on tight to feel the burn. Rummaging in my sleeping bag for the wine, I found something else in there: Ena's copy of *The Women's Room*. She's left a message inside the front cover:

> *Hey, Ems! I finished this. It's really cool. You should read it and learn from it. We can all be strong women if we work at it. Even you, little Em! Ena xxxx*

That last line's like being slapped in the face. What does she mean by that?

How must I have come across to her?

Am I so obviously the walking wounded?

I HATE THE FRENCH SHIT.

I hate him so much for making me like this.

I hate myself for letting him do it to me.

Should I hate Ena, too, then? But she doesn't owe me anything. To her, I was just this weed, this victim, this weakling girl she had a couple of drinks with.

She saw right through me.

I'm transparent, like tracing paper.

KATE

2013

Kate almost didn't go to Starbucks.

She filled the intervening days with her usual refuge activity of cleaning the house. She pulled everything out of already pristine cupboards, scrubbed them out and replaced their contents more neatly. She steam-cleaned each of the four bathrooms and the sauna. She stripped and waxed the maple floorboards of the guest level.

But all the activity failed to chase the date, time and venue for the meeting from her memory. It kept repeating itself in her mind like a mantra:

Upstairs, New Oxford Street Starbucks, midday, Thursday.

She tried to obliterate it with alcohol, sitting alone each night drinking one, sometimes two, bottles of wine. Mark was away on business and Tilly was busy either working or saying goodbye to friends in far-flung corners of London, so there was no one to curb or criticise her excesses.

When she woke up hung-over and alone on the Thursday morning, she thought perhaps she might just not go out. The idea of leaving the house suddenly seemed like an enormous challenge to her. She found the West End hard to bear, anyway.

All that noise and dirt; all those people squashing around her with their smells and their germs.

She had dared to begin to hope that, with the help of time, and the success of Martha's Wish, she had made some headway at being more like the almost normal woman she had learned to be before Martha's death. But no. Just the sight of Beattie's name pulled her all the way back to the horrors of the distant past.

And Beattie had said she was desperate.

She had no idea what it could be about. But she couldn't keep away. She had to go and see her.

It had been a long time. Time enough to forget, perhaps. But not really.

You don't forget those sorts of things.

'Pull up here, please,' she said to the taxi driver, a little before they reached Starbucks. Despite the relentless, ice-pick rain, she needed a few steps to right herself.

As she drew the collar of her mac around her ears and put up her umbrella, the taxi took off, aquaplaning on a puddle and soaking her legs. By the time she pushed open the coffee-shop door, she was regretting her decision to walk the last couple of hundred yards.

One of the issues she had with crowds, other than the sheer press of their humanity, was that she always had a sense that everyone was looking at her. The only way she could cope with this was by mentally hazing the space between herself and the world. It reminded her of when she used to get stoned – the fogginess gave a greater objectivity.

Of course, with her famous picture doing the rounds, the staring problem was now more real than imagined. She had taken pains to make herself less recognisable with a sheepskin hat and the dark-rimmed glasses that she normally only used for reading. But, even so, she was certain that a man glanced oddly at her as she passed him in the street, despite the fact that he was hurrying past her, huddled against the cold and the wet.

As she entered the warm, coffee- and vanilla-scented interior, she forced herself back into focus. She hadn't been able to face breakfast, and the smell of lunchtime paninis warming up made her feel queasy. She glanced around to see if she recognised anyone, but of course Beattie had said she'd be upstairs. To put off the moment, she queued for a chamomile tea.

'In or to go?' the barista asked.

'In,' she said, passing up the final possibility of escape. The barista set out a china cup and saucer.

The upstairs room was crowded and fugged with the steam rising from cups and wet coats. She had to take her specs off, because they were entirely clouded over. Juggling glasses, cup and rolled-up umbrella, she stood at the top of the stairs and cast her eye around.

And there she was. Sitting at the far end of the room, her back to the wall, looking out, but not yet seeing her. She was unmistakably Beattie, despite the extra pounds and years, and the change in her hair, which, like Kate's, was now fair and wavy. There was also a tension in the way she held her body; her face looked strained. Hardly surprising, though. Kate was sure she didn't look so relaxed herself.

She waited until Beattie's gaze settled on her. Then, without a smile, Kate nodded and headed over towards her. As she approached, Beattie stood with a stiffness that suggested some minor mobility problems. Kate focused her anxiety on how to greet her. A kiss would be wrong, surely? But a handshake seemed too formal, somehow.

Beattie short-circuited the moment by stepping forward and

drawing Kate to her in an embrace. As she was pressed to this unfamiliar, soft body, Kate smelled cigarettes and a perfume she didn't recognise. She tried not to appear too held-back, but she really wasn't a hugger.

'Thank God you came,' Beattie said as she held her, her voice deeper and more gravelled than it had been.

'Good to see you,' Kate lied, breaking away to take off her hat and coat. 'Long time no see.'

'Sure is,' Beattie said, removing her own coat from the seat she had saved for her. This meant that Kate had to sit with her back to the room, which was never her favourite arrangement. But there was nothing she could do about it without appearing unhinged or high-maintenance, neither of which seemed to be a good idea for this meeting.

The two women sat and looked at each other in a silence that didn't quite deliver its threat of being uncomfortable. Even allowing that she was a few years older than Kate, Beattie was considerably more weathered. Deep lines grained her face, and her skin was thicker, coarser. Kate supposed that this was probably down to the cigarettes she could smell on her. Or sun exposure, perhaps.

Above dark rings, Beattie's eyes were still green, but, inevitably perhaps, the colour had faded from them over the years. She was nervy, too, which reminded Kate painfully of the last time she had seen her. She kept biting at her bottom lip, running her teeth along the edge, grimacing slightly. For a moment, Kate thought perhaps she might have developed a tic, but it wasn't that. She was nervous about something. Though that was hardly surprising, given the circumstances.

'How are you?' Kate said. The minute the words left her mouth, she cringed at their inanity. That wasn't what she wanted to ask.

'I'm fine,' Beattie said, smiling. But Kate could see this wasn't entirely the truth. 'It was that charity picture,' she said. 'That's how you were found.'

'Found?'

Beattie reached over with her right hand and, in a move that was shocking in its intimacy, pushed up Kate's sleeve and held her by the elbow. Then, with her free hand, she revealed her own forearm.

And there they were, the matching tattoos, their Triskelions, their marks of Hecate, the Triple Goddess.

'You haven't changed all that much,' Beattie went on, her American accent sounding more southern than Kate remembered. 'Apart from the hair, of course. But that's what clinched it.' She traced her finger around the curlicues of ink on Kate's arm. 'Not many of these around on this sensitive bit.'

'Ridiculous place for a tattoo.' Kate smiled, retrieving her arm. She rolled down her sleeve.

'Remember how it hurt? Jesus, Jake cried, I swear,' Beattie said.

At the mention of that name, Kate jolted like she had been hit.

'Why are you here?' she asked, once she had gathered herself back together.

'I've got some news for you. Something has come up. We're in a mess, Emma.'

'I'm Kate now.'

'Sorry, yes, Kate.'

Kate waited for Beattie to say what she had to say. She was certainly drawing the moment out. Her clothes, she noticed, while not brand new, were of a quality: Donna Karan coat, Mulberry handbag. And, although her hands showed her age, her nails were neatly manicured. None of this should matter, but Kate was relieved that, like her, Beattie seemed to have found a comfortable life.

Eventually, Beattie took a sip of her cappuccino. 'This charity of yours. You lost your daughter, huh?'

Kate nodded. What did this woman want?

'I'm sorry for your loss.'

Kate didn't like it when people said that. It always sounded like they were making out it was her fault. It felt like they were ramming it down her throat.

But Beattie wasn't to know that.

'You have another daughter, yes?' she said. 'Tilly?'

'How do you know that?' Kate frowned.

'Some website back home.'

Beattie pulled up a page on her phone and passed it across the table to Kate. It was a photograph of her, Mark and Tilly coming out of the restaurant they had eaten in after the *Hello UK!* interview. Kate, who had recently thrown up, didn't look too good. In fact, she was actually scowling. The picture was captioned *Face of Kindness*?

'Is that your husband?' Beattie said. 'He's hella handsome.'

'I had no idea someone was taking our photo. Sorry. That's just freaked me out.'

'Yeah, weird, isn't it? Rat-asses, aren't they, the press? Sorry. I didn't mean to upset you. She looks like a lovely girl, too.'

'She is.' Kate took a sip of her tea, then cradled the cup in her fingers.

'I've got daughters, too. Here.' Beattie pulled a wallet out of her handbag and showed her two passport photos of two plump, staid girls in what looked like their twenties. 'Good girls. Not like we were,' Beattie said, tucking the photos away again.

'Are you married?'

'Was. My husband was a surgeon. But, rest his soul, he got

taken away.' Beattie smiled again, and Kate realised that what she had taken for tiredness in her eyes was more like sadness.

'I'm sorry.'

'Oh, it was over a year ago. I'm beginning to learn how to live without him.' Beattie drew her arms around herself and shrugged. 'It was hard. It gets easier. You'd know that from losing your little girl.'

'Yes,' Kate said, finding herself rubbing her nose.

They sat in silence for a few moments, the background noise in the coffee shop – soft rock, lovers' chatter, a child's prattle – surrounding them like a muffled blanket. At last Kate couldn't bear it any longer.

'So tell me what this is all about, Beattie. What's this news you've got for me? I thought the idea was that we weren't going to see each other ever again.'

Beattie put her hand on Kate's elbow. 'I didn't want to do this, but you need to know. He's on to you, too, now.'

'What? Who?' Kate said. 'What are you talking about?'

Beattie leaned forward, put her lips to Kate's ear and whispered the words she had come from the other side of the Atlantic to tell her.

Words Kate never thought she would ever hear.

Words that changed *everything*.

Kate's cup seemed to take thirty-three years to hit the floor. When it finally landed, it clattered and smashed, splashing hot tea over the legs of the man sitting behind her.

'I'm so sorry,' she said as she tried to get up to grab a napkin to help him. But then the floor came up to greet her. On her way down, she caught her temple on the corner of the table and then she knew nothing more.

EMMA

1 August 1980, 6 p.m. Athens. Peta Inn roof, parapet.

I can't bear to look at *The Women's Room*, so I've tucked it under my mattress. Using my Swiss Army knife, I've opened the wine and popped a couple of Valium. The wine tastes like rat's piss, and it's been so warmed by the sun in my sleeping bag that it's almost hot. Even so, I've managed to put away half the bottle. I feel a lot better now.

I'm here on the parapet, swinging my legs over the side, looking at what's going on down below. It's late afternoon and more people are coming out from the backpacker hostels lining the street, all going off together in their little groups, no doubt to have fun out in the bars *Let's Go* says line the hills up to the Acropolis. I can hear Australian and American accents, Dutch, German.

All so fucking happy.

An old Greek man in the café across the street stares as a girl goes by in a see-through cheesecloth dress and no bra. She's asking for it. She should wear a black shroud like me.

If only I were a strong woman like Ena said I could be. I'd go out there on my own into the early evening streets and make new friends, find a gang, belong with other people. Tell that girl to cover herself up, perhaps save her, perhaps be her friend.

But there are no 'other people'. It's just me.

I want to go home.

But that would be so lame, Emma. You told everyone you were coming out for at least four weeks, and everyone said you were mad, and you told everyone they were just blinkered. Remember?

That was who I was, Ena. I *was* a strong woman. I was the driven, brave girl, the intrepid. The one who worked hard and got great marks and was the first ever to get a Cambridge scholarship from her school but who was more than just a swot, the girl everyone wanted at their parties, the girl who took drugs and danced the night away and looked down on the local boys. The girl who was better than all that.

I was born in the wrong town, to the wrong people. I should have been the offspring of intellectuals in London or Paris or New York. Not a bloody electrician and a supermarket cashier in fucking Ripon. Perhaps then either all that bravado would have settled more fully into me to become *actual* courage, or I would have realised in time, before I ended up here, on this parapet, that I was only bluffing.

Is this all fall-out from The French Shit?

Or is it because I am completely useless?

1 August 1980, later – can't see my fucking watch. Athens. Peta Inn roof, parapet.

OK, so I've nearly finished the wine and I've swallowed a couple more pills and I'm sorry about the handwriting.

I'm still up here. Smoking, drinking, writing and swinging my legs over the edge of the parapet.

These Karelia make my eyes water. But they're so cheap, and they come in this sweet little box that reminds me of the Sobranies I once had to smoke for the school play.

I've taken off my sandals because I was worried they might fall off my feet down to the street. If I half close my eyes, the lights and

96

colours underneath me from the shops and the cars all swirl together. It's quite lovely.

There's still no one else up here. Perhaps no one wants to come up here while the wrecked English girl with the Sid Vicious haircut is around. They don't want to be contaminated by her.

Jesus. My handwriting.

I think it would be quite nice just to let myself drop. All I'd have to do is shift forward a bit. It wouldn't require much effort. It'd just be a letting go, really.

No one would miss me, would they? Except Mum and Dad, but I wasn't planning on seeing them much anyway after I went to Cambridge. They've had the best of me they were ever going to get.

So that's the end of the wine, then.

That tall, skinny, long-haired boy from The Milk Bar is on the roof of John's Hostel across the road (it's the only place in the street cheaper than Peta Inn, but *Let's Go* says to avoid it like the plague). At least, I think it's him. He's watching me again. I looked over at him, but everything's a bit blurry.

Will I be able to read this back? Who cares?

Are his arms waving all over the place, or is it just my imagination?

Dear Mum and Dad. I'm sorry. I love you. I was a total let-down. You're better off without me.

KATE

'Kate.'

She woke to a strong smell of antiseptic. Her head was pounding and she didn't seem able to move her arms. Nearby she heard a beeping and a shuffling; quite far away someone – not herself, she realised after a second – was moaning.

'Kate.'

She opened her eyes. Mark was leaning over her.

'You had me worried there, Katie.'

Frowning, she extricated her arms from the tightly tucked-in blanket that had been constraining them and propped herself up on her elbows. She was in a cubicle, on a hospital bed. Her husband was there in his business suit.

'Ow.' She gasped as her blood caught up with her movement and throbbed into a very painful temple.

'You took a nasty blow to the head,' Mark said. 'You've been out for nearly an hour. They want to keep you in for a couple of nights, so I've got you a nice room on the private ward.'

'What about Tilly?'

Mark smiled briefly. 'Tilly can look after herself. I've told her what happened and she'll be in to visit when her shift's over.' His iPhone, which was, as ever, in his hand, buzzed. 'Damn,' he said, glancing at the screen. 'I've got to take this. Sorry.'

Before Kate could ask him what the hell she was doing in a hospital, he ducked out of the cubicle and was replaced by a young female doctor with a long blond ponytail.

'Ah, Mrs Barratt. Welcome back to the world of the living,' she said as she wrote something in her notes at the end of the bed, taking readings from the monitors Kate now realised she was wired up to. 'All good.'

Without warning, she reached forward and put a thumb on Kate's right eyelid. Kate flinched, but resisted the urge to bat her away.

'I hit my head?'

The doctor nodded. 'You've got quite a concussion, and I think we're going to have to give you a couple of stitches up here.' She put her hand near the point of most pain on Kate's forehead. 'Do you remember passing out?'

Kate shook her head.

'You were upstairs in Starbucks on New Oxford Street.'

Kate blinked. Upstairs. Starbucks, New Oxford Street . . . upstairs, New Oxford Street Starbucks, midday, Thursday.

Then she remembered: Beattie.

Beattie.

Who had given her the shocking, unbelievable news.

The beeping machine attached to Kate's chest picked up tempo.

'When did you last eat?' the doctor was asking.

'What?' Kate said.

'When did you last eat?'

Kate tried to focus her mind. 'Um . . . yesterday? I don't really have breakfast and I hadn't had lunch yet . . .'

'The thing is, Mrs Barratt, you are rather underweight. You probably fainted because you're not getting enough calories.'

'I'm fine,' Kate said. Though she knew that, since Tilly had sprung her Bombshell, she had hardly kept anything down. These were old tricks, and she knew them well.

'You're probably not aware that you have a problem. There's nothing in your notes to indicate any reason for concern in the past.'

Oh yes I am and yes there is, Kate thought. But she didn't say anything. Why would she?

'I'm keeping you in for observation for concussion. I'm also going to get the Mental Health Team to drop in on you while you're here.'

Mental Health? Kate couldn't believe that this girl, who wasn't much older than her daughter, was talking to her like this. 'You can cancel that,' she said. 'I'm not seeing a shrink. I'm just naturally skinny and I forgot to eat.'

The doctor raised an eyebrow and wrote something on her notes. 'Not eating properly and maintaining such a low weight puts enormous pressure on your system. The reason you fainted was that your heart simply didn't have the strength to push blood to your brain. Unfortunately, you then hit your head, which has resulted in the concussion.'

'That's not why I fainted,' Kate said, her voice low.

The doctor ignored her. 'I want you to have this.' She stood and handed her a leaflet from underneath her notes. 'And I'll be referring you to your GP. I would strongly recommend that you follow this up.'

She left and Kate looked at the leaflet. *Addressing Adult Anorexia*. Knowing it wouldn't tell her anything new, she crushed it into a ball and let it fall to the ground. When it came to things to address, she had far more important candidates.

Alone, she closed her eyes again. In among the hospital hubbub, she could hear Mark speaking emphatically on his phone. A knot tightened inside her. How had he found out she was here? Had he met Beattie? Had she told him who she was? Had she blown her cover?

And then the relief came flooding through her.

She had no need for cover.

Beattie's words, shocking as they were, had set her free.

Somehow, the death she had held in her hands for thirty-three years had not happened.

But how to explain any or all of it to Mark?

It was impossible.

She wasn't who he thought she was.

Her whole life with him had been a lie, and there was no going back.

'Jesus, sorry,' Mark said, coming back into the cubicle and pocketing his iPhone. 'You leave the office for half an hour and the world falls apart.'

'How did you find out I was here?' Kate said.

Mark pulled up a chair. 'Claire found my number on your phone and called me.'

'Claire?'

'Your old school friend. The American?'

Kate breathed out. Of course. Beattie wouldn't have revealed anything like the truth to Mark.

'She was worried that it was the shock of bumping into her that floored you.'

'No, no,' Kate said.

'But now we find out it's because you haven't been eating

properly. I thought you were looking a bit too fashionably thin lately.'

'It's the Tilly stuff.'

Mark sighed with a note of impatience. 'You mustn't worry about all that. She's going to be fine.'

Perhaps she will, then, Kate thought.

Because everything had changed.

She wasn't sure of anything now.

She had been like a boat, her anchor wedged in horrible, jagged rocks at the bottom of a stagnant bay. Now the chain holding her in one place had ripped and she was floating free. No, free was the wrong word. She was floating lost, in uncharted water.

Mark handed Kate a Starbucks napkin with some curved, looped handwriting on it. 'Claire gave me her address and phone number – she's staying at the Waverley Hotel in Goodge Street. Over to see the sights, she said. Poor woman.'

'Poor woman?'

'Didn't she tell you? Or perhaps you can't remember with the concussion. Her husband died last year, and this trip is supposed to help her get over it. I told her she must come round and visit when you're back home.'

Kate looked away. Her life – which no one in the know would ever have described as straightforward – had, in one short encounter, disintegrated into the surreal.

'You must have a lot of catching up to do, bumping into each other after so many years. It'll do you good to have someone to talk to. A friend.'

'Yes.' Kate wondered what the rest of what Beattie had to say was. She had brought her the best yet most shockingly unimaginable news, but she had also come to warn her.

He was on to them, she'd said.

The story still wasn't over, was it?

'She said she recognised you straight away. I've always said you've hardly aged.'

'But that's just you,' Kate said, trying to pin her attention to his conversation, trying to keep things light.

'She said you hadn't changed at all. I imagine she has, though. She's not weathered the seas of time all that well, has she?'

'Shh,' Kate said, forcing a smile.

He looked at her, narrowing his eyes. She felt small and pale under his scrutiny. 'You look worn out, Kate. Martha's Wish is taking it out of you. And we should get a cleaner to help you with the house. You should take it easy.'

He was always saying things like that. She thought sometimes that he would only consider his job as her protector done when she was sitting on the sofa all day, doing absolutely nothing. But she was too painfully aware of her privilege and her lack of productivity to end up like that. After all, it wasn't something she had been born to.

'Are you going to be all right?' He reached over and squeezed her hand. The invisible golden threads of his work were pulling at him.

'You go back to the office,' she said. 'I'll be fine.'

He left, without, she noticed, kissing her. When had they stopped kissing goodbye?

But she was glad to be on her own. She had a lot to process. If only she had known sooner.

For thirty-three years she had lived thinking she was responsible for a death.

Everything she was today had been defined by that thought.

She was not the person she had thought she was.

She tried it out in different ways.

She was not a murderer.

She had not killed anyone.

Except, of course, she thought with a jolt, Emma James.

She had well and truly finished off Emma James.

PART TWO

BEFORE

1

2 August 1980, 5.30 a.m. Athens. Peta Inn roof.

It's happened again!

Everything has changed AGAIN. Everything is completely, wonderfully, different.

This crazy travelling world just seems to be totally up or totally down. At least it's not boring, or bland, or beige, I suppose . . .

So, of course, I didn't jump off the roof. Or I wouldn't be writing this, would I?

I did seriously think about it. But when it came down to it, I couldn't do that to my parents. Just thinking of how glad they were to hear from me yesterday morning made me think again. Perhaps if I had a brother or sister I might've let myself go over. But I'm the only one they've got. The one they've chucked all their hopes and dreams into. If nothing else, I owe it to them to keep on living.

Just as well. Because if I had jumped, I wouldn't have had this evening!

So I can't sleep because I stupidly took a couple more slimming pills half an hour ago. But the good thing is that I feel I can write and write and write! Which is just as well as I've got lots to put down. I'll start at the beginning and write as much detail as I can remember. I want to record this night for the rest of my life.

I stayed up on the parapet – over there, in fact, just yards from where I am now on my bunk – for another hour after writing my goodbye note to Mum and Dad.

I sat with my hands clenching the rough stone surface, my shoulders hunched up around my ears and my chin slumped on my chest. It got darker and a bit cooler. After a while, the world stopped swirling quite so much, and I looked up. The lights on the roof had been switched on and I was more or less spotlit. There was a group of people on the roof opposite, sitting on a line of chairs, their feet up on their own parapet, swigging from beer bottles and smoking and laughing amongst themselves. I think they were watching me in case I did something interesting. I looked down at the street, which seemed even further away than it had in daylight. A girl glanced up at me, put her hand over her mouth, and pointed me out to her friend.

Feeling a little foolish, like a bad actor in a cheap melodrama, I swung my feet round and slipped off the wall onto the roof. I needed to get away from the edge, just in case I changed my mind again.

Sleepy from the wine and Valium, I looked over to my bed. At some point while I'd been sitting on the parapet, Mick the acid-casualty Australian must have slunk in and climbed onto his mattress right next to mine, where he lay, snoring, out and away on something. I couldn't face lying next to him up there.

So, with no particular plan, I grabbed my bag and ran for the stairs. I didn't much like the thought of going out into the night on my own, but what I had nearly done to myself freaked me out. I needed to get away, down onto the ground, quickly, before I changed my mind again.

I bombed as fast as I could down the stone stairs, but on the second floor I stumbled and fell, twisted my ankle and tumbled down five or six steps. Luckily, someone coming in the opposite direction broke my fall.

I'm going to try to remember every single word we said . . .

'Whoa,' he says.

I look up and see he's the tall skinny boy from The Milk Bar. The boy from John's Hostel roof. He's startlingly beautiful close up.

Even in the dim stairwell, I can make out the extraordinary blue of his eyes.

'Ow,' I say, catching my ankle behind me (which still really hurts now by the way).

He smiles. 'Where were you off to in such a hurry? You had the hounds of hell at your heels.'

It's a question I can't answer, because I have no idea where I was going. That, and something about the kindness in his voice – warm, American, sincere – makes me crumple. I just burst into tears. He wraps his arms around me and holds me.

It might sound a bit Mills and Boon, but that's what it was like. He held me. My first touch since Marseille. The tender touch I wanted. The tender touch that, even before The French Shit, I'd never known. I don't come from a family of huggers or kissers. I don't do all that.

Normally.

'What is it?' he says, his lips in my hair.

'It's stupid,' I say, or something like that. 'It's nothing.' My voice is thick with pills and wine.

'It doesn't look like nothing to me. Tell me.' He's rubbing my back. It feels safe, though, brotherly, lovely. Not threatening in any way.

'It's just—' The tears overtake me again. 'I don't know what I am or where I'm going.'

Eventually, when the worst of my tears are over, he takes me by the shoulders and looks at me.

'What's your name?'

'Emma James.'

'I'm Jake. Jake Mithras.'

'Hi,' I say, laughing through the remains of my tears, because it seems odd to be introducing ourselves after such an intimate moment.

'Do you wanna go get something to eat, Emma James?' he says, wiping the wet from my cheeks.

I nod.

'I know just the place. Come on.'

He takes me by the hand and leads me down the stairs and out through the front door onto Nikis.

And there we are: two people, people together, a couple of people, a couple. Part of the throng of pairs and groups of backpackers and travellers winding their way up along the dusty road into the narrower pedestrian twists and turns of the Plaka, looking for food, drink, action.

As we walk, he tells me about himself. He's twenty-one years old and has recently graduated from UCLA, majoring in philosophy. He grew up in San Diego and is in Greece to discover an ancient way of life lost to 'dumb Americans'.

'Look,' he says, as we pass some patchily spotlit ruins of a temple partially fenced-off behind a bunch of café tables filled with beer-swilling tourists. A couple of mangy street dogs loll on the steps up to the pillars, almost identically mirroring the postures of two crumbling stone hounds next to them. 'You wouldn't get something like that in California – the ancient past, casually muddled up with the present. If we did have anything that old, it would be kept preserved, set behind Plexiglas, sanitised. I've been here two weeks and my mind is totally blown. Are you staying here long?'

I shake my head. 'I want to head out to the islands, find a simpler way of life.'

'Me too!' he says. 'There's places out there where they still live like they did back in the olden times, where they still even speak a sort of Ancient Greek.'

'Really?'

'Sure.' He turns towards me and smiles, giving me no choice whatsoever but to smile back at him. I like him. He's got this soft mouth, with an exaggerated cupid's bow that looks almost girlish. But there's something else there in his face, something edgy that makes me think he might come up with a surprise or two.

Of course, after The French Shit, I've got my antennae up. But the size of this boy – he must be at least six four to my five one – makes me feel protected, rather than threatened. I feel OK with him. He is, at the very least, someone to be with.

And anyway, what could have gone wrong tonight? Out there in the bustling, jostling street, all noisy with harsh northern European languages mingling with the fluid, looser shapes of Spanish, Italian, Greek.

I hadn't noticed it last night with Ena, but the smells of Athens at night are unbelievable – you walk from raw sewage to incense to charcoal-grilled lamb. Then, after passing the rancid patchouli and dandruff stench of a hippy unwashed since setting off overland from Pune, you get the relief of a cascade of jasmine, which in turn is swamped by the reek of death, probably from an unseen, unlucky one of the millions of stray dogs and cats that throng this city.

And, all the way, the pavements are crowded with the rammed tables and chairs of countless bars and tavernas. The gaps between are filled with people selling just about anything you could imagine – second-hand dentures, hand-braided bracelets, cheap plastic toys. And every couple of hundred yards, the way is blocked by a crowd watching a street performer – a guitar-playing German student, perhaps, or a barefoot gypsy girl dancing to her brother's wild violin.

Eventually, Jake leads me across a little park dotted with old men and even older women, sitting cooling themselves on stone benches under cypress trees exhaling their woody oils after a day roasting in the heat.

Look at me. I'm really writing!

I tense slightly at being taken off the main drag, with its safety net of people, but Jake squeezes my hand and points to a string of coloured fairy lights hanging in trees rising behind a crowd of glossy-leaved shrubs.

'There. Kostayiannis. Best lamb chops in town.'

He takes me through a gate in the bushes and we're on a gravel terrace set with old wooden tables and chairs. Waiters bustle around the diners – and there are many straight-looking Greeks in amongst the travellers and hippies – bearing plates piled high with grilled meat and puffy flatbreads.

And suddenly I realise I feel hungry. Not just hungry, emptied out, like I haven't eaten for a week. Which, thinking about it, apart from the vomited binge on chips from earlier on, is about true.

We sit down and Jake smiles at me.

'They don't have a menu, but I know just what to order. You do eat meat?'

I nod.

'You're gonna love this.'

'Why are you being so kind to me?' I ask.

'I saw you. I was on the roof of John's over the road. Man, you looked so down. I couldn't bear to watch you any longer. I was scared you were going to jump.'

'I nearly did.'

He orders a jug of village wine and some food. They bring the wine first and he pours me a glass and sits back and puts his hands together on his chest, as if he's some psychiatrist.

'So, Emma. Tell me about it. Why are you so sad?'

I look at him and wonder if I should tell him about The French Shit. I can't, though. I'm never going to tell it to anyone. I've got this feeling that if I don't talk about it, then gradually it will all fade away and not exist any more.

I shouldn't really write about it here, then, either, I suppose. But maybe shutting it away in this notebook is a good thing. And perhaps one day I might be able to make something out of it. I might be able to incorporate it into my great novel or something. That would be a victory of sorts, wouldn't it?

So I don't lie to Jake. I just leave out the bit about being raped and kicked and spat on in an alleyway in Marseille.

I tell him about how I'm not cut out for lone travelling, how I've been away for just thirteen days, but how it seems more like a lifetime, how I'm lonely and lost, and how I'm tired of being targeted by men and scared to go out because of it. How my big adventure that I saved for and looked forward to all year has come crashing down around my heels. And then I tell him about Ena and how what I see as her rejection of me was almost the final straw. How I'd thought the world a kinder place and what a shock it's been to find out the truth.

When I finish, he reaches across, takes my hand and looks me in the eye. 'Poor Emma James.'

I nod. I feel light. I have all but told him the truth and I feel purged. A tiny, tight kernel of hope forms in my throat, making it almost impossible for me to swallow my wine.

* * *

Halfway through my story, Jake orders more wine, but it isn't until we've nearly finished the second jug that the waiter brings our food – perfect, thinly cut, herby lamb chops, pink on the inside, caramelised from the grill on the outside, creamy, cool tzatziki, a plate piled with thin chips, and a Greek salad.

I decide I am going to eat one chop, ten chips, and a handful of salad, without the cheese.

Jake takes the first bite from his lamb, then stops and looks across the restaurant at something behind me.

'Look,' he says. I turn to face the object of his attention. 'Your twin just walked in.'

2

2 August 1980, 7 a.m. Athens. Peta Inn roof.

So: I'm STILL AWAKE. The others'll be up soon and if I don't watch out, I'll be too tired to have fun.

Stupid. Stupid. Stupid. Shouldn't have done the whizz.

My hand's aching from all the writing, but I've got to keep on. I'm like Hemingway, or Kerouac, or Tom Wolfe and the Electric Kool Aid Acid Test and the Merry Pranksters.

So, then. This is what happened next, in my best prose style:

Standing at the entrance to the taverna some thirty yards away from us, casting around for a place to sit, is a girl who, indeed, as Jake says, looks almost exactly like me, right down to the calamitous hairdo. Even her clothes are similar – she, too, wears a big black baggy T-shirt dress, although hers is accessorised by a gigantic shoulder bag slung across her body. She catches my eye and her mouth opens a little, her expression almost mirroring mine.

She stops a waiter as he passes her, his hands full of piles of empty plates, and asks him a question. He looks around the terrace, and they exchange a couple of words. While Jake and I have been talking, every table in the place has filled up. The waiter shrugs and bustles off into the kitchen.

The girl hesitates for a moment, then comes over to us.

'He says I should sit with you guys,' she says, shrugging. 'Is that OK?' She talks like Rhoda off the telly, so I guess she's from New York.

She's not so like me close up. Where I have quite unimpressive features – smallish and not very well defined – this girl has a very striking face – dark, dramatic eyebrows, full lips and almond-shaped green eyes. But she *is* around the same height as me and, even though she might be a few pounds heavier than me (it's hard to tell in these baggy dresses), we're of a similar build.

Jake looks at me, an eyebrow raised. 'You OK with that, Emma?'

'Sure,' I say, moving over to make space for her, although I'm a little sad at having to share him.

'Thanks so much,' the girl says, 'I've just arrived in town and I don't know anyone. I hate coming out on my own.'

'Me too,' I say. 'I'm Emma, this is Jake.'

'Hi,' she says. 'I'm Beattie. I like your hair, Emma.'

Beattie's story is this:

She is, indeed, from New York. She's a drama student at Tisch – an 'awesome school' in New York City – and had been due to do 'The Grand Tour' with a boyfriend, but 'the rat-ass' dumped her at the last minute, citing 'commitment issues'.

I love how she talks!

She decided to come over anyway, and, at the start, enjoyed travelling – first to London, then Madrid, Florence, Pisa, Rome and Venice. But she's feeling the strain of continually arriving in places on her own, never spending time with anyone she's known for longer than two days.

So we've got a lot in common, then.

I like her, a lot.

We sat there, telling each other about our lives until the last of our fellow-diners had left – way beyond midnight. So long as we kept buying wine, the waiters didn't seem to mind us still being there – they had plenty to be clearing up.

Beattie did most of the talking. The way she spoke about Italy – the art she had seen, the food she had eaten, the people she had met – made me cross at myself for missing out on all that.

'To behold Leonardo da Vinci's *The Last Supper* is like standing in front of God,' she says, her hand to her chest. 'Right there in the flesh.'

'You went to Milan too?' I say, ready to come out with my story of the train station at night, the horrible hotel, the pounding on the door.

'No, I headed south straight off,' Beattie says. 'Milan is just like this big industrial city.'

'But *The Last Supper*'s in Milan,' I say. I know this because it was one of the things I had planned to go and see. One of the things I had denied myself. That The French Shit had denied me.

'Is it? Oh my God.' She laughed. 'My brain's all fucked, I guess. With all the travel, the moving, the seeing so much stuff. And this wine!' She gestures at her glass. 'I meant the Sistine Chapel, the Michelangelos on the ceiling. Jeeze.' She slaps her forehead and we all laugh, our voices echoing round the empty courtyard.

Then the waiter brings out the bill, along with a carafe of Metaxa and three small glasses. His expression apologetic, he says we can stay sitting at the table, but he needs us to pay so he can get some sleep.

'I'll get it,' Jake says, reaching into his jeans pocket for his wallet.

'You sure?' I say, but not too forcefully – my share of the bill would have blown my budget for the day *again*, something I'd done once already with my morning visit to the chemist. I've been making too much of a habit of going over my carefully planned daily allowance. I'm going to have to sit down soon and do a re-calculation if I'm going to spin my traveller's cheques out for my full month away.

That thought hitting me now, so soon after I wanted to go home to my parents, is a mark of what a sea change this evening's been for me. Something inside me already knows I've found some travelling companions, some muckers, some mates.

Jake paid, the waiter said 'Kalinichta' and limped wearily inside the taverna, shutting and locking the door behind him. A few minutes later, the lights strung in the trees around us went out and we were left in the warm moonlight, with only the sound of crickets, distant, barking dogs and the occasional putter of a passing moped for company.

We sat and smoked and talked and drank our Metaxas and slapped at the mosquitos closing in on us. Beattie leaned back in her chair and stretched her arms up above her head. I noticed then that her black T-shirt dress was of a much finer material than mine, and she clearly had no bra on underneath. My eyes flicked to Jake, who seemed oblivious. In fact, throughout the whole evening, his attention had hardly veered from me. I even picked up a hint of resentment in his attitude to her – as if he felt she was intruding on us. It was only subtle, but I could feel it.

It was quite nice, actually . . .

But it's better if she is here. I don't think I could be on my own with a man for any period of time. Jake seems trustworthy enough at the moment. He seems completely lovely, in fact. More than completely lovely . . .

But how do I know at this stage that I can trust him? And there's that edgy thing about him that I can't quite put my finger on. Something a little odd. I haven't got any evidence, but I can just feel it. And if there's one thing I've learned from that alleyway in Marseille, it's that I should trust my instincts more.

So it's far better that there is another girl here to act as a buffer and support. On top of the fact that I really like her, having Beattie around could also be useful.

'I love you guys,' Beattie says, looking at both of us. 'I don't want tonight to end!'

I'm with her on that (and look! It still hasn't ended, even now, not for me, at least. I'm still writing it up!).

'We could go up this hill I know,' Jake says. 'It's a great place to watch the sunrise.'

'And I've got this.' Beattie pulls a bottle of ouzo out of her big shoulder bag.

'And we could mix it with these,' I say, placing my pills on the table.

Jake picks up one of the blister packs of Valium. 'Cool,' he says.

'Help yourself.'

He pops two out and washes them down with his Metaxa.

Beattie picks up the pack and reads the ingredients, which are printed on the side in both Greek and English. 'My mom takes this shit. Should we be mixing it with alcohol?'

'Don't worry. What was it this Australian girl I once knew said about it?' I say. I put on a drawling, cod Australian accent, enjoying the mockery. '"It really kicks up your buzz."'

Jake catches my eye and smiles. He knows I'm talking about Ena.

'Well,' Beattie says, her Oz miles better than my crap attempt. 'If it "really kicks up your buzz", then I'd better get on it.' She takes two pills out and passes them on to me.

'Take us to your hill, then,' I say to Jake, as we get up to leave our table. 'And tell us everything you know about Athens.'

'This place just gets under your skin, man,' he says. 'There's so much to see it freaks me out, and then the heat, and the guys you meet every day, it's just insane.'

We trip across the little park, now deserted except for two

backpackers in sleeping bags, looking very uncomfortable using their rucksacks for pillows.

'They won't last all night,' Jake whispers as we pass them. 'They'll either be robbed or picked up by the police. And you don't want to mess with the Athens police force, believe me. Stories I've heard from guys who have. It's like *Midnight Express*.'

'Jesus, that movie,' Beattie says, laughing. 'When Billy pushes the guard back and the hook goes smash right through his skull.'

We carried on, stumbling and talking rubbish, while Jake led us up through the narrow winding streets of the Plaka. I've got a terrible sense of direction and had no idea where he was taking us, except that it was very definitely uphill. Most of the houses we passed were shuttered up for the night, although there was the odd Greek voice coming from behind high walls, and the occasional thump-thump of some late nightclub.

Most of the tourists had gone home to their hotel or hostel beds. In their place were the cats. They were everywhere – slinking along walls, peering up in gangs from grassed-over ruins, dozing on the steps of Byzantine churches.

The night was still and airless; the air pressed in on us. Even without the oppressive heat of the sun, the going was hard work. Or perhaps it was the Valium and alcohol cocktail we had swallowed. Or the fact that we were smoking as we walked. We had to break out the slimming pills to keep ourselves going.

3

2 August 1980, 8.30 a.m. Athens. Peta Inn roof.

For fuck's sake.

Break out the slimming pills indeed. Been for a pee, my hand is hurting from all the scribbling and there's still no sleeping going on. Like Coleridge, then, but with no person from Porlock to interrupt my writing. Most of the hippies have woken now because of the heat, but Beattie is just snoring on. Sweet. How I envy her.

But at least I can get all this down . . .

Jake leads us up a narrow, steeply climbing street. 'So I spent some time the other night with this guy who had been here for, like, months,' he says. The buildings are behind us now. To our right is a stone wall, and between the olive trees lining the other side of it, we can see the shapes of the city way below us.

'He was broke, stuck here working in some bar trying to get the air fare together to get back to Jefferson City or some shit hole of a place. He said this is the place the Greek kids come and hang out at New Year. It's the best view you can get of the city. It's called Areopagus Hill, but the Greek kids call it *vrahakia*, which means little rocks.'

We round a bend in the street. Jake leads us past some gates which, he says, are the entrance to the Acropolis, then we cross a gravelled area and we're standing at the foot of what looks in the dark like a small mountain with steps carved into the side.

'We go up,' he says.

'Oh man,' Beattie groans. 'Shall we humour him, Em?'

'We'll never hear the end of it if we don't.'

'Be careful, the rocks are really uneven,' Jake says. 'You'd be better taking those off.' He points to Beattie's leather sandals. 'You don't want to fall.'

And there it is again, the weird look in his eyes. There is definitely something odd about this boy.

But even so, I do think he fancies me. And I do him.

Oh God, I do him.

We scrambled up the steep stone steps until we reached the top of the rocks – which was a lot closer than I'd thought from the ground. I nearly fell twice at the top – the going was extremely rough, and I was pretty drunk and whatever. But the view was amazing. Behind us loomed the Acropolis with the Parthenon sitting on top, lit up like some sort of fairy castle, and stretching from left to right in front of us were the twinkling lights of Athens, backdropped by distant mountains looming blue into the night sky.

Up there, high above the smog cloud that cloaked the city, I felt I could really breathe properly for the first time since Marseille.

Being on those rocks early this morning felt to me like some sort of rebirth.

'Take care,' Jake says.

He's a little up ahead of Beattie and me, leading the way. 'You can't see it in the dark, but there's a pretty steep drop over there.' He disappears behind the lip of a rock.

'Jake?' I call, worried that he's failed to follow his own advice.

'I'm just here,' he says, as I crest the peak. He's curled himself into a rounded hollow, almost like an armchair. 'You get the best view from here.'

I drop down so that I'm sitting next to him. He puts his hand on my shoulder – which makes me prickle with pleasure – and points. 'Can you see the glow of the dawn over there?'

'Hey!' Beattie arrives on the rocks behind us. 'Thought I'd lost you guys! There're some goddamn Greek kids coming up behind us.'

'So we're not alone up here,' Jake says.

'Nope,' Beattie says. She seems a bit pissed off about it.

'Not necessarily a bad thing,' he says. 'More people up here to chase away the ghosts.'

'Whatever,' Beattie says, slipping down to join me and Jake. The three of us sit, backs to the cool rocks, like a family watching TV on their sofa, me in the middle, my leg resting against Jake's. The Greek kids settle themselves in another hollow a little way from us. It feels like we're an audience waiting for a play to begin.

'What a beautiful city,' I say. I'm almost a bit teary because of it.

'Yeah, but you don't want to stay too long,' Jake says. 'It sends you crazy. That guy I met was totally demented.'

'The heat's enough to drive you mad,' I say, nodding. 'And it's so full-on all the time.'

'What are your plans?' Beattie asks me, pulling the ouzo out of her bag and unscrewing the lid. She seems edgy. Her foot's tapping out a crazy rhythm on the rock. That'll be the speed, I suppose.

'I want to go out to the islands,' I say. 'I want to visit the places mentioned in the *Odyssey* and the *Iliad*. I want to be a lotus eater!'

'You what now?' Beattie says.

'I used to love the Greek myths when I was younger. It's why I'm here,' I say, which isn't exactly true, but while I'm speaking I totally believe it, the drugs and the drink leading me on – I want to seem more interesting, I suppose. 'But basically I just want to find some-where completely unspoilt and just chill for a bit. There are places where they live like they did back in the olden times, you know, even speak a version of Ancient Greek.' It's only when I finish that I realise I've just parroted what Jake told me earlier. I glance over at him, but he just winks back.

'Hey, now I get you,' Beattie says, passing me the ouzo, which I'm drinking, even though it tastes completely disgusting. 'Sounds cool. And you, Jake?'

He nods and I notice how long his eyelashes are. 'Exactly the same.'

'Hey, we could go together, all three of us!' Beattie says, putting her arm around me.

'Great idea.' Jake does the same and I'm sandwiched between them, really enjoying the feel of my new friends.

And that's how it happened. We've almost automatically become a threesome. We popped a few more slimming pills and, as the dawn crept across the sky, its paleness disguising the fact that it was actually the rising of a sun whose heat would have us pinned down by midday, we made our plan.

We're going to stay in Athens for another two nights while we work out which island will meet our needs, which are (we decided):

1. Not touristy, authentically Greek (we talked a lot about authenticity)
2. Sandy beaches
3. High cliffs

Number three was added by Beattie, who said she just wanted to lie out flat on sand and do very little after all her chasing around Europe, but that occasionally she needed to climb something to avoid running to fat.

Jake seemed to find that irritating. In fact, I don't think he likes Beattie very much. I can't see why. She's a bit full on, but I sort of admire that.

By the time the horrible ouzo had gone, we had been joined by quite a few other people – travellers as well as Greek kids. In my heightened state, I remarked that the rocks had taken on a holy aspect, as if they were some sort of temple, conveying something quite solemn to the birth of this friendship of ours.

'A sort of consecration,' Beattie said, taking my hand.

I felt a rumble in my stomach: a stir of something not unlike love.

4

2 August 1980, 10 a.m. Athens. Peta Inn roof.

Jesus, my hand is hurting from all this writing. Writer's cramp from writer's spew: a sort of reverse writer's block. Writer's bulimia!

Nearly ready at last to turn in, though. I've taken a couple of Valium, so I hope that'll help.

So it turns out that Beattie is also staying at Peta Inn! She arrived from the railway station after I ran into Jake on the stairs. The level of coincidences between me and her make me even more convinced that our meeting's been preordained somehow, that we were fated to meet.

The three of us tripped home, hand in hand, with me in the middle all the way. I like being in the middle!

Luckily, Ena's bed was still empty when we got back here – it must have been about five in the morning and everyone else on the roof was still asleep: legs, arms and other body parts drawn out of their sleeping bags by the dawning heat. Beattie moved her stuff from the bed she took earlier, crawled into the bunk under mine and took a couple more Valium.

By the time I returned from the bathroom, she was fast asleep. That's when I took the extra slimming pill. I guess it was because I didn't want the night to end.

So that worked, then.

I'm knackered now, though. I've made a makeshift sunshade by tying the corners of my PLO scarf to the bed-ends so I've got a sort of low-lying tent to shade me from the sun.

Jake's still over at John's Hostel, but he says he'll move over here after he's taken a nap. People are beginning to get up now, but Beattie's still out for the count. The great thing is that for the last half-hour, Mick the hairy Australian has been slowly packing his rucksack. He says he's off to the Peloponnese. Sparta. He says he 'wants to see some rock down there they used to throw sick babies off of.'

He asked if I'd like to 'split the joint' with him. It was a tempting offer, but I declined. I've got a far more exciting plan in place. The next few weeks – at least – are sorted with Beattie and Jake. I'm going to have the time of my life. Who knows? Perhaps we might even stay out here, spend months, years, even the rest of our lives like this, travelling around the world, taking things as we find them.

There are worse ways of living a life.

Mick's gone now. I've thrown my sleeping bag onto his empty bed to reserve it for Jake. I like the idea of him sleeping next to me up here. We could hold each other's hands and swim off into oblivion and then there would be no one else but me and him and we would ride away on our bunk-bed boat to

5

2 August 1980, 4 p.m. Athens. National Gardens.

Oops. Woke up at midday, sweltering, with my face pressed up against this book and my cheek all inky!

So here we are in the National Gardens.

Jake and Beattie are on either side of me, sleeping. I'm sitting here, smoking and writing. There's absolutely no wind at all today so we've come here to escape the heat that makes your skin feel two sizes too small. The trees and dense shrubs provide a sort of barrier against the smog so the air's almost fresh compared to out on the streets.

We're not on our own in this little fenced-off clearing – there are about thirty other people here, mostly other travellers. But there's also a sprinkling of Greek tramps. Everyone except me is stretched out fast asleep on the grass. I've only slept for about two hours since Areopagus Hill. It was Jake, really, who woke me this morning, clattering around installing his stuff in the bunk next to mine. I didn't mind, of course; I've got him on one side and Beattie's underneath me. What more could I want?

It's a total new start for me.

Anyway.

It's peaceful here now, but it hasn't been like that all afternoon.

My new friends have surprised me, but it's actually just made me like them more. I thought it was just Jake, but it turns out they're *both* quite edgy, actually.

It started when we were talking about how far we would go with things.

'I guess I can't help myself,' Beattie says, swigging from one of the beers we've brought into the National Gardens with us.

'What do you mean?' Jake's lying on his back on the dusty grass, his face covered by a straw cowboy hat. When he speaks, the hat wiggles in a way that makes me smile.

'It's just I have to keep pushing things,' Beattie says. 'Do you know what I mean?'

'Give me an example,' I say, lighting up a Karelia.

'I'm always looking for a way to make a situation more exciting, more dangerous.'

Jake sighs beneath his hat. His arm is still against mine. The nearness of him makes it quite difficult to concentrate on what's going on. I'm itching, and it's not just my mosquito bites.

'It started back home,' Beattie says.

'What?' I ask.

'This hunger for danger.'

'That so?' Jake says, sitting up and leaning his shoulder into mine.

'Sure.' Beattie's eyes flick to the point where Jake and I touch.

'Back in New York City?' Jake asks.

Sometimes when he speaks to her, I hear scorn in his voice. I hope my friends are going to get on. It'll be awful if they don't: I don't think I could choose between them.

'Of *course* back in New York City.' Beattie rolls her eyes at him in a way that makes me think she's picked up on his snarky tone as well. 'Me and my friends, we have this riff on situations. We call it The Dangerous Game.'

'What do you do?' I ask.

'Well, it started off just simple stuff, like, say, lifting a lipstick from the drugstore. Then it got bigger – we learned to pickpocket, and that was pretty cool, but we got so good it didn't really give us the buzz any more. Then we'd do stuff like, I don't know, go have conversations with these dudes hanging out on street corners, like up in Harlem. Like there we were, rich white kids from the Upper East Side, playing ourselves, but a stupid version of ourselves, really badly buying drugs in a totally uncool way that would get the dudes all het up. That was hilarious, but then it started getting tricky. One kid I know had a knife pulled on him. Another got taken down an alley and had his face trashed. That was too much, really, so we stopped all that. But we kept on with other stuff, like climbing onto the ledge outside my friend's apartment on the fortieth floor. Running across the subway track. Yeah. Streaking through Central Park. Spitting off the Empire State Building. Dangerous shit like that.'

'We never did anything like that in Ripon,' I say, and laugh.

'Like Russian Roulette but without guns,' Jake says.

'Exactly.' Beattie flashes an almost-too-much smile at him.

'Wow,' I say.

Beattie lies back and stretches herself on the grass like a cat.

'Lie back, Ems, it's so much cooler down here.'

I lie down and allow the world to spin behind my eyelids. Shortly, Jake stretches out too, lying beside me. His hand nearly touches my own – I feel the electricity of his presence just beyond my fingertips. The sad thing is, though, that if we're to stay a threesome for the island trip, Jake and I can't really get together. Whatever he and I want (and I'm pretty certain he wants the same as me), it will have to wait until . . . until what exactly?

'Do you think of the future at all?' I ask them both as we lie there. 'Or the past?'

'No,' Beattie says.

'It's weird, isn't it?' I say. 'It's like I can't imagine myself being, or having been, anywhere else other than with you two, right here and right now, lying on this grass, looking up at that palm tree.'

'I know what you mean,' Jake says. 'It's like nothing I ever did was ever real until I got to now.'

'God.' Beattie rolls over to face us, propping her head up on one hand. 'Will you two listen to yourselves. Have you quite taken enough drugs today yet?'

At that I start giggling, and Jake joins in. Soon the three of us are curled up on the ground, shaking with laughter, Beattie on one side of me, Jake on the other.

Then the odd thing happened.

A siren starts at the entrance to our fenced-off part of the garden. The gates open, and in stream three uniformed park attendants, one with a megaphone, shouting something so distorted that, even if it were in English, I wouldn't have understood it.

While he shouts whatever it is at us, the other two men go around the lawns shaking the sleepers awake and making those lying down sit up. They come over to us and a rough pair of hands pulls me up by the shoulder. I gasp in pain, because it still hurts where The French Shit pressed down on my ribcage. I'm still pretty badly bruised there under my T-shirt dress.

As soon as I make a sound, Jake jumps to his feet, like someone's flipped a switch inside him. 'Hey, man. What the fuck are you doing?' he says, towering over the park attendant, who, with his bulging eyes and large double chin, has something of the air of a squat frog.

'No sleeps,' the man says. 'No allowed sleepings.'

'Don't touch her like that.' Jake's whole body twitches. I'm scared he's going to hit the little park guy.

'Cool it,' Beattie says. She steps in and puts a restraining hand on Jake.

The park attendant sneers something at Jake, his throat blooming with indignation.

'Don't talk to me like I'm a piece of shit on your shoe, man,' Jake says, shaking Beattie off and taking a step towards him. 'DON'T touch her and DON'T talk at me like I'm shit.'

The man may not understand Jake's words, but he doesn't mistake his tone. He leaps out of his reach, pulls a whistle out of his pocket and blows two short blasts. His two companions steam over to join him, flanking him on either side, arms folded, eyeing Jake.

Time stands still as the three men face the – my? – tall boy. The crickets, which have been carrying on their racket almost constantly in the bushes, stop, leaving nothing but silence.

A walkie-talkie crackles in one of the men's pockets, making us all jump, then the silence falls once more. The other people in the park, all of whom have meekly obeyed the park guys, now watch the action closely, no doubt hoping for a fight to pierce the boredom of the long, hot afternoon.

Jake's rubbing the tips of his fingers together, like he's rolling invisible cigarettes. Something tightens in him. He's like a catapult pulled right back. While I don't fancy the idea of him launching into the park attendants and landing us all in the shit, and while being so close to potential violence is kind of scary, I can't help but be fascinated by this new side of him.

I like that I have this fierce friend on my side, protecting me. I like that his affection and loyalty are rare and precious, not fripperies he hands out unquestioningly.

Then Beattie steps into the hiatus, positioning herself between Jake and the men, smiling at the first park attendant.

'Please,' she says, her voice sweeter than I've ever heard it – almost flirtatious. 'He's just very tired.' She turns to stroke Jake's arm.

'He needs to sleep.' She mimes sleep by tucking her hands at the side of her head. Then she reaches into her bag and pulls out a thousand-drachma note. Reaching forward to shake the man's hand, she palms it to him.

A thousand drachs! That's nearly three days' budget for me. I had no idea Beattie was so loaded.

She stands back, puts her hands on her hips and, smiling up from a coyly lowered face, stretches her chest out in her white T-shirt. From the looks on their faces, not one of the park attendants fails to notice that her breasts are almost completely visible through the thin fabric. 'Just two hours' sleep, OK?'

I like that. I like that she used their stupid dog-sex-hunger as a weapon against them.

The first park attendant glances down at the note in his hand and audibly swallows.

'*Endaxi,*' he said, pocketing the money and holding up two fingers. 'Two hour. Next time, police. Understand?'

'*Efharisto,*' Beattie says and, astonishingly, she steps forward and kisses the man on the cheek. He goes bright red, turns to signal to his mates, and leads them off sharply, out of the garden.

'Yeah, man!' the German hippy near us says, giving Beattie a peace sign before stretching himself out on the lawn to resume his siesta.

'You're such a douche, Jake,' Beattie says, rolling her eyes at him.

So they've gone back to sleep again. I wish I could, too. But I'm too excited, I think.

And how come Beattie has so much money she can just flash thousand-drach bills around like that?

6

3 August 1980, 11 p.m. Athens. Peta Inn roof.

Ouch. My eye hurts, my body hurts and I know tomorrow I'm going to have the biggest come-down/hangover of my life.

Another weird, slightly scary thing happened tonight. These friends of mine are nothing like the boring lumps of Ripon!

The past day and night have been a bit of a blur. We've worked our way through all the pills I bought on the nearly throwing-myself-off-the-parapet night (which seems such a long time ago), and I guess we've each drunk a couple of gallons of Amstel beer. I've been too wasted to write and my memories of how we have passed the time are, unsurprisingly, somewhat blurred.

I'm a bit of a lightweight with drugs and alcohol. Whatever I take, I reach a point where I know I have to stop, because if I don't, there will be a vomiting or a passing out.

Jake and Beattie are different. They both seem to have endless appetites for intoxicants. With Beattie, who's a great talker, booze or pills just stoke her fires – I reckon she could quite literally go on for days.

And Jake's one of those people who seem to change completely when he's wasted. When he's straight, he's still the calm, strong, level guy who saved me after the aforementioned parapet incident. But with enough alcohol inside him, he seems to reach a point where he's possessed: his blue, blue irises go dark and his face looks like someone else's. That's when I see the wild and scary (to other people) part of him.

Or is it scared, rather than scary? It's impossible to tell.

And so this is what happened tonight . . .

We were sitting outside Manos's Bar on Kidathineon. It's a backpacker pub, one of those places that the Greeks and the straights don't go near. Manos is a grey-skinned, greasy old man in a stained T-shirt who sits at his bar, flicking his worry beads over his wrist, looking at us all as if we're animals in some kind of zoo. But he's happy to keep serving us beer after beer after beer whenever we put our hands up in the air, bringing the bottles over on a dirty tray (no glasses), waiting over us until we pay his over-the-odds prices. It's only when people fall asleep – or pass out – that he turfs them out, and that's simply because they're no longer in a position to pay him for any more beer. The poor drunk kid then either slumps in the dust or picks himself up and staggers off in search of his filthy hostel bunk.

It's not dignified. But it's a load of fun and it goes without saying that we love Manos's. You can be as loud and as outrageous as you want. And even though we bitch about the price, the beer's still cheap compared to back home and he's open all day from ten in the morning until the last person leaves the following morning. He plays nothing but The Police's *Reggatta de Blanc* over and over again. But I don't think I could listen to 'Bring on the Night' enough in my life. Secretly, I've made it mine and Jake's song. Because one day our night will come, I'm sure of it. When I get over what The French Shit did to me, when Beattie's gone her way. After all, she's got to get back to college, whereas Jake's finished, and I've not started yet, so I'm not fully committed. Who knows where our lives will go in the next couple of months? Call me a fantasist, but . . .

Lots of bars here don't really want young travellers because of how we get. From what I've seen, Greeks rarely just sit and drink beer like us. For them, alcohol goes with a four-hour meal, which they don't start until eleven at night, whereas we see food as a necessary evil that has to be taken from time to time to soak up the alcohol. Until tonight I hadn't actually eaten since my lamb chop dinner. How many nights ago was that? One? Two? They're all melting into each other here.

Feels like I've been here forever. I can only just about vaguely remember Ripon (thank God).

Anyway, we sat at the same table at Manos's today for going on eight hours, drinking beer after beer, smoking, finishing off the pills and enjoying the goings on at the table next to ours, where two bearded German longhairs in cut-off denims were listening to a tiny shaven-headed Australian drunkenly slur on about how his mate had abandoned him.

'He just took off, man,' the Australian says. 'We're out drinking, get stoked, and then bam! I score with this chick, take her out to this park for a blow job – and man, that chick could really blow, if you know what I mean –'

That's how he really spoke. I ask you. It cracked us all up.

'– And when I get back to the club he ain't there no more. Reckon the cunt's got jealous, you know what I mean? But it's been three days now and we're supposed to be flying back tomorrow, you know?'

'That kind of shit happens so much here,' Jake says quietly to us, so the Australian can't hear him. 'People just get pissed with their friends and slope off some other place.'

'I don't blame that jerk's friend for leaving him,' Beattie says.

'Yeah. Tosser,' I say.

At one point, Beattie gets up and fetches us three gyros from the kiosk next door – soft, doughy flatbread stuffed with shaved-off

136

spit-roast lamb, chips and tzatziki. She and Jake fall on theirs like hungry wolves, but I just pick out a couple of bits of lamb from mine. It's pretty greasy.

'You don't eat much, do you?' Beattie says, eyeing me above her napkin-wrapped handful of bread and meat.

'It's the heat,' I say. 'I just don't feel all that hungry. Plus, I'm so full of beer, I slosh if I jump.'

I get up to demonstrate, putting my belly up against her ear. But I stumble and lurch into the Australian's table. He's now telling the story of a fight he had with a thief in India.

'I socked the eye sockets out of him!' he announces, as if it were the punch line to the world's biggest joke.

So I'm partly unsurprised when, as a response to a surprise jolt from behind (i.e. me bashing into him), the Australian jumps up and, without checking who his 'attacker' is, or why it's happened, he turns and whacks me in the face, knocking me back against our own table and sending the twelve empty Amstel bottles we've built up spinning and flying to the pavement, where they smash with a racket like some sort of experimental Pink Floyd track.

The strike takes the wind right out of me. As I struggle to find my bearings, my hand clasped over the eye that caught the punch, I hear Jake's chair clatter to the ground. He jumps to his feet, eyes blazing like police lights, and his fist is on its way across the air in front of my nose to meet the Australian's sunburned jaw.

'You don't hit a girl, man,' he yells, as he makes contact. Perhaps it's the drugs, or perhaps everything really does slow right down, because I'm sure I see the Australian's face vibrate three or four times with the impact of the blow. The final quiver of his head trails a thread of snot and blood behind it as the rest of his body follows its trajectory into the air and across the table. He almost lands in the laps of the startled Germans, who jump up as if afraid to get the casualty's weaselly bodily fluids onto their immaculate kurtas and minuscule shorts.

'You do not hit a girl!' Jake cries again as he launches himself on top of the Australian. He takes the neck of the guy's frayed T-shirt in one hand, and shapes the other into a fist, ready to bring it down again on his head.

'He's nussing to do viz us,' the Germans say, backing off into the shadows with their shoulder bags. Then they turn on their heels and run away.

Beattie, who by this point is down on the pavement with a protective arm around me, starts yelling, 'Stop it, Jake!' and – I almost laugh at the cliché – 'He ain't worth it!'

But Jake goes right on ahead, slamming his fist down into the Australian's face, centrally on his nose this time.

Most of the other drinkers at the bar are standing now, keeping clear of the immediate area around Jake and the Australian. Passers-by stop to gawp, bottlenecking the pedestrianised street.

Jake hits the Australian again.

'Stop him,' one woman shouts to no one in particular.

'He'll kill him,' another says.

But no one makes a move to stop him. He's too fucking scary.

As Jake goes in to hit the Australian a fourth time, Beattie jumps to her feet and launches herself at him, tugging at his shirt, trying to drag him off his victim.

Again, I want to laugh at the sight of tiny Beattie trying to pull six-foot-four Jake away from the mini-Australian, who's only a bit taller than me and Beattie. It doesn't seem like a fair fight in any way at all, but then the Australian recovers from his initial shock, comes to, and proves to be a wirily vicious fighter, jabbing and striking to try to get away from Jake's lengthy but scrawny body.

Then Manos, the bar owner, weighs in and somehow pulls Beattie and the Australian away from Jake, while all time letting fly a stream of Greek: *Malacca* this and *Malacca* that. He flings the Australian onto the pavement and spits on him.

'Police will come,' he snarls. 'Close me down and arrest you. *Pusti Malacca.*'

'Take it easy, man,' the Australian whines, scrambling to his feet. 'He's a fucking maniac,' he shouts, pointing at Jake, who lurches towards him. 'Fucking maniac.'

'You're the fucking maniac,' Jake slurs, stumbling over another chair that got tipped over.

Before Jake can reach him, the Australian scurries away into the shadows of an alleyway opposite the bar.

Manos lets go of Beattie and starts to wave his arms in the air, still cursing after the Australian.

The whine of a siren and strobing blue lights on the white-painted buildings at the end of the road warn us a police car's on its way. A wedge of stoned/drunk tourists block the disco-beating street, so it's making slow progress. Alarmed by this – the police have the power to close down disreputable bars – Manos runs about the tables in an oddly nimble way that verges on the dainty, picking up empty bottles, sweeping away the broken glass, shooing away drunkards.

Beattie's panic at what's just happened, and, no doubt, at what could potentially unfold if the police are to ever reach the bar, galvanises her into action.

'OK, we split,' she says, grabbing Jake by the hand and dragging him away from the bar's tables and chairs. 'I'll look after this idiot asshole. You pick up our gear,' she says to me. She slips into the crowd with him. Not wanting to lose sight of them, I quickly scoop up all our bags and dive into the throng, which, the floor show over, is beginning to move along.

At the end of the street I almost stumble into the police car. Two fat, sweating policemen are inside, leaning their elbows on the open windows, the driver lazily pushing the horn while the siren whoops intermittently above them. If anything they look bored, not at all in a hurry to reach the scene of the crime. Perhaps they know Manos, and are giving him time to sort himself out before their arrival. In any case, they're not at all interested in me – I'm just one more grubby young tourist. I get right past them, drunken, stumbling gait, three bags and all.

But I can't find Beattie and Jake anywhere. I walk up and down Kidathineon a couple of times, but they're nowhere. It's as if the street's swallowed them up. I suppose they're thinking the same about me. There are loads of people and the alleyways around are a kind of maze.

As I search for them, the full impact of what has physically happened to me begins to dawn. Once again, I have been attacked. My eye hurts like hell and I'm cold and shaky, even through the heat of the night. Out on the street, alone again, the fear comes back. Not only do I have the memory of The French Shit haunting me, but there's also the very real possibility of bumping into The Australian Shit and having him recognise me. I hug our bags to my chest and run, stumbling on the cobbled streets, back in what I think is the direction of the Peta Inn.

Eventually, more by chance than design, I found my way back here. Ignoring the couple of other people sitting around chatting, I've climbed up onto my bunk bed and now I'm burrowed into my sleeping bag, writing this.

I'm back home.

It's two hours since I got here, and there's still no sign of Beattie and Jake. I hope they're OK. But I can't stay awake any more. Perhaps they've gone on partying. Like I said, I'm a lightweight. At least, from the way he reacts to her, I don't have to worry about Jake fancying Beattie!

The world has gone all spinny and I have to sleep.

Goodnight, Emma.

7

4 August 1980, 2 p.m. Athens. Peta Inn roof.

So when I woke up this morning, it wasn't to Jake's face in the next-door bed, but Beattie's. I peered over my mattress: Jake was sleeping underneath. It was a little disappointing, but what the hell, at least they were there. At least they had come back to me, not done an Ena.

Shortly after I'm awake, Beattie opens an eye and looks at me.

'Shit, man,' she says. 'That's one fuck of a shiner.'

As we climb out of our bunks, I ask where they got to and she says Jake had popped more slimming pills than he should have, so it took her hours to bring him down. She'd put him on the bottom bed so he'd have a bit of shade.

'He'll sleep for hours now,' she says as we leave him snoring with a note at his side telling him we'll be back later.

We staggered up a steeply winding street in the Plaka, with desiccating hangovers. The morning heat was already blistering and my black baggy dress was soaked with sweat. I've worn it day and night for over a week now. Really must wash it soon, although everyone stinks here, it's inescapable.

There's not a single mirror in the Peta Inn. I quite like this: it's a sort of escape from the ever-present tyrant of my own reflection. But when, like this morning, I catch sight of myself in a shop window, it can be quite terrifying. I'd forgotten what I'd done to my hair, and I looked too thin even for my own exacting standards. I was quite a shock to myself. And I saw how alarming my right eye is: it's puffed almost shut, with a deep black stain going down into my cheek, blending through purple to an almost fluorescent yellow outline.

I look barely human.

I'm feeling so disjointed, what with the shock of realising what has been done to my face, an achy neck from some kind of whiplash from the punch, an appalling hangover that's putting everything into a sort of time-lapse and the perspective-flattening effect of viewing the world through just one eye. It's like I'm not quite living in my own head right now.

'Jake was out of order last night,' Beattie says, leading me on, up the hill.

'But that Australian Shit was a total jerk,' I say.

'He sure made a mess of your face,' Beattie says. 'But Jake, like, just lost it, didn't he? It was like nothing else I've ever seen. He's very protective of you, isn't he?'

'Yeah, I suppose.'

'Something going on there?'

'No!' I blush, but it's probably hidden by the bruise and the fact I'm beetroot red with the heat anyway.

Beattie looks at me, one eyebrow raised.

'What was he like last night after you lost me?' I ask, to change the subject.

Beattie frowns and bites her lip. 'He was set on searching out that Australian. Going on about how only freaks hit women, and how he was going to make him pay.'

'You didn't find him?' I ask, alarmed at the thought.

'Nah, thank God. We ended up in some bar further up in the Plaka, some scuzzy little disco dive upstairs with stupid coloured lights and one idiot Dutch girl running the music, serving the drinks and dancing like a maniac in between. I think she thought she was giving some sort of floor show.'

'Oh.' I feel a spike of jealousy. I didn't think they'd actually have gone into a bar together.

'I mean, we looked for you and all, but I just reckoned you'd go back to Peta Inn. And Jake needed calming down. He was totally wired, in no fit state to be wandering around the streets alone.'

'But I had your bags with your money and shit.'

'Aha! But I found this,' Beattie stops, rummages in her bag and pulls out a tooled leather wallet. 'Five thousand drachs in it. About a hundred and twenty dollars.'

I gawp at her.

'Aw, don't look at me like that, Ems. There was no ID in it. So no chance of handing it in anywhere. Whoever I gave it to would just have taken the cash out themselves. Might as well put it to good use.'

I nod, biting my lip.

'We can put it toward our escape fund. Get outta this place.'

She put the wallet back in her bag and led me off again, as if walking would somehow make me agree that there was absolutely nothing wrong with what she had done.

But worse was to come.

The sun was really too much for us by then. We slipped into the shelter of a gift shop. It looked tiny on the outside, but inside it was cool and cavernous, smelling of the leather sandals and belts that crowded the walls.

* * *

The shopkeeper, a boy about my age, eyes us briefly. Then, I suppose not finding anything interesting to ogle in two unwashed, punk-cropped backpackers – one with a humdinger of a black eye – returns to reading his book.

'Let's play the Dangerous Game,' Beattie says under her breath.

'Eh?'

'Steal me something.'

'What?' I shoot back at her.

Not being the kind of girl who hung out in the gangs that ransacked Woolworth's after school, I'd never stolen anything in my life.

'Go on. Just something tiny, just for me,' she says, exercising her glottal stops. While I've been taking up a few Americanisms, she's trying out my Ripon accent with its flat a's and elongated vowels. She says the habit of collecting accents has been beaten into her at drama school.

She moves over to a stand nearer the boy shopkeeper and bends forward to examine some postcards on the bottom of a spinning stand, positioning herself so that he can see right down her baggy vest front to her breasts.

Although my mother would say she needed to, Beattie doesn't wear a bra, so the boy is treated to, as my mother would also say, 'a right eyeful'.

I know she's giving me my moment and, although I know it's wrong, I don't want to let her know what kind of wimp I actually am. Also, the hungry look in the boy's face as he ogles Beattie wins him no favours with me.

So I reach out and pick up a tooled leather hair clasp, one of those curved things with a wooden prong that holds a ponytail. It has *Hellas* burnt into it in Greek letters. My cheeks burning, I palm it into my bag. Then, too casually, I carry on browsing, rifling through ceramic thimbles with the Parthenon painted on them, pens with a Greek-flagged ship sailing up and down them in a bubble of liquid, key rings with a satyr's phallus attached. Then I come to a basket full of blue glass eye things with long blue tassels attached.

'I'll take one of those,' I say, picking one out and giving it to the boy.

Beattie looks at me like I'm crazy.

'It's OK,' I say, flicking my eyes to my bag.

'You have weakness and evil?' the boy says as he takes my fifty drachs.

'What?' I flush.

'*Mataki*.' He points to the glass eye, which he's wrapping carefully in paper striped blue like the Greek flag. 'Evil eye. It guards against.'

'Ah. But Emma,' Beattie says, still pretending to be from Yorkshire rather than Manhattan, 'you should have haggled.'

'Oops,' I say, batting my eyes at the boy. Playing the game.

The boy smiles again and I realise he has very kind brown eyes.

'What are you reading?' I ask him as he gives me my change.

He holds his book up. It's *Tess of the D'Urbervilles*, in English.

'I love that book,' I say. 'Your English must be very good.'

'I try,' he says. 'Plenty to practise on here.'

He points into the back of the shop, where I see, in the shadows, shelves of second-hand books, mostly in English.

'Wow,' I say, going over to take a closer look.

'I buy and sell,' he says.

'I've got five books back at the hostel which I've done with. Would you buy them off me?'

'If they're not too shitty condition,' he says. 'Or I swap. One of my books for two of yours.'

'Cool,' I say. 'So where have you got with *Tess*?'

While Beattie personifies boredom, the boy and I chat about the book. I'm pleased to find that he agrees with my theory that Hardy objectifies Tess.

'Hey, come on, Emma, we gotta meet Jake in ten minutes,

remember,' Beattie says, coming over from where she's been dawdling at the back of the shop, and pulling on my arm like a nagging child.

'Oh,' I say. 'No one told me.'

'Bye,' she says to the boy and pulls me out of his shop.

'I'll be back with my books,' I say to him.

'I look forward to it,' he says, as we step out into the sunlight.

'What was that about?' I ask Beattie.

'You were going on for ages.'

'So?'

'I was bored. And anyway, I'm sure Jake wouldn't want you to get too cosy with that booky Greek kid.'

'What does that mean?'

'You know *exactly* what that means, Ems.'

'Look. There's nothing going on—'

'Yeah, yeah, yada, yada. Yeah. Look at me. Gooseberry Bea.'

'That won't happen,' I say. 'I promise.'

We sit down at a café a few streets away from the shop and order a couple of beers.

'What did you get me, then?' Beattie holds out her hand.

'I feel really bad about this,' I say as I pull the hair clasp out of my bag. 'The boy turned out to be so nice.'

'So? He was nice before you lifted it.'

I place the thing in her palm.

'Well, it might be a lovely keepsake for the future.' She turns it over in her hands and smiles. 'Not much use right now, though.' She demonstrates how pointless a clasp is when your hair is about one inch all over.

'Oops.' I hadn't really thought about anything other than going for something small enough to fit in my palm.

Our beer arrives and we both take long, thirsty draughts straight from the bottles.

'I'm going on a diet,' Beattie says.

'What? Why?' I say. 'You're just the right size.'

'Nah,' she says, grabbing a tiny pinch of flesh at her belly. 'Look at that. Gross. I'm going on the Emma diet. I'm just going to eat what you eat. I'd love to be as slim as you.'

I shift uncomfortably. She's only seen me shrouded in this black thing. I know what I look like naked. It isn't a pretty sight.

'Still, plenty of food in this though, eh?' She tilts her bottle at me. 'Keeps me going.'

'Oh yeah. I got you something, too.' She reaches inside her bag and pulls out the first volume of Robert Graves's *The Greek Myths*. She holds it out to me, smiling.

'You didn't?'

'Course I did. While you two were yattering away out front, I made the most of my time in back. I remember what you said on the rocks about all that mythology stuff. Take it. Go on.'

I have no choice but to take the book from her hands. The way she's holding it out is drawing too much attention. I flip through it. She chose well. It's very scholarly and thorough – just the thing for me. It'll be a great thing to read before Cambridge – if I ever get around to it, of course. It's been, what, three days since Ena left me *The Women's Room* and I haven't even started it. I've not read a word of anything.

'Don't I get a thank-you?' Beattie says, folding her arms and sitting back in the cheap plastic chair.

'You shouldn't have, Beattie.'

I mean this not in the English polite manner of receiving a gift, but quite literally – I really wish she hadn't stolen the book from the boy.

'In any case,' I say, 'it hasn't gained us anything – I was going to go back and swap my old books. I would probably have chosen this one anyway. Now there's no way I can go back to that shop.'

Beattie roars with laughter. 'You are soooo straight,' she says. 'Seriously, Emma, do you really think it's all about getting the thing?

I mean, honey, this hair slide is completely fucking useless, but the fact that you took it for me means the *world*. It's the *buzz* that's the important thing. The thrill of taking. And who's to know whether old Romeo there'll notice anything missing from his precious shop anyhow? His head's way too firmly inserted in the clouds. Did you see the way he went back to his book after we walked in? If that was me, I'd be on us like white on rice. Go on, tell me you didn't feel the buzz when you lifted the hair thing?'

I shrug. I felt something, but it hadn't been entirely pleasurable. However, I don't want Beattie to suspect I'm as boring as I actually am, so I give her a little half-smile.

As promised, we headed back to the hostel to fetch Jake, who said he wanted to go down to The Milk Bar for lunch. This, we have decided, is our new place – we're giving Manos's a wide berth in case The Australian Shit decides to come looking for us.

But I was feeling pretty sick at heart by then. Even though it was lovely to see Jake, and I would have liked to have spent the rest of the morning with him, I needed a rest from Beattie. So I said I had a headache – which I did – and, while they went off for lunch, I lay down where Jake had been sleeping, hanging my big PLO scarf from my own bunk above to shade me and give me a bit of privacy. His sleeping bag has the sweet warm scent of him, so, hidden by my scarf, I'm holding it close to me, as if it contains him. When I've finished writing this up I'm going to try reading the book Beattie stole for me, but I'm pretty sleepy now.

8

5 August 1980, 2 a.m. Athens. Peta Inn roof.

And boy, did I sleep.

It's only much later in the afternoon, when the heat's gone off the day, that I wake to what I think is a mosquito just outside my makeshift sunshade. But then I realise it's someone giggling. I lift aside the scarf and there are Beattie and Jake crouching on the next-door bunk, their knees almost right in my face, passing a bottle of ouzo between them.

Just for a minute they look like they've been caught out.

Hmmm.

'Aha!' Jake says. 'She rises!'

'What are you two up to?' I say, smiling. By the size of their pupils they're pretty speedy.

'Ta-da!' Beattie holds out a palm full of silver coins.

'What's that?'

'Spoils. Yours. From your books.'

'You didn't?' I say.

'Sure. We wanted to ask you first, but you were so out of it, we decided to go ahead anyway.'

'We went in your rucksack. I hope you don't mind?' Jake says.

'Of course not.'

And I really didn't mind. What's mine is theirs. The only thing I don't want them to see is this journal, but I keep it in my day-bag pillow while I'm sleeping. And The Women's Room – which I really want to read, despite Ena's inscription – was safe, still tucked under my mattress. I could see it from where I was lying on the lower bunk. What I only realise now as I'm writing this – because when we got back tonight I wanted to look up ferries and things – is that in among the books they sold was my Let's Go, which initially I thought was a bit of a bummer. But I suppose I don't need it now I've got Jake and Beattie. We can find our own way, together.

'Anyhoo,' Jake says. 'It worked out well, because the gift-shop guy was all like, "you stole my book" at Beattie. But she told him it was you and that you'd like just disappeared off to Turkey owing her money, but had left the books, so she thought she'd bring them in and see if she could get something back for them.'

'When he told us about the stolen book, I offered him two of yours in exchange, like some sort of good girl,' Beattie says. 'But he was so cute, he just said that since you'd ripped me off too he'd buy all five off of me. So there you go.'

She tips the coins into my hand.

I blink and shake my head.

'You OK, Em?' Jake says. He looks a little crestfallen at my reaction.

'I mean, like, I was doing you a favour,' Beattie goes on.

Well, it can't be undone. And in any case, I'm not planning on seeing that boy again, so I decide just to fold my mortification away. Perhaps I'm being too English about it. Too hung up. Beattie would say that, probably. She might be right.

'So, then, what's up for tonight?' Beattie says, shifting over to the end of my bunk.

'The beach?' I look at my handful of money. 'I reckon I've just about got enough for the subway fare.'

'Cool,' Jake says. 'We stopped at the drugstore on our way back, so we're all set.' He hands me the ouzo bottle and a couple of pills and smiles at me with his blue, blue eyes and somehow all the problems that Beattie has dumped in my lap seem to melt away.

She can be a bit of a liability, though. What would it be like if it was just me and him? If she'd never bumped into us at that restaurant?

We didn't ever get to the beach, of course. We just ended up in The Milk Bar all evening, getting wasted.

9

6 August 1980, 2 p.m. Athens. National Gardens.

Beattie's done it again.

This morning, after a lost day and night of drinking and pills, Jake had another lie-in. That boy can sleep! He's conked out again now, while I write, between me and Beattie – who is also sleeping. We're in the National Garden again, his beautiful cheek resting up against my thigh.

When he's this close I can imagine him touching me more, and kissing me. I really would like that, I think. The idea of sex scares me, though. I'm not sure if I could cope with that, not after The French Shit. So I'd like Jake and me just to hold hands and kiss and perhaps he could put his arms around me. Perhaps it would get to the point where I could tell him what happened to me and he would understand and wait until I was ready.

Am I in love, I wonder? Am I in love with Jake?

Anyway. Back to what Beattie did (second instalment).

So, earlier on, she and I left Jake another note and headed off to The Milk Bar, where we started with a couple of coffees – Nescafé for her and a *metrio* for me (a Greek coffee that's not too sweet, which I really, really like). She had a yoghurt and honey as well, but couldn't persuade me to take one. They're massive and full of fat and really expensive. It would be a waste of drachma. I've completely thrown my budget to the wind the past couple of days and, even with Beattie's 'found' money, I've really got to be careful now.

'Have you noticed how Jake changes when he's out of it?' Beattie asks me, licking runny honey off the back of her spoon.

I nod. 'He's one of us, though,' I say quickly. I can't bear the thought of her saying something bad about him.

'Certainly.' Beattie leans forward, puts her hand on mine and whispers, 'I even think it makes him kinda interesting.'

'Me too,' I say, smiling at her. *Do* I have a rival here, I wonder? Do I have to keep my eye on her?

I drain my *metrio* and take a Karelia out of its dainty, white box. Man, are they harsh, though. But I'm getting used to the taste: the roughness may even be anaesthetising my throat against the hot, thick dust of this polluted city.

'Fuck it,' I say, and I wave at the waitress and order a beer.

It's only an hour off midday – we're in the last bit of shade before the sun fully hits the street – so it feels almost reasonable to be moving straight from breakfast of sorts to alcohol.

'Make that two, will ya?' Beattie says to the girl serving us, who can't be more than twelve years old. Then she gets back to talking about Jake. 'It's like his normal gentleness gets overtaken by some kind of dangerous guy,' she says.

The girl brings us our beers.

'At least he's on our side. All that fighting at Manos's was only because he was defending me,' I say.

'Your hero! Ta dah!'

'And me, a damsel in distress.'

'At jeopardy from a pissed-up Antipodean.'

I blink. Beattie entirely copied my accent with that last line. She's got a real gift – not only has she mastered Ripon, but she also softens her own quite deep voice to something much lighter and more like my own. What's also uncanny is the way that, when she does me, she takes on my character too. Jake pointed it out last night, and, although it's hard to recognise your own mannerisms, she's got me down to a T.

We sit in silence, drinking our beer. A dog cocks its leg in the street just in front of us and pisses on the pavement. We watch as the thick yellow stream runnels through the dust, heading towards a barefoot, purple-clad boy squatting on the ground with a tatty velvet board of shitty earrings for sale. He seems oblivious as the piss hits his foot and pools around his baggy trouser bottoms.

The sun nudges the morning shadows further towards the wall, scorching Beattie's leg. She leans back in her chair and puts her hands behind her head.

'We've gotta get out of this place,' she says. 'It's doing my head in.'

Despite her wildness, I really do like Beattie. And up until what happened next, what she'd done hadn't been *so* bad. She made amends for the book she stole, and she was right about the wallet she found – the money would only have been taken by someone else. Looking at it like that, the only person who had really done any wrong was me, nicking the hair clasp.

But then . . .

A girl and boy roll up along the street, almost entirely swamped by their luggage of two heavy backpacks, a day sack – which the girl wears on her front – and a large pouch dangling from the man's neck. When they reach The Milk Bar they stop and, panting like dogs from the heat, stick their noses into their guidebook – the same edition of *Let's Go* as mine was. I wonder if perhaps it's the actual copy, bought from the gift shop, but theirs is in a lot worse state than mine.

'Is this it?' the boy asks the girl.

I recognise his accent as being from somewhere up near where I come from.

'Aye,' the girl says, firmly placing her as Yorkshire too.

'Do you speak English?' the boy asks us. 'Can you mind these for us while we go in and order?'

They dump their rucksacks at the table next to ours and go inside.

Given what happened to the lost wallet, I wonder briefly whether we're the right kind of people for them to entrust with their stuff.

But I don't know the half of it.

They come back out followed by the young waitress, who has two Amstels on a tray for them. They sit and drink, then the boy leans over towards us. 'Bloody hot, intit?' he says.

The girl waves at us from her seat. 'I'm Laura, he's Tom.'

'I'm Trudy and this is Joanie,' Beattie says, smiling as I frown at her.

'Where you from?' I ask.

'Harrogate,' Tom says. 'Going back on the Magic Bus tomorrow at the crack, worst luck. I could have stayed out here for ever.'

'No way!' I start, imagining that the three of us would start on a long conversation about places, people and events we had in common. 'I'm from—'

'You just arrived in town?' Beattie asks, interrupting me and offering them a cigarette.

'Just got back from the islands. We've been out there two months now. I'd forgotten what a dump Athens is,' Tom says.

'We've been blinded by beauty,' Laura says. Her face, mostly hidden by a beaten-up straw sunhat, is like a little elf's. 'You look sort of familiar,' she goes on. 'Where're you from?'

Beattie leans across between us, obscuring Laura's view of me.

'Can I get in more beers?'

'Cheers, love,' Tom says.

She nods at the waitress, motioning at our empty bottles. Then she turns the back of her head to Tom and Laura and mouths the words 'Dangerous Game' to me.

As the girl comes by with four more beers, Beattie sits back and angles herself towards Tom and Laura. 'Which islands have you visited? We're heading out soon, so if you've got any recommendations . . .'

'Well,' Tom says, 'we discovered a little piece of heaven on earth.'

It's a strange turn of phrase. One I wouldn't have put in the mouth of someone so ordinary-looking. But people surprise you sometimes, don't they?

'Really?' Beattie says.

Tom nods and takes a swig of his beer. 'Place called Ikaria. Hardly any tourists at all, just a handful of backpackers like us. The people are right friendly, hitching is a cinch, you can camp just about anywhere and they've got some of the bloody best beaches and mountains in the whole of Greece.'

'You have to go to this beach called Nas,' Laura interrupts. 'And the honey is out of this world. It's like butter.'

There's something drippy about her I don't like at all. She reminds me too much of home.

'And the best part is,' Tom says, 'we found this little farm where we picked tomatoes in exchange for a hut to sleep in, two hundred drachs a day each and as much food and wine as we could fit inside us.'

'We didn't spend a penny!' Laura says, patting her day sack. 'Almost all the money we brought with us, we're taking back home.'

'Cool,' Beattie says, and I think *Oh no*.

Tom unzips his backpack and pulls out a map, which he unfolds onto our table.

'There,' he says, pointing to an island not far off the coast of Turkey.

'Is it anything to do with Icarus?' I ask, and all three of them look at me, frowning. 'You know, Icarus, who didn't do what his dad said, flew too close to the sun, melted the wax on his wings and fell into the sea and drowned.'

Tom shrugs. 'I wouldn't know. I'm a chemist.'

And Laura just giggles.

'It's got great surf,' Tom says.

'But you have to be careful,' Laura adds. 'The currents are awful dangerous around the north coast.'

I'm surprised by this. I've always thought the sea around Greece was calm and blue, but then I guess those stories of storms in the Odyssey must have some grounding in fact.

'And are there cliffs and sandy beaches?' Beattie asks.

'Loads,' Tom says. 'It's a bit windy, but apart from that, it's paradise on earth.'

'Perhaps we've found our place,' I say to Beattie.

'Talking about which, we've not got anywhere to stay tonight. Any ideas?' Tom says.

I'm just about to recommend the Peta Inn when Beattie jumps in.

'There's a really good place up Mitropoleos called Funny Trumpet Guest House,' she says. 'It's meant to be the best in Athens. If they're full, you can keep heading up that way.' She gestures with her hand towards Mitropoleos, which is in the complete opposite direction to Nikis, where we're staying. 'There's loads of cheap places up there. But don't take your backpacks while you look — it's way too hot for that. Just leave them here and we'll mind them for you till you find somewhere.'

'Would you?' Laura asks, her little white teeth showing through her pretty smile.

She actually looks fit to drop. A lot of travellers arriving in Athens do – especially the smaller girls, for whom lugging round twenty-five-pound rucksacks in the midday heat is a serious challenge. Even if it weren't for being attacked so regularly, my neck and shoulders would still hurt from carrying my rucksack.

'Sure,' Beattie says. 'I know what it's like. It feels like running free when you can leave the baggage for a while.'

'Cheers,' Tom says. 'Let me buy you a couple of beers to say ta.'

'Listen to Mr Moneybags,' Laura says, giggling.

He signals again to the waitress for two more, and she brings them to our table to line up against our unfinished drinks.

'Leave that, too.' Beattie points at the day pack Laura is still wearing clamped to her front. Laura looks at Tom, who nods.

'Thanks,' she says, taking it off and handing it to Beattie, circling her freed shoulders.

'Weighs a ton,' Beattie says, putting it down at her feet.

'It does pull on my neck a bit.'

Tom places a pile of coins on the table for our beers while Laura fishes out a map and gets Beattie to point out where Funny Trumpet is.

But I knew that Beattie was sending them off on a wild goose chase. Funny Trumpet is indeed supposed to be the best hostel, but everyone knows you have to book up in advance well before you turn up. There was no way they were going to find a bed there.

We watched them drift off along the street like sunburned children, freed of all their luggage except the pouch, which Tom kept around his neck. The shops were all closing for their long afternoon breaks and, apart from our poor, hardworking girl waitress and an old man dozing on a chair in the shade of a closed greengrocer's awning, there was not a Greek to be seen. The muzz of morning beer mixed with midday sun descended on me. It's a great feeling. The trick is to keep it topped up with just enough alcohol to stop it turning into a headache, but not so much that you start slurring, become incoherent or fall asleep.

'What was all that about?' I ask Beattie as soon as Tom and Laura are out of earshot.

She sits back and taps the side of her nose.

'But why did you make up names for us?'

'So they won't be able to find us,' she says. Then she hauls the day pack up onto her lap, unzips it and rummages around. 'Stupid girl, leaving her bag with me.'

'What are you going to take?' I say. 'Not her passport and stuff?'

'Nah. We need her to be able to go home on the Magic Bus tomorrow. Just stuff like . . . Ah.'

She pulls out an envelope that had been tucked away at the bottom of the bag.

'"Almost all the money we brought with us, we're taking back home",' she says, patting the day bag and copying exactly Laura's thick Yorkshire accent and simpering tones. 'Oh no you ain't, honey.'

And I just sit there, my mouth hanging open, as she counts out two hundred pounds in twenty-pound notes and slips the remaining forty back into the envelope, which she places back right at the bottom of the day pack.

'What?' she says, catching my shocked expression. 'It's not like they'd budgeted to have this much. I'm doing them a favour. Life should never be too easy.' She stands up. 'Now we'd better clear outta here before they get back.'

'What about their stuff?' I ask her. 'Someone could just steal the rest of it.'

Beattie sighs and goes over to have a word with the waitress. As we leave, carrying the bottles Tom bought us, I look back and see the poor girl lugging the big rucksacks into the safety of The Milk Bar kitchen.

That's almost the worst part of it. If anything is discovered to be missing before Laura and Tom leave for home tomorrow, we – as in 'Trudy and Joanie' – are not going to be the first suspects.

We went back to Peta Inn, woke Jake, who was, amazingly, still asleep, snoring and sweating on his bunk, and we brought him here to the Gardens for the afternoon, stopping to buy some more beers on the way.

'So we can celebrate,' Beattie says.
    I don't feel much like celebrating.

10

7 August 1980, 10 a.m. Athens. Peta Inn roof.

Last night was great! Sore head again, but well worth it.

We found this rooftop bar up above a thundering main road. It was high enough to catch a slight breeze and had a lovely view of the Acropolis rising above the city streets. Beattie was on top form and I almost felt able to forgive her for what she did earlier. I began to get that feeling again that the three of us are special; spiritual, almost.

OK, I was pretty pissed, but whatever.

We talked on and on about Ikaria, making our plans, weaving a picture of the idyllic, clean life we would lead away from the city, which, lovely view or not, is filthy and stinking. We've decided to go the day after tomorrow. We'll just head down to Piraeus, jump on a boat and set off.

We shared a couple of flasks of Metaxa with an off-duty bouzouki player at the next table. As the night wore on, he started playing and we sang along, making up lyrics to his traditional tunes until our voices were hoarse.

We didn't leave until gone four in the morning, when the light had begun to creep into the night, silhouetting the Parthenon and making us realise that we were ready for sleeping. We stumbled back towards Nikis Street, still with the song in us, muffled by a pleasing blanket of booze and Valium.

Jake started singing, 'I've Bin Stone Before', and we all joined in. Gong. *Camembert Electrique*. Pretty esoteric but we all know it. You see? Magic. Like our threesome was meant to happen.

And now I remember something that until now has completely escaped me. Am I having blackouts? Jesus, I thought that only happened to serious old alcoholics, not young girls who like to have fun.

After we've been going for a while, I stop and take a piss behind a tree.

As I stand and straighten my black dress, I catch sight of a poster someone's tacked to the trunk of my makeshift toilet.

DO YOU KNOW THIS MAN? it says in English. And underneath is a drawing of a youngish male face.

'Hey,' I say to Jake and Beattie, who have moved on to an awful rendition of Pink Floyd's 'Great Gig in the Sky'. 'Come here.'

They both stagger over.

'Don't we recognise this guy?' I say, pointing at the picture on the poster. 'Isn't that The Australian Shit who punched me?'

Beattie pushes in front of me to peer at it, leaning against the tree to steady herself. 'Nah,' she says. 'Face is all wrong, see?'

Perhaps the face *was* the wrong shape. It was hard to tell in the dim street light. And to be honest, my memory of that night in Manos's bar was *also* a bit blurred by drink – not to mention the whack in the face.

We carried on back, taking the direction we thought was right for Nikis. It wasn't, however, and we ended up in some dodgy area on the wrong side of the Plaka. We retraced our steps and it must have taken us at least two hours to find Peta Inn, even though the bar had only been a fifteen-minute walk away when we set out.

As we go into Peta Inn, I see another copy of the DO YOU KNOW THIS MAN? poster, pinned up among the TRAVEL PARTNER NEEDED and SLEEPING BAG FOR SALE notices on the board at the hostel entrance. The rest of the poster, which I hadn't read out in the street, says that the drawing is taken from a body found in a clump of bushes near the Agora. Apart from a tourist map in English, there was nothing to identify him.

Jake takes a look, and shakes his head.

'Nah, Ems, Beattie's right. Not that Australian cunt at all. It's not his eyes, or his nose.'

I'm just relieved that I was wrong. I don't want to have to start bothering with going to the police and all that shit.

But it *was* the same guy. The longer I think about it, the more certain I am.

OK. I've just been down to take another look, just to put my mind at rest. But, this morning, the poster isn't there any more. Perhaps they've found out who he was, then.

11

8 August 1980, Midday. Athens. OTE office, Patission Street.

Shit. I woke up this morning and remembered I said I'd phone my parents like five days ago. The old dears'll be worrying, and we're off to Ikaria tomorrow, and God knows if they've even got phones out there.

So I came down here to place my reversed-charge call.

But I've been waiting here in this stinking hot hall for TWO HOURS.

I've got no idea why it takes so fucking long just to place a call.

I'm supposed to be meeting Jake and Bea right now in that new bar we found last night. They'll be there now, and I'll be missing out on all the fun. And I don't want Beattie spending too much time alone with him.

It's not that I don't trust him. Or her.

But.

Oh hell. Nothing's happening here at all.

Fuck it. I'm out of here.

12

9 August 1980, 10 p.m. Athens (still). Peta Inn roof (again).

Today was going to be the moment we made our move to Ikaria. We meant to get up early and leave town before the sun got too high. But by the time we'd prised ourselves from our beds, waited for Dimitri to haul our rucksacks out of the store and packed our stuff up, it was nearly midday, and we were still here on the roof.

On our way down the stairs with all our gear, Beattie says that if Dimitri isn't at his perch behind the reception desk we'll play the Dangerous Game and do a runner. I'm not too keen on this because we've been staying here for a week or something and he knows who we are. Also, he has the air – unusual for a Greek – of being a man who won't let being ripped off rest too easily. And, as I tell her, at some point we're going to have to pass back through Athens when we return.

'If we return,' Jake says, and we laugh.

But, thank fuck, there's little chance of Beattie having her way. I haven't ever passed the front desk, day or night, without Dimitri being there. And, sure enough, there he was, perched behind the scarred wooden counter, smoking and poring over another porny mag, the creep.

* * *

We paid and stumbled out into the street, talking a little too loudly and a little too fast, thanks to the pills we'd taken to help us on our way.

We stopped in at our new favourite bar – I never did find out the name – for a farewell drink. Of course, the one beer turned into three, and then we wandered around for about half an hour looking for Monastiraki station. So it wasn't until about three that we managed to catch the train out to Piraeus.

The carriage was rammed and stifling. We had to stand, pressed in against people who were even stinkier than us. Of course we hadn't thought to bring any water, and, as the beer/speed dehydration kicked in I felt as if the last drops of fluid in my body were soaking into my rucksack (which I had to keep on, because there was no room to take it off).

So when I step off the train at Piraeus, the world disintegrates into black dots and I fall to my knees.

The next thing I know, Beattie's cradling my head in her lap, pouring some water into my mouth.

'What happened?' I ask.

'Crap, Emma. You just blacked right out,' she says. 'The guard said he wanted to call you an ambulance, but I managed to talk him out of it. Said you do this a lot.'

'Thanks,' I croak.

Despite the water, my lips feel numb and crisp, as if they belong to someone else.

'Girl, you haven't eaten anything since those fries last night,' Jake says from somewhere to my right.

In fact, I only ate two of the fries he's talking about. He and Beattie wolfed down the rest.

'We're going to get some food in you if it's the last thing we do,' Beattie says.

So they lead me out to a bar near the Piraeus subway station, on the busy main road that runs in front of the port. Despite the heavy traffic and a reeking blue cloud of diesel from a ferry engine running in the water about a hundred yards away from where we're sitting, the air is lighter and fresher than it is in Athens.

Beattie orders a Greek salad, three portions of fries and some souvlaki. The meat looks burned and tough, but I manage to force down a couple of the chips and a few pieces of tomato and feta. Jake has asked the waiter to bring a litre of house red wine, too, which costs just fifty drachma.

'It's very restorative, red wine,' he says, pouring me a large glass. 'More of a medicine than a drink.'

Although my digestion is working hard to take the solid food on board, my head's mostly landed back on my shoulders, and I'm able to organise my thoughts a little.

'Do we know what time the boat leaves?' I ask, accepting another slug of wine from Jake.

Beattie shrugs. 'I guess we have to go ask somewhere.'

'You mean you don't know?' Jake says, turning to her.

'Not exactly. But this *is* like where the boats go from?'

'Jeeze,' Jake says. 'Blind leading the blind.'

'What's that supposed to mean?' Beattie says, frowning, her back suddenly more erect.

'I just thought you were on it,' Jake says.

Beattie rolls her eyes and spears a chunk of grilled pork with her fork. 'Is it me has to arrange everything, then?' she says.

I nearly laugh. They're bickering like an old married couple, like my parents, even.

We finish our meal, pay – despite Beattie's unsurprising suggestion that we do a runner – and, lugging our rucksacks, we skirt around the port until we find a kiosk with TICKETS and LEFT LUGGAGE and BEST DEALS! written above it in English.

The blonde, immaculately made-up woman in the booth tuts and jerks her head back when we ask her about boats to Ikaria. 'Boats to Agios Kirikos only Friday and Tuesday,' she says, returning to what she had been doing – filing her nails.

Today is Saturday.

'No, we want to go to Ikaria, though,' Jake says.

'Agios Kirikos is the port in Ikaria,' she says, tutting again.

'How was I supposed to know that?' Jake says, spreading his hands wide.

The woman shrugs and slips her emery board back and forth over her index fingernail.

The sound makes my teeth feel fizzy.

'Cow,' Jake mutters, just loud enough for her to hear as he turns away.

Shockingly, the woman hisses at him.

Sighing, Beattie muscles past him and buys three tickets, deck class, for the Tuesday ferry to Agios Kirikos. I pull Jake aside while she does the deal. He has offended the woman enough and needs keeping in check.

'Great,' Beattie says, coming over to join us and looking gloomily at the indecipherable Greek on the three pieces of card the woman eventually handed to her. 'We've got to wait out three more fucking days.'

'Shall we go back to Athens?' I say.

'I'm not staying in this asswipe of a place.' Jake gestures around the ugly port. 'It's a total heap of shit.'

'Seems like we've got no choice, then.' Beattie sticks out her lip.

'Hey,' I say, putting my arms round both of them, feeling the electricity from where my bare forearm touches Jake's shoulder. 'Don't be so down. We have fun in Athens, right? It's not so bad.'

'Yeah, but I want to be on a boat on the ocean,' Beattie says. 'I want to go to the island right now.'

'Me too,' Jake says.

'There, there, children,' I go, smiling. 'We can go on Tuesday. It's only three days away.'

I suggest that, since we're in Piraeus, we might as well have a look around. It looks more authentically Greek than the parts of Athens we've been hanging out in. And there probably won't be that many foreigners, if we move away from the port area.

So we go back to the woman who's sold us the tickets and, for a hundred drachs each – which is a total rip-off, but Beattie and I stave off Jake as he starts to tell her that (after all, it's not like we don't have enough cash now) – we dump our stuff with her. Then we set off to explore the dusty, monochrome grid of streets behind the port.

'What now?' Jake says, as we stop at the edge of an unremarkable square.

'Look!' Beattie says, her face lighting up for the first time since the disappointment of not being able to get on a boat. She points to a small shop next to a bar at the other side of the square with a sign saying TATTOOS above its door. 'That's more like it.'

'What?' I say.

'Let's get inked,' she says. 'It'll be our Dangerous Game for the day.'

'We have to do a Dangerous Game every day?' I ask.

'Sure. We paid the hotel, we paid the restaurant. We're running the risk of being too safe today.'

'Isn't that danger enough?'

'I need a drink,' Jake says.

'Well, let's go in that bar, have a couple beers and decide what we're going to have done. We can all have the same thing, so we're bound together forever, till death do us part.'

Jake and I look at Beattie. Then, one by one, we smile. It's a good plan. A *great* plan.

We set ourselves up at a little table outside the bar. You can tell it's not a tourist place because, instead of the Police, Blondie, Queen and Hot Chocolate tracks that blare out of the bars in Athens, the sound coming from inside is that of a TV football match. Two sullen elderly men slump in the smoky interior nursing Greek coffees and neat ouzos, their eyes glued to the screen. We sit outside, in the sunshine. When our beers arrive, they come with a plate of mezes – slices of sweaty, rubbery cheese and mystery salami with a sprinkling of wrinkled olives. Unappetising as it looks, Jake finishes the lot off before I've even managed two sips of my beer.

'It's got to have something to do with three,' Beattie says of the tattoo. 'For the three of us.'

'Triangle?' I say.

'Too boring.'

'Tricycle?' Jake suggests.

'Jeeze.'

'Triad? Trident?' I say.

'Triple A?' Jake says.

'The Automobile Association of America?' Beattie says. 'Give me strength.'

'Triskelion?' I say.

'What?'

'Triskelion. It's like this.' I pull a napkin from the plastic beer-branded holder on our table and sketch it out – three spirals, arranged in a triangle shape and connecting in the middle. 'The mark of Hecate.'

'You know all this totally weird stuff,' Beattie says.

'I had to do this costume design for the three witches for some homework on *Macbeth*. Hecate lived in the Greek Underworld and was like the goddess of witches. And she always appeared as three: a lion, a dog and a mare, or three beautiful women – always looking in three different directions, over the earth, sea and sky, or the past, present and future. It's her symbol.'

The others gaze at it for a minute. Then Beattie looks up, smiling.

'That's it!' she says. 'Perfect! And we'll have it here.' She holds out her right forearm and points to the inner part.

'Ow,' Jake says, pinching his own arm in the same place, leaving a couple of nail impressions that make me feel strangely hungry. 'The hurty bit.'

'Let's not do this,' I say as Beattie leads the way into the tattoo parlour and we see how filthy the place is. The white on the chequerboard lino floor is almost indistinguishable from the black, and there are hundreds of flies buzzing around a crackled, plastic-coated display of mostly nautical tattoo motifs that's pinned up on the wall. Opposite is a shelf bearing an assortment of grubby figurines and dolls covered in tattoo designs – some sort of weird, cack-handed promotional tool, I suppose.

'I love this guy,' Beattie says, pointing out a large green Scottie dog with an intricately patterned heart on his backside. Behind us, four mismatched vinyl chairs make a sort of waiting room, facing a curtain of multi-coloured metal chains that clatter in the breeze, partly concealing a doorway.

The door to the street swings shut behind us, setting off an old brass bell on a spring. We stand there, stewing in the sweaty little room, looking around. I've almost got used to the sewage smell of the streets of Athens and Piraeus, but in the tattoo parlour it's almost unbearably concentrated, and mixed with a nasty sweaty body odour.

We sit on the vinyl chairs, me trying not to gag.

'Here,' Jake says, handing round a blister pack of Valium. 'This'll help.'

'Are we crazy?' I say, swallowing the pill without water. 'We'll pick up a nasty disease or something.'

'It does look kinda grimy,' Jake says, scuffing his foot on the floor to shift a used tissue under his chair.

'Jeeze. You two,' Beattie says.

Jake tuts, gets up and goes over to examine the wall of designs.

'Hello?' Beattie calls out. '*Yassoo?*'

Somewhere in the building a dog starts to bark. Then something stirs behind the chain curtain. A few minutes pass, then a greasy-skinned man in a stained vest staggers through from the back room, a cigarette stuck to his lip.

'*Yassoo,*' Beattie says again. 'Do you speak English?'

The man purses his lips and gives a little nod. 'Whaddaya want?' His accent is a lot like Beattie's.

'Tattoos?' Jake says.

'For all of us,' Beattie says. 'All three?'

'She sixteen?' he says, nodding at me, licking his too-pink lips.

'I'm eighteen,' I say.

'Seriously?' Beattie says. 'I thought you were the same age as me.'

'How old are you, then?'

'Twenty-one.'

'Hey, same as me,' Jake says to her.

I had no idea she was that old. Or him. I feel kind of proud that my two best friends in the world are in their twenties.

'You wanna tattoo or you wanna stand and talk?' the man says.

'How much for this?' I show him the Triskelion I had drawn on the napkin. 'To have here.' I point to the inside of my forearm.

'What size?' The man picks his nose and examines his findings.

'About this big?' Beattie says, making a circle with her thumb and forefinger a bit bigger than a ten-pence piece.

The man shrugs. 'Two thousand.'

'Each?' Jake says. 'You gotta be kidding, man.'

In the end we bargain him down to two thousand drachma for all three, which he insists on us paying upfront.

'What if we don't like it?' Beattie says.

She was annoyed about having to part with the money: she'd probably been hatching a running-away plan. But the man just shrugged again and said that we would like it, that he was the best tattooist in all of Piraeus.

Jake goes first, on the basis that he claims already to have one tattoo, in a place that neither of us has seen, but – as he puts it – we might if we got lucky. Beattie and I push him towards the back room, and we sit making faces at each other as we listen to the whirr and buzz of the needle and the occasional curse from Jake. When he comes out, he looks strained and pale – but excited.

'Look!' he says, holding out his arm for us to see. 'This guy is some kind of artist. He's got it perfect. Perfectly symmetrical.'

He's right. Underneath its bloom of blood and swelling, the design is indeed flawless.

'Next!' the tattooist calls from behind his chain curtain. Beattie and I look at each other.

'I'll go,' she says and strides into the back room. Jake takes her seat, which is next to mine.

'Did it hurt?' I ask, tracing the design on Jake's arm with my fingertips, enjoying the contact.

'A little,' he says. Then he brings his other hand up to my cheek. 'Don't do it, Emma,' he says.

'What?'

'You don't have to get it done if you don't want to,' he says. 'Don't let her force you into it.'

'She's not forcing me into anything.' I pull away from him.

To be honest, I'm getting a bit fed up with his attitude towards Beattie. She's a natural leader, and he has some sort of issue with that. But it's unfair on her and I find this idea he's got that I can't stand up for myself a bit insulting, too.

'I'm doing this of my own accord,' I say. 'I've always thought about getting a tattoo and this is completely the right time and place. I don't want to forget these days and you guys, not as long as I live.'

Jake sighs and lights a cigarette.

* * *

I was lying, of course. I've never considered a tattoo before, and, even before I had it, I was playing the scene in my head of when my parents see it. They'll hate it. They think tattoos are for rough sorts. My mother once pointed out a woman on the bus with a little black bow inked on her ankle.

'She's only good for one thing,' she whispered to me.

Beattie comes out proudly displaying the bloodied design on her arm. It matches Jake's completely.

'Be careful,' she says to me, as I stand to meet my fate. 'He's a bit of a creep.'

I waver for a moment. Can I refuse to go in? Clearly not. Not to go ahead will set me apart, spoil the balance we have.

'Fuck him,' I say, under my breath, not loud enough for the tattooist to hear in his little backstage booth.

'Good girl,' Beattie says.

She hoots with laughter when I pull my *mataki* evil eye out of my bag and hold it out in front of me as if it were a cross and the tattooist a vampire.

I part the metal curtains and go inside. He's sitting by what looks like a repurposed dentist's chair, smoking another cigarette, knocking back a glass of what could be water, but which is more likely, from the alcoholic fumes in the room, some sort of spirit.

And he really does smell awful. An oniony, turdish stench of un-washed hot-climate armpits. The fan spinning behind him just circulates the stink.

'Sit down,' he says, motioning to the chair. I do as I am told and he presses a button to recline me.

'Do I need to be lying back?' I say.

'Easier for me,' he says. 'Bad back.'

I watch out of the corner of my eyes as he dabbles his needle in the ink, his concentration mostly on the TV positioned over my chair, which is showing the same football match the old boys were watching in the bar.

Then he turns and smiles at me, treating me to a gust of heavy breath and the sight of the black gaps where most of his teeth should have been. He bares the underside of my forearm and lies it on the armrest of the chair.

'You nervous, little girl?'

I smile politely and nod. All I want to do is run away. It's all coming back to me, horribly. I can feel the rasp and scrape of the stones of the wall as I was pressed into it. I can feel the panic rising.

'Drink,' he says, offering me a bottle from beneath his chair. 'Go on.'

It feels impossible to refuse, so I tip the bottle to my lips. It isn't disgusting ouzo, for which I'm thankful — instead, it's something far rougher, far fierier.

'Ha!' The tattooist laughs as I choke on the stuff. 'Is *Raki*, spirit of my home island, Kriti.'

I grip the evil eye in my hand as he puts his needle to my skin and it starts buzzing. The pain is like sunburn being stung by a wasp. I can't stop myself crying out.

'Stay still, or I fuck up,' the tattooist says. He leans against my arm, but he is at such an angle that his shoulder presses into my breast. I try to tell myself that this is entirely different to Marseille – I have volunteered for this. But the feeling of being constricted, of painful things being done to my body, is too much. I'm scared I'll hit him.

'Stop!' I say.

He lifts his needle and looks at me.

'What's the matter now?' he says.

'I want Jake to be in here with me,' I say. The only way I can see it through is with him in here.

The tattooist shrugs.

'Jake!' I call, and he is there in an instant, the chain curtains clattering behind him.

'Will you hold my hand?' I ask, my voice small, my eyes motioning to the tattooist's shoulder, which still presses against me.

Jake gives the man one of his looks, which makes him move a little away from me. Then my lovely boy sits at my side, holding the hand of my free arm, and I suddenly feel safe. That's how he makes me feel. It's how I can cope with Beattie and all the trouble she nearly gets us into. Because Jake is there.

He's got my back, as he'd say.

The session seems to go on for ever, far longer than it's taken either Jake or Beattie to get theirs done. But in the end, when I'm near to passing out with the smell, the pain, the endless buzzing of the sharp needle, the tattooist lifts his instrument and stands.

'All done,' he says, standing up and turning his back to us to put his tools and inks away. I hold my arm up against Jake's.

'Awesome,' Jake says.

I nod.

We are identical.

By the time we get out onto the street, it's dusk.

As we make our way to pick up our rucksacks, I notice Beattie has a carrier bag dangling from her hand.

'What have you got there?' I ask her.

'Here? Oh, it's just my new pet,' she says, lifting out the tattooed green Scottie dog. 'He was too good for that creepy little old man. I've liberated him.'

We both stop and look at her.

'What's the problem?' she says, looking at us. 'It's good news for you chickens. We've done two Dangerous Games today, so we can have a day off tomorrow.'

* * *

Riding back on the subway, each jolt of the train set off the pain of the tattoo, which stings like someone's pressed a hot iron against it. But it feels oddly great! I've read that people who self-harm say they do it to make themselves aware that they exist. Where the hurt inflicted by The French Shit and The Australian Shit made me feel ill and defeated, this pain – pain I have bought for myself, my own choice – works for me. I feel more alive than ever before.

Perhaps Beattie's right. Like the pain of the tattoo, playing the Dangerous Game also wakes me up. It's a good thing. No one's really been hurt, have they? I promise myself I'm going to be less judgemental, less responsible, less goody goody, less concerned about what everyone else thinks.

I'm going to burn in the light of the flames, like Beattie!

The tattoo is my blood bond on that.

We got back to Peta Inn and, luckily, our beds were still free up here on the roof. It's like we never left.

We're tired, sticky, and our arms are sore. So we've turned in early.

In Athens, and in bed by ten. Who'd have thought it?

13

10 August 1980, midnight. Athens. Peta Inn roof.

It's still a little muggy now, but last night was the most airless I have known it here. If I didn't know better – *Let's Go* said that it hasn't rained in Athens in August for over a thousand years – I would have suspected a brewing storm.

So, yet again, I had a sleepless night, sweating and smoking to keep the FUCKING MOSQUITOES off me.

Something lovely happened today!

Low because we should have been arriving in Ikaria this morning, we crawled out of our tangled beds when the sun got too hot and slumped on our two top bunks, me and Beattie on one, Jake on the other, sharing a bottle of wine that Beattie had somehow got hold of. Wine for breakfast. Nice.

They'd slept better than me, but were still pretty groggy. And we'd all been bitten to shreds. Some of Beattie's bites have got infected, too, so they're like pus-filled blisters. I want to pop them, but she won't let me near them.

'I stink,' Beattie says, putting her nose to her armpit.

'Me too,' I say.

'I didn't like to mention it,' Jake says.

'Asshole.' Beattie spills some of the wine from her bottle over her head, then she flops back, wine flicking from her hair all over her already-stained mattress. 'I need a shower.'

'Me too,' I say. 'But I don't know if I can face it.'

The one Peta Inn shower is filthy and gross. It also has no lock on the door and only a horrible, mildewed curtain between the cubicle and the rest of the bathroom. I tried it once when I first arrived, but, too scared of someone stumbling in on me *Psycho*-style, couldn't even bring myself to switch it on, which was annoying, because Dimitri charges fifty drachma for ten minutes of hot water, which he controls from somewhere behind his desk.

Jake's offered to stand guard outside the door, but I don't want to impose on him like that – the corridor outside is dark and stifling, and anyway, if someone did try to get in, I wouldn't want to be the cause of another fight like the one with The Australian Shit.

'Hey, we could have one together,' Beattie says to me. 'We can watch out for each other, save money and give Dimitri a thrill at the thought.'

'I don't know ...' I hug my knees. I'm not too keen on people seeing me naked. I've got what you might call hang-ups about my body. But I really do need a wash and, anyway, we'll soon be on a beach on our paradise island, our bodies exposed to the sun. At some point Beattie and Jake are going to see the rack of ribs on me, the hipbones that I know protrude at my back. They can't have failed to notice – my arms and legs are a pretty good indication of what's going on underneath my black dress.

'Aw, come on, Em,' Beattie says, sliding off her bunk and pulling her washbag out from where she stashes it underneath the bottom bed. 'This is going to be fun.'

Knowing she won't take no for an answer, I grab my own stuff and follow her down the stairs to Dimitri's desk.

'Hey, Dimitri,' Beattie says, sidling up to him, her arm around me. 'Em and me here want to have a shower.'

'One hundred,' he says, glancing up from a magazine spread of naked women doing things to each other. Charm is not one of his strong points.

'You don't understand.' Beattie leans on his desk so that her breasts squash together into a cleavage at the neck of her vest top. She beckons at him with one finger so that he has to move in closer. 'We want to shower together,' she whispers.

Dimitri gulps, blushes and raises his eyebrows. Beattie moves her hand up to my hair, which she strokes as if I were some sort of cat. He looks at her breasts, then at her hand.

'Seventy-five,' he says.

'Oh, come on, Dimitri.' She rubs herself up against his desk. 'We won't use any more water than one person. In fact' – again she leans in towards him, her finger tracing the body of a naked young woman in his horrible magazine – 'we won't be using water all the time we're in there.'

'Please, Dimitri,' I say, trying to copy Beattie's seductive act. I'm pretty useless at it, though.

He looks at us. The thought of what might be going on in his mind makes me feel quite ill.

'*Endaxi,*' he says at last. 'Fifty. But just this once, OK? No more times than this.'

Beattie pays and we run upstairs laughing.

'Stupid asshole. All men are the same,' Beattie says as we burst into the shower room. 'Think with their dicks. You just gotta use it, though, Emma.'

'Jake's different, though, isn't he?'

'Oh yes,' Beattie says, looking at me seriously for a second. 'Jake is very different.'

She pulls all her clothes off and I see her body. She's fairly slim, but unlike me there's no sticking-out bones. And she's got proper, round breasts, not skinny little pockets like mine.

As Beattie turns the shower on, I take a deep breath, pull off my baggy black T-shirt thing and step out of my pants. She can't disguise the little intake of breath that escapes her at the sight of me. Not only the bones, but also the bruises and grazes still fading from Marseille, and all of it set off by my black eye.

'Oh, Emma,' she says. 'What happened to you?'

'I fell,' I say. I can't tell her. I wish I could, but I can't. 'I fell down a bit of a cliff when I was in France.'

She puts her arms around me. 'Poor you.'

I can't help it. I start to cry. And Beattie holds me, letting me let go. For me, this is the moment that cements our friendship. Her reaction to the state of me isn't revulsion, as I had expected – as I always expect of anyone – it's compassion. Behind that wild, pushy, Dangerous Game-playing loudmouth is a truly good heart.

If only I could get Jake to see that.

The shower, which has been running hot all this time, has fogged up the little bathroom.

'When we get to the island, everything will be OK, Emma,' Beattie says, when I have calmed down a little. 'Me and Jake'll look after you really well. We'll have you back eating again, and everything will be OK.'

I actually think it might, now.

She leads me into the cubicle and, very gently, washes me. The tenderness she shows me in that shower nearly makes me cry again. I haven't been touched with such care since I was a baby. She looks at me with level green eyes that seem to reflect me back at myself, and she rinses the soap from my back, squatting to clean my legs, then between my legs.

* * *

I'm sure she didn't intend it to be sexual – she was just cleaning me with care and love – but I actually felt something when she touched me. It was almost like she was erasing some of the brutality done to my poor body. Perhaps I could manage sex if I only do it with a woman? After all, those morons at school used to call me a lesbian.

But I don't fancy women. I fancy Jake. I love Jake.

There you go.

I LOVE JAKE!!!!!

When Beattie is done, she wraps me in my towel then goes back in the shower to wash herself.

I stand on the other side of the shower curtain towelling myself down, watching her silhouette through the mouldy plastic, my throat so swollen with love and gratitude that I think I might stop breathing. For the first time in my life I have found a friend – two friends – who really understand me, who know instinctively how and who I am. My new, cool family.

And the day after tomorrow we go to paradise!

14

12 August, 2 p.m. Somewhere in the Aegean Sea. Ferry.

Yep. That's right. We've finally got away from Athens!

The boat left at six this morning – far too early for us. We didn't leave enough time to get to Piraeus by subway, so in the end we had to blow some cash on a cab.

'It's no biggie,' Beattie says, as the taxi she has just hailed screeches to a stop just inches away from my feet. 'I found another wallet last night.'

I don't get this at first. Because we had such an early start today, we took it easy and turned in early yesterday. We had souvlakis from this little hole-in-the-wall grill place at the other end of Nikis Street, where you can see the meat cooking on charcoal grills and they make their own tzatziki. I ate almost a whole one – except for the bread. That, along with two Valium, meant that I fell fast asleep at ten. I thought Beattie and Jake had done the same.

As the grumpy taxi driver watches us lumping our rucksacks into the boot, Beattie explains to me that she and Jake weren't able to sleep, so after I'd passed out they went off for a farewell-to-Athens walk, taking in a couple of bars.

It's stupid, because I really did need to sleep, but I wish they'd woken me up and taken me with them. I feel sort of jealous, I suppose. Left out.

But I've clearly got nothing to worry about. Whatever went on last night has hardly drawn them together.

'You go in front,' Beattie orders Jake, as she holds the back door open for me to climb in.

'Yeah, whatever you say, as ever,' Jake mutters.

'Chill out, asshole.'

He looks daggers at her.

What the hell's going on between them? It's a pity, because this is our big adventure, and the bad air between them is threatening to spoil it.

After he slops into the seat next to the driver, Beattie jumps in next to me and leans forward. 'Piraeus,' she tells the driver. 'Fast.'

The taxi driver tuts, revs his engine, and we lurch off into the grey dawn streets.

'So in the last bar some douche had left this wallet stuffed full of notes,' she says to me.

'Was there any ID in it?' I ask.

'Nope. Or else I would have tried to get it back to its owner, of course, Emma,' Beattie says, rolling her eyes at me like I'm stupid.

We arrive at the port with five minutes to spare before our boat takes off (or whatever it is they do).

The taxi driver won't open his boot until he has his extortionate thousand drachma fare in his hand.

Jake starts to argue with the guy, rubbing his hands on the back of his grubby baggy combat shorts, itching with anger, and I'm thinking *oh no, not again*.

'Don't be a *douche*, Jake. We don't have time to argue with the little shit,' Beattie says, pushing past him and peeling notes into the waiting hand of the taxi driver, whose demeanour is so sour it's hard to tell whether he understands what she's just said or not.

After a little confusion, we find our boat, and beetle up the ramp just as it closes, sealing us in. The sailor operating the winch says something jovial to us in Greek. Already we're away from Athens and everyone just seems so much nicer.

Except, perhaps, Bea and Jake . . .

As well as being the cheapest, Deck Class has to be the best way to go. We've rolled out our sleeping bags and mats and got the beers in. I'm between Bea and Jake, but I'm finding it pretty exhausting keeping everything light because they haven't yet spoken a civil word to each other. We've got fourteen hours of this, for fuck's sake.

I've given up trying to broker peace between the two of them and instead I've spent some time watching the ever-changing scenery of sea, distant islands floating in the hazy air, and closer land where I can make out houses and white strips of beach. There is so much blue, everywhere, in the sea and the sky – and in Jake's eyes, which, even in this foul mood he's in, seem to suck it up and soak it all in.

But you can only gaze out at the view for so long. With the lack of conversation I've finally started reading *The Women's Room*. It's about Mira, who starts out as a wild student who doesn't behave how girls were meant to behave back then and so gets a reputation for herself. But now she's this middle-class housewife in New Jersey. She can't work, doesn't do anything really other than keep a really neat house and clean children while her husband goes off into the world and studies to become a doctor.

It's interesting, but it doesn't seem all that relevant to girls my age. We'll all have careers and everything will be equal for us.

I do feel sorry for Mira, though.

The boat has stopped at five islands so far. Each time we hang silently on the railings, watching the dotted houses of the port town hover into view, the scene getting closer and closer until we can pick out a straggle of foot passengers and vehicles waiting on the dock for us.

But we're not allowed to stay and watch them get on. Beattie says it's important that we get back to our patch of deck before boarding commences, because, as she puts it, 'some fucker's going to muscle in on our pitch.'

Jake doesn't do as he's told, of course. But I've been following her back each time. Just to keep everything sweet.

Man, though. She does like to be in charge.

15

12 August 1980, no idea of the time. Paradise.

Well, this is perfect here and now. We've found our beach.

But when we arrived in the late afternoon, first impressions weren't so great. We'd built Ikaria up to be some mythical idyll with whitewashed buildings and happy, smiling locals who'd point us in the right direction. But, in fact, Agios Kirikos, the main port town, struck us as pretty run down, just a functional place full of normal Greeks going about their business, shopping, going to school, putting out their rubbish.

Not one other backpacker or tourist got off the boat with us. We seemed to be the only foreigners in town, and people were quite openly staring at us. I suppose we cut a bit of a strange sight – two short punky girls (one pretty beaten-up looking) and an almost laughably tall and skinny boy with long, curly hair and weird blue eyes. Fairly normal in Athens, but we're like aliens here.

Deflated, we sat on the birdshit-splattered terrace of a bar on the quayside, got some beers in and watched our ferry chug off into the distance to other islands, some of which we could see floating on the horizon, blending into the sky more like a watercolour painting than real life.

* * *

'What we going to do now, then?' I ask, rubbing lotion into my sunburned legs. Out on the boat deck you don't feel the heat of the sun with the sea breeze, but it's fierce.

'Looks like a shit hole,' Jake says gloomily.

'Oh quit it, Jake,' Beattie snaps.

'We should've stayed in Athens, if this is what it's like.'

'This is just the main town.' I touch his arm. 'It'll be different when we get away from here, out into the countryside.'

'Yeah. What's the name of that place that drippy dork girl talked about in The Milk Bar? That great beach?' Beattie says.

I shrug. Neither of us can remember. I know I have it written down somewhere in my notebook, but I don't want to get it out and start flipping through it, with them looking over my shoulder.

'And how big's this goddamn island anyhow?' Jake asks, sprawling on his chair, all legs and arms.

None of us know. We haven't really done our research. We'd just assumed that Ikaria would be perfect, and we'd instantly get the size of the place, sort of know it all at once, the minute we stepped foot on it.

We drain our beers and wander down a narrow shopping street, just off the harbour. In the back of a kiosk selling cigarettes and magazines we find a map of the island, which turns out in fact to be about seventy kilometres long. Massive.

We just thought you'd be able to walk round it in a day.

We also discover that Agios Kirikos is on the south coast and there's this string of interesting-looking beaches towards the west. Beattie says we're going to hitch out and find a nice quiet beach to spend the night on.

So, after a visit to a supermarket for as many supplies as we can carry along with all our gear, we stand on the coastal road leading out of town, ready to stick our thumbs out.

After about twenty car-less minutes, a rusty old pickup truck appears, slows down and stops, crunching into the gravel at our feet.

Even with Jake beside me, I'm apprehensive about getting in. I've never hitched before, but I've heard the stories. But then I see that the driver is a toothless old man and, crammed in beside him, are three young children and a youngish woman.

Luckily, the old man can speak English – in fact, like the creepy tattooist, he has an American accent.

He translates our request to go to a quiet beach for the woman (who I take to be his daughter) and they launch into a long, animated exchange.

'We take you there. Best beach in Ikaria,' the old man finally says, and gestures with his head for us to jump in the back of the pickup, which is partly filled with empty crates.

'Awesome,' Jake says, not entirely enthusiastically. But he gives me a leg-up into the tall vehicle and when Beattie asks him to do the same for her, he does.

Progress!

The way the old man drove! Beyond the town, the road started rapidly to climb uphill. The going was rough, bumpy and full of potholes, but he didn't slow for any of them, so we were thrown all about in the back, bashing against crates, thumping into our rucksacks. At times it felt like we might be chucked clean out of the van. My bruises have got bruises, etc.

As we headed away from the town, the landscape framed itself on a different, wilder scale. The road skirted in and out of the deep ravines of a black, almost vertical mountain, which reared above us to our right, and crumbled straight down to a rocky shore to our left. And the wind howled around us, lifting loose bits of sacking in the back of the van, catching Jake's hair (out of the three of us he has the most on his head by far), whipping it into his firmly closed eyes. He gripped his rucksack, his knuckles white.

'The old boy probably does this trip every day,' I say, trying to reassure him.

I'm surprisingly calm. I'm not a good road traveller – I used to puke all over Dad's car when we went on Sunday drives – but Jake looks like he's on the verge of passing out, and it's easier to be strong if someone else needs you.

'And he wouldn't endanger the lives of his grandchildren, would he?' I nod at the children, whose heads we can see bobbing around in the rear window of the driver's compartment.

'How do you know they're his grandchildren and not abducted or something?' Jake says, his eyes still shut.

I'm not sure if he is joking or not. It's hard to tell with Jake. It's getting harder, actually. Since we left Athens, almost by the hour, he's got jumpier, more edgy, like there's something bearing him down. It could be seasickness. Or perhaps he's feeling the same tension as me, about us not having got together yet. I hope it's that.

I wish I knew.

It will happen, though. I'm sure of that.

'At least there's no other traffic.' I stroke his clenched hand, relaxing his fingers so they curl round mine.

He opens his eyes and smiles at me. I feel the tingle that his touch stirs in me.

Beattie laughs cruelly. 'You're such a damn pussy, Jake.'

Scary or not, the views were spectacular, and so long as I didn't look down, all the terrifying detail about sheer drops and crumbling roads was hidden by the sides of the van. All I could see was the Ikarian Sea rippling and shimmering, and I calmed myself by breathing in the delicious, herby, salty air – which smells like sticking your face in a packet of oregano.

This is what I've been looking for all the time I've been travelling. Beattie's right: this island's going to cure me.

I'm going to relax, start eating properly, drink and smoke less and, gradually, Beattie will understand, and Jake and I will become a couple and I'll be able to let him in.

After about an hour, the van draws to a halt on a blind bend that seems to tip over a cliff and into the water. We clamber shakily out on the roadside. A path disappears over the edge of the rocks, and the old man tells us that it leads to a perfect beach: white sand, limestone and granite rocks, and 'very special water'.

I ask him to mark the spot on our map, and he also circles a village a little way inland, pointing out a track that leads to it. We'll find a shop and a taverna up there, he says.

We say our thank-yous and Jake – oh Jake – helps me on with my rucksack. I notice that when he touches me now – when Beattie isn't watching – his hand lingers. This island is our chance.

We stumble down the path – it is mostly slippery smooth rock, but there are some steps cut into the steeper parts – zigzagging down until we reach this glorious, sheltered sandy beach, hugged all around by a curve of high, steep cliffs. The only sign of human activity is a rough stone slipway and a rusty boat winch that doesn't look as if it's been used for decades.

The sun's nearly down now and, thanks to our supermarket shop, we have one candle, one big bottle of water, twelve bottles of beer, three cheese pies and enough cigarettes to see us through the night. All that's needed for life, really.

It's beautiful here. Perfect. We're like Adam and two Eves in our own lovely Eden. It's a different world after Athens. The only sound is the gentle slap of the waves on the sand, the cliff shelters us from the wind, it's warm enough, but not too hot, and the air is fresh, with NO BLOODY MOSQUITOES. But the best thing is the cave. We have a little limestone cave to sleep in!

First, though, we have to drink our beer and relax. I'm writing this while Beattie and Jake are out swimming – she went to the left, he to the right.

I've stayed behind, of course. I can't swim.

16

13 August, night-time. Paradise again.

Ooh look, a new notebook. I've still got ten pages left in the old one, but I went and left my bag up in the village taverna tonight. At least, I hope that's where it is.

Just for the record, I can't write the exact time any more because Beattie has persuaded me to stop winding up my watch. Time is for squares, apparently.

The village is a bit of a walk — over an hour of uphill slog. Beattie really didn't like it and bitched almost all the way up there.

Every time she complained about how far it was, or how steep, or how shitty the road was, Jake muttered something under his breath, or tensed his shoulders.

It's odd, and I don't understand it. It's so lovely here; why would they feel worse than in Athens? Sure, we had fun back there, but being here on the island, living on our beach, just seems so much healthier and simpler. I could stay here for ever.

I've even had this little thought that they might be fighting over me. They might both be jealous of each other. Who'd have thought it? These two exotic creatures both wanting a piece of little Emma James.

Oh, put your swelling head away, Emma.

But still I can't help thinking what it would be like now if Jake and I had never met Beattie. We'd have walked to the village hand in hand. We'd be here now, in this cave, curled up together, instead of him sleeping over there, and me here, next to Beattie.

Aw, but she looks so sweet when she's sleeping – more how she really is beneath that snappy, domineering exterior, like who she showed me she was when we were in the shower. I love her so much as a friend. I'm *glad* she's here. And anyway, me and Jake can wait.

We've got the rest of our lives.

So, in other news, I ate tonight! There wasn't a menu, so the waiter – a boy about my age, who introduced himself as Giorgos – took us in to the kitchen, which looked like it hadn't changed for centuries. A middle-aged woman – who is so like Giorgos she must be his mother – stood at an ancient-looking stove, stirring a stew in a giant cast-iron pot. On the wall above her head there was some sort of religious icon of the Madonna, and beside that an ancient shotgun, hanging from a richly embroidered strap.

The mother – Giorgos introduced her as Elpiniki – pulled great earthenware dishes from the oven, unleashing smells of meat and wine and cinnamon and nutmeg, and put them on the scrubbed wooden kitchen table for us to choose our meal. We all had the same: a lamb stew with onions and nutmeg. It was delicious, and I ate half the bowlful!

'The waiter seems to like you, Emma,' Beattie says as we're finishing our food.

'Oh, I don't think so,' I say, darting a quick look at Jake, who is concentrating a little too hard on his plate.

'Sure he does. Look at him.'

I turn towards the boy, who is about my age. Our eyes meet and he quickly glances away, a blush creeping across his cheeks. He's actually rather beautiful, a proper Adonis, with olive skin, thick curls and a classic profile. If it weren't for Jake . . .

'Asshole,' Jake mutters and Beattie and I laugh.

The boy comes over to take our plates.

'Where you come from?' he asks us, his accent almost too thick to be decipherable.

'America,' Beattie says quickly.

Jake sits back in his chair, smoking and looking bored.

'You stay here?' Giorgos asks.

Beattie and I tell him about our beach. Through gestures and the few words of English he has, he tells us that he fishes off that beach and he'll bring us some *barbounia* next time he's out there.

We say that will be awesome, and he heads off with our plates.

'What the fuck's *barbounia*?' Jake says. 'Some sort of missile?'

'Some sort of fish, I hope,' I say.

'Asshole,' Jake says again.

'Jealous?' Beattie says.

And Jake tells her to go fuck herself.

I really have to do something with my friends . . .

At the village shop, which was still open even though it was really late, we bought bread, three six-packs of water, tomatoes, cheese, honey and three enormous plastic bottles of stinkingly cheap wine. Then we lugged it all back down the hill, which was pretty scary in the dark, because I hadn't thought to bring my torch.

It was only when we got back down here that I realised I'd left my bag behind.

I'm sure it'll be OK. Giorgos will have picked it up. He'll know it was mine. My only worry is my diary — I'd die if anyone read it. Still, I don't reckon he's got enough English to make sense of it.

I've been thinking about Jake and Beattie, about what's going on between them. Perhaps it's not me. Perhaps it's because they're such urban animals. Looking at them both sleeping, they look completely out of place away from buildings and beds and bars. If *barbounia* are fish, they're like *barbounia* out of water here.

But they'll come round. It'll just take them a short while to get used to it. And if it *is* about me, well, I'm just going to have to make sure I divide my attention fairly between them both.

For me, it's magical. I'm here in our cave, writing by flickering candlelight, although I hardly need it because the moon is full and fat, lighting up the white walls of our new home. The only sounds are the odd sigh and whimper from my sleeping friends, the sea hushing the shore, and the wind rushing in the mountains far above us. The cave both amplifies and softens these sounds, and everything seems as if it is a beautiful dream.

I truly believe that if I were to die here, I would be happy.

17

14 August, 1980, 5 p.m.(?) Ikaria. The beach.

I'm sick.

Something I ate, possibly. But we all had the same last night, and I'm the only one who's ill. It's more likely just a bug. Or perhaps my system saying it's had enough of all the abuse I've been doling out to it over the past fortnight. Anyway, I've emptied myself out both ends and now I'm all shivery and feverish.

Bollocks.

At least it's forced Jake and Beattie to work together a little. They've made me a shady bower from driftwood and sleeping bags, so I can lie on the beach, where a cool breeze can get at me. I don't know where they are. Off swimming, perhaps. Together, I hope.

I've no idea how long they've been gone. Time's taken on an odd quality today.

I've hung my evil eye on the entrance to my little shelter, to make sure I don't get any worse.

Been reading *The Women's Room*. Mira has found herself and gone to university, but she finds living a new, freer life really hard. Won't be like that for me, thank God. I'm more like Chris, the daughter of the uncompromising feminist Val. Though, unlike her, I had old-school parents. But that's all behind me now. I've been reborn into the lives of my friends. Anything's possible for me.

My head's pounding and the sleeping bag I'm lying on feels squelchy with my sweat.

I close my eyes and it feels like I'm on a boat, rocking on a stormy sea. I've just lain here all day, listening to my shallow, wheezy breaths and marking how the sound distorts, as if someone's playing around with volume and bass.

Can't write any more.

OK, something amazing has happened.

I'm just dozing under my shelter when I feel a touch on my arm. I open my eyes and there's Jake, his face close to mine. He's out of breath, like he's been running. He helps me sit up and gives me a fresh bottle of ice-cold water, which I gulp down.

'Emma,' he says.

He takes my hand and looks at me.

'I need to tell you something, Emma.'

At his touch, and the seriousness of his tone, I feel my empty stomach churn, as if it's trying to eat itself up.

He looks at me with those wide, lovely eyes, those eyes that seem to steal the colour from the Greek sky and concentrate it into something even bluer. Then he sighs.

I swirl under that gaze. He leans over and puts his forehead to mine. Then – I can't believe he does this – he kisses me, gently at first, but then it becomes more than that. I find myself knotting my fingers into his dark curly hair. It's like coming home, this kiss. It's what we've been heading for since the moment I ran into him on the staircase in the Peta Inn.

It's everything.

He pulls away and puts his forehead to mine again, his eyes closed.

'I've wanted to do that for so long,' he says.

'Me too.' I pull him to me again.

I pull him to me!

I kiss him and I run my fingers, at last, up his back and into his hair. I swing myself round so that I am straddling him. I feel him, his erection, press against me, into the space between my thighs.

But he holds me away. 'You're so lovely and kind and clever. I—'

I push towards him and cover his lips with mine. We kiss again, joining everything together.

I know it's wrong for all of us. The way things are between him and Beattie, this will bust up our little group, our gang of three, our Triskelion.

It's certainly not being fair with my attentions!

If he and I become a couple – as it seems at this moment, as I reach down for him and he moans, his dark head thrown back against the rocky wall of the cave – it will be the end of everything.

Then his fingers find their way between my legs and, despite everything I want, I freeze. I am not ready to be touched there.

'I'm sorry,' I say, and he lets me gently move his hand away. 'I'm sorry.'

'No, it's—' he starts to say, but I silence him with a kiss and I feel like I *could* perhaps . . . but then he moves his lips away, takes my face in his hands and looks at me. I see he has tears in his eyes.

'Listen, Em, I've got to tell you something, something you're not going to believe at all—'

'Hey, where did you get to, Jake-o!' Beattie appears out of nowhere, dropping to her knees so that she is next to Jake at the edge of my shelter. At the sound of her voice, I jump away from him, as if we have been caught doing wrong. Which, in a way, I suppose we have.

She takes in the scene in front of her. 'What's going on?'

'Jake's just getting an eyelash out of my eye,' I stutter.

'I'm great at eyelashes. Let me see.' Beattie elbows Jake out of the way, kneels at my side and pulls my eyelid down. Several painful moments follow, of her prodding and me pretending that I can feel it.

'Perhaps it's gone round the back?' I say.

'You sure?' she says. 'I could see if I can find something to make into an eye bath.'

I shake my head. 'It's fine.'

Free from her attentions, I look for Jake. He's sitting over by the entrance to our cave, smoking a cigarette and drinking a beer, looking daggers over at Beattie.

Oh, Lordy.

18

14 August 1980, night. Ikaria. The cave.

My fever's really on one now. I need paracetamol or I'm scared I'll end up hallucinating, or having a fit. It happened to me once when I was younger. I've tried cooling down with seawater, but it's really not doing the trick.

I've finished *The Women's Room*. I said I identified with Chris. I didn't realise how much we had in common: it turns out that, like me, Chris is raped by a stranger. I cried so much when I read that bit. But I'm luckier (stronger?) than her. She lets it change her whole life. Whereas I'm determined not to let The French Shit ruin mine. With Jake's help, I can pull through all this. You see, women and men need to live together and work together, or it all ends in unhappiness.

Beattie and Jake have gone up to the village, to get some more supplies and to eat. I hope they get on OK together. I asked them to see if they could find my bag. It's got all my money in it, not to mention my first journal and my passport.

I've tried to start *The Greek Myths*, but I just can't get into it. It's all about the creation of the world, about the Goddess of All Things rising naked from Chaos. Sort of know how she feels, but it's all a bit beyond me at the moment.

Shivery.

So this is weird.

I've found something really odd.

I looked in Jake's rucksack for paracetamol. I was sure he wouldn't mind. He's sort of my boyfriend now, after all.

There was nothing in the outer pockets, so I decided to look in the main body of the bag, where, sweetly, he keeps his stuff all neatly folded. I didn't want him to know I'd been rummaging around, so I lifted things out carefully, placing them in a way that'd help me get them back in the same order.

Holding a T-shirt to my nose, I inhaled his scent. Like some lovesick teenager.

I pulled out a nylon pouch, like a washbag, and opened it. Inside there was a bottle of Tylenol – which the pack says is paracetamol. I fished out a handful of the pills, took two and was about to put the bottle back when I saw that the pouch also contained two passports.

I shouldn't have looked at them, but I did. The first was Jake's, although you wouldn't be able to tell it from the photograph because, like my own, which was taken when I was fourteen and still a child, it looked like another person altogether.

But the other passport was Australian. When I opened it, my skin prickled into goosebumps that had nothing to do with my fever. Unlike Jake's, this photo was a very good likeness of its owner. Unmistakable, in fact.

It was The Australian Shit. The man I thought I recognised in the drawing on the posters back in Athens. The man whose body was found dumped behind bushes at the Agora. I remember thinking he was weaselly, mean and pinched-looking, but in his passport he looks more innocent. You can see he was someone's son.

And now, if I was right about the posters, he's dead, unidentified, lost to his parents.

And Jake has his passport.

My hands shaking, I put aside a handful of Tylenol. Then I replaced the things in Jake's rucksack exactly as I'd found them.

Was this the thing he was going to tell me – the thing he said I wouldn't believe, before Beattie joined us and he scuttled away? Some sort of confession?

How the hell did Jake get that passport? I've tried to think back to the evening when The Australian Shit hit me, but the days and nights have got jumbled in my mind, and I haven't got my first journal to check the facts right now. Wasn't that when Jake and Beattie went out after I'd fallen asleep? When they found that wallet? Did Jake stay out longer than Beattie that night? Or did he go off on his own when she was asleep?

And then it's just possible that they found the Australian's passport that night, perhaps dropped, or lost in a mugging gone wrong. Beattie does seem to have a talent for finding other people's valuables.

But then why didn't they tell me?

And isn't that just too much of a coincidence?

Oh God. Now my mind's working overtime. Fuck.

Despite what went on between us earlier (and even thinking about it, even now, I get a little tic of something – desire? – in the back of my throat), Jake is still something of a mystery to me. It's hard to get a word in edgeways with Beattie always there, but even so, he's not very talkative, and seems to have become even less so as the days pass.

And there are the points when he loses it.

Have I been blinded? Has my whole perception of him been coloured by the fact that the first time I met him he practically saved my life? And, of course, that I fancy him?

Have I been a stupid little girl?

And, although it feels like a lifetime, I've known him for less than two weeks. How much can you get to know a person in that short length of time? Especially when we are all of us away from anything we can call home, with no touchstones, no familiar points to hook ourselves onto, nothing to help us say 'yes, that's me', let alone, 'yes, that's him'.

And what do I know about Jake's touchstones, anyway? Virtually nothing. While Beattie is happy to tell us all about her crazy life back in New York, and I've told them bits about Ripon, as far as I can remember (which might not be saying much), Jake has not once talked about his life back home.

What do Bea and I know about him? Except – and this is the worrying thing – how out of control he can get.

I can't think straight.

I need to talk to Beattie about all this.

19

15 August 1980, not dawn yet. Ikaria. The cave.

This is terrible. Terrible.

The waves slap the rocks. Somewhere up the mountain a rooster is calling too early. A dog's howling too.

Beattie is finally sleeping next to me, like a poor, drowned rat. Even now I can feel the pain and the hurt coming off her in hot waves. I've had to prise myself away from her arms.

I wonder if perhaps she has caught my fever.

But it's not that. It's what Jake's done to her, of course.

I'm awake because I'm too stunned to sleep. Also, I'm keeping guard.

I have no idea where he is. Up on the mountain somewhere. I don't care. I just don't want him to come down here.

Can I excuse his behaviour? Put it down to drink or pills?

No.

I really liked him. I *really* liked him. I thought I loved him.

But there's no excuse.

Are all men such bastards? Will they only ever think of one thing?

Do they all feel they have the right to use us like this?

After Beattie came back down to the cave and told me what Jake had done, I couldn't believe it at first. It seemed impossible, so out of character, so not like the boy who had kissed me just hours earlier.

I thought he was different.

But he has this wild side . . .

And then there's the issue of the Australian's passport . . .

I never really knew him, did I? Hardly surprising, with all the drinking and the pills and the sun and now the fever. How can you get to know someone when you and they are out of it most of the time?

Jake.

What he's done.

She's showed me the bruises, the red scrapes on her back and buttocks, where he dragged her over the rocks. The mess he's made of her forcing himself on her, before she got away and ran down here to me.

To me. For me to protect her.

They could be my own injuries after Marseille. They are almost identical.

'Where is he?' I ask her.

We're not fit to stand up to him physically – even combined, we don't measure up to him.

Beattie points in the direction of the mountain. 'He's probably passed out up there. He was so out of it. It was like he was a different person.'

We know he can get like that, but we never thought . . .

I wonder what might have happened to me if she hadn't interrupted him with me earlier. I might have got it all wrong. Might I have been the one beaten and bloodied instead of her?

As she tells me what happened, I wash her cuts and grazes in our drinking water and rub aftersun – the only ointment I have – on her bruises. I also give her a couple of the Tylenol I stole from Jake's rucksack.

As I do this, I tell her about the Australian's passport. Her eyes widen and her hand creeps over her mouth. Seeing Beattie so scared, so on the back foot, is frightening.

'Do you think . . . ?' she whispers.

I nod, gravely. I ask her to tell me what happened.

They'd eaten supper at the village taverna and polished off two litres of wine between them. It was a busy night – they're working up to some sort of big festival tomorrow, so there was lots of noise and dancing. Elpiniki got some local firewater out and Bea and Jake (the monster Jake) matched the locals shot for shot – helped by a couple of slimming pills they took to keep them going.

In the end, Beattie felt sick and dizzy, so Jake suggested they come back down to the beach. But when they got out of earshot of the village, he pulled her off the road into the forest. Laughing, she had followed him, but as soon as they were in the trees, he jumped her. She managed to struggle free, and ran, yelling as Beattie would, back towards the road, but he caught her, put his hand over her mouth, tore at her skirt and dragged her to the ground, where he forced himself into her.

He was blind drunk, she said. Like another man, as if a demon possessed him.

When he'd done that, he tried to turn her over to do God knows what to her. But as he twisted her she got hold of a rock, which she brought down on his head. That was how she got away. She had no idea where he was, but she just ran downhill, praying that she'd be able to find her way back to the cave to warn me, in case he was thinking of coming and doling out the same treatment to me.

Just as she's telling me this, almost on cue, I hear footsteps crunching along the beach towards us.

Beattie stops talking and makes me put out the candle. I peer outside. It's unmistakably Jake: tall, curly-haired, staggering slightly, his tread heavier than usual.

Beattie's face is close against mine, stone pale in the moonlight, all the suntan drained from it. She shakes her head and grasps my arm.

'Tell him you're trying to sleep,' she mouths.

I can smell her fear.

'Bea!' Jake calls from outside. 'We need to talk.'

My heart pumping like it's about to break my chest, I look quickly at Beattie. She shakes her head again.

'Beattie?' Jake asks again, louder, closer, this time. His shadow falls across the cave entrance. Beattie scoots behind me.

'Jake?' I make my voice sound groggy.

'Emma! Are you OK in there?'

'I was just nearly asleep,' I say.

'Have you seen Beattie?'

Beattie shakes her head violently, mouthing 'No'.

'No,' I say.

'Good. OK. You sure you're OK?'

'I'm fine.'

'You get to sleep, then. I'm just going back up the cliff,' he says. 'To keep an eye out for her.'

'I hope she's OK.'

'She went on ahead of me. She was pretty wasted. I'll check the path. You try to get to sleep.'

'OK. Good night, Jake.'

'Night, then. If I can't find her, I'll wait up on the top in case she's lost and calls out. See you in the morning.'

We hold our breath as his footsteps crunch back across the beach, until we can hear him no more.

'That's weird,' I say.

Then Beattie loses it, shaking and crying, running her hands through her hair.

I hold her.

'I hate him,' she says, sobbing on my shoulder.

I hate him too.

While I've been sitting guard here, waiting for sunrise, I've looked back over what I've written these past few weeks. Somehow, despite all that Jake put her through, Beattie managed to keep my bag – which the taverna boy Giorgos had handed over to her – over her shoulder. She held onto it through everything. She knew it had my life in it; she couldn't let Jake get his hands on it.

That's the kind of friend she is.

That Emma of the early parts of the first journal was a different person. She was just a little girl, so stupid. So blind to anything that could go wrong.

So entitled. That's the word.

I realise now that women aren't entitled to anything. It's a long fight, all the way.

I realise that now because of what happened in Marseille. What happened to Hardy's Tess, and Mira and Chris in *The Women's Room*. And what's happened to my Beattie, now.

These moments will never be forgotten.

20

15 August 1980, about 8 a.m. Ikaria. The cave.

Still no Jake, thank God.

We've made our plan.

It was beautiful to see how putting it together gave Beattie strength.

We're going to play the worst ever Dangerous Game. It'll teach Jake a lesson; let him know how awful we know he is.

Then we're going to take all his gear and leave him stranded on the island with no money, no ID, no stuff.

Make him pay.

And that'll be the end of him in our lives.

Better that, as Beattie says, than go to the police and all that, and have him tied to us for months more. Cut and run. It's the best way.

I'm not going to mourn what could have been between me and him. I just feel like I've had a lucky escape.

Beattie's gone on ahead now and I'm waiting for him to come back. He will at some point, she said, because he has no food or money.

I've got the map to the island. Beattie has shown me where she'll be waiting, up on the cliff, a headland about a mile along the coast. She found it when she and Jake went off when I was first sick.

I'm to lead Jake to her.

'Tell him you want him or something,' she said, smiling grimly. 'Seduce him up there. Act like nothing has happened. He'll probably give you some bullshit, but don't listen to him. He's fucked up.'

My fever's still knocking me about.

I've taken a couple of slimming pills to give me strength.

I'm so fucking scared.

21

15 August 1980, 9 p.m. Ikarian Sea. Ferry.

Everything is over.

I don't know what I'm going to do.

I've thrown everything overboard, into the sea. My rucksack, all my gear, *The Women's Room*, *The Greek Myths*, everything's gone except the clothes I'm wearing, my passport, my money and these journals.

I'm done with it all.

I can't get my head round everything that's happened, so I'm going to try to write it out in order. Perhaps then I can make sense of some of it. I'm on my third Amstel and it's pretty choppy out here tonight, so I hope I'll be able to read this when I'm able to face it all again.

I'm not even sure how reliable I am, if I've got a grasp on things. I'm still pretty ill, spaced out, not sure what's real and what's not.

Am I trying to defend myself?

* * *

Jake. Beattie.

Did we ever really know each other? Or were we just three strangers thrown together until our ugly parts showed?

My ugly parts showed.

And some.

So Beattie was right. She left me in the cave this morning and went up to the cliff. Sure enough, an hour later, I hear Jake's footsteps on the beach, coming my way.

'Hi,' he says, from outside.

I crawl out of the cave to greet him. He looks bleary. And he has an egg-sized lump on his forehead. That would be where Beattie hit him with the stone.

I want to run away as fast as I can. But I hold my ground.

'What happened to you?' I ask him, trying to show concern.

'Oh this . . .' he says, touching the lump with his fingers as if he has only just noticed it was there. 'I fell over last night on the way down the hill. Beattie didn't come back, did she?'

I shake my head. 'Do you think she's OK?'

Jake frowns.

As Beattie and I have planned, I suggest we go and look for her.

'Are you strong enough?' He places a hand on my shoulder and I try not to flinch at his touch.

I nod.

'It's better you stick with me, anyhow,' he says. 'I don't want to leave you on your own down here if I'm not nearby.'

I don't really know what he was playing at, pretending to be so caring. Perhaps he was a real psychopath, or schizophrenic or whatever it is. A split personality. The thought makes me shudder when I think of the times I spent alone with him.

But that doesn't really matter now, does it?

Nothing matters any more.

I duck inside the cave to grab a bottle of water. I also open my Swiss Army penknife and stash it in my pocket, just in case he's planning something like the attack he launched on Beattie. As a final thought I grab my evil eye, to protect me.

Ha.

'I need to talk to you, Em,' Jake says, as we climb up to the road.

'Not now,' I say, thinking he might be wanting to make a confession.

I couldn't deal with that. I really would rather be dead.

'Let's find Beattie first,' I say.

He looks wretched, but he nods. 'Probably better we do.'

We continue up the hill.

The village is surreally quiet. The taverna's still shut, the streets empty, and Beattie, of course, is nowhere to be found.

'So where is she, then?' Jake asks.

I repeat what Beattie and I prepared. 'Perhaps she took the wrong turning on the way down the hill? You know, where the paths fork?'

'Possibly.' Jake doesn't look at all convinced.

I'm trying not to sound as jumpy as I feel. If he thinks about it, he'll wonder what I know about forking paths on the way down. I only made the journey back from the village once, and it had been dark and I'd been drunk.

But he doesn't think about it.

'It's worth a try,' he says. He touches me, his knuckle grazing my cheek, his eyes searching out mine, which can't quite meet them.

The blue in his eyes isn't beautiful any more. It looks dangerous now, evil, like cold stone.

'Are you OK?' he asks me.

I bristle. It's as if he's decided that he's my boyfriend and he's going to look after me.

Well, of course he would, Emma, after you'd been so stupid with him, for fuck's sake.

I'm trying to act how I would, had I not known what he's done to Beattie. So, with difficulty, I don't pull away from his touch. Instead, I just smile gratefully at him and nod.

'Just a little spaced. And worried about Bea.'

But what did he think he was up to? What did he imagine he might do to Beattie – and me, possibly – when we found her?

Well, whatever he had planned, we had decided that he wasn't going to get away with it.

Oh, God.

We follow the path back down the hill, away from the village.

'Here's the fork,' I say. 'It'd be easy to make the mistake at night, take the wrong turning.'

Jake halts suddenly and grabs my hand. I just manage to stop myself from shrieking.

'Look, Em. I need to tell you—' he starts, but I put my finger to his lips and, trying so hard that I almost burst a blood vessel, look love into his eyes.

'Not yet. Let's find Beattie first.'

'But it's to do with her.' He looks frantic.

'Shh,' I say. 'Let's find her first. Perhaps she's hurt herself.'

I lead on, hurrying down to the next headland, where the bluff juts out a hundred feet above the sea, before dropping straight down to the rocks below. We cross an olive grove, avoiding the nets spread out beneath to catch the fruit. Luckily, the path is difficult and narrow and we have to walk in single file, so he can't hold my hand. The wind roars in my ears, so any attempt by him to say anything to me is pointless.

It's hard going. Lightheaded with hunger and fever, I hear my heart working overtime to pump enough blood round my body to keep climbing. I touch the blue glass evil eye in my pocket, but it doesn't make me feel any stronger.

We reach the foot of the scrubby path up to the towering bluff. As we crest the hill, the wind blasts hot dust into my face, taking my breath away.

And Beattie is nowhere to be seen.

22

15 August 1980, 11 p.m. Ikarian Sea. Ferry.

This part is so hard to write. I've had to down another beer to get to it. On my way back I chucked my Swiss Army knife and my evil eye into the sea. I'd forgotten they were still in my pockets. Fat lot of good either of them did me, really.

On the top of the cliff is one lone tree. Some sort of oak, I think. As it was growing, the wind must have pushed the trunk down and away from its roots. It looks like a giant hand clawing the earth.

I stop and look around. We're on the highest point along the coast. Churned by the wind, which has blown fiercely all morning, the sea heaves and froths what must be a hundred feet below us, crashing onto a rocky shore strewn with fallen chunks from the cliff we're standing on. The islands in the hazy distance hover like an expectant audience. A fishing boat, a tiny blue-and-white speck riding the distant waves, is the only sign of any other human presence.

We're on the cliff. But Beattie isn't here.

A cold panic sets in on me. Have I got the wrong point? Have I brought Jake up here to end up alone with him? What kind of danger have I put myself in?

Jake hands me the water bottle, which I take, keeping him at arm's length.

Where the hell is Beattie?

I drink, hand the water back to him and he takes a swig, tipping his head back.

As he removes the bottle from his mouth and wipes his lips, Beattie steps out from behind the tree. She stands and glares at him, her big bag slung over one shoulder. I know that in it is the equipment we have prepared.

At the sight of her he jolts and drops the bottle. Caught by a gust of wind, it flies off the edge of the cliff.

'Hi, Jake.' Beattie's eyes shine like go lights.

'Easy, Beattie,' Jake says, stepping in front of me, holding his hands out. I poise myself, ready to spring should he jump her.

Her eyes on mine, Beattie reaches into her bag.

This is my signal. I leap forward and push him as she rushes towards him. Totally taken by surprise, he has no time to struggle. Making the most of his confusion, I grab his arms, and Beattie swiftly ties them together behind his back, tightly winding my tent guy rope round and round his wrists.

'What the FUCK are you doing?' Jake says, struggling to get free, but it's too late. We have him. Beattie kicks the back of his knees, making him buckle to the ground.

With extraordinary strength she pushes him forward and he smashes face-first to the ground. She pulls my PLO scarf from her bag and throws it to me. While she sits on him, straddling his back, I tie it securely over his eyes, knotting it up in his hair.

'What are you doing, Emma?' he screams at me.

I kick him. Just like The French Shit did me. Hard. He deserves it.

He deserved *that*, anyway.

'I know what you did to Beattie,' I shout above the roar of the wind.

'What?' Jake says. As if he doesn't know what I'm talking about.

'You think you can just take what you want and get away with it,' I yell. 'I saw what you did to her. You bastard.'

'What the fuck are you talking about, Emma?' he says. 'Beattie? What the fuck?'

'Rapist,' Beattie says, pulling his hair. 'Creep.'

'What? No!' Jake says. 'Emma, you've got to believe me, I didn't touch Beattie. She—'

'SHUT UP!' I yell at him and kick him again.

It feels so good, like I'm getting back at my own attacker as well as Beattie's. It also feels great – at this point – that the two of us, two tiny, scrap-haired girls, have overpowered this tall, violent boy.

'So you're going to blame it on your victim, then, Jake?' I tell him. 'She provoked you, did she? Was her dress too short or her top too low?'

My throat is still sore from the shouting I did up there on that cliff.

Jake struggles underneath Beattie. I think he's crying behind my scarf.

The thought of that makes me feel very good. I want him to suffer so much.

'Please, Emma. Please believe me. I didn't do it. I didn't touch her. You have to believe me, she's lying—'

'HA!' Beattie says, looking at me. 'Denial. What did I say he was going to do?'

'And what about the Australian?' I say. 'The boy you killed in Athens?'

'I DIDN'T TOUCH HIM,' Jake shouts.

'I SAW you touch him. I SAW you beat him up.'

He turns his head towards me, trying to look at me underneath our makeshift blindfold. 'But you didn't see me kill him, because I didn't fucking kill him, Em. You have to believe me.'

'Shut UP.' I kick him again. I don't believe him. Why would I? He's lied and lied and lied.

Beattie hands me the knickers – her soiled knickers from the night before, and pulls his head up by his hair as I stuff them in his mouth and tie them in place with a belt of Beattie's.

'Like that, do you? My underwear in your disgusting mouth. Pervert,' Beattie shrieks into his ear.

Then Jake suddenly bucks, throwing Beattie off him. His hands still tied behind his back, he scrambles to his feet. Turning, he charges blindly at her with a muffled roar, his head down. She jumps easily out of the way and trips him up. Unable to save himself with his hands, he topples forward onto the ground, slamming his chin on a rock.

As he lies there, dazed, blood at the corner of his mouth, Beattie jumps on top of him again, gripping him firmly with her thighs.

So those were his true colours, revealed. While he played the lover boy with me, he attacked Beattie.

What was that about?

I've thought about it over and over and I've come to the conclusion that after we arrived on Ikaria he tipped over into some sort of psychosis. I don't know what triggered it. Being too far from home? All the drinking and the pills? Or just some random chemical imbalance that happened to trigger itself at that exact moment, when it was most dangerous to all of us.

For a second, I waver, watching him trapped there, bound on the dusty, rocky earth, blood mingling with spit around the gag where he has cut his lip or bitten his tongue. For a second, I feel pity. What if he *is* sick? If he can't help himself?

But then, as Beattie pulls the ouzo and Valium out of her bag, her dress rides up and I see the purple, blue and green bruises, the cross-hatching of scratches and cuts that almost entirely cover her left leg and, I know, her back and buttocks, too.

He did that. And worse. A lot worse.

We roll him onto his back. I kneel, jamming his head between my knees. He struggles to get free, but we have him now. He's not going anywhere.

Beattie pops ten Valium out of the blister pack. I undo the belt, prise the knickers out of his mouth and, by pinching his nose and forcing his chin down, hold his jaws open. Beattie throws the pills at the back of his throat in a way that reminds me of Mum worming the cats back home. Then she unscrews the bottle and fills his blooded mouth with ouzo. I force his jaw shut and we make him swallow. We keep on going until all the ouzo is used up, and Jake is groaning and retching.

I fix the gag back on him, although it is hardly necessary. He is already nearly insensible with the dose of drugs and alcohol we have just dealt out to him.

Throwing the bottle to one side where it smashes on the rocks, Beattie, all afire, rips his T-shirt, and tears it off him, past his bound arms. Then she scrambles to her feet and pulls off his trousers, leaving him completely naked.

This hadn't been in the plan, but it seems the right thing to do.

His thin, muscular body looks deceptively beautiful in the sunlight, struggling on the ground out in front of me.

His fear and his pain are more beautiful to me at that moment, though.

Evil. That's what it was. He was evil, not ill.

I have to remember that.

He tries to curl up to hide his withered penis.

* * *

221

Perhaps he thought we were going to castrate him. I'm not saying that the thought hadn't crossed my mind – it would have saved other women he might have come across.

Beattie motions for me to get up. Then, pulling him by the hair, she tugs him to standing where he staggers, the blind drunkard of our making.

It feels good, seeing him like that. Vulnerable, exposed, like I had been in Marseille, like Beattie was last night.

'We're going to play the Dangerous Game,' Beattie says, launching into the next part of our plan. 'Make you pay for what you did. We're going to lead you on a little walk up here on this cliff. Right to the edge. Then you're going to jump off.'

Jake whimpers. He's crying again, cowering, shaking his head. We have him.

We weren't planning to *really* make him jump over the edge.

We just wanted to make him *think* he was jumping.

That was my contribution to the plan, thanks to Miss Higgs who taught me *King Lear* for my A Level, who made us act out the scene where Edgar does the same thing to Gloucester.

We wanted to give Jake, quite literally, the fright of his life. We reckoned he'd either collapse in terror, or, failing that, the ouzo and Valium would take him out long enough for us to get back to the cave, clear out all his and our own stuff and disappear on the midday ferry.

That was the plan.

Again, Jake whimpers, pleads.

'Shut up, *coward*.' Beattie nods to me. 'Turn him.'

I get hold of him and whirl him around four or five times.

As he stands, swaying and dizzy, I pull out my penknife and

rest the point on his back, at the base of his ribs.

'If you don't do as I say,' I say to him. 'I'm going to stick this knife in you.'

He's shaking his head like he's trying to escape into another dimension.

'Take a step,' Beattie yells.

'Do it.' I jab the point so that it makes a tiny indent in his skin. A tiny nick.

Falteringly, he takes a small step towards the edge of the cliff, which is about ten yards away from us.

'Another,' I shout.

We keep on at him. About three yards away from the edge, we tell him to stop.

'Can you feel the wind?' Beattie cries. 'Can you smell the sea beneath you?'

A flock of seabirds wheels right over our heads, screaming at the rushing air.

'I'm going to count to three,' I tell him. 'And you're going to jump. If you don't, we're going to push you.'

And this is where our plan goes wrong.

Somehow, Jake manages to free his hands from the guy rope. Without warning, he turns and rams into Beattie, sending her flying backwards, away from the edge. Then he rips off his blindfold, tugs the gag from his mouth and wheels round in my direction, his eyes like cold, blue fire, his mouth a bloody hole.

It all happens too quickly. I think he's going to attack me, so I rush at him first and push him away from me, back up towards the cliff edge. Unsteady on his feet because of what we've tipped down his throat, he tumbles and trips backwards. Disoriented, thinking he's falling over the edge of the cliff, he lets out a muffled scream and his body totters, half falling, half running in strange, almost comical backwards steps.

But it isn't funny at all.

'Jake!' I scream and run towards him, trying to grab him. But, because he is naked, there is nothing to hold on to.

He's still stumbling, upwards and backwards towards the actual edge of the cliff.

And then he stumbles beyond it.

Time hangs still. He hovers, suspended over nothingness, his face awful, full of the realisation of what has happened, what is about to happen. This is a picture I know I will remember all my life. Then I blink. When I open my eyes, he is no longer there. He's disappeared beneath the craggy lip of the bluff.

I don't know what to do. I'm rooted to my spot. I pray that perhaps some bird, or some freakish gust of wind has somehow scooped him up and saved him.

He deserved to suffer for what he did. Really suffer. But he didn't deserve to die.

No one *deserves* to *die*.

Beattie scrambles to her feet, and looks at me, her mouth open in shock and disbelief.

The wind howls around our ears, blowing grit into our eyes as we creep towards the cliff edge.

We look down. The white of the stony shore and the reflected sunlight shooting up from the boiling sea into our eyes makes it hard to see at first.

I think for a moment that he isn't down there, that somehow it has been an awful dream, a fevered hallucination. That none of it has happened at all.

But then the dazzles clear from my eyes and reveal him to me: splatted on a flat white rock, all the way down on the shore, his legs splayed at strange angles, one arm pinned under his body, bent at a horrible angle. I can't tell if it is blood pooling around his head or if it's his hair. Perhaps it's both.

I try to imagine he's sunbathing, but even through half-closed eyes it doesn't look like that.

'What do we do now?' I ask Beattie, who is just staring down at him, her face drained of all colour, her teeth working away at her lip.

She sits back on her heels, shields her eyes from the sun and looks straight at me. I notice there are tears rolling down her cheeks.

'Is he dead?' I ask, the full horror of what we have done hitting me as if I, too, have tumbled over the edge. 'Have we killed him?'

Beattie is sobbing now. Her face contorted, her eyes shut, she nods.

I reach for her, to try to comfort her, but she pulls away, scrabbling to her feet and running down the slope, away from the edge of the cliff, towards the tree, which she grabs on to as if it were the only thing holding her to the earth.

I take one last look at Jake and watch as a giant wave comes out of nowhere and washes his body from the ledge, and into the sea.

He is gone.

'What do we do now, Beattie?' I scream into the wind. 'WHAT DO WE DO NOW?'

She hunches into the tree as if she's trying to bury herself in its branches. For a second I think Beattie, the girl with the plans, the girl I have come to rely on, has no idea what to do next.

But by the time I reach her, she's still grasping the tree, but she is able to look at me, her eyes terrible, her mouth a gash in her face.

'It's all over,' she says. 'You pushed him over.'

'I didn't mean to, I—'

I don't know exactly what I am saying or what I mean at this point.

'You did it for me?' she asks.

'I – I –' My brain feels like scrambled eggs, I don't know what happened, what I did or why I did it.

Beattie steps forward and puts her arms around me, tight, like a vice. She takes my breath away. She kisses me, full on the mouth. Then she steps backwards, away, and points towards the road.

I'm scared; I don't know what she's doing.

'Get out of here fast, Emma,' she says. 'Cover your tracks.'

'But . . .' I say, reaching out towards her.

'Go. This never happened. We never met. We'll never, ever see each other again.'

She turns to me like a tiger, her forcefulness making her seem twice the size of me.

'Get out of here,' she yells. 'GO.'

I stand there dumbfounded, shaking my head. But she launches herself at me, her fists flailing. 'We should never have met. You have to get out of here before . . .'

'What? Before what?'

'Go, Emma. Go. This is your last chance. Go away and forget we ever met. Forget about Beattie, forget about Jake.'

She slaps me hard round the face and, reeling, my eyes stinging, in shock, I stumble away.

I have got away. But I will never, ever be able to forget.

PART THREE

AFTER

2013

One

Mark told Kate she was to do nothing for a week when she got back from hospital. She complied for the first day, which she spent lying in bed, bolstered by pillows, gazing up at grey nothingness through the glass atrium and listening to the distant rumble of the city.

But as the concussion and shock receded, the details of her meeting with Beattie bored into her brain.

Somewhere in the world, Jake still existed. She had been certain she had killed him, but somehow, by some freak chance, he had survived.

What was she supposed to make of all that?

All the lies she had told, all the people and prospects and hopes she had turned her back on. And he wasn't dead.

She had no idea whether to rejoice or to weep.

* * *

Tilly came and went that first day, tiptoeing in with cups of tea and pieces of fruit and toast to tempt her. But mostly she was left alone. She didn't see Mark. Although it was a Saturday, he was at the office as usual.

Sophie PR sent over a big bunch of lilies, unaware of Kate's problem with cut flowers. With the delivery came a little note – Sophie's words but written in the looping hand of a young florist – saying that she would be writing the *Kate Reports* blog posts until she was 'up and firing on all cylinders again'.

Kate wondered when that might be, but was grateful that one more source of guilt had been lifted from her shoulders.

The next day – Sunday – she couldn't bear it any longer. As soon as Mark and Tilly were both out – he to Surrey to play golf with a client, she to serve those chips to those National Theatre actors – she pulled out the Starbucks napkin with Beattie's phone number on it and called her.

'I was so worried about you, Emma,' Beattie said, a little breathless, as if she had run for the phone. Or perhaps it was just the catch of a smoker's throat. Behind her voice, Kate heard the sound of traffic.

'I'm sorry.' Kate picked her holey stone up from her bedside table and ran her thumb over its smooth edges as she spoke.

'Oh honey. It's hard to take in, isn't it?'

'Yep.'

'I know exactly what you're going through. I was the same when I found out.'

'What happened? You said he's on to us. What does that mean?'

'Look,' Beattie said, 'I can't talk about it here. What do you say I come by and perhaps I can show you?'

'Show me?' Kate hesitated. Was it wise to bring Beattie into her house? To mix the oil of her past with the water of her present? But then, as far as Mark was concerned, she was an old school friend. In any case, he wouldn't be back at least until supper time, and Tilly was on a long shift, so she and Beattie would have the whole afternoon to themselves.

'OK,' she said. 'Can you come now?'

'Can I make you a coffee?' Kate showed Beattie into her kitchen.

'Thanks.' Beattie turned around, taking in the space. 'What a beautiful home you have, Emma.'

'Can you try to call me Kate?'

'Oh gosh, I'm so sorry. It's just I've thought of you as Emma all these years.'

As Kate reached for the coffee beans, she realised that, so successfully had she erased her early life from her conscious mind, she had hardly thought of Beattie at all until now. It was unsettling in the extreme to have everything back here, in her house, forced in front of her nose like this.

'It's just—' She turned and smiled apologetically at Beattie. 'No one in my life knows anything at all about what happened.'

'No. I know. It's the same for me. I'll try.' Beattie sighed, shivering a little and hugging herself, running her hands up and down her arms. Kate reminded herself that her former best friend had said she was desperate, and it had something to do with Jake. She had to face up to her responsibilities towards Beattie. Her selfish desire not to have her nice little boat rocked was neither here nor there.

Beattie moved in front of the big family photograph on the kitchen wall. 'Is this your little girl?' she said, gently touching Martha's face. 'She was so pretty. I'm so sorry for you.'

Wanting to avoid talking about Martha, Kate stopped what she was doing and turned to face Beattie.

'I'm sorry, Beattie, but I don't really understand why you're here. You've told me Jake's alive. But what of it? What do you need to warn me about?'

Beattie looked to the floor.

'I'm so sorry, Em— I mean Kate. I didn't want to come in here and mess everything up. But I'm in such a state. I didn't want him to get you unawares.' She looked up and Kate saw tears in her eyes.

'What do you mean, get me?' Kate said, feeling the need to lean back against the kitchen counter. 'What is it?'

'Jake's *alive*, Kate.'

'I know. You said. But isn't that a good thing? Doesn't that mean we can live the rest of our lives more easily?'

Beattie shook her head. 'He's alive. But he's mad.'

'Mad how?'

'Mad furious.'

Kate rubbed her temples. Of course. Of course he would be mad furious. She had tried to kill him. They had left him for dead. 'But why now? After all these years?'

'Do you have that coffee?' Beattie said. 'I need some help with this.'

'How about this?' Kate pulled a bottle of Sauvignon Blanc from the fridge.

Beattie raised an eyebrow and nodded.

Old habits die hard.

Kate fetched two glasses.

'I still can't really believe it,' she said, when they were sitting on the living-area sofa, each cradling a large glass of wine. For the first time in years she had a tingle-lipped craving for a cigarette.

'It's hard to take in, I know. I'm sorry.'

'I feel like I need to see him.'

'Of course you do. So you can believe it's true.'

'It's not that I don't believe you, Beattie, it's just – he looked so *dead*.'

'He's told me the whole story.'

'You've spoken with him?'

'Oh yes. He tracked me down a while back. Likes to Skype me. He enjoyed telling me it all, watching me squirm. This fisherman rescued him, apparently,' Beattie said. 'And then he was flown to some god-awful hospital in Athens, where he stayed for two years. First they thought he'd never come round, then that he'd never walk again, but he proved them wrong on both counts.'

'Unbelievable.' The thought suddenly struck Kate that they could have saved him, had they not panicked and run away. The thought that they had had a choice back then, and they had chosen to abandon him.

But, a tiny voice piped in her head, *didn't he deserve what he got?*

She tried to bat it away.

'I know. It's too weird, isn't it?' Beattie said. 'You could come back home with me and we could visit with him, if you want. I've not met him face-to-face yet. I've not dared.'

'No,' Kate said quickly. She did not want to go 'home' with Beattie. The stories she'd have to tell Mark and Tilly, the preparations she'd have to make, the facing of people, the shock of the flight; then, oh horrors, the arrival and confrontation . . .

'I've got some photos he emailed me, though,' Beattie said. She pulled an iPad out of her handbag.

Kate steeled herself, but nothing could prepare her for the shock of what she saw. Until that moment, whenever she thought of Jake – and where she had mostly managed to push the thought of Beattie from her mind, *he* had been a regular, unwelcome visitor both to her waking and sleeping hours – she pictured a tall, skinny boy with thick, curly dark hair. It was almost entirely the opposite of what she saw in the photograph.

If time hadn't been kind to Beattie, it had been positively brutal to Jake.

It was what Tilly would call a 'selfie' taken with a webcam, and it showed a fleshy body, barely contained by the camera frame, spilling over the edges of what appeared to be a wheelchair; a great bald bullet head held at either side by a padded support; a mouth lolling open in the middle of a vast beard, purple lips parted by a loose tongue.

'I thought you said he could walk,' Kate said.

'He could after the accident *we* caused him,' Beattie said.

After her years of wrangling with the fact, Kate could have argued Beattie's use of the word accident. But she let it go.

'But that was just the beginning of his story. He hasn't had a lucky life.'

'So it seems,' Kate said, looking again at the screen. 'But are we sure this is really Jake? It doesn't look like him.'

'Emma, he was twenty-one when we thought he died.'

Kate mentally corrected this to *when we thought we killed him*.

'He's mid-fifties now. People change. But look.' Beattie swiped the screen until the photograph closed up on the man's sharp blue eyes. 'No one I have ever met since has eyes like this. Not this colour. Not that look. There's no way anyone could fake those eyes. Tell me that's not Jake.'

Kate peered at the screen. Much as she wanted all of this to be some elaborate hoax, Beattie was right. Looking into those irises was like stepping back in time. She even experienced a ghost of the thrill she remembered from when she was eighteen, immersing herself in that blue, believing herself to be in love with the person behind them.

And was he still there, that boy, somewhere inside? Or had she played a part in ripping him to pieces – not physically, as she had once thought, but psychologically? What was he like, the man in there?

'And there's this,' Beattie said, scrolling to the next photograph, in which Jake displayed his right forearm to the webcam, showing the Triskelion tattoo. Instinctively, Kate put her hand to her own ink. There was no doubt. This was Jake. Or what remained of Jake.

'It's him, believe me,' Beattie said. She shivered again and looked away from the image. 'I wish it wasn't, but it is.'

'What is he doing, Beattie?' Kate asked. 'What does he want?'

'He calls it reparation. He wants his life back.'

'What do you mean?'

'He's bled me dry, and now he says it's your turn.'

'What?'

Beattie's iPad screen changed, and the jaunty sound of an incoming Skype call – familiar to Kate because it was how she kept in touch with Mark when he was away on business – was accompanied by another onscreen photo of the obese bald man in the wheelchair.

'What's this?' Kate said, her eyes shimmering with horror.

Beattie passed a hand over her face. 'I'm sorry, Emma. I don't want you to think I've led him to you. He found you himself and would've let you know far more brutally. I came to warn you so that you're ready for him. Imagine if this all just came out of the blue.' She thrust the screen into Kate's hands and moved quickly off the sofa, onto an armchair opposite.

'What do I do?' Kate said. 'What do I do?'

'You have to answer. If you don't, we'll both be in trouble.'

'What?'

'Please,' Beattie said, her voice tiny, strangled in the back of her throat. 'He made me come to you.'

Kate froze, holding the screen away from her body as if it carried some terrible disease.

'Please answer, Kate,' Beattie said.

Kate looked at Beattie once more. She seemed to have shrunk into the big armchair, where she looked almost childlike. Her white shirt gaped a little at the front to reveal the stain of a bruise on her chest. The skin around it looked fragile, delicate, old.

Kate took a deep breath and pressed the reply button.

Two

'Click the video on,' a wheezing male voice said from the darkness of the Skype window.

Kate stabbed at the screen and there he was.

Jake_1959.

Looking directly at her.

'Well, hello there, Emma.'

The connection was bad. His image was blurred and broken, his mouth seemingly unable to keep up with his words, like a badly synched film. This was not entirely unhelpful for Kate; it eased what she was witnessing from horror story to actual, live fact.

'Hello, Jake.'

'Is that all I get? My tiny Em, my little girl, my true, true love. The One.'

Had he thought that too?

Kate swallowed, hard. He could only speak between in-breaths. Protruding from the beard that covered most of his features, a tube led from the base of his throat to some machine that whirred and pulsed beyond the reach of the webcam. Under the Yankees baseball cap that shielded the hair-free part of his face, a small microphone partially blocked Kate's view of his mouth.

That mouth that once had touched her own lips.

She tried to conceal the shudder that ran through her body.

It was cowardly and selfish, she knew, but she would have preferred to look at his rotting cadaver, dug up from the grave, rather than this.

Although, of course, had he died, he would be nothing but dust now.

Was he more than that here?

Kate put the vicious thought from her mind. Of course he was. He had aged; he was disabled. But he was alive. And that had to be a good thing, surely?

He lifted his right hand from the mouse, levering the forearm up from the elbow into a modified greeting wave. On the underside of his arm, as fresh as the day it was scarred into his skin, was the Triskelion – the matching part of the three of them: Jake, Beattie, Emma.

'What happened to you, Jake?'

'Didn't you hear?' he said. 'I got pushed over a cliff by my gal and left for dead.'

Kate looked down at her lap.

'LOOK AT ME,' Jake roared suddenly. 'LOOK AT WHAT YOU'VE DONE WITH ME AND TELL ME WHAT YOU'VE GOT TO SAY.'

The delay between his words and his image made him appear still to be talking after he had stopped. In another situation it would have been amusing.

She lifted her eyes to meet his. He had tilted his head slightly – it appeared he had a very little movement up and down – and there they were, out from the shadows of the baseball cap, those blue, blue eyes, like a cat's, like an Ikarian rock pool. It was the first time she had looked into them since he had charged her on the cliff top.

She couldn't say for sure, but, under the mike and the beard, he seemed to be smiling. Behind him she noticed a dark wall covered in American football posters and pennants. It looked like a schoolboy's bedroom, rather than that of a grown man.

'I'm sorry,' Kate said. 'I'm really sorry.' The moment the words left her lips she knew they were utterly, pitifully, inadequate.

He laughed. Or at least she thought the wheezing, choking sound he made was laughter. 'I bet you are. Real sorry. Sorry I'm still here?'

She covered her eyes. 'No, no. That's not what I mean.'

There was a pause as the machine whirred. It seemed he could only use the out-breath to speak. Everything was unfolding excruciatingly slowly, like some nightmare that you know is going to last through until the alarm goes.

'So which part of it are you sorry for? Pushing me off a cliff and killing me?'

Kate sat there and waited for the whirr, hiss and in-breath.

'Or not realising that you hadn't actually succeeded, and leaving me for dead?'

'I'm sorry for all of it,' she said, her voice as small as she felt.

'SAY IT PROPERLY. Sorry for WHAT?'

'I'm sorry for pushing you off the cliff.'

'And thinking you'd killed me? SAY IT.'

'And thinking I'd killed you.'

'AND LEAVING ME FOR DEAD?'

'And leaving you for dead.'

'And leaving me for dead. On eight, fifteen, eighty, in Ikaria, Greece.'

'Yes.'

Jake wheezed with laughter. 'Engraved on your mind, no doubt. As it is on mine. Good girl. Say that S word again.'

'What?'

'The S word, Emma.'

'Sorry.'

'That's it. And again.'

'Sorry.'

'More.'

'Sorry, sorry, sorry, sorry, sorry.'

'Ah. Sweet music.'

There was a long pause while Jake's machine whirred and buzzed.

Then, finally, he spoke.

'Apology not accepted.'

Kate looked away.

'So then, little Em. Or should I say "Face of Kindness"? That's a nasty little cut you got there on your head. How many stitches?'

'Seven.' She put her hand up to her forehead. The wine mixed with the hospital-prescribed painkillers had numbed the pain. But it still felt tight, and immobile.

'I see you never took up eating, then? Or is something eating at you instead? I so hope you're not ill. I'd hate anything to happen to you now we've just met up again.'

'I'm not ill.'

'No cancer or nothing?'

'No.' She had actually expected something of the sort to happen to her over the years, but, in spite of everything, her body had remained defiantly healthy.

'Oh, I'm so glad. Life's treating you good, then. Apart from the knock on the head.'

Kate closed her eyes.

'Hey. Don't feel guilty. We can't all have the luck.'

Silently, out of shot of the iPad camera, Beattie edged forward and poured two more glasses of wine. Kate nodded her thanks to her.

'Is that my little Bea playing barmaid?' Jake said, suddenly. 'Hey honey!'

Beattie recoiled in disgust and put her hands over her ears.

'Show her me,' Jake said.

As Kate trained the iPad on her, Beattie straightened herself out and put a weak smile on her face. 'Hi, Jake,' she said.

'Oh, hello there. Lovely to see you again. I hope you're faring well after your – ah – accident.'

Beattie reached inside her shirt and rubbed her collarbone. 'I'm fine, thank you.'

'What?' Kate said.

'Oh, didn't she tell you?' Jake said. 'Put me back so I can see you now, Em. I've had enough of looking at *that*. My, you've aged so much prettier than her. Mind you, you always had one over her in the looks department. Yeah. So poor old Beattie here had a slight incident with some guys who appear to have been following her around. Huh, Beattie?'

Beattie got up and moved over to the window, where she stood, looking out, hugging herself and rubbing the back of her neck. For the first time, Kate noticed that she was limping.

'What did you do to her?' she asked Jake.

'Me? Do I look like I can do ANYTHING to ANYONE?'

Kate looked at him as he drew more oxygen from his machine.

'What happened to you, Jake? After – after Ikaria?'

'I survived. Clearly.'

'But I thought you could walk again, after the hospital and everything.'

'After the hospital. But not after everything, honey. Beattie, I'm surprised you haven't told Emma here my whole story yet.'

'I thought I'd leave it to you,' Beattie said, without turning round.

'I don't feel like it. You tell it.'

Beattie stayed where she was, her eyes fixed on the world beyond the window.

'BEATTIE. LET HER KNOW,' Jake said. Kate couldn't work out if it was anger or the breathing machine behind his sudden outbursts.

Beattie turned and looked at Kate. Her face was as white as the wall behind her.

'Come and sit by her so I can see both of you,' he said. 'Don't you know it's rude to talk behind a body's back?'

Beattie and Kate looked at each other. Like a schoolgirl called before the headmaster, Beattie did as she was told.

'Tell her then, Beattie. It's quite a story, you see, Kate, and my speech comes a little slow, as you have probably gathered.'

'So.' Beattie held her hands in her lap as if she were praying. 'So, Jake was in hospital in Athens for two years.'

'Two years, one month and six days,' Jake corrected her.

'And then he got out and he stayed on in Greece.'

'I don't go back home because, as you may remember, I have no ID, no passport, nothing. By the time I come out of the coma which saw me as good as dead for SIX MONTHS AND TWO DAYS, no one has any idea who I am. Not even me, to start with. I don't even know I'm American. I have no language. The upside of all this is that in this no man's land state I find it easy to learn Greek. *Itan efkolo na matho Ellinika*. It helps me understand my physiotherapist's instructions so that gradually, painfully, I can learn to walk again. Proceed, Beattie.'

Kate looked at Beattie, who was clearly finding this equally hard to listen to. It was like being in court, or at the gates of hell, being made to account not only for your crimes, but also for their consequences. Over decades.

'So, he got a job,' Beattie started to say.

'As a humble plongeur in some two-bit tourist taverna,' Jake added.

'Then he fell in with this, like, group of Americans, some, um, sect.'

'*You* call it that,' Jake said. 'But I call it The Fellowship. They saved me. They were the saviour of me. Unlike some people.' He bared his teeth at Kate in a cold grin.

'They were sort of Buddhists. He learned forgiveness.'

'HA!' came the breathy voice from the iPad.

'And they brought him back to the States.'

'Yeah, I'd worked out by this time where I was from,' Jake said. 'The memory has this extraordinary ability to regenerate. Neural pathways can reform, reroute themselves. Find their way back home: remember. I remembered what had happened to me. WHAT YOU HAD DONE TO ME.'

'They brought him back to live on a sort of ashram near San Francisco, where he found a wife and learned computer programming.'

'You put it so baldly, dear Beattie.' Jake cast his eye over Kate. 'Where is the romance in this woman's life? She has no soul, Emma. Not like you.'

Emma felt Beattie stiffen beside her.

'It took me a while, Ems, TO LEARN TO TRUST PEOPLE AGAIN. But eventually I found my wife, a good woman. Marnie. She looked nothing like you, Emma. Perhaps that's why I went for her. God knows I didn't need any reminders. And, oh, the children. Didn't you mention my kids yet, Beattie? This stunted dick, Emma, that you'd have left limply attached to a corpse, actually went on and created life. For a little while you could even say that from the outside I looked happy. I had a family, a community in the ashram in the Bay Area, a job. A damn good job, riding the digital revolution through the nineties.'

'Good,' Kate said. 'That's good.' She just wanted to turn away, to run upstairs to her bed, pull the duvet over her head and sleep, like Mark had said she ought to. Could she rewind? Could she un-invite Beattie?

'But, as you can see,' Jake rolled his eyes as if showing her the room around him, 'there wasn't what you'd call a happy ending. Is there ever really, though? Doesn't it always go messy in the end? No. All the chanting and dharma in the world couldn't save me, could it, eh? Tell our Emma what happened, my little Bea.'

Beattie drew her hands up to the back of her neck and scratched, as if she were trying to rid herself of some parasite. 'He had this anger inside of him—'

'Oh, yes, the anger,' Jake said. 'And that was there because of what, Emma?'

Emma looked away from him. 'Because of what we did to you.'

'Correct. It was there because of what you have done to me. Proceed, Beattie.'

'The anger wouldn't go away.'

'You BET it wouldn't.'

'When he had a bad time, he'd hit out at his wife.'

'When he had a particularly bad time, he'd hit out at his wife Marnie and his children Zeb and Moon,' Jake said. 'He wasn't proud of this. One night he broke Marnie's nose and his little Moon's arm.'

Kate felt a hot fat tear fall on her cheek.

'Charges were pressed,' Beattie went on. 'He got four years.

244

When he came out of jail, The Fellowship wanted nothing to do with him, and they'd disappeared his wife and children somewhere safe, away from him.'

'I wasn't happy.'

'No,' Kate said.

'And so I tried to finish the job you started.'

'What do you mean?' She leaned forward so that her face was right up against the screen. She was finding it hard to breathe.

'He jumped off a bridge,' Beattie said.

'Not any old bridge, Ems. The Golden Gate Bridge. The Golden Gateway. But not for me, it seemed. Once again, Emma, death turned me away. Perhaps it was because of unfinished business. Who knows? So that's how come I end up like this. Bruised, bloody but unbowed. List my afflictions, Beattie, if you will.'

Beattie's voice was now small and hard. Kate could see she was hating this, hating him. What had he done to her? How could he do anything, in the state he was in?

'Jake is tetraplegic. He has mobility in his right arm, below the elbow, and limited movement in his neck. He needs assistance to breathe.'

Jake gargled on his tube by way of illustration.

'He needs twenty-four-hour assistance for all his day-to-day living.'

'That's eating, shitting, pissing, that sort of thing,' Jake chipped in. 'Luckily the only sexual feelings I get are in my brain. But that's sort of eclipsed now by anger and, what shall I call it? Oh yes. A burning sense of injustice, if that's not too floral a way of putting it. And, Beattie, tell our mutual friend here about the financial side of things.'

Beattie looked at Kate. 'Because his injuries are judged to be self-inflicted, he is not covered by his health insurance. He has high day-to-day care, medical and living expenses . . .'

'Crippling, even!' Jake performed a machine-assisted, wheezing form of a laugh.

'And he also has outstanding medical and rescue bills to pay.'

'And there are other things I need, too, like a properly adapted house to live in, a better chair, an adapted car. It's extraordinary how possible an independent life would be for me if money were not the issue it is. I would almost be normal. And this – and I can see by the way your little pale eyes are narrowing that you have already guessed – is where you fit in, dear Emma. Beattie has been helping me to the best of her abilities, but she assures me she is nearly at the bottom of her relatively meagre wealth bucket. Though I see she is able to fly across the Atlantic and wear pretty smart clothes and stay in a pretty smart hotel.'

Beattie tutted in exasperation.

'But—' Kate said, reason suddenly coming back to her, 'your injuries are a result of your own actions. You are the person responsible for them.'

'Really?' Jake said, unsmiling. 'Is that what you really think, Emma? Do you think people just throw themselves off bridges for no reason? Put yourself in my position. What would you have been feeling? Huh?'

'But you were fucked up before we got up that cliff in Ikaria.'

'Language, Emma. I thought you'd have learned some sort of restraint in all these years of being the fragrant Mrs Mark Barratt, the doting mother of the lovely aspiring actress Tilly.'

At the mention of her daughter's name, Kate felt a curd of anger rise inside her.

'You tried to rape Beattie. You attacked her.'

'Oh, *this*. I was completely wasted at the time,' Jake said. 'And she led me on.'

'That's not true, Emma!' Beattie said.

'She wanted it. She was jealous of you and me. She threw herself on me.'

'No!' Beattie roared.

'I know what he did, Beattie,' Kate said. 'I remember how he hurt you.'

'Did I deserve to die for kissing a girl who wanted it anyway?'

'She didn't. And it wasn't just kissing.'

'Where do you draw a line? At what point do you say I deserved to die? How many penetrations does it have to be?'

'And there was the Australian.'

'Huh?'

'You killed the Australian.'

'I didn't touch no Australian.'

'So why did you have his passport?'

'I found it, Emma. Don't you ever find things? If you thought I'd killed him, why didn't you ask me? Huh? Or do you believe in executing someone because you've put two and two together to make five?'

'It was an accident!' Kate said. 'I didn't mean you to fall.'

'YOU PUSHED ME! You pushed me off the edge of a high cliff. What did you think was going to happen? Icarus's daddy comes along on his waxy wings and whisks me to safety?'

Kate put her hands over her ears. 'I don't want to go over all this again. Do you think I've just breezed through life? Living with the thought of having killed you?'

'Oh, poor Emma. My heart bleeds.'

Kate gripped the iPad. She wanted to fling it to the floor, as if doing so would get rid of him.

247

'Just look at it this way, then, Ems. You pay me, you do your penance. It's my gift to you. You can buy your way out of the hell you've created for yourself.'

Kate closed her eyes and tried to still her heart. No one spoke for a while.

'Hey, Emma?' Jake said at last, his voice a singsong. 'Whaddaya say?'

She looked at him levelly. 'So what do you want?'

'I'll let you know. Ta-ta, love, as I believe you say over there.'

With no further warning, the screen went blank.

The two women sat there in the silence, the grey, late afternoon light bleeding weakly around them. It felt to Kate like a tornado had just whirled through the house. So much so that when she looked up and away from the screen, she expected to see her surroundings as devastated as she felt inside.

Instead, everything in her large, open-plan living area was still in its perfect, allotted place. The order she worked so hard to maintain still existed.

But it looked all wrong now.

She glanced at Beattie. 'Is he serious?'

'Oh yes. I'm afraid he is.'

'What has he taken from you?'

'My savings. The life insurance pay-out from my husband's death. Other stuff. Luckily, my kids are done with college, or I wouldn't have anything left to see them through. I've given him everything I have. But still he says he needs more. He's very persistent.'

Beattie stood up, turned her back to Kate, and pulled her blouse up and over her head.

Her arms bore the tell-tale dots where hands had grabbed and wrenched them, and purple, blue and yellowing bruises patterned her pale fleshy back from where her waistband dug in, to the points where her bra straps cut into her shoulders. She turned, and Kate gasped. The word MURDERER had been carved into the soft flesh of her belly, denting and ridging where it was healing into scar tissue.

'They done me over good, huh?' Beattie said, pulling her top back on.

'They?'

'He puts his one good arm to good use. He's turned his programming skills to big-time hacking, so he's got this network of people round the world he can call on, people who owe him favours. Some of them aren't too friendly. Some of them see no problem in jumping on a middle-aged woman to teach her a lesson. I knew he had them watching me – they don't have to worry about me going to the police, after all, do they? But then I missed a payment – because I just didn't have the money – and he set them on me.'

'How did he find you?'

Beattie sat next to Kate on the sofa. 'Once he decided he wanted to track me down, it took him three hours. Just three hours, after thirty-three years. Like you, just in case, I'd changed my name—'

'To Claire McCormack?'

'Claire Cohen, actually. McCormack is Ed's name. Was. Yep, I changed my name. But the paper trail is there for anyone with the skills to get at it. Easy for someone like him. The funny thing is that I live in San Francisco, forty minutes from his apartment. We could have bumped into each other on the street anytime. Had he been able to get out. But you truly disappeared, didn't you? Went to great pains to change your identity.'

Kate frowned. 'Yes, but how—'

'Jake told me. He set out to find us both, but drew a blank

with you. He wasted no time in pointing out that you were clearly far cleverer than me.'

'I came back and didn't contact anyone.' The words felt strange in Kate's mouth: this was the first time she had uttered them out loud. 'I couldn't go on being Emma James. She didn't deserve her bright future. So she just disappeared. As far as everyone except you and Jake knows, she never returned from Greece. Her parents never knowingly saw or heard from her again, her university place went unfilled. She became one of the missing.'

'No way,' Beattie said.

Kate nodded. 'What really happened was that I hitched up to Calais, stowed away in a lorry at the docks, went straight to London, slept on the streets for a bit then landed up at a squat. I got a job in a pub, a cash job, under a made-up name – it was easy back in those days before everything was on computers. It didn't take too long, moving in the circles I found myself in, to connect with someone who could sell me an identity for the money I had left over from Greece. A dead girl, a baby, who died shortly after birth a year before I was born. Katherine Brown. I had her National Insurance number, a new passport, everything. There is no paper at all linking me to Emma James. Nothing.'

'Wow,' Beattie said. 'You were way more resourceful than I would ever have given you credit for back then.'

Kate tried not to feel stung by this. 'I think the idea that I was a murderer sort of knocked the naivety out of me.'

'And what do they know about you? Your husband and daughter?'

'They think my parents were killed in a car crash when I was seventeen and that I had to give up school and go out and get a job.'

'How long have you kept that story up?'

'Mark and I will have been together thirty years this year. Married for twenty-five of them.'

'Like me and Ed. We met just a little before you and Mark did.'

'We all need someone we can lean on, I suppose.'

'Especially us, eh?' Beattie took Kate's hand. 'Oh Emma. It's so good to see you again. If it hadn't been for that photograph of you and those cute little African girls, we'd never have met again. I'm sorry, though, that I brought Jake with me. I wouldn't have chosen to force all this on you. Not for all the world.'

Kate shook her head. That damn photograph. Her greatest wish was always that Martha hadn't died. The thought stabbed her unawares every day. But for the first time, it formed for a different reason. If Martha were still alive, Martha's Wish would not exist. Therefore that photograph wouldn't be a thing in the world. And with no photograph, Jake wouldn't have found her and she wouldn't have to be here now, having her past rubbed in her face like a festering old rag.

But, of course, Martha's death was part of Kate's payment for that past. It was what she truly believed. An eye for an eye.

So wasn't all this inevitable, preordained?

The equivocating thoughts rolled on, knotting into an unsolvable tangle. Without that past, the past that saw the resurrection of tragic, dead baby Katherine Brown, there would have been no Martha, no Tilly, no Kate. And would she wish that all away now? To do so would be like murder all over again.

She got up, opened another bottle and poured Beattie and herself another glass of wine. It was too much to take in.

'But if it weren't for finding you, Kate,' Beattie said, 'I don't know what Jake would have done to me. I doubt if I'd still be standing. His finding you has saved my life. And probably my daughters' lives too – he knows where they are and what their movements are.' Kate saw her eyes flick over to the kitchen, to the photograph of her family.

'He'd use Tilly to get at me, wouldn't he?' Kate said, her throat tightening. Beattie pressed her lips together and nodded. 'He's truly scary, isn't he?'

'I have nothing left to give,' Beattie said. 'But still he wants more.'

Kate watched her as she sat back, drank her wine and took in the tall, beautiful windows, the acres of white floor dotted with expensive Italian furniture, crowned at the far end by an epic, glossy kitchen. She saw her eyes lingering on the artworks, the costly splashes of colour on the towering white walls of a room that had once been the assembly hall for three hundred primary school children. Entirely Mark's thing, the pieces included a Jeff Koons, an Isa Genzken, a Dan Colen, a Tracey Emin, and a Damien Hirst spot painting. And these were only a small part of the story, too. Kate was aware of this. In pride of place in the bedroom hung a small orange and red study by Rothko. She didn't much care for the pieces – her art appreciation stopped with the Impressionists – but Mark said they were excellent investments.

She knew what Beattie was thinking as she took it all in.

But instead of remarking on all the opulence, her old friend turned to her and smiled weakly. 'At least we're not murderers, then.'

'We? It was me who pushed him,' Kate said.

'But I would have, had I got there first.'

'That's not the point. I pushed him, and all these years I thought I had killed him.'

'But you didn't!'

'No. But look what I did.'

'*We* did, Emma. It was both of us.'

'Yes.'

'I thought we were such a gang back then, the three of us.'

Kate nodded, unconsciously touching her tattoo. 'We were friends for life, remember?'

'Not a day has passed when I don't wish it had turned out differently,' Beattie said. 'I ask myself was it something I did? Did I give him an idea I was leading him on? I know you liked him. But I had no idea how he felt about you. He told me about it when he first found me again. I know one thing, though: his attack on me wasn't about love. It was something darker – anger? Hate? I don't know what I did to provoke that, but—'

'Stop this. It wasn't your fault, Beattie.' Kate hugged herself on the sofa. 'And nothing happened between me and Jake. Not really. I didn't want to spoil what we had, the three of us, edge you out. You were far more important to me than that.'

Beattie took her hand. There were tears in her eyes. 'But if he felt like that about you –' she nodded towards the iPad – 'what did he call you – "my true, true love"? Then why did he do that to me? Why did he attack me? To scare me off?'

'I don't know,' Kate said. 'I suppose we never really knew him.'

Beattie sighed and looked at her. 'I never trusted him back then, you know. Not really.'

'No,' Kate said. Though she had trusted him herself beyond all reason. Beyond all the signs that she should not have. She had trusted him blindly, stupidly, until it was too late.

But perhaps he would say the same of her.

Weren't they both as bad as each other?

Three

Pleading exhaustion, Kate managed to get Beattie out of the house soon after they finished the second bottle of wine.

'I'll call you tomorrow,' Beattie said on the doorstep. 'You rest up now. You look so pale.'

As soon as she was alone again, Kate climbed up to her office, got down on her hands and knees, pulled aside the rug in the middle of the floor and prised open the floorboard that only she knew was loose. Reaching in, she pulled out two notebooks – ancient, tattered, dog-eared, kept unread for thirty-three years. She held them in her hands for minutes, looking at them, daring herself to open them.

But she couldn't bring herself even to lift one front cover. She couldn't face meeting Emma James again. She was gone, and that was the end of it.

Ashamed at her cowardice, and feeling as if she was burying some sort of deadly landmine, she tucked the notebooks back into their hiding place, replaced the floorboard, and straightened the richly embroidered kelim on top.

She crept down the stairs to her bed and lay huddled there,

drifting in between sleep and a horrible awareness of what was going on in her waking world.

Mark texted to say that he was taking his client out for dinner because, having thrashed him at golf, he wanted to smooth the waters. Mark was like that: it was why he was so successful.

She was glad to be alone.

For the first time ever, she had told someone else what really happened to her after Ikaria. She drew her knees to her chest and curled up tightly, her surroundings looming over her, outscaling her.

Had Emma James been told when she was a child lying in her tiny room at the front of her parents' Ripon council house that one day she would have a bedroom like this, with a vast, vaulted glass ceiling and the Rothko on the wall – not that she would have heard of Rothko back then – she would have just laughed in disbelief, dismissed it as fairy tales.

Katherine Brown, that catch-all, everywoman name, had opened the door to this world. As Kate, she met Mark when she was twenty-one. Not all that long in the great scheme of things after she had left Emma, Jake and Beattie behind. But back then it seemed like a lifetime, because in a way it was.

Fed up of the squats, pubs and intoxicant diet of cheap Red Leb, rollups and synthetic lager that constituted her life post-Ikaria, Kate Brown had scrubbed herself up and applied for a job as a secretary at a City bank. She already had the skills – her mother had insisted on her taking a typing and shorthand class in case 'the exams and that' didn't work out – but she knew that, with a little grooming, her looks would help her out as well.

Mark had been her boss. He wasn't like the other – frankly obnoxious – young men at the bank. He didn't bray and brag and try to weasel his way into her knickers. Best of all, he was moved by her terrible family tragedy story. To lose both parents at once like that: his eyes misted. A Cambridge man, he was exactly the kind of boy she would have set her sights on had she been able to take up her university place.

At one point, shortly after landing the job at the bank, she slipped into a library and looked at the Cambridge University English prospectus. All she actually seemed to be missing out on by not going there was a hell of a lot of medieval literature. She convinced herself that she wouldn't really have enjoyed that.

Mostly, though, she was far too busy to stop and think about what she had given up. She had to lose the vestiges of her accent, develop and maintain a credible backstory, work out what constituted good taste for those for whom money wasn't an issue.

Mark helped enormously. He saw her as his own personal project. He took to saving poor, tiny, orphaned Kate as heartily as she had since taken to rescuing girls like little Mariam and Bintu.

Three weeks after she started working for him, he asked her to see *Cyrano de Bergerac* with him at the Barbican and, as she stood talking to him in the interval over the glasses of champagne he had paid for, she realised that he could offer her the life she wanted – and needed – to help her out of the hole she found herself in.

A self-eradicated girl, she saw that he had the means to help her to be someone again. His money and ambition and clear devotion to her would make this far easier to achieve than it would have been without him.

Without him.

If those last two days hadn't happened in Ikaria, she would

still have been Emma James. Would she have got together with Jake? Would he then have kept his looks? He had been the most beautiful boy.

But no longer, except, possibly, those eyes. Time and cruelty were thieves of everything in the end.

Perhaps she would have been better suited to learning Anglo Saxon and frolicking around with *Beowulf*. But who was to say? Turning back the clock was not an option. She believed there was only one chance at life, and she had made a complete, almighty cock-up of it. A cock-up that seemed to want to keep on cocking up.

She lifted her head and looked at her alarm clock. It was eight o'clock in the evening and she needed to eat. All she had put inside herself that day had been wine.

Swinging her legs around to the edge of the bed, she stood carefully, knowing that she would see black dots as she rose.

She made her way down to the kitchen and fixed herself a bowl of yoghurt and blueberries, which she carried up to her office.

The strange turret room suddenly seemed absurd to her, with its circle of windows, each punctuated, stabbed into, by ranks of cacti, prickly fingers flipping the bird to the world. Was that on her behalf? What arrogance, she thought. And coming from a woman whose whole existence was so tenuous, built on the shifting sands of her own feeble making.

She crossed the room, carefully walking around the kelim on the floor. Then she sat down at her laptop and made herself pick at her berries as she downloaded her emails.

There was no Martha's Wish mail, not on the personal, nor the website account. Patience must be intercepting them for her, possibly on Mark's instructions. While this had no doubt been motivated by kindness, it depressed Kate. She was being looked after like a child. No one wanted anything from her.

Then she looked at her home email account. It hardly ever saw any traffic, but something was coming in, and the sender was Jake Mithras. The one person who wanted something from her very much indeed.

How had he got this address? It wasn't published anywhere.

No doubt, though, anything was traceable if you had the power he seemed to have over the Internet.

It was chilling.

The email was bulleted and straight to the point. This was what he needed:

- $2.5m for outstanding emergency services and medical bill
- $500,000 for independent living equipment
- $500,000 to set up a fund for care services, supplies, personal maintenance and on-going expenses

After providing her with bank account details for someone called Stephen Smith, he signed off.

Kate looked at the list. It was a lot of money. But then she and Mark *had* a lot of money. It would make a dent in their wealth, but it wouldn't bring them down.

Did she have a choice? She had seen on Beattie's body what Jake was capable of. She shuddered when she remembered Tilly's name in his mouth.

She took a deep breath and tapped in the password for the account aggregator software that Mark's people had installed for her. It let her see all of their personal investments on one screen – a good thing, since Mark's one requirement of her management of the money he handed over was that she spread it around various banks and investment vehicles.

The password Kate used everywhere was M@rtha1997. She was still always everywhere, Martha. Kate wondered, as she typed her daughter's name, if she would ever cease to exist for her. If Jake could come back from the dead, then couldn't Martha? Couldn't she? Wouldn't that be fair? Couldn't she have a refund of the eye for an eye she'd paid for that she didn't really owe?

Shaking the madness out of her head, she looked at the total of all their instantly accessible investments. It was absurdly, obscenely healthy. She could entirely cover Jake's demands and still have twenty thousand or so left over. The tax year had just ended and, as usual, Mark would soon be tipping his bonus into their own accounts for her to manage. For the past six years this had been upwards of a million, and Kate had no reason to think that it would be any less this time round. So, very shortly, a good sum of cash would be coming in to replace the money paid out to Jake, and it was highly unlikely that Mark would ever suspect a thing.

She leaned back in her chair and breathed out, letting her shoulders settle away from the position they had assumed around her ears. Her neck ached. She ate two more blueberries and felt a faint twinge of nausea.

Did she have a choice, though? Was there an alternative to paying up?

She could afford to, and it was her obligation. The only way Mark would find out would be if he looked at their accounts, which, in all their time together, he had not once done. He was quite busy enough ploughing most of his profits back into his fund, building up their personal wealth that way. He saw the money he handed out to Kate in much the same way a fifties husband would have viewed his wife's housekeeping money.

So no one would suffer, everyone would win. Jake would

get off Beattie's back, Beattie would be able to breathe again and so, ultimately, would she, Kate.

And, most importantly, Jake's unspoken, but heavily implied, threat to Tilly would no longer exist.

Perhaps he was right, too. Perhaps this was the way she could buy her way to heaven.

But she needed to think about it first. Leave it for a day or two, wait for it all to sink in. She had not yet fully processed the thought that Jake was still alive, let alone what sort of monster he had become. He hadn't given her any deadline, and, in any case, it would take a couple of days to release the money from its various holding places. She wasn't going to rush into it.

She tried out the thought that she was a victim. It was a role she had always forbidden herself because she reckoned she had earned everything bad that had happened to her: she had deserved to miss out on her education and the love of her parents; she had deserved to lose Martha; she even put what had happened to Emma James in Marseille – Kate Brown/Barratt had never put a name to it – as a sort of down payment against what she had committed in Ikaria.

Yet, since she was innocent of the murder she had put at the root of all those losses, didn't these demands Jake was making turn her into a victim of extortion?

It was a perverse yet liberating idea.

So long, she thought, with a chill that ran right through her, so long as Tilly is safe.

And for the first time she saw that the fact that her daughter was going away, out of harm's way, was a good thing.

260

Four

'I don't understand,' Kate said, looking at the gift Mark had just given her. It was wrapped in shiny paper printed with cupcakes, and done up with a rosette of curlicued ribbon – hardly his normal style.

It was Monday evening and the first time she had seen him since he had set off to play golf the day before. In order to stop her mind from churning itself into soup after all the Jake stuff, she had taken a couple of sleeping pills on the Sunday. So she had been out cold whatever time Mark had returned from taking his client to dinner. And, as was his usual habit, he had slipped out of bed and off to work before she surfaced.

She was glad of the hiatus. It had given her a chance to reassemble herself. As soon as she heard the front door slam behind Tilly, who was on day shifts, she had pulled herself from bed and started on the housework. Putting everything to a clean order was her way of keeping a grip on her world. For the second time in a week, she pulled everything out of the kitchen cupboards and bleached their insides, enjoying the sting on her cracked and chapped fingers. She stripped the beds and re-made them with the beautifully ironed linen that turned up every week from the laundry service. All this work stopped her thinking too much, and she was glad of it.

Mark had texted to say that he would be home by eight, an event so rare that it was worth making an effort for it. Tilly's message followed soon after: she was staying over at a friend's house in Bow. At six, Kate stood under the shower until she nearly felt like she belonged to her new, non-murderer self. She blow-dried her hair, put on the almost bare make-up she had perfected over the years, and slipped into loose silk trousers and a cream cashmere jumper. Checking in the mirror, she saw the work had paid off: only the stitched gash – like a grotesque black caterpillar sitting on her forehead – suggested that this was anything other than a relaxed, elegant woman, entirely at home in her own skin.

'It's not from me,' Mark said, nodding at the present, which Kate had now opened to reveal a book. *I Want to Disappear*, it was called, with a subtitle of *Why Women Starve*. It looked self-published, with a glossy, fussy cover.

'Claire said you might find it helpful,' he said, standing in the kitchen and sipping the gin and tonic she had made when she heard him slam the front door.

'Claire?'

'She called me at the office this afternoon to say she'd dropped by on you.'

'What?'

'I gave her my card when we met at the hospital. I told her what the doctor had said about your weight.'

'And you know that's rubbish, don't you?'

'You are thin.'

'I've always been thin. I'm naturally thin. Clothes look better on me like this.'

'I can't deny that.' Mark leaned forward and ran his hand

over her hair in a gesture that felt to Kate only a small step away from a pat on the head. 'So a little after the phone call, Serena signed for this parcel. There was a note from Claire stuck on it, explaining that one of her daughters had suffered an eating disorder and this book helped both of them get through it.'

'Really,' Kate said, turning the book over in her hands, working hard not to feel irritated that Mark and Beattie had been talking about her behind her back.

'It was very sweet of her,' Mark said.

'Yes.'

She was relieved at least that Mark had revealed that he knew about Beattie's visit. She had been intending to tell him that she had been alone on Sunday. Even she, the seasoned liar, would have had difficulty wriggling out of that situation. She put the book down on the counter and started making the dressing for the Caesar salad she was putting together.

'I also thought it might be nice if she came round for supper tomorrow,' Mark said. 'I could come back early. It'd be great to meet someone from your mysterious past.'

'But that's the night before Tilly leaves!'

'And it would be great for Tills to meet an old friend of yours, too. She'd love to hear the truth about when you were young.' Mark smiled. 'All we've got is your word on what happened.'

'But I wanted it to be a special evening for Tilly, though.' Kate poured the dressing on the salad and tossed it furiously, crumbling the croutons. 'Damn,' she said, as a piece of lettuce fell on the floor.

'You wanted it to be special for you, you mean,' Mark said. 'I'm sure Tilly couldn't be bothered one way or another. She might even have other plans, you know, like seeing friends or something.'

'And I haven't got anything in.' The thought of what an evening with Beattie, Mark and Tilly could turn out like was too much for Kate to contemplate.

'Don't worry. We'll get something delivered,' Mark said. 'And I'll tell Tilly she has to be here, no excuses. It'll be fun.'

Fun.

Kate looked gloomily at the mess she had made of the salad.

'Anyway. She'll be here about seven,' Mark said, moving to the kitchen noticeboard and unpinning a menu. 'Shall I order from the Lebanese place?'

'Why not?'

So he had gone ahead and invited Beattie for supper without even consulting her. Of course. She had been so passive all these years, allowing him to first shape then look after her. Why on earth would he think that she even had a view?

Oh, Martha's Wish was a palliative, sure. She did good work for the charity. But apart from that, she had bedded herself down as the big man's wife. It made an excellent hiding place, and, besides, she had a gift for it. She was always well turned out, not at all demanding, and kept the house clean and tidy and beautifully decorated. She made him believe he was an excellent lover, and yes, she supposed she loved him. It was a good partnership.

She hadn't yet fully decided to do so, but if she *were* to pass all that money on to Jake behind Mark's back, she would utterly transgress all the unwritten rules of this marriage. Something of the old Kate – the Emma deeply buried inside her – felt a frisson of excitement at that thought.

Could she justify herself like that? Could she tell herself that he deserved it for having had it so easy from her all these years?

As if to confirm her thoughts, Mark moved towards her and put a smooth, clean hand on her cheek. 'You look pale, Kate.

Are you sure you should be up? Why don't you go to bed after supper. I've got some reports to look at before I turn in, anyway.'

As Kate lay sleeplessly in her bed, the moon full and bright above her, the thought came again to her that Jake's disabilities were of his own making, not hers. Sure, for him to be in the mental state to want to kill himself might have its roots in what had happened to him on Ikaria. But that was thirty-three years ago! He couldn't seriously blame her and Beattie for everything bad that had happened to him since?

Propelled by this thought, she slipped out of bed and silently tiptoed upstairs to her office turret. She didn't want Mark, who she assumed was still working in his basement study, to hear and come at her with awkward questions. He'd be cross about her getting out of bed when, in his view, she should be resting.

Sitting at her desk in the darkness, she shook the mouse a couple of times to wake her computer. Outside she heard the wail of police cars, and saw their blue lights flooding the air above the road to the river. A helicopter buzzed over her, joining the ground forces with a roaming searchlight.

It was a jungle out there.

She fired up the email software and looked again at the figures Jake had quoted. Two and a half million dollars for emergency services and medical bills? Wasn't there some sort of scheme that picked up the bill for that sort of care in America if you couldn't afford it?

She looked up an American disability aids website. The half-a-million dollars Jake had demanded would buy their whole inventory.

There was no doubt about it: his figures stank.

Not only was he being unreasonable, but he was also

greedy: he was taking both her and Beattie for a ride. This was blackmail.

Something hardened inside her. She wasn't going to allow this to happen. She needed to reason with him.

She quickly drafted a reply to his email, saying that she agreed to help him out, but she needed to see evidence of his figures. She was as polite as possible, but to the point. She pressed send, checked that it had gone, then quietly took herself downstairs to her bed, took a couple of pills and fell fast asleep.

Five

'She's late,' Mark said, as he and Kate sat at the kitchen island waiting for Beattie, having finally given in and broken out the champagne and pistachios. 'And where the hell's Tilly?'

Mark always turned up on time, and considered anyone who did otherwise to be enacting some sort of betrayal. But Beattie's tardiness was the least of Kate's concerns. Had she had any say in the matter, she would never have let this dinner take place. At one point she had thought about pleading weakness and taking to her bed, but that would only have put the matter off and made it worse for her in the long run.

No. However much it would feel like she was standing with her feet in two different worlds, she needed to face up to it. If she were ever going to explain Beattie's presence in her current life, she was going to have to plunge into the evening.

She had called Beattie that morning, ostensibly to thank her for the book.

'I'm so sorry about tonight,' Beattie said as soon as she picked up the phone. 'He asked me out of the blue. I know it's going to make things very awkward for both of us. But what could I do? I called him because I was concerned about you – you do look so frail, Emma. When he told me what the doc said to you, I couldn't believe the coincidence. Jessie my eldest had exactly the same thing. The book was so useful to us. I do hope it helps.'

'Thanks. It looks interesting,' Kate said. She had, in fact, hidden it under a pile of magazines, but she didn't want to appear impolite or ungrateful for Beattie's concern. 'So how are we going to survive tonight?'

'I guess we'll play it by ear. I'll take my lead from you, and go along with whatever you say.'

Kate blinked. For a moment she doubted if she had it in her to create such an elaborate and impromptu deception in front of both her husband and her daughter. Then she came to her senses. Of course she could. It was what she had been doing all her life.

But she had never had to rely on anyone else before. She hoped Beattie was up to it.

The front door slammed and a clattering in the hallway heralded Tilly's arrival. Kate offered up her usual thanks that her daughter had got home safely. The roads between the bus stop and the house were the worst inner city sort: dark residential front gardens and great blocks of flats rising from empty concrete courtyards. There were so many murky spots for attackers to hide, or to drag you away to. When Tilly started working at the National Theatre, Kate had wanted to pay for a cab to get her home at night, a plan that had been firmly rejected.

'What's the point of me going out to work if you then pay half my day's wages to get me back? It's a bit sick, Mum,' Tilly had said. 'Everyone else in the whole of London has to get home under their own steam, and so will I.'

Kate couldn't really argue with that. But she had signed both Tilly and herself up for a self-defence course and extracted a promise from her daughter never to use headphones at night, to walk down the middle of the quieter streets, and to keep her wits about her. Kate had enjoyed the classes, although she wished she had taken them when she was Tilly's age.

'God, can I have some?' Tilly said, breathlessly making her entrance and spying the champagne.

'"Hello, Mum and Dad. How are you?"' Mark said, getting up to fetch her a glass.

'What's got his goat?'

'Our dinner guest is late,' Kate said.

'Oops. Cardinal sin,' Tilly said.

'It's not a big issue,' Mark said, tetchily pouring the champagne for Tilly. 'How was your day?'

'Jesus. A nightmare.' Tilly knocked back her drink. 'It was someone's birthday and the Ayckbourn matinee cast were doing tequila slammers. Like a bloody zoo. At five-thirty in the afternoon.'

'The horror,' Mark said.

Kate was just offering Tilly a pistachio when the doorbell rang, making her jump and drop the bowl.

'Damn!' she said.

'At last,' Mark said.

'Fashionably late, Pa,' Tilly said, as, still in service-industry mode, she fetched a dustpan and brush to deal with the spilled nuts.

'It was just the bloody food,' Mark said, returning to the kitchen with two large carrier bags. 'Where the hell's your friend got to, then?'

'Perhaps she mistook the time, or something,' Kate said,

glad of the grace being granted by Beattie's late arrival.

'It's so unlike an American, though.' Mark sorted the meat and rice dishes from the salads and handed them to Tilly, who slid them into the oven to keep them warm. 'Or at least any that I know.'

'Claire was never much of a time-keeper,' Kate said, trying on the old school-friends disguise. 'She must have been late for every single class.'

'I thought people grew out of that sort of thing,' Mark said, dumping salad onto a platter.

The doorbell clanged again, and, once more, Kate jumped.

'That'll be her,' Tilly said, heading for the stairs. 'I'll get it. And Dad? Calm down, dear.'

'Cheeky cow,' Mark said.

When did they start talking to each other like that? Kate had no idea.

'Shit!' they heard Tilly gasp from the hallway. 'Dad!' she yelled up to the kitchen.

Mark and Kate looked at each other, then rushed to the stairs.

Beattie was leaning in the front doorway. Her nose bled into a cut lip, which in turn spilled blood onto her good camel coat. Deep grazes in her knees merged with the ripped nylon of her tights, and she had the beginnings of a black eye.

Kate still remembered how that felt.

'What happened?' she said, rushing to catch Beattie as she stumbled into the house.

'Damn kids mugged me,' Beattie lisped through her split lip. Mark took her other arm and they helped her upstairs.

'Go ahead and sort out the sofa,' Kate said to Tilly. 'Put a blanket over it and get some cushions at the end for B— Claire's head.'

'Bastards took my bag,' Beattie said as Kate settled her down on the throw Tilly had arranged over the clean white sofa.

'We need to get you to a doctor,' Mark said, pulling out his phone.

'No, no, I'm fine. Just a little shook up.'

'But they hit you!' Tilly said.

'They just shoved. It was the fall that hurt me. Nothing's broken.'

'Your eye, though . . .' Kate said. Beattie looked at her and, almost imperceptibly, shook her head.

'I'll call the police, then,' Mark said, taking himself out of the room.

'No need,' Beattie said, but he had already gone. She turned to Kate, panic in her eyes.

'Tills, could you get Claire a brandy, please?' Kate asked. 'There's some in the dining-room cabinet.'

Tilly rushed off, glad for something to do.

'It was Jake's guys again,' Beattie whispered hoarsely as soon as they were on their own. 'Different individuals, but they all look kind of the same. They jumped me just round the corner from here.'

'No!' Kate said, her eyes wide.

'They said you hadn't paid up yet. Said this was just a taster. A warning. Said I'm to tell you –' Beattie looked away.

'What? What?'

'I'm to tell you to look after your daughter.'

Kate put her hands over her mouth and looked in horror at Beattie's beaten face. She had heard nothing from Jake since she had emailed him asking for proof of his figures. She had imagined that he might be redrafting his demands in the face of her questions. But here was his sign to her that he wasn't prepared to negotiate. However unreasonable his demands, he had her – and Beattie – over a barrel. There was no way they could tell anyone about his blackmailing without incriminating themselves, which meant he could use as much force as he wanted to make her pay up. And here, now, was the proof of that.

'I'm so sorry,' she whispered as Mark came back into the room, still on the phone.

'What did they look like, Claire?' he said.

'Young. Black,' Beattie said, and shrugged. 'Sorry. That's all I took in.'

Mark repeated the information into his phone.

'And how many were there?'

'Three.'

'She says three.' He listened for a minute, then turned again to Beattie. 'And when and where exactly did it take place?'

'About half an hour ago? I'd just turned off the road that leads here from the bus stop.'

'Bridge Lane?' Mark asked.

'I – I think so.'

'I hate that bit at night,' Tilly said as she came back from the dining room with a stiff measure of brandy for Beattie.

Mark spoke to the police operator. Then he listened, nodding, writing notes on a pad he had brought in with him.

'Yes, she can walk. OK, yes. Yes. She'll be with you. Yes.' He clicked his phone off and turned to Beattie. 'They can't send a car out at the moment – there's some sort of riot or something going on in Woolwich. We've got to take you down to A & E to get your injuries registered. Then we'll get you to the police station, and they'll take a full statement. They gave me a crime number, which I've put at the bottom there.' He tore the top sheet off the notepad and handed it to her.

'Come on then, Claire,' Kate said, going to help her up. It was wrong, she knew, but her major feeling was one of relief that she was going to be spared the discomfort of a dissembling dinner.

'Let her have a drop of brandy first, Mum,' Tilly said, handing the glass to Beattie. 'She's had a terrible shock.'

'Yes, yes of course,' Kate said.

'But I was so looking forward to dinner with you guys,' Beattie said, sipping at the brandy. 'The food smells delicious.' She winced as the alcohol touched the cut on her lip. 'And I'm starving. I haven't eaten all day.'

'Well, they didn't say anything about going straightaway,' Mark said. 'I'm sure we can eat first. Then I'll take you.'

Kate hoped that no one heard the tiny groan that escaped her lips.

'Thank you,' Beattie said, in tears now. 'You're very kind.'

'It's nothing.' Mark patted her awkwardly on the shoulder. 'Kate, have we got something we can clean Claire here up with a bit?'

'Of course,' Kate said. She ran up the stairs to her bathroom, her head reeling. Here was another fiction – the mugging – that she and Beattie had to maintain for the evening. She hoped they both were up to it.

Mustn't drink too much, she told herself.

As she climbed back down to the living room with the first-aid box and Dettol, Beattie's gruff voice rose up the stairs to greet her.

'. . . And she was so clever at school – straight A's all the way!'

She entered the room and found Mark and Tilly sitting on the armchairs facing Beattie, who was now lying back down on the sofa.

'Such a pity she had to leave before her A Levels. It was awful what happened to her parents – they were such sweet people. Always welcomed me into their home. I was a little lost, being an outsider – my father's firm moved him from New York to set up the UK branch when I was fifteen. We only stayed three years in the end. Oh, hi, Kate.'

Kate put a thin smile on her face. At least Beattie had taken the burden of leading the stories off her shoulders.

'That's the most I've ever heard about Mr and Mrs Brown. Kate prefers not to talk about the past,' Mark said.

'It's not my favourite subject,' Kate said, filling a bowl with boiled water.

'I would like to have known her back then, though.'

Kate couldn't read the look Mark gave her. Was there regret in it? Or just curiosity? Did he find the present-day Kate lacking? She poured a good slug of Dettol into the water.

'She was quite something,' Beattie said, looking at Kate warmly.

'I bet she was.'

'Enough!' Kate said, blushing as she brought the bowl and first-aid box over to Beattie.

'I'll sort out the food,' Mark said, discreetly moving over to the kitchen so that Kate and Tilly could help Beattie off with her tights.

'I'm so sorry, you guys,' Beattie said. 'Messing up your evening like this.'

'It's hardly your fault,' Tilly said.

Beattie winced as Kate set to work on her knees with the Dettol water and tweezers, dabbing and picking bits of grit out of the gouges.

'So you went back to the States then, after Gloucestershire?' Tilly asked her.

Kate held her breath – she had forgotten to warn Beattie that she had relocated her childhood to the Cotswolds. But she didn't miss a beat.

'Yep, to Minnesota. We were forever moving around.'

'Lucky you,' Tilly said. 'I've never been anywhere really.'

'Apart from to stay with your uncle in New York and to West Africa to visit the school,' Kate said, putting plasters on Beattie's wounds.

'But mostly we just go to Cornwall,' Tilly said, rolling her eyes.

'We've got a house there,' Kate said.

'How lovely,' Beattie said.

'Open a bottle of red, will you?' Mark called over to Kate from the kitchen.

When Kate returned to the sofa with the wine, corkscrew and glasses, she found Tilly sitting on the floor telling Beattie about her Greek plans. With all the stress and excitement of Beattie's predicament, she had nearly forgotten that tomorrow was the day her daughter was leaving.

'Mum's not keen, for some reason, but I think she's coming round.'

'Oh, you've got to be allowed to spread your wings,' Beattie said. 'I learned that when Jessie took off for three months in South East Asia. I didn't want her to go at all – I'd heard all these horror stories about what happened to young American girls out there. But of course she was fine. And she says that she would have gone even if I'd have stood in front of her and physically barred her way. Believe me, honey,' she turned to Kate, her bearing matronly, 'you can't stop your young ones flying the nest.'

'It's a little different for Mum, though,' Tilly said. 'With Martha and all that.'

'Of course. Your poor little sister. Your Mom told me about her,' Beattie said.

'Wine?' Kate said. Even though she was so close to Beattie and Tilly, she felt she needed to declare her presence, to stop them talking about her in the third person.

'Yes please,' Tilly said.

'Yes please, Kate,' Beattie said. 'So where are you planning on going in Greece?' she asked Tilly.

'Oh, Athens, Delphi, Thessaloniki, Sparta. Then I'm going to hit the islands, see if I can find a perfect beach with not too many tourists.'

'Ah, the authentic Greece. I know just the spot,' Beattie said.

No, no, Kate's heartbeat fluttered up into her throat as she drew the cork from the bottle, *please don't.*

But it was too late.

'You've been to Greece, then?' Tilly asked, handing the pistachios to Beattie.

'Oh yes. I'm what you might call a Grecophile, honey.'

'Where do you suggest, then?'

'Well. There's this lovely little island called Ikaria.'

Kate couldn't believe what she was hearing. As she poured the drinks, the neck of the bottle slipped from the rim of the glass, spilling red wine all over the expensive white rug.

'Mum!' Tilly said, jumping up.

Beattie might simply have been trying to be helpful, but it was so dangerous to mix up fact and fiction like that.

'I'm sorry, I—' Kate said. Perhaps she wasn't as acquainted as she was with the rules of living a lie. Although hadn't she said that her own family knew nothing of her past?

'Ha!' Tilly smiled at Beattie. 'Mum spilled the wine because she doesn't like us talking about Greece.'

'Oh?' Beattie said, looking at Kate.

Kate tried to laugh, although she felt like being sick. 'It's hard to say goodbye to my girl.'

'I'm not going for ever, Mum.' Tilly rolled her eyes and headed off towards the kitchen area. 'Dad,' she said. 'Mum's spilled wine all over the rug!'

'Why the hell did you tell her about Ikaria?' Kate whispered sharply to Beattie. 'It's the last place on earth I want her to be.'

'Sorry,' Beattie said. 'I didn't think.'

'Clearly.'

'I'm so sorry, Emma.'

'It's Kate!'

'God, I'm sorry. Kate. I'm just a little shook up right now.' Beattie looked devastated.

Kate's knuckle rubbed at her nose. She thought she'd come round to Tilly's departure, but Beattie's stupidity had made her superstitious dread rear its ugly head all over again.

Mark and Tilly marched into the living area. He brandished a tub of salt, while she waved a roll of paper towels above her head.

'Salt's the thing,' Mark was saying.

'Listen, Dad, I spend my life clearing up after pissed actors knocking over their wine. Believe me, this is the method that works.' Tilly wadded up a great long piece of kitchen roll and placed it over the wine stain. 'Claire was telling me about some island she knows in Greece. What was it called?'

'I – um – the name's slipped my mind,' Beattie said, frowning.

'But you just said it!'

'I—'

'Claire's had a bit of a shock, Tilly,' Mark said.

'Wasn't it something like diarrhoea?' Tilly said. 'Icky—'

'Wasn't it Ikaria?' Kate said, stepping in. Beattie's clumsy attempts to backtrack, while well intentioned, were only making things worse.

'Yes,' Beattie said, frowning slightly. 'That was it.'

'I've never heard of it,' Mark said.

'Not many foreigners have,' Beattie said. 'It's why it's so special.'

'When did you go?' Tilly asked, stamping on the kitchen roll.

'Oh, a long time back. When I was, what, twenty or so,' Beattie said. 'Just a little older than you are now. I had a great time. It's the most beautiful place.'

'Named after Icarus?'

'Yep. He fell into the sea just nearby, and his poor old Pop Daedalus buried him on the island.'

'I'm going to go there,' Tilly said.

Kate knocked back a big slug of wine.

'You just make sure you keep in touch with your Mom now,' Beattie said. 'Let her know what you're getting up to, where you're going and all that. Be a good daughter.'

'Of course,' Tilly said. She peeled the paper from the carpet with a flourish. Almost all the wine had been absorbed.

'Oh, she's a good daughter,' Kate said, as Mark knelt to sprinkle salt over what remained of the stain. 'The best.'

Better than she had ever been herself.

How it must have been for her parents never to see her again, never to know what happened to her. When she was pregnant with Tilly and facing her own impending parenthood she had hired a private detective to see how they were doing. She had thought perhaps that she could somehow make some sort of amends, possibly funnel some money their way or something. The short investigation revealed that they had, in fact, died within six months of each other, less than five years after she had staged her disappearance. The official line was that her father had been taken by a coronary and her mother a stroke. But Kate had added their deaths to her list of culpabilities. It had been hearts that had killed them, hadn't it? Broken hearts.

Mark stood, brushing lint from his knees where he had knelt on the rug. 'Grub's nearly up. Are you all right to sit at the table, Claire?'

'Of course,' Beattie said, putting out a hand. 'Help me up, will you, dear?' she asked Tilly, who handed her father the wad of wine-stained kitchen towel and stepped in instantly.

During the meal, Kate felt observed in every way. For one thing, everyone else at the table was watching how much she was eating. She knew, too, that Mark and Tilly would also be trying to picture her as a schoolgirl, friends with this strange American woman. She could also feel Beattie looking at how she, Kate, interacted with her family. She felt like she was a bad actor in the wrong play: utterly unconvincing on every level.

The only way to survive was by taking control and driving the conversation around the safer routes. So she asked Beattie about her life: what her children were up to (Jessie was a dentist and Saira was nearly a lawyer), how she was coping after the death of her husband (it was taking her a while to adjust), and what it was like living in San Francisco (it was really cool). Even so, after all this expense of energy, she still encountered some difficult moments. At one point, Beattie went to push up the sleeves of her polo neck jumper, which would have revealed her Triskelion. Kate, who was sitting opposite, managed to tap her leg under the table just in time and point out her own tattoo. Mercifully Beattie took the hint.

'Would you like some more, Claire?' Mark asked, holding the plate of lamb kebabs up for her.

'Oh no thank you, Mark. It was delicious, but I really need to watch what I eat.'

She smiled over at Kate, who had just hidden a lump of meat under a lettuce leaf.

'So what did you think when you bumped into each other in Starbucks, then?' Mark said, as he and Tilly cleared the plates at the end of the meal.

'I couldn't believe it,' Kate said. 'Claire was sitting across the room. I thought I recognised something about her, but I couldn't quite put my finger on it. Then she came up and asked me if my name was Kate and I recognised her voice instantly. It hasn't changed one bit.'

'Whereas you even look exactly as you did when you were at school,' Beattie said, resting her chin on her hands and smiling warmly at Kate.

'What were you doing in the West End, though, Mum?' Tilly said. 'You never go there.'

'Oh, I was on my way to Heals, to find some new cushions.'

'We should get you to A & E, Claire,' Mark said, shutting the dishwasher.

'Can I get my iPad before we go, please, Dad?' Tilly said. 'I want Claire to show me something.'

'I don't think—' Kate said.

'Of course,' Mark said.

'No rush.' Beattie beamed at Tilly.

Tilly ran upstairs while Kate sat tight-lipped at the table.

'I don't think you should come with us, Kate,' Mark said. 'You look awfully worn out. You need to go to bed.'

'You did very well at supper, though,' Beattie said, leaning over the table and putting her hand on Kate's. Kate knew this was rubbish. Beattie had either not been watching her cut her food into tiny pieces and hide it around her plate, or she was just being kind.

'Can you show me the island you were talking about?' Tilly said, bounding back into the kitchen, her iPad in her hands. 'Ikaria?'

Beattie took the screen from Kate's daughter's hands and moved her finger around it. 'Just there,' she said, pointing. 'Tucked down to the left of Samos.'

Kate watched as Tilly zoomed in on the island. Her eyes shone with an excitement that she remembered only too well in herself at that age.

'There are so few buildings,' Tilly said.

'A lot of the island is mountainous and uninhabitable,' Beattie said, 'but look along the south coast – see those beaches? Some of them you can only get to by scrabbling down a mountainside. Completely deserted.'

Kate could barely mask her exasperation. Didn't this woman know when to stop?

'Wow,' Tilly said.

'But what about food and water?' Kate said. 'You couldn't stay somewhere like that for long.'

'Oh, but you find ways around that sort of thing,' Beattie said. 'You have to be a little together, but nothing's impossible.'

'Where did you stay?' Tilly said, and again Kate found the word NO circling her brain as Beattie scrolled along the screen. She was sitting opposite the two of them, so she couldn't see exactly where Beattie was pointing, but she had a pretty good idea.

'Just there. See?' Beattie said. 'There's a great cave to sleep in on the beach. And, if I remember rightly, there's a village about a half-hour walk up the mountain. Look.'

'I'm so going there!' Tilly said, taking the iPad and bookmarking the map. 'Thank you so much, Claire!'

'No problem, sweetie.' But as Tilly gazed at the screen, Beattie glanced apologetically at Kate.

'Time to go,' Mark said.

'Can I come?' Tilly said.

'Best not,' Kate said. 'It could take hours and you need to be fresh for tomorrow.'

'Have a great time in Greece, honey,' Beattie said, kissing Tilly on the cheeks.

Kate walked Mark and Beattie to the front door and stood and watched as he helped her to his car. Despite her bulk, Beattie looked tiny as she limped along beside him.

Beaten down Beattie.

She had to be careful that the same thing didn't happen to her.

As she cleared away the last things from the dinner table, she noticed that on top of the champagne, two and a half bottles of red wine had been drunk. Tilly and Mark had taken only one glass each. So she and Beattie must have shared the rest. So high were her nerves, though, that, even taking the high tolerance she had built up over the years into account, she didn't really feel as drunk as she deserved.

She called in on Tilly's room on her way upstairs to propose a special goodbye breakfast the following morning, just the two of them.

'That'd be great, Mum.' Tilly was sitting at her dressing table and brushing her hair. 'But I'm going into work early to say goodbye to the morning shift.'

Kate forced a smile and restrained herself from asking

why the morning shift was more important to Tilly than her mother. She knew, of course: it was all part of the process of withdrawal that a child had to go through. Soon she would only see her every few weeks, and later, perhaps, when Tilly had her own family, she would come home for one or two days once or twice a year.

She knew she should be grateful even for that. It was more, after all, than she had permitted her own parents.

'I love you, Tills.'

'Love you too, Mum.'

Kate leaned forward and kissed her on the head. Her daughter's hair smelled of argan oil and apples. She filed this sense-memory away, to be retrieved should she need it.

Just in case . . .

Just if . . .

Blocking the horrors from her mind, she climbed the stairs to her own floor, where she crept into her bathroom, bent over the toilet and made herself throw up the small amount of food she had eaten that night.

At least that was one thing she could keep a grip on.

Six

After cleaning her teeth to get rid of the taste of vomit, Kate took a long, hot shower to soothe away the evening. It didn't work. Her fingertips still itched; the guilt at what she had caused to happen to Beattie still ate away at her concave stomach.

At least, she thought, as she towelled herself dry, Tilly was going away in the morning. At least she wouldn't be walking down Bridge Lane at night for another six months, when all this would hopefully be in the past, where it belonged.

She went down to the kitchen, filled a large glass with the remainder of the third bottle of red and took it up to her office, where she found an email from Jake.

Skype me, it said. Just that.

Like a finger click from her past.

As she stared at the screen wondering what she was going to say to the man she was beginning to think of as The American Shit, she thought about Beattie's split lip, about the look on her face as she stood in the doorway earlier that evening, her knees tattered, her palms ripped.

The whole thing was monstrous. It was thirty-three years

after the deed he was demanding that they pay for. She had to stand up to him or they would be lost.

Firing up Skype, she found that Jake_1959 had asked to be her contact and was there, online, waiting for her call. She supposed – possibly cruelly – that with his disability he had little else to do in his life other than hound her and Beattie. He could make it his full-time job, if he wanted.

She called him and waited. She was just about to give up when he answered, his image looming full into view on her large monitor.

She sat back a little, keeping her distance. Then, emboldened by the wine, and before he had a chance to get a word in, she launched herself at him.

'How could you do that to Beattie? I can't believe you. You send me completely unreasonable demands and then you expect me to jump when you whistle and do what you want straightaway without question? Don't you think I've got a right to know that you're going to use my money well? I know you and your appetites. I – I –'

She stopped, her legs trembling. Jake, too, was shaking. His whole body was in spasm, as if he were having some sort of fit.

She leaned forward and squinted at the screen. Was he all right? Was something happening to him? Might he be suffocating? Was his breathing machine letting him down? She watched carefully, willing it to happen.

Waiting to watch him die in front of her eyes. Again.

But, with the terrible rattle and whoosh of the breathing apparatus, she realised that, far from dying, he was laughing.

Laughing at her.

This could have – should have, perhaps – fuelled her anger, but instead she felt as if she were crumpling, shrinking. She saw her image in the corner of the screen getting even tinier in her big, expensive back-friendly work chair. Tears pricked at her eyes.

'Oh my dear. Oh little Em,' Jake said, after he had regained his composure. 'My, can't you just stamp your little foot until it hurts? Where did you learn to speak like that? From your wealthy, powerful, perfect husband? Or is there some rich-bitch wife/entitled mom school?'

'You set some thugs on Beattie,' she said, hearing her voice squeak over the vowels. 'Again.'

'Did I? Oh, oh, I'm sorry. Did they get carried away? Oh, I do hope she's OK.'

'She's at the hospital now.'

'Hospital? What? In case she can get some compensation? That greedy little fuck.'

'Don't talk about her like that, and no. The police need to have a doctor's report on her injuries.'

'Police? Oh, please don't tell me you're doing something stupid. I know you're careless. Evil, possibly. But I didn't have you down as stupid.'

Evil. Kate looked down at her hands, which hung over the keyboard like sparrow's claws. 'She told Mark she was mugged, so he called the police.'

Jake tilted himself forward so that his face was very close to the camera. She could see right up his nostrils, where a lump of something clung to a hair. How could she once have desired this flesh?

It wasn't because of his disability, she told herself. If it were Mark in that position, she would take care of him and feel exactly the same about him as she did now he was strong and active. Even – though she didn't manage to wholly convince herself on this point – if he were to balloon in weight and lose himself under a forest of facial hair. Not that, if she

286

were caring for him, that sort of thing would happen.

So then there she was again, tied up in knots because, if she had loved Jake and if the terrible things hadn't happened, then perhaps, even if he had ended up disabled for some reason or another, at least he would be slimmer, with better hair.

She almost laughed out loud at the depths of her shallowness.

'Jake.' She put her hands flat on the desk and positioned her face right up against the monitor. If it weren't for the world wide web spanning the distance between them, they would be as close as lovers. 'You brought all of this on yourself. If you hadn't attacked Beattie, then none of the rest would have happened. Perhaps,' she said, looking straight into his startling eyes, 'we would be together now.'

'Oh Emma,' he said, his voice hoarse. 'You're killing me.'

She threw herself back in her chair. Was he taking the piss? Was he being serious? She didn't know. She had no idea how to approach him.

'Tell me,' he said, 'who did Beattie say mugged her?'

'Some kids.'

'Some black kids?'

'Yes.'

Again Jake started shaking. 'Oh, good ol' Bee. We can rely on her for some Down South casual racism, heh?'

'She comes from New York, remember.'

'What?' Jake stopped shaking. His chin fell into his neck. 'Oh OK. Yeah, New York. I always think of her as Southern, with all that la-di-dah genteel middle-aged shtick she seems to have built up around herself. She's a total drag now, ain't she, Emma? An energy drain. A vortex. Don't you think? Not like you, I bet you've still got it when it counts, eh? Still a little firecracker.'

'Don't try to turn me against her,' Kate said, rubbing the back of her neck. 'It won't work.'

'Oh, you're so faithful. Such a good friend after all these years.'

'You are so full of hate, aren't you?'

'WOULDN'T YOU BE?'

'I don't want to talk about this any more. It just goes round and round in circles.'

'Well,' Jake said, levering himself slightly away from the camera, 'let's get down to business. You think, Emma, that you can make demands of me.'

'I just asked for—'

'Well, you listen here. You forfeited your rights to ask anything of me thirty-three years ago on a cliff in Greece. OK?'

'But—'

'You really lucked out, didn't you? Good health, the impossibly good-looking, kind and loving husband. The clever, pretty daughter. All that money. The lovely place in Battersea, the beautiful house with the far-reaching blue sea and sand views in Cornwall. Strange name, *Gwel an Mor*.'

'How did you—?'

'They tell me it looks lovely.'

'WHO tells you?'

'My homies. My peeps. Surely Beattie told you? It wouldn't be like her to miss out on a bit of melodramatic gossip. These people I exercise my arcane computing skills for are not the nicest of guys. But they bear immense gratitude to me, and they help me out in whatever ways they can. And you should be grateful too, at what I'm offering you.'

'What do you mean, "offering" me?'

'You don't believe you deserve any of all that luck you've landed, do you? And rightly so. That silly little charity of yours is just your small way of feeling better about it all, isn't it? Because even little Martha's tragic death didn't help, not really, did it?'

He had to stop talking to take another in-breath. Then he continued:

'Emma, my LOVE. Remember: my offer is to help you out here. With your reparation. You pay me what I need, without asking too many questions, and, hey, you feel better. Who knows, you might actually start to enjoy yourself a little more. Remember what happened on Ikaria? The day before you tried to kill me?'

'I didn't try to kill you.'

'Semantics. Remember when we kissed?'

Kate closed her eyes.

'You enjoyed that, didn't you?'

She nodded. The tears, which had threatened to engulf her since she realised he was laughing at her, finally appeared.

'But I don't think you've been able to enjoy yourself, since, have you? Whatever's eating Emma James? Eh?'

Kate said nothing.

'Not talkative? Oh well. We can get round to that some other time. I'm pretty pooped now, and I should imagine that you are too, after the evening you've had.'

'How do you know so much about me?'

'Takes one to know one, doesn't it?'

'I'm nothing like you.'

'Really? I would have said we were both of a piece.' He paused again, while the machine gave him breath. 'This is what happens next. I want that money in my account in three days. What happened to Beattie was just a hint at what this old crip can do. I am serious. Believe me. If you do not let me have my money, you will really, really regret it.'

He did something with his good hand and a message popped up on the screen.

'I've just sent you a link to a YouTube video. It's private at the moment, but I've made sure you can use it, my Face of Kindness. Or should I say Kate62.'

'You know my YouTube account.'

'Why wouldn't I? There's a load of stuff I know about you, Ems. Like I say, the video is private at the moment, just between you and me. But I can easily, easily make it more widely available should I deem it necessary. In the meantime, I wish you well, my lovely Emma.'

He moved to disconnect himself, but then he paused, frowning, as if struck by a new thought. 'Oh yes. Do you know that your daughter walks home at night with her headphones on? You really should discourage that, Emma. It's not at all safe. Not for a pretty girl like that.'

Anger cut through Kate's tears, sizzling them like a hot knife.

'ALL RIGHT!' she said. 'All right. I'll get the money to you. But it'll take five days.'

'It will take three days.'

Kate rubbed her stinging eyes.

'All right. Three. But I want your word that when you've got it, you'll not bother us any more. Not me. Not Beattie.'

Jake's eyes twinkled as he looked at her. 'You have my word, Ems, then, if that's what you want. Three days, mind. And don't forget to look at that little YouTube clip, will you?'

'Why are you so—' Kate started to say, but the familiar Skype parting sigh evaporated him from her screen.

With both hands, she scratched her scalp until it nearly bled. Her stitches throbbed, her skin felt as if it might crackle right off her.

Dreading what she might see, she clicked the link Jake had messaged her.

Looming up into the YouTube window was her own, thin, worried face, sitting exactly where she was at that moment – it was almost as if she were looking at herself in a mirror. The background noise was different, though. Instead of the traffic that rumbled ceaselessly up and down Battersea Bridge Road, there was the sound of Jake's breathing machine, and a shuffling sound that could or could not have been a dog somewhere near the microphone.

'No, no. That's not what I mean,' her mirror-self said.

'So which part of it are you sorry for?' Jake's voice rumbled close to the microphone. 'Pushing me off a cliff and killing me? Or not realising that you hadn't actually succeeded, and leaving me for dead?'

Kate watched herself. The lump in her throat – was it an Adam's apple or a swollen thyroid gland? She had never really noticed it before – bobbed up and down as she swallowed.

'I'm sorry for all of it.'

'SAY IT PROPERLY. Sorry for WHAT?'

Her reply – her confession – was distant, crackled, out of synch with her lips. But there it was. Filmed. Posted. Ready to show the world unless she paid up.

The bastard.

Her heart thumped against her ribs. She wanted to get on a plane, track him down and really kill him, properly this time.

But what good would come of it?

She didn't believe in evil. But if she did, what Jake was doing was exactly that.

She put her forehead on her keyboard and, once more, she wept.

Seven

Despite the weariness that came with feeling that her entire being had been wrung out, Kate had to take three pills to knock herself out.

So she didn't wake when Mark came in from looking after Beattie. Nor, once again, did she even stir when he got himself up and disappeared to the office.

She had the consolation of knowing that he had been home, though. As was his nightly habit, he had thrown two of his three pillows onto the floor when he went to sleep. Following her own morning routine, she replaced them when she made the bed in her classic five-star hotel turndown style.

She performed a couple of yoga asanas, just enough to raise the grogginess that clasped at her like a shroud. Then she stood in her walk-in wardrobe deciding what to wear for her visit to the bank. The night before, after watching her YouTube performance, she had transferred almost all the cash from various accounts to the current account she shared with Mark, which, thankfully, he never looked at or touched.

The sum she then had to transfer to Jake so far exceeded even their private bank's Internet floor-trading limit that she would have to go in and authorise it in person. So today, after taking Tilly to the airport – something she was now viewing more with relief than trepidation – that was where she was heading. She planned to explain the money transfer away as something to do with a property development project in the States.

Planning her wardrobe for the day, she laid out a simple woollen tunic and matching trousers to wear to take Tilly to the airport at eleven. For the afternoon, she chose a well-cut Prada suit which she had worn a couple of times in the past for meetings with potential Martha's Wish donors. It made her look business-like and in control, a far cry from what she was actually feeling.

She laid the suit out on her bed, and selected shoes, stockings and the simple gold necklace Mark had bought her when he first saw her in the suit. He enjoyed accessorising any special outfit she bought – so much so that most of her jewellery had been acquired this way.

She shouldn't feel so uneasy about the bank visit – she was an old hand at playing the rich woman. Even so, the role always seemed to require some effort.

Still in her workout clothes, she ran upstairs to her office and found her passport and birth certificate, ID for the bank, to safeguard against money laundering. She looked at her papers – real enough but certainly false – and admired the irony that they would do the trick.

Her mouth hangover-rough and dry, she decided to make herself a cup of tea before she showered.

But when she opened the door to the kitchen, she almost yelped with shock. She had thought herself alone in the house. But there was someone else sitting at the kitchen island, bundled in one of her snowy-white guest dressing gowns, eating a bowl of her own special muesli. Kate's initial instinct was to bolt for the door – Jake's comments about his 'peeps' being 'not necessarily nice' rose high in her mind.

But then the figure turned to face her and Kate saw, with some relief, that it was only Beattie.

'Oh, hi, honey,' she said, swivelling round on the tall white stool. A couple of stitches protruded from her lower lip and her black eye had bloomed to the colour of a Victoria plum. 'Yes. I'm still here, I'm afraid. I'm really sorry. It was a hellish long evening. The hospital took hours: the ER looked like a battlefield, loads of kids with knife wounds, drunken women bleeding and screaming. It was like hell. And the police station was pretty much the same. I tried to insist, but Mark wouldn't hear of me going back to the hotel. He's very forceful, isn't he? Very insistent, once he gets an idea.'

'Yes,' Kate said, putting on the kettle.

Beattie held her hands in front of her and examined the grazes on her palms. 'You don't expect it from a moneyman, but he's almost suspiciously kind. And your guest suite is gorgeous. Better than my hotel by a million miles. So thoughtful too, to provide dressing gowns and slippers and toothbrushes and whatever a body needs.'

Kate nodded. She liked to keep everything on the guest floor ready for visitors. Although, since Martha died, she had fallen out of the habit of playing hostess – the rooms had seen only a handful of occupants in all that time.

'You don't mind me helping myself to breakfast?' Beattie indicated the muesli. 'I was just so starving.'

'How are you feeling this morning?'

'Bit sore, but I'll survive. They just cleaned me up, then I made up some story for the police.' She smiled. 'I was so vague, I don't think there's any chance of them picking up the wrong boys.'

'Tea?'

'Do you have any coffee? I don't really do tea in the mornings.'

Kate reached down for the coffee beans. 'I'm going to the bank today to move the money over to his account,' she shouted above the noise of the grinder.

'That's a relief, then, hun.' Beattie passed her hand over her forehead. 'God bless you.'

Kate winced. Beattie's gratitude clearly showed that she put the previous night's attack down to her not instantly giving in to Jake's demands.

'I could get my taxi to give you a lift back to your hotel after he drops me off.'

'Ah,' Beattie said, awkwardly running the nail of her index finger over her stitched lip. 'Um, you see, I'm not at the hotel any more.'

'What?'

'Like I said, Mark is quite insistent,' Beattie said. 'He told me that, particularly as Tilly is off and away, you'd both love to have me here as your guest. Someone's going round to pick up my stuff and bring it here this morning – Mark got me to call the hotel last night to authorise it. He's also going to settle my bill for me, because he thinks those boys stole my purse with my wallet in it. Jake's guys did in fact take it, so he is actually helping me out of a tricky situation.'

Kate carried on making the coffee, her back to Beattie. How could Mark not consult her first before inviting Beattie to stay? This was going to complicate everything. Every time she looked at her, it was like having her nose rubbed in her past. And she'd have to live this whole new subset of Beattie-related lies whenever Mark was around.

Beattie slipped off the kitchen stool and took Kate's hands.

'I'm so sorry, Emma. Believe me, I didn't want to move into your space. I know it's going to make everything really awkward for you. But he just wouldn't take no for an answer. And, to be honest, not having to pay for the hotel is going to be a real help. Thanks to Jake I'm right up against it, as you know.'

'When are you due to go back?' Kate said.

Beattie looked at her feet. 'So my passport was in my purse. I'm going to have to get it back or buy a new one. Mark said he'd ask his secretary – Serena, is it? – to sort out an appointment at the embassy. But I'm afraid I didn't buy a return ticket,' she said. 'I couldn't really afford it. And I didn't know how long all this was going to take.'

'Well, it's nearly all over,' Kate said. 'I'm getting the money to Jake this morning, and I've got his word that this'll be the end of it. I'm happy to get you a ticket back home just as soon as we get you sorted with your passport.'

'Thank you so much.' Beattie hugged Kate tightly, then stepped back, dabbing at her eyes with the dressing-gown belt, leaving a little smudge of mascara on the towelling. 'Both of you – you're so kind.'

But it wasn't really kindness that was motivating Kate, more a desperate wish for this episode of her life to be over.

'Here's your coffee,' she said, handing Beattie a mug.

'Thank you so much,' Beattie said again, taking it back to her bowl of muesli. Kate sat opposite her, cradling her cup of tea. She knew she shouldn't be worrying about such a thing, but at least there was no danger of Mark taking a fancy to her friend. In the chunky dressing gown, with her hair unbrushed and her facial injuries, Beattie looked rough as hell and at least ten years older than her. She was also, Kate reckoned – and this was a calculation she was used to making when she looked at other women – two and a half times her weight.

Checking herself, she tried a more humane train of thought: poor Beattie, with her dead husband and grown-up kids. She must feel quite alone in the world.

As if she could read Kate's thoughts, without warning, Beattie put her coffee down and covered her eyes with her hands.

'What is it?' Kate put an arm out across the counter, alarmed. 'What?'

'I didn't want to tell you this. I'm too ashamed,' Beattie sobbed. She reached out and wound her hot, wet fingers around Kate's. 'You see, I don't have a home to go back to. The girls don't know it, but I had to sell our house. There's nothing left for me in San Francisco; just a storage facility full of the furniture I couldn't get rid of.'

'You had to sell because of Jake?'

Beattie looked at Kate and nodded. 'He's like that, Emma. He took everything I had and then he wanted more. He blackmailed it out of me, with threats that he was going to tell everyone what you and I did to him, and those creeps trailing me all the time, everywhere I went. I'm so scared he's going to do it all over again to you.'

'He gave his word. I'm paying what he asked for and no more,' Kate said. 'And let that be the end of it. If he's had all that money from you, he has more than he'll ever need.' She looked at Beattie and tightened her grip on her hand. 'Don't be scared.'

The thought struck her that, as with Martha's Wish, good could come out of terrible events. She, Kate, had it in her power to look after this poor creature in front of her, to use the shadow of Jake's awfulness to be kind and good.

She stood, walked round to Beattie and took her in her arms. 'Don't worry about a thing. You can stay here as long as it takes for you to get yourself sorted with a plan. As long as it takes for you to feel safe from Jake.'

'Will that ever happen, though?' Beattie said, her face pressed against Kate's shoulder.

'Of course,' Kate said. 'Of course it will.'

'I don't know what I'd do without you,' Beattie said, holding Kate tight.

'Oh!'

Kate could hear the gasp all the way upstairs in her shower room.

'Oh,' it came again.

She threw a towel around herself and ran downstairs to find Beattie in the hallway, an open empty suitcase in front of her and a sheaf of papers in her hands. A brown envelope lay at her feet.

'What is it?' Kate said, stopping on the stairs.

'It's Jessie and Saira.' Shaking, Beattie handed over the papers.

What Kate saw – holding the print-outs away from her eyes because she didn't have her reading glasses on – was a series of photographs of Beattie's daughters going about their daily business. In one, the bigger of the two was unloading plastic carrier bags of food into the boot of a station wagon. In another, the other young woman, who had permed dark brown hair and weary eyes, was in a café laughing at someone out of shot. The images had the grainy quality of photos taken from a distance.

'Jesus,' Kate said, handing the pictures back.

'He's got people *that close to them*.' Scowling, Beattie pulled out one of the sheets and held it up for Kate to see. It was of the larger daughter unlocking a front door, the station wagon now parked in the driveway. Both car registration plate and house number were clearly visible. 'That's Jessie's house.'

'How did you get these?' Kate asked.

'Mark's driver just brought my stuff back from the hotel. Didn't you hear the doorbell?'

'I was in the shower.'

'I took the liberty of answering. I thought it might be him. But he said this was all there was in my room. My empty suitcase and this envelope full of pictures. Everything else has gone.' Beattie's voice started to rise in pitch. 'Disappeared. All my clothes, my papers, my toiletries, everything. He's taken it all. They must have gotten my key from the purse they stole. I've got nothing now but my torn dress and bloody coat from last night.'

Still clinging on to the photographs of her daughters, Beattie sat on the stairs and sank her head in her hands. Gently, Kate took up position at her side and put her arm around her.

'What did the hotel say?'

'They told Mark's guy they'd be happy to help me with my insurance claim, but they aren't responsible if I kept my key in my bag rather than handing it in at reception.'

'Oh Beattie, I'm so sorry.'

'I haven't any insurance, Kate. I was doing all this on a budget. It seemed like an unnecessary expense. But the worst of it is these pictures.' She threw the pile of papers onto the hall floor. 'He knows where both my daughters are. If he lays a finger on either of them . . .'

'It won't come to that, Beattie. I'm getting the money to him today and I'm sure we can find you something to wear. This'll be over by tomorrow.'

Beattie put her hands in front of her face and shook her head. 'I don't deserve all this kindness. I'll never be able to repay you.'

Kate held her tight. 'Don't worry about anything, Bea. I've got this.'

A shadow fell across the frosted glass of the front door. It was Tilly, back from her trip to say farewell to her co-workers. By the time she had unlocked the door and entered the hallway, Beattie had stuffed the photographs back into the suitcase and the two women were standing there in line, like a reception committee.

Eight

'We need a trolley,' Kate said, heaving Tilly's rucksack out of the boot of the Audi.

'I'm fine, Mum, really,' Tilly said, taking her bag from her and swinging it onto her back.

Beattie, who had been having some trouble getting out of the low-slung car, finally popped out onto the pavement.

She was something of a sight. The only clothes Kate could find that went anywhere near to fitting her were a pair of stretchy leggings and an oversized structural sweater dress that she had never worn herself because the space around it made her feel like an orphaned child. She had also loaned her some large sunglasses to conceal some of the bruising on her face. The expensive clothes looked cheap, stretched over Beattie's body, and with her split lip and the yellowing skin around the edges of the Dior frames, the carefully groomed woman Kate had met just six days before in Starbucks seemed to have been replaced by some sort of escaped convict.

'What time's your plane, honey?' she asked Tilly for what Kate thought was the fifth time.

'One-fifty,' Tilly said. Being a better person than her mother, she didn't seem at all annoyed at having to repeat the answer yet again.

'Oh, sorry, I asked that already, didn't I? It's just I get so overwhelmed by airports and all that. Since Ed died. I don't know. They just make me nervous.'

It was extraordinary to Kate how Beattie had changed since they were both young. This dowdy, dithery, housewife figure had been the feisty one, the leader, the queen bee of their little threesome. Or at least that's how Kate remembered it. Hadn't this same thing – this narrowing of horizons – happened to her, though? It was so hard to see oneself objectively. She was certainly more adventurous back then. More foolhardy, she corrected herself. They had all changed: she, Beattie and Jake. All in different ways, but all for the same reason.

The Jake Effect.

She looked around her at the rows and rows of cars parked by people who had left them to travel all over the world. Why couldn't life be simpler? It seemed absurd, when you could talk to anyone over a computer, to have to go up fifty thousand feet or however high it was in a big metal bird and move to a different place.

Yet here was Tilly, all ripe and ready to go. Kate tried to recall her own wanderlust, how she felt when she took the train down to London to set off for Dover. Of course, her parents didn't give her a lift or anything, like she was doing for Tilly. They had no idea. They couldn't even begin to understand what she was up to.

'Come on, Mum,' Tilly said, large rucksack on her back, small bag strung across her front like a baby carrier. She turned to Beattie. 'She's always going off like this. Into a dream world.'

'Oh, but she's sad to see you go,' Beattie said. 'All discombobulated.'

Kate locked the car and they set off for the departure lounge. On the travelator Tilly strode in front of them, walking fast, swinging her arms. From the back, she looked like a soldier going into battle. She seemed so sure, so steadfast.

Kate told herself it was absurd to worry about her. A kid brought up in London, used to walking the city streets at night, a girl who had been working all hours for the past six months, dealing with drunken famous actors at the National Theatre. She wouldn't make the same mistakes as wet-behind-the-ears Emma James.

Tilly will be fine, Tilly will be fine, she chanted silently. And, most importantly of all, she would be out of Jake's clutches, in the far reaches of Europe, until it was all over.

'Have you got your phone and your iPad?' she asked as they stepped off the end of the travelator.

'Yes, Mum. And my passport, and my debit card, and my euros, and my insurance documents and three pairs of knickers.'

'Only three?' Beattie said, putting her hand to her chest. 'My.'

'One to wear, one to wash and one to dry,' Tilly said, as they approached the easyJet baggage drop.

She really did know what she was doing, this girl. Kate tried to fill the big balloon of emptiness expanding inside her with gratitude that Tilly was being delivered to safety. They checked in her big rucksack and moved on to the security channels.

'Are you sure you've got no liquids in your bag?' Kate asked.

'No tweezers or sharp things?' Beattie added.

'Jeeze. It's like having two twittering mother hens instead of just the one!'

Kate had much rather it had been just her and Tilly at the airport. Ever since she heard her daughter's plans, she had imagined this morning as a scene played out between just the two of them. But Beattie had been too nervous to stay on her own at the house. She swore that a car she had seen on the street earlier, when she had been out having a cigarette, belonged to Jake's people.

'Why?' Kate had asked.

'Tinted windows,' Beattie said darkly. 'They all have tinted windows.'

Kate shrugged it off. Most of the young men around the neighbourhood had tinted windows in their cars. It was no big deal.

'Don't leave me here,' Beattie had pleaded, holding on to Kate's arm. 'Not till you put the money in Jake's account. Please.'

So it was that Beattie was the first to get a goodbye hug from Tilly.

'I'll make it to Ikaria,' Tilly said, holding her hand.

'Get there early. It's glorious in the spring,' Beattie said. 'Flowers everywhere. And you can make the most of the lovely walking because it's not too hot.'

Kate frowned. How did Beattie know all that? Had she been back there? She couldn't imagine that she had. Or perhaps, like her, she had looked out for the island – regularly entering the name into search engines, exploring it in Google Maps. It had been in the news recently too, due to it having one of the highest concentrations of centenarians in the world. Not dying, it seemed, was commonplace in Ikaria.

And how ironic that, despite her best efforts at never, ever mentioning the place, Kate was now seeing her daughter off to go right there.

'I'll see how I get on in Athens,' Tilly said. 'I want to see the sights and keep an open mind.'

'Hey, perhaps you'll meet someone nice,' Beattie said, smiling over at Kate.

'I hope you get your passport and that sorted out soon, Claire,' Tilly said. 'And make sure Mum and Dad look after you properly.'

'Oh, I'm sure they will.'

Tilly kissed Beattie on the cheek one more time, let go of her hand and turned to Kate.

'Um, well, I'll just go get a coffee, I reckon,' Beattie said, diplomatically moving away.

Tilly put her arms around Kate. While not tall, she had an inch on her mother, which, even after a lifetime of being shorter than everyone else, made Kate feel the lesser person of the two of them.

Her nose stung, and then her cheeks were wet and she was sobbing on her daughter's shoulder.

'I'm sorry,' she said. 'I didn't want to be like this.'

'Listen, Mum, I'll be careful. I know my way around. I know not to take sweets or lifts from strangers. I'll keep in touch every day.'

'Promise?' Kate said, looking up and leaving a string of snot on Tilly's jacket.

'I promise.'

Kate fished a tissue out of her handbag and wiped the mess she had made from Tilly's shoulder.

'I've got to grow up, Mum.'

Kate nodded.

'You'll be fine,' Tilly said, bending to kiss her on the cheek. 'Text me when you land, won't you?'

'Of course. And I'll Skype as soon as I get Wi-Fi.'

'Good girl.' Kate pulled out the hundred euros she had stashed in her wallet and curled Tilly's fingers around them.

'Mum, I've got plenty of money.'

'No, I want you to have it. Get a taxi from the airport, and buy yourself a couple of good, hot meals.'

'Oh, OK,' Tilly said. 'If you insist.'

She turned to go.

'And Tills?'

'Yes, Mother?'

'If you don't want to come back through France and all that, we'll be very happy to pay your airfare back from Greece.'

Tilly sighed. 'Thanks, Mum. I'll bear that in mind.'

She had nearly reached the security gates when Kate caught up with her and stopped her again.

'Take this,' she said, putting her holey stone in her daughter's hand. 'We found it on the beach by *Gwel an Mor*, remember?'

Tilly looked blankly at her mother.

'It's for good luck. Keeps the evil spirits away.'

'Mum, you are such a loony tunes sometimes.'

'Take care, darling,' Kate said, kissing her one last time on the cheek.

'Can I go now?' Tilly said, not unkindly.

Kate stepped back and watched her daughter weave through the retractable barriers to the security channel. A sturdy female guard stopped her to have a word. Kate was just about to intervene and go up and demand what the hell this woman was cross-questioning her daughter about, when Tilly shook her head and kept on going. She showed her boarding pass, turned and waved, and then she was gone, just a blur behind a frosted-glass screen.

As Kate stood there gasping and gulping and dabbing at her eyes with a tissue, she felt an arm snake into hers. She looked round with tear-filled eyes to see Beattie standing beside her with two cups of coffee on a moulded cardboard tray.

'Skinny latte cool with you?' she said, smiling softly at Kate, who took the drink from her.

'Let's not let Jake know where she's gone, eh?' she said to Beattie.

'Now why on earth would we do that?'

On the way out of the departures hall, a youngish woman with a small crucifix hanging on the outside of her purple polo neck jumper rushed up to Kate.

'You're the Face of Kindness, aren't you?' she asked, taking her by the hand. Kate froze. Was this something set up by Jake?

'She is indeed,' Beattie said, smiling at the woman, oblivious to any possible threat in the situation.

'I just wanted to say thank you. Thank you for all you are doing for the poor girls of West Africa. Whatever anyone else says, you are a great person. The world needs good people like you.'

She clasped Kate's hands again and, before hurrying off, gave a little bow, a sort of genuflection.

Kate stood there perplexed. She hadn't thought about Martha's Wish for days. She'd forgotten all about the school-girls and the buildings.

She was a fraud and a liar.

Nine

'They're back,' Beattie said later that day as their taxi drove out of the gates to Kate and Mark's house and past a white Ford Mondeo parked at the side of the street. Two figures lurked inside, outlined behind tinted windows. 'I must have scared them off when I spotted them this morning. But they're back. Watch.'

Kate turned and, as their cab reached the end of the street, she saw the Mondeo pull out.

'Hopefully just keeping tabs on us,' Beattie said, tugging at the neckline of the too-tight sweater dress.

'Hopefully.' Kate's bones jolted as the taxi splashed through a pothole and turned onto the main road leading up to the river. The Mondeo merged into the thick, rain-soaked traffic three cars behind them.

It was still there, at about the same distance from them, when they reached the Strand branch of the private bank where Kate and Mark held their accounts. As their cab pulled up, their stalker sped past and turned the corner up ahead of them.

'Satisfied that we got to the bank, I guess.' Beattie stumbled out of the car and stepped under the shelter of Kate's umbrella. 'My, it's a beautiful building.'

It was. A sleek swathe of glass in a row of Regency grandeur, its impeccable wall of windows reflected the two women and the entire street behind them. With the distance offered by this, Kate could see what an odd figure Beattie cut. As an outfit, what they had cobbled together wasn't so bad. On the right person – bigger than Kate and smaller than Beattie – it would have emitted the edgy chic favoured by women of their age, who had grown up in the punk era. But the hard edges of the clothing brutally stretching over Beattie's soft hips just looked frumpy and wrong. She looked like a sheep in the clothing of a fox.

Feeling the commanding structure her own Prada suit offered, Kate remembered how and why she had selected it. It was hard enough feeling authoritative with stitches on her forehead. But, like a tatty accessory, Beattie's shambling, beaten-up appearance would instantly undermine all her efforts.

'Here,' Kate said, fishing a twenty-pound note out of her bag. 'Go into that café over there and I'll come and join you afterwards. They do marvellous little Portuguese custard tarts.' She had never tasted one herself, but she had it on Tilly's word how delicious they were.

'Are you sure?' Beattie said. 'Sure you don't want any support in there?'

'I'm fine, honest. They know me very well.'

'It's just,' – Beattie rolled the twenty up into a tube – 'I don't want to be on my own out here. Not with them being so close by.'

'I'll walk you to the café,' Kate said. 'It's always packed, so nothing can happen to you once you're in. And I'll come and get you afterwards.'

'OK.' Beattie looked doubtful.

'Come on. It's nearly all over. Just a couple more hours.'

She ushered Beattie across the road and into the warm, sweet-scented café, found her a seat near the back, away from the windows, and ordered her a large latte and one of the tarts.

'I'll be as quick as I can,' she said, before stepping out onto the street.

It felt different to be outside on her own, knowing that the Mondeo and its drivers might be nearby. The rational part of her brain told her the car might not have had anything to do with Jake – the fact that they were 'followed' could just be one of those coincidences of journey, timing and direction that must happen every day. But the thought that she had not yet been physically hurt – was virgin territory in that respect – gave her a superstitious inkling that her turn might be coming up.

Why had she given her holey stone away to Tilly? Surely she was the one in more need of it?

She hurried along the pavement towards the bank, where she was shown inside by a doorman in a bottle-green uniform.

The transfer was actually more problem-free than she had anticipated. The story about sending the money to someone called Stephen Smith, who was building a property for her in the US, seemed entirely plausible, the ID did the trick, and the bank manager, a woman about ten years younger than her who sported a fearsome, bright red manicure, even complimented her on her suit. 'Prada, isn't it?' she said.

Kate smiled and nodded.

Feeling as if she had just relieved herself – which, in many ways, she had – she stepped out onto the street, her fingers crossed that Mark wouldn't somehow find out what she had been up to. The downpour had eased off, and a rainbow arced its end into the gap between the buildings at the Trafalgar Square end of the Strand. Any sense of release drained quickly from her, however, as a white Mondeo with tinted windows turned onto the main drag from a side street a little way from where she was standing. It cruised slowly towards her then stopped in front of her, right by her toes.

Kate had no idea what to do. Should she run? To where, though? She certainly didn't want to lead them to Beattie. The driver's window wound down a couple of inches to reveal the top of a bald head.

'Emma James?' the man inside said, his voice high and reedy, his accent nasal and odd, possibly Essex.

'What?' Kate said, reluctantly moving closer to the car, in an attempt at keeping the exchange intimate. She didn't want to respond too openly to a name she hadn't used when in the bank.

'He says good,' the man said. 'Good girly, he says.'

'Can I have Beattie's passport?' Kate said suddenly. If she could get that from him, then Beattie could go home quickly and, with a little help from Kate, find herself somewhere to rent and get herself back on her feet again, hastening the end of this whole horrible chapter.

But the man just closed the window of his car, revved the engine, and sped off, raising a wave of puddle water that splashed against the trousers of an elegantly dressed elderly gentleman passing on the pavement.

'Farking cunt,' the old man said, waving his walking stick at the retreating Mondeo.

Marks and Spencer's was overheated and reeked cloyingly of roast dinners. Kate's suit felt too tight and she longed to take off her Louboutins, which were the kind of shoes you could only stand in for half an hour before feeling as if some sort of medieval fire torture had been conducted on the balls of your feet.

She felt embarrassed and ungenerous taking Beattie here, rather than, say, Harvey Nichols, but they did need to buy several outfits and M&S was better suited both to Beattie's style – if you could call it that – and the size she would need, which Kate estimated as a UK eighteen.

But Beattie loved the shop. 'It's like JC Penney but a million times nicer,' she said, fingering an overdone scarf in the Per Una section.

'What takes your fancy?' Kate asked as they waded through the racks and racks of clothes.

'You dress so beautifully. You choose for me.'

To Beattie's effusive displays of gratitude, they managed to fill a shopping trolley with possibilities. Kate sat on a vinyl armchair outside the changing rooms and handed items through to her to try on – they had exceeded the fitting-room garment limit of six many times over. Every now and then, Beattie would step sheepishly outside the cubicle and show herself for Kate's verdict. The rejects – which amounted to most of their initial selection – she handed out so that Kate could hang them up.

Kate looked at a pair of tailored trousers Beattie had not been able to get into, and thought that she could fit into them twice. The thrill of triumph she felt at that thought repulsed her. Such ideas did not make her a winner over Beattie. If anything, it was the reverse.

So what was it about Beattie that made her want to despise her? And then, as she pegged the trousers back onto their hanger, she realised that it was because Beattie had so fully allowed herself to become a victim, the role Kate had spurned throughout all the challenges of the years. Alongside raising her remaining daughter to be healthy and happy, she considered that to be her life's victory. And now, here was Beattie, whirling into her life, dragging her down with her personal fears and her battered face and her state of having allowed everything to be taken from her.

It was heartless to think it, but Beattie was like an evil talisman. Kate wanted her away from her as soon as possible. After this blip – the Jake Effect blip – she wanted to enjoy the rest of her life in peace. She had paid and paid and that was that.

And as if to herald the coming new age, at that very moment a text arrived from Tilly:

Arrived safely xxxxx

Kate texted back:

Get a taxi into town! xxxxxx

Instantly the reply arrived:

Yes, Mother xxxxx

In the end, Beattie chose a series of loose, flowing clothes in creams and taupes – colours that made up the major part of Kate's own wardrobe. Unconsciously, she had selected for Beattie styles very like those she would choose for herself. And oddly – given their physical differences – they also looked good on Beattie. The result was that Beattie looked like a distorted, lower-rent version of herself – when not in her sharp Prada suit, of course.

They stopped in the food hall, because Beattie said she wanted to cook supper for Mark and Kate, to say thank you.

'I will pay you back,' she said, as Kate used her card to pay for her purchases. 'I promise, Emma.'

'Don't even think about it,' Kate said.

'You're so kind.'

No. No, I'm not, Kate thought.

'I have to say that you're taking all this very well,' Kate said as finally they made their way towards the shop exit, taking up the whole aisle with the bulk of their carrier bags. 'Having all your things taken, and all that.'

'It's only stuff.' Beattie leaned into Kate a little so that their arms brushed. 'And I'm so lucky to have such a good and generous friend.'

'And now we've paid Jake off, we don't have to worry about him hurting us or anyone we love,' Kate said.

'I hope you're right about that,' Beattie said.

Kate stopped. They had stepped out on to the crowded street, right into the pedestrian flow. A woman with a briefcase bumped into them and crossly veered around them.

'What do you mean by that?'

'He's a very greedy man, Emma.'

They both looked glumly out at the river of pedestrians, which had diverted its flow around the obstacle they presented, as if they were an island.

Ten

'I've paid the money into your account.'

'Good,' Jake said. It was a particularly bad Skype connection. His image kept freezing.

Kate raised her eyebrows.

Was that it? He could at least show a little gratitude. It was a hell of a lot of money, after all. But he clearly had other things on his mind. Immobile as he was in his chair, he exuded the energy of an excited puppy.

'Hey, little Em, I've got great news,' he said, his face beaming broadly across the monitor.

'What is it?' Kate said.

'Guess who I've found?'

Kate shrugged. The way Jake had his fingers tangled in the web, it could have been anyone. 'Elvis?'

Jake laughed, a large, throaty, surprisingly un-wheezy guffaw and, for a second, she thought she glimpsed the beautiful boy she had once loved.

The meaty smell of Beattie's cooking snaked through Kate's office. She found this evidence of her friend's presence strangely comforting, because, while her weakness and gratitude wasn't exactly wholesome, it gave Kate the rare feeling of being the stronger person – as if she had budded powerful, capable wings for Beattie to shelter under.

'Elvis! I love it,' Jake said, once he had taken the breath again from his machine. 'You are a scream, little Em. No. It's even better than that. It's someone else who, like you, was once close to me. Well, some *people* who were close, in fact. Three people.'

'I've no idea,' Kate said, not wanting to play his game. She felt an unfamiliar rumble in her stomach and realised that the cooking smells were making her hungry, one of the many feelings she thought she had eliminated from her repertoire.

It was nearly all over. She was nearly free. She wanted to switch Jake off and forget about him.

'Think, girl. Who else was I looking for as well as you?'

'Not your family?'

'Clever girl! Yep. I have located Marnie, Zeb and Moon. The Fellowship are smart at covering tracks – not as smart as you were, but pretty good. But if you know how to look and where to go, and if you have some people who can actually WALK on the ground for you, then anything's possible.'

He inhaled again, grasping at the air, much quicker than usual – as if he had news he couldn't wait to share.

'I've spoken to them, Emma! Can you believe it? The kids are looking great! They even seem happy to see me. And Marnie – well, I'm no threat now, am I? It's not like I CAN HURT HER ANY MORE. Hey, she even looked a little tearful when she saw the state of me.'

'I'm sorry,' Kate said.

'Oh, sorry. Sorry. You don't have to feel sorry any more, Emma! That's the great liberation I offer you, hun. Oh, the kids, they are so bright. Chips off the old block.'

'How old are they?' It seemed she had to go through with this conversation now.

'Zeb's sixteen, and Moon's fourteen. Marnie wants them to go to college. I want them to go to college, but then hey, what Daddy wouldn't? The problem is they don't have any cash – The Fellowship just provides board and food and bare basic expenses in exchange for Marnie's work in the kitchens. There's nothing spare. Plus, of course, there's The Fellowship stance on education. Back when I was with them, they needed the men to go out and earn cash, so I was able to train in my craft. But no longer. Having moved more or less fully into self-sufficiency, these days they disapprove of formal schooling beyond the basics, preferring the children to move unquestioningly into servicing the community. But Marnie, who trained as a teacher before she met me, has kept Zeb and Moon up to speed. Hey. Do you know, Emma, how much it costs to put a child through a good school in the good ol' U S of A?'

Kate leaned her head back against her seat, closed her eyes and sighed. Beattie had been right. It wasn't over. 'You want more money.'

'A lot more than it's going to cost you and Mark to send sweet Tilly to read drama at Bristol University.'

'But you gave me your word this would be the end of it.'

'HA! The word of a dead man? Not worth the breath that forms it.'

Kate didn't move.

'You see, my dear,' he went on, 'I'm offering you the chance to do even more for me. You *know* how good it makes you feel. And I know how PASSIONATE you are about education for disadvantaged kids. WELL, THEY DON'T GET MORE DISADVANTAGED THAN ZEB AND MOON.'

'How much?' Kate said, her eyes still closed.

Jake composed himself and lowered his voice. 'Well now, it seems indelicate to discuss money face to face. I've put it in an email for you. It really would be better for everyone, for *all* of our children, if you read it very, very carefully. If you have any questions, just whistle. I'm not going anywhere.'

Kate refused to answer or to look at the screen. After several minutes' silence, Jake sucked in some air and broke the standoff.

'How's little Tilly doing, Ems?'

'She's fine, thanks.'

'Still enjoying working in the National Theatre staff canteen?'

'Yes.'

Kate tried not to smile. It seemed Jake didn't know everything about her life, then.

'And how is dear Beattie settling in?'

'Beattie?'

'She's moved in with you, I believe.'

So he knew *this* detail. She could fully imagine that he had guys sitting in that Mondeo watching the house day and night. How long would it take him to find out that Tilly was away? But he wouldn't be able to discover where she was, surely?

Then a sickening thought occurred to her. Had he hacked into her computer? Could he see her emails? Listen to her Skype calls?

'HOW'S BEATTIE? I SAID,' he roared.

'Beattie's doing fine.'

'I do like the feeling that I've brought old friends together, like a little TETRAPLEGIC CUPID. I'm sad I can't be there, in fact. We'd have a ball, the three of us. Just like back in the day.' He leaned in towards the camera, so that all Kate could see was his mouth, surrounded by the ragged whiskers of his moustache and beard. His teeth, she noticed, looked remarkably good for someone in his physical condition.

'Remember the island?' he said. 'How we thought it had been put there just for us? How, when we got on that boat, we felt we were escaping the world? Remember our beach, Emma? With the cave and how we kissed and then you pushed my hand away, like some little pricktease?'

Everything inside Kate tightened and she felt as if she might be going to suffocate.

'What was it, little girl?' Jake said, spittle flecking his lips. Lips that once had been full and cherubic but which now just looked fat and thick. 'Why didn't you want poor Jake to touch you?'

'I – I – it wasn't you. It was me.'

Again, he roared with laughter, ending with a gale of coughing and spluttering. 'The classic phrase! Oh, Emma, did you never grow up?'

Kate sat there, her mouth held in a twitching scowl that she knew would dissolve into tears if she let it go. The Emma in her wanted to blurt it all out, to tell him what had happened to her in Marseille, and how that had made it impossible for her to let him near her, but Kate held her back. She refused to explain herself to this – this – unable to bear it any more, she stopped the call, slamming the mouse down to disconnect.

Immediately an email buzzed into her inbox: Jake's new demands.

- $2m for each child (total $4m), to be established into a fund for college fees, living expenses and to compensate them for their violent, miserable, disabled father.
- $1.5m for my ex-wife Marnie, to enable her to extract herself from The Fellowship and to live independently.

- $2m to enable me to buy a suitably adapted house on the East Coast, to be near my poor, estranged family.

Remember, Emma. This is non-negotiable. I give you two days to get the money to me. Once more: NO NEGOTIATION.

Seven point five million dollars. Five million pounds. In two days. Kate wanted to laugh at the absurdity of the sums. But instead, all she could do was look at them, aghast. Jake's first demands had been within her reach. But this was too much. She just didn't have access to that sort of cash.

Her mind raced on. What could she sell without Mark noticing? The art on the walls – which would have easily covered what Jake wanted – was completely out of the question. Mark was the collector. He knew exactly what they had and where it hung. It would be impossible even to move a picture or sculpture without him noticing, let alone get rid of it. There was a graphic Tracey Emin drawing of a naked woman on the living-room wall. Identifying too closely with the self-loathing nature of the work, Kate had once tried to move it to one of the guest rooms. But Mark had been quite put out. He'd patiently explained to her as he returned it to its original position that he had bought the piece specifically with that distressed, bare-brick wall in mind and couldn't she see how badly it fitted against the smooth plaster in the bedroom?

Perhaps she could stage a burglary, pretend the Rothko had been stolen from their bedroom wall and get rid of it somehow on the black market. But the potential complications of that strategy – and the fact that she would be layering another whole stratum of deceit over her relationship with her husband – ruled that plan out.

Jewellery, then? But again, Mark had bought every single

piece she possessed, and often suggested this or that necklace or bracelet to go with an outfit. She thought about perhaps re-mortgaging either the house or the Cornish cottage, but it wouldn't raise enough, it would take far too long, and then there would be the repayments to explain away.

She sat at her desk. The smell from the kitchen was now that of cakes baking. Her hunger deepened.

Seizing her keyboard, she replied to Jake's email.

I don't have this sort of money.

Immediately, the reply came back.

I said two days, no negotiation. You know I have my eye on pretty little Tilly walking those London streets at night, as well as not quite so pretty nor so little Jessie and Saira in their ugly suburbs.

You'll think of something.

Eleven

'How'd it go?' Beattie said as she stood at the stove.

The kitchen looked as if a group of giddy children had smashed a giant piñata full of food in it. Every sleek, glossy surface was smeared, the floor was littered with peelings and open packets; spilled spices and flour dusted the work surfaces. At least five kitchen gadgets had been used; each one stood caked in something gloopy.

Kate felt the itchiness that such disorder set off in her – if she wasn't careful, she'd start scratching herself.

'Oh, fine,' she lied. 'He's happy.'

She had decided on the way downstairs that she wasn't going to tell Beattie about the new demands. If she did, she'd never see the back of her.

In any case, by the time Beattie did leave, she would have found a way around this new problem, she was certain. She would just have to, as Jake had put it, think of something.

'Oh, I am so relieved!' Beattie turned to her, one hand to her chest, her face glistening from the heat of the stove. 'I really had this idea that he was going to keep on and on taking money from you until you were ruined as much as me.'

'I think he's finally satisfied.'

'Hey! We can breathe again,' Beattie said, turning back to the fritters she was making, and Kate knew she had made the right decision in not telling her.

'Wine?' Kate said.

'A celebration?'

'Indeed.' Kate stooped to take a bottle of Rioja from the wine rack. She felt far from celebratory, but this was the story she had chosen to tell. 'In fact,' she said, changing her mind and heading for the fridge. 'I've got a nice bottle of bubbly in here. Let's go for that.'

'Far more suitable.' Beattie pulled a plate out of the warming oven and scooped the batch of fritters – Kate thought perhaps they might be sweetcorn – onto a pile of earlier creations.

'They smell heavenly,' Kate said. They did – all sweetness and salty butter, like a real version of that ersatz cinema popcorn aroma. She popped the cork on the champagne and poured out a glass each for her and Beattie.

'Do you mind if I smoke in here?' Beattie said, pulling the packet of cigarettes Kate had bought her from the handbag Kate had bought her.

'Um, I'd rather you didn't,' Kate said.

Beattie frowned. 'I thought Mark smoked, though.'

'No. He gave up ten years ago.'

'Oh. I thought –' Beattie shook her head then smiled brightly at Kate. 'Ah. He just looks like a smoker. I'll just step out onto the terrace, then.' Beattie took her glass and her cigarettes towards the French windows at the other end of the living area. 'Oh, a message came through on your phone, I think. It pinged in your purse over there.'

It was unlike Kate to leave her phone lying around – or her

handbag, come to that. It was a sign of how distracted she had become.

She glanced at the message. It was sent by Mark at six-thirty, saying he was on his way home: an event so rare at that early hour as to be extraordinary. It was probably his way of saying sorry for not asking before inviting Beattie to stay. Or perhaps he wanted to check that she was all right after saying goodbye to Tilly.

He was a good man, she thought. Like Beattie said, almost suspiciously kind.

It took an enormous effort, but she managed to restrain herself from clearing up the kitchen while she waited for Beattie to finish her cigarette – she knew that to do so would seem rude. Instead, she sipped her champagne and looked at the Martha's Wish website on her phone. It had been days since she'd checked it, longer since she'd contacted the office. Patience had posted the Face of Kindness image on the home page to accompany an article about how successful it had been for the charity, and how the donations kept rolling in. She outlined what possibilities the extra money opened up for the charity.

Kate shook her head. It was depressing that a sentimental photograph could make people cough up when the shocking facts about poverty and lack of opportunity for West African girls had failed to have anything like that effect.

'What was the text?' Beattie said as she came back in again, bringing cold air and an acrid waft of tobacco smoke with her.

'Mark's coming home for supper,' Kate said. 'Which is most unusual. We should feel honoured.'

'I asked him,' Beattie said.

'What?' Kate said, surprised.

'I called him a while back and asked him. I want to say thank you with this meal.'

'Oh. OK.'

'He has been very kind to me. Well, you both have.'

'It's nothing. Really.'

'Especially because he has no idea . . .'

'Indeed. What time is it now?'

'Seven-thirty.'

Kate frowned. 'He said he'd be back by seven. It's not like him to be late.'

'Oh, anything could have happened. The traffic was pretty bad when we were coming back.'

'But he's on his bike.'

'On his bike? Isn't it too far for that?'

'He can normally do it in fifteen minutes. Keeps him fit, he says.'

'Oh well, I don't know. Perhaps he got waylaid on his way out of the office.'

'Maybe,' Kate said. Apprehension buzzed around her fingertips like an angry fly.

'How long did Jake hound you for?' she asked Beattie as she sat at the kitchen island to drink champagne and watch her make more of a mess of the kitchen.

'It started nearly three years back.'

'I hadn't realised it was so long.'

'Believe me, it seems like a lifetime. Ed was still alive then, of course, so it was real hard sneaking the money out of our accounts without him noticing. I had some things to sell – a little of my mother's jewellery, for instance, but I didn't have any money of my own.'

'You didn't have a job at all?'

'Nope. I was a homemaker. I guess I just wanted to hunker down after all that stuff in Greece. I didn't want to get out there and battle or anything. Ed earned enough, and I loved my babies.'

'I felt exactly the same,' Kate said. 'It's funny, that, isn't it?'

'I guess so. I never went to a shrink. Did you?'

'No.'

'I guess we both had what you'd call post-traumatic stress disorder, from what we thought we did to Jake.'

'What *I* did to Jake.'

'That's what you say. But I'll say it again: I would have pushed him, had I got there first.' Beattie narrowed her eyes, but she really didn't have the knack of looking mean. 'I really wanted him dead after what he did to me.'

Kate frowned. She hadn't meant to push him over the edge, though. She had merely wanted to keep him away from her and Beattie. But was she remembering correctly? It all happened so quickly that perhaps she only believed it had gone like that to save herself from the worse truth.

In any case, it didn't matter, because Jake was still alive.

She had to hold on to that fact, whatever problems it caused her.

She had not killed him.

She was not a murderer.

'What happened to you after Ikaria?' she asked Beattie, who was now dunking chicken pieces in egg, then throwing them into an over-spilling bowl of breadcrumbs.

'Well, now,' she said. 'I wasn't nearly so brave as you, Emma. I mean, you totally reinvented yourself, didn't you?'

Kate nodded.

'I thought about giving up my drama school place. But then I thought, well, we had his ID. No one on that island knew who he was, or who we were, come to that.

'Shall I tell you something? I met Ed on the plane coming

326

back to New York from Athens. He was a junior doctor at St Vincent's, and had been enjoying something of a more civilised time in Greece than we had. I didn't plan anything. I just told him my name was Claire Cohen. So that was it. When I got back, that was who I was. It wasn't unheard of for a drama student to change her name.'

'What did your parents say?'

'My parents? They thought it amusing. Then Ed and I got married the following summer, after I graduated, and we moved down to Georgia. I didn't get any acting jobs. I don't think I was honestly cut out for that life anyway. Not after all that happened. Instead, I got pregnant, kept a lovely home and learned to cook like a Southern mammy.' With a slotted spoon, she lowered the breaded chicken into a pan of hot oil.

'It all smells delicious,' Kate said, wondering how you could keep a 'lovely home' when you cooked in such a chaotic matter.

With the chicken pieces sizzling in the pan, Beattie turned to Kate. 'I've never told anyone this. And I didn't want to tell you earlier, before Jake backed off. But I think he was responsible for Ed's death.'

Kate could hear her heart pick up a beat. 'What do you mean?'

Beattie's eyes glistened. 'He was killed in a hit-and-run. Mown down at a crosswalk. The driver got away and no one got the license plate. It may just have been some drunk kids or something, of course, but I have this idea that it was Jake's guys. I was refusing to pay at that point, see. Well, not refusing, unable. I couldn't find any other money.'

'But that's murder. That's way beyond intimidation.' Kate registered that, despite the state-of-art under-floor heating in the kitchen and the fierce heat emanating from the stove, goosebumps were prickling on her arm.

'I asked him if he had done it, but he denied it. Perhaps he had only meant to scare me, and it went wrong.'

'We know how that goes, don't we?' Kate said.

Beattie nodded gravely. 'Jake got the result he wanted, though. I could pay him after Ed died, because of the life insurance. And, of course, with no Ed to object, I was free to do what I wanted with the house. Or, rather, what Jake wanted.'

'Jesus.'

Kate looked at the clock on the cooker. It was gone eight now. Mark was over an hour late. Where the hell was he?

She closed her mind against the image of him, winged by a speeding Mondeo with tinted windows, thrown through the air to land cheek first on the gritty road, caught in a flying fall, the realisation on his face the same as that she had witnessed all those years ago on someone else's: the awful look she had never truly been able to escape, even in the midst of the most joyous days of her life, when she had two young daughters and the darkness was in abeyance.

A sharp alarm filled the air, so high-pitched that she had to put her hands over her ears. 'What's that?' she said, panicked, looking at Beattie.

'You seriously don't know?' Beattie asked her, as she switched off the hob and moved her pan of fat to a cooler place. 'It's your smoke alarm. I've set it off with my deep-fat frying. I'm always doing that.'

She moved around the room opening windows, then she climbed on a chair and flicked a tea towel at the screaming alarm, a white box protruding from the ceiling.

Kate had never heard the smoke alarm before because she had never fried anything in deep fat. Also, she rarely used the oven and never made toast.

'Mark had better be home soon.' Beattie lifted the golden,

crispy portions of fried chicken from the pan and placed them in a warm dish. 'This keeps, but it's far nicer fresh . . .' her voice trailed off.

'What is it?' Kate asked.

Beattie had stopped, tongs in hand, and was standing over the platter of chicken, her shoulders shaking. She turned to face Kate, tears spilling from her eyes.

'Oh Emma. This was Ed's favourite food. It's the first time I've made it since – since –'

'Oh, Beattie.' Kate swept round the kitchen island and put her arms round her.

'I miss him so much,' Beattie sobbed into Kate's shoulder. 'I've been so scared.'

'It will pass,' Kate said, holding her tight. 'It's nearly all over with Jake and soon we'll be able to live our lives again.'

'Hello?'

Kate looked up and saw Mark standing in the kitchen doorway, frowning slightly.

Beattie hurriedly stepped out of Kate's arms and dabbed at her eyes with her sleeve. 'Sorry, Mark. I was having a little moment and Kate was looking after me.'

'So I see,' Mark said.

'Thank God you're back,' Kate said, moving towards him and kissing him on the cheek. 'I was beginning to get worried: you, the bike, rush hour.'

'Queen of the worst-case scenario as ever,' Mark said.

Although he was clearly physically unscathed, he didn't look altogether happy. Had he heard them talking? Kate felt the stab of worry that had plagued her entire life with him, but now carried a far more deadly weight than ever before: *had he found her out?*

329

He looked round at the state of the kitchen. 'Jesus, what happened here?'

'Remember? I'm cooking you supper,' Beattie said in a singsong voice Kate had only ever heard her use on Mark.

'Fantastic,' he said, with little enthusiasm.

'Kate's been very kind,' Beattie said. 'She's shown me around, taken me clothes shopping so I'm not naked.'

'I heard about your room being ransacked,' he said. 'What bastards.'

'It was my own fault for keeping the hotel key in my purse. Never again.'

'You look worn out,' Kate said. 'Champagne?'

'I'll get myself a vodka,' he said, running his fingers through his hair. Kate noticed he had a slight tic in his right eye. She had seen this twice before: during Martha's illness and when his father fell down dead from a heart attack shortly after their wedding.

'Is everything OK?' she said.

'Fine,' he said.

'You sit down, Mark. I'll fix your drink for you,' Beattie said, going to the fridge.

Mark mumbled his thanks and perched on a stool, tapping his fingers on the kitchen island worktop.

'I'll set the table, then,' Kate said, heading for the cutlery drawer. 'What is it, Mark? You look shattered.'

'Oh, just some crap at work,' he said. 'But it's the last thing I want to talk about right now. Worst part is, I've got to go back in again after supper.'

'What? Oh no.'

'Tell me about it.'

He slipped to his feet and paced around the vast living area, looking out of the windows, examining the self-loathing

Tracey Emin, the Damien Hirst spots.

Again, Kate felt a flush of guilt. Had he read her mind about selling the artworks? Did he know? Was that why he was so edgy?

She didn't think she could go on like this much longer. The layers of deception were spiralling out of control.

'Do you *have* to go back?' Kate said. He had clearly only come home early to be polite to Beattie. It was ridiculously over-solicitous of him.

But they were unused to visitors, which was why he was putting himself out so much. Despite the lavish guest suite, their only overnight guests in the past eight years had been a couple of business associates of Mark's who were more friends than colleagues and a Martha's Wish fieldworker who needed somewhere to stay in London for a couple of nights. The young woman had been completely charming, but the way she eyed the expensive furniture set in vast spaces and her comments on the quality of the guest suite's toiletries had made Kate feel uneasy, as if she weren't giving enough of her wealth away. Looking through her guest's eyes, she had even detected a certain smugness in her own face in the big family studio portrait on the kitchen wall.

Having outsiders around exerted a pressure on her she could do without. She was far happier with just her fast-dwindling family for company.

'I have completely and utterly no choice,' Mark said, forcing a weak smile as Beattie handed him a glass filled with ice, vodka and a couple of lurking lemon slices.

'Did Serena have any luck with the embassy?' Beattie said, turning back to a sauce she had going in a double boiler. The excessive brightness of her tone must have been an attempt at lifting Mark's mood, but Kate knew that sort of thing wouldn't swing with him.

Sourly, he pulled out his iPhone and checked his calendar. 'Nine next Thursday morning.'

'Can't it be any sooner?' Kate said.

He turned to her. 'They're very busy, apparently. In any case, Claire's welcome to stay, isn't she?'

'Of course. It must just be very frustrating for her.'

'Oh, it doesn't bother me!' Beattie said. 'It's so lovely staying here with you guys.' She clapped her hands. 'Dinner time, Mom and Dad!'

Kate looked at her, puzzled.

'Oh, don't mind me,' Beattie said. 'It's what me and Ed used to say to each other.' She wiped a knuckle across her eye, smudging tear-wetted mascara onto her cheek. Then she smiled a little too brightly and set to serving up the food.

They each carried a laden plate to the table. Along with the sweetcorn fritters and fried chicken, there was fried banana – Oxford Street Marks and Spencer was clean out of plantains – buttered kale in place of the collard greens they also didn't sell, corn bread which looked more like a cake, biscuits which were more like savoury scones, and gravy, which was more a sort of meaty white sauce. Kate knew she wouldn't be able to eat all of the food on offer. In fact, the quantity on her plate made her nervous. But that unaccustomed hunger yawned in her stomach. She decided as she sat at the table that she would eat slowly and steadily then stop when the last of her two dining companions had finished. She didn't want an issue to be made out of the food, or her eating of it.

'I haven't dined like this since I visited a client in Savannah,' Mark said, tucking into his chicken. Kate noticed with relief that his eye was now still. Perhaps he had just been hungry. Perhaps that was all there was to it.

'You were in Savannah?' Beattie said, clapping her hands again. 'I lived there for seventeen years!'

They carried on talking about the Historic District and the trolleybus, and the deliciousness of the figs. With Mark relaxing, Kate stood her guard down, stopped listening to the conversation and turned her worry back to the two knotty problems of eating the food on her plate and meeting Jake's new demands.

She could feel her belly distending. Her stomach, unused to carbohydrates – well, unused to food, really – was as full as it could possibly be. Yet, for some reason, she couldn't stop cutting and chewing and swallowing.

'Isn't she doing well?' Beattie said, drawing Kate out of her stupor.

'It's the most I've seen her eat for years,' Mark said, smiling at her.

Dessert was a homemade key lime pie with thick pastry and luminous green filling. Kate managed a mouthful. As he finished the last morsel on his plate, Mark's brief relaxation evaporated and his eyelid recommenced its rhythmic batting.

'I have to go now,' he said, suddenly getting to his feet. 'Thank you for a delicious meal, Claire. I hope I can stay sharp with all of that inside me.'

'Why don't you take the car?' Kate said.

'I'd rather cycle. Clears the mind.' On his way to the door, he stopped and turned to Kate. 'Will you be awake when I get back?'

'I'll do my best.'

'That'd be great. See you later, then.' He clattered down the stairs, his tread heavier than usual. Then, with the slam of the front door, he was gone.

'Doesn't he wear a helmet?' Beattie asked, helping herself to another slice of pie.

'Never,' Kate said, frowning after the space Mark had left behind him, wondering what it was he wanted to talk to her about later on.

'He really should, you know.'

Twelve

Having spent two hours scrubbing the kitchen clean, Kate sat up in bed with a notepad, trying to list ways out of the hole Jake had her in. All she could come up with were:

- *Plead with Jake*
- *Expose Jake*
- *Tell Mark*
- *Kill self*

It wasn't extensive, but those appeared to be her options, all of them impossible except, possibly, the final one. But she couldn't dump parental suicide on Tilly, and anyway, if she did that, wouldn't Jake out the truth anyway and bring shame on her family? She sat there for a while, doodling around the page, racking her brains for another way around the problem.

After a while, she came up with one more:

- *Kill Jake*

After all, she had done it once already.

But her stomach clenched at the idea. She realised that, horrific as the situation she found herself in was, the fact that she was released from the burden of being a murderer had started to fix something deep inside her.

Then another item for her list came to her. But it was so terrible – worse by far than any of the other solutions – that she didn't even dare write it down. The frightening thing about it was that, out of all the alternatives, it was the most achievable.

The front door slammed and she heard Mark's heavy step on the stairs. She only just managed to slip the notebook into her bedside drawer before he blundered into the bedroom.

This was not his usual mode of entry late at night. Normally he would tiptoe in to avoid waking her up. She knew this, because she would often pretend to be asleep, not wanting him to press himself upon her with all the energy he seemed to draw from his working day. Tonight, though, it seemed like the energy transfer had been reversed. He looked awful: grey-skinned, hood-eyed and – despite his beautiful, bespoke suit – shabby. As he shut the bedroom door she caught a gust of whisky and tobacco.

So Beattie had been right. He was still smoking. Perhaps he had even shared her cigarettes the night before, when they went to the hospital and the police station.

For a fleeting moment, Kate forgot that she had no cause to be jealous of her.

'I need a shower,' Mark said, leaving Kate on her own in the bedroom, sitting upright, worrying and wondering what it was that was eating at him.

After a while, the shower door opened. The Florentine count's bespoke scent followed Mark as he crossed the bedroom to his wardrobe.

'I need pyjamas tonight,' he said.

'What's the matter, Mark?' she said as he stumbled into his pyjama bottoms as if he had become so unused to putting them on that he had lost the knack.

He threw himself on the bed and exhaled. Despite the shower and the expensive toiletries he had not entirely obliterated the tobacco smell. She turned to face him.

'What is it?'

'There's trouble.'

'Yes?'

He continued to look up at the ceiling, avoiding her gaze. 'This is strictly confidential.'

'Of course.' The blood bloomed on her cheek – what was he about to say to her?

'OK. I'm in the shit. My fund's thirty per cent down and we've been winging it for quite a while.'

She let out an audible sigh of relief, which, had he been in a state to notice it, he would have found puzzling. 'Why down?'

'Oh, China, gold, low interest rates, limited liquidity, bad bets. Do you want to know the details?'

'Not really.'

'Good.'

'Can you get out of it?'

'Not sure. The Americans are wanting to pull out.'

'New York?'

'New York and Savannah.'

'Gosh.'

'And the Japanese, in amongst a lot of politeness, are also threatening to withdraw.'

'Oh.'

'And my big UK pension fund, too.'

'How long have you got, do you think?'

'A month. Six weeks.' Mark closed his eyes and breathed out. 'I'm going to JFK tomorrow, first flight, to try to stall the situation.'

'OK . . .'

'Sorry. It's totally last minute. Serena booked my tickets this evening. I'll be gone three days. But at least you've got Claire to keep you company.'

'Don't worry about me. But your shirts . . .'

'It's not about shirts, Kate,' he said.

She looked away and ran her fingers down her cheekbones, feeling their sharp edges. Then her knuckle strayed to the tip of her nose. She didn't like being told off like that.

'Look,' he said, taking her hand and turning her to face him. 'Kate, love. I'm under big stress here. I don't know how much more of this I can take. My heart's fluttering all over the place, my blood pressure's sky high.'

'Your blood pressure?'

'I saw the doc last week. Dizzy spells.'

'But why didn't you tell me?'

'You've not been so well yourself. I didn't want to worry you.'

'I thought we had no secrets,' she found herself saying, but he wasn't listening.

'But I need to tell you now. In case . . . It's in my family, isn't it? My father. And my grandfather.'

He took her other hand as well and turned so that he was kneeling on the bed, facing her. To see him like this, no defences, not in charge . . .

For the first time ever – not ever, actually, she reminded herself, but since Ikaria – she felt the butterfly wings of desire play inside her. She extracted one hand and moved it up to his face. But he retrieved it and held it still on the bed. 'Look, Kate. We need to act.'

'What do you mean?'

'Where do we stand with cash? Have you looked lately?'

'Um, about two?' she said, trying to breathe steadily. She

338

looked down at the bedcovers, unable to meet his eyes. Was he going to want to see it? Was she going to be able to get away with this?

'Really? I thought it was more than that.'

She shook her head, relieved that he had so little idea.

'I'm going to sell the best artworks. Bonham's have got a twentieth-century auction coming up soon and I've had an email valuation of fifteen million on the collection. We need to liquidate and get the money out.'

'Even the Tracey?'

'Even the Tracey, I'm afraid.' He smiled. He knew she hated it. 'I've set up an offshore account so if the shit hits the fan we can still feed ourselves. We need to move our cash out of the UK as soon as possible.'

'Give me the details. I can do that,' Kate said, quickly.

'Can you do it tomorrow?'

'I can do it yesterday.'

He didn't know how true this was.

'That's my girl.'

He let go of her hands, turned on his side and settled down on the bed, facing away from her.

Feeling quite unhinged by this new development, she ran her fingers along the cool skin of his back, breathing in the scent of him.

He half turned and kissed her on the top of her head, and she moved down to touch his neck with her lips.

'Do you mind if we don't?' he whispered. 'I'm done in, and I've got to be up in four hours.'

'Of course not.' She withdrew her hand.

'Spoon around me,' he said, and she did as she was told.

Thirteen

'Hey, Patience.'

Mark was on his way to New York, and Kate had two days to go until Jake's deadline. Having told Beattie she needed to work, she sat at her desk, on the phone to the Martha's Wish office. The trousers of her velvet tracksuit felt a little tighter than usual. This, she supposed, was a good thing.

She was worried about Mark, of course she was. He could lose his business, and the stress was clearly playing on him. But the reprieve offered her by his instructions to clear out their UK accounts and his plan to sell the art outweighed all of that. Whatever happened, they could survive on that money. The artworks would bring in so much that the relatively small amount she had diverted from their funds wouldn't even be noticed by Mark.

However, the artwork sale wouldn't address her own immediate problem, which was finding five million pounds in less than two days. Not at once, anyway. But she still had that plan, the plan so awful that it didn't make it onto her list.

'Kate! How are you?' A machine whirred behind Patience's greeting. An office printer, perhaps.

'I'm back on it.'

'That's great!'

Beyond the windowsill cactus garden it was mid-morning; the whole of London was encased in fog: shapes of buildings bled into the air.

'I'm up for the blog post this week.'

'Oh, that's OK, Kate. Sophie PR's written the next four weeks already.'

'Oh. Good.' Kate didn't know why this annoyed her so. Sophie's action was a kindness – they hadn't known how long she was going to be off sick. However, she would be charging for it at her extortionate agency rates, depriving small African girls of a school. But this didn't irk her as much as the feeling that she was being squeezed out.

Using her annoyance as momentum, she forged on.

'I feel like I'm out of the loop,' she said. 'With everything that's been happening lately, with Face of Kindness and all that, and the incredible public response Sophie wrote about on the blog.'

'Oh, it's been amazing,' Patience said. 'We'll have to have that celebratory team meal soon.'

'Indeed.'

'We can't spend it fast enough.'

'How much has come in, exactly?'

'I need to put it all together, but it's millions, not thousands.'

While Kate was taking this in, there was a knock at the door and Beattie came in.

'Excuse me just one second, please, Patience.' Kate put her hand over the receiver and smiled at Beattie.

'I thought you could do with a coffee, hon.' She tiptoed across the room and placed a steaming cup at Kate's side.

Kate mouthed her thanks at Beattie and watched as she

crept back out the door. When she was sure that she had left, she turned her attention back to Patience. 'We don't have the infrastructure for spending that sort of money, though, do we?' she said, dipping her toe in the water of her plan.

'No. We're going to have a trustees meeting soon to reassess our priorities for the coming year.'

'That's what Mark and I were talking about last night. In fact, he's got this great investment opportunity that would be a perfect place to house the money until we're ready to spend it.'

'Really?'

'We should make the most of it. Not let it rot in our reserve account.'

'But would the money be safe?'

'Guaranteed return of capital, easy access and potentially up to twelve per cent for the first year, which Mark actually says is a conservative estimate.'

'Sounds too good to be true.'

'Mark does know what he's talking about.'

'Of course. I didn't mean—'

'It's a limited window, though. He says they're going to go like hot cakes when the word's out. Do you think you could get the actual picture to me as soon as possible?'

'Of course,' Patience said. 'I'll get a report to you by next week.'

'The window is *extremely* limited,' Kate said. 'Is there any way you could do it by the end of the day?'

She heard Patience sigh, and the clatter of a keyboard. 'I guess it could be done. We're pretty busy, though . . .'

'This is the best thing for Martha's Wish,' Kate said.

'OK. Is it ethical, though, this investment?'

Martha's Wish had no guidelines for where their money should go before it was spent. But morally correct investment was one of Patience's things, and since she was in charge of the day-to-day financial side of the charity, it had become a major unofficial policy. So the charity kept its current and reserve accounts with a small ethical bank, a move that Mark had nearly vetoed, saying that they could earn more bloody interest at any of the major institutions. Kate had talked him out of it. Keeping Patience happy was, to her, more important than half a per cent on an interest rate.

'Of course it's ethical! Patience, we've been working together for seven years. Do you think I'd approve of anything else?'

'No, of course not. Sorry.'

'It's renewable energy. A big flotation. I can bike the literature over if you'd like to see it. Put your mind at rest.'

'No, no, I trust you,' Patience said, as Kate had been 99 per cent sure she would. The one per cent error margin could have been dealt with by a bike messenger going astray story.

'Great, because we've got to get a crack on.'

She hung up and put her head in her hands.

It was dicey – really dicey. But she had no choice. There was money and she could get at it. It was a bad thing to do, but she would pay it back as soon as they shifted the horrible artworks, and no one would be any the wiser.

It wasn't as bad as murder, after all. Hadn't Jake implied a threat to Tilly if she didn't pay up? Even if he had no idea where she was right now, he knew exactly where she was going in the autumn – he'd named both her university and the course she was doing. So wasn't this really little Martha looking out for her big sister? Wouldn't that be Martha's wish?

She closed her eyes and the part of her that had been born a Catholic – Emma, she supposed – crossed herself.

Fourteen

Kate now had to wait until Patience got back to her. She paced the circle of her office floor, unable to decide what to do. To make the time pass more quickly, she could have gone downstairs and worked through her normal Thursday cleaning tasks. But if she did, Beattie would insist on helping, and she couldn't face dealing with that.

Restlessly, she sat again, opened a new browser window and searched for Tilly's hostel on Google Earth, but was disappointed to see that she couldn't zoom in to Street View. She hadn't heard from her since the text she had picked up while she was in Marks and Spencer and she ached to talk to her. But if she called, she ran the risk of being accused of being a neurotic mother.

Then, almost as if Kate had summoned it, Skype started singing and Tilly's face popped up: a photograph taken last year in Cornwall: long, yellow curls blowing in the wind, smile almost bursting her suntanned face.

'Where have you been?' Kate asked, trying not to sound like she was flinging accusations.

'I tried to contact you,' Tilly said. 'I emailed, and I

Facebooked and I tweeted and I DM'd on Skype . . .'

Kate glanced at the bottom of the Skype window. There she was, Tilly, trying to contact her at six the evening before, then later on at eleven, twelve and one-thirty.

'Oh, sorry, darling. But I was expecting you to phone.'

'I've lost my phone, Mum.'

'Oh no.'

'After I texted you yesterday, I put it back in my bag. But when I went to text you again, when I got to the hostel, it wasn't there. Someone must've nicked it.'

'Oh *no*,' Kate said. Was it all starting to go wrong already for Tilly?

'It's not the end of the world, Mum! It's insured. And at least I've got the iPad.'

'I suppose so.'

'And here's a funny thing,' Tilly went on. 'That hundred euro you gave me? Well, it's all gone. I got completely ripped off by the taxi driver. My guidebook says it shouldn't cost more than thirty to get to the city centre from the airport. It was quite funny, really. We had this big old shouting match in the street outside my hostel, me threatening to call a policeman, trying to get the people around to help me, but they were actually just beggars and druggies and couldn't give a shit. There was even some man lying in the doorway next to the hostel passed out with a needle still in his arm. Gross.'

'Oh, Tilly!' Kate put her hands over her mouth.

'In the end the taxi guy looked like he might get violent, so I had no choice but to hand over the money. I made a big show of writing down his number, though. Said I was going to report him. Arsehole.'

'You should do that.'

'Well, too late now. I'm on my way out of here.'

'What do you mean?'

'It's fucking boiling in Athens, Mum. They're having a crazy heatwave at the moment. The hostel guy said it's never been this hot in April before. The Greeks are really lovely, though. So friendly, so welcoming. I feel like I've come home. But I can't stay here, it's just sweltering. So I'm going to go out to that island Claire told me about until things cool down a bit. There's no way I'm doing sightseeing in this.'

'You're going to Ikaria?'

'Yep. Got my ticket for the night boat this evening.'

Kate's disquiet that Tilly was heading so quickly to the place of her own downfall was completely outweighed by relief that she was putting even more distance between herself and Jake's clutches. The further away she was from civilisation the better, as far as Kate was concerned. Even if it meant she had to be in Ikaria.

'Look after her, Martha,' Kate said under her breath after they had said their goodbyes.

'Emma! Lunchtime!' Beattie called from somewhere out on the landing.

'But she's insured, right? For the iPhone?' Beattie placed a giant turkey club sandwich in front of Kate.

'Yes. But it's the fact of being robbed. It's horrible. And she's going to have to survive without a phone now until we can get a new one to her.'

'Can't you just wire her the money to buy a new one?'

'Tilly wouldn't allow that. She's determined to be independent.'

'They are at that age, aren't they?'

'Too right.'

'I'm so jealous of her, being in Athens. Remember sitting up by the Acropolis, watching the dawn?'

'Areopagus Hill? Yes.' Kate recalled the closeness of Jake, how it hadn't been enough.

'It was our playground, wasn't it?'

'Yes. After we three met. But—'

'But what?'

'When I arrived, I was in a terrible state. I had a lonely couple of days.'

'Why were you in such a state, honey?' Beattie sat opposite her and leaned towards her, elbows on the worktop, slightly frowning, searching out Kate's eyes. But Kate didn't return her gaze; she could only keep looking at the ceiling down-lighters, to keep the tears at bay.

Was she just about to tell Beattie the thing she had never let slip to a single person, that she hardly ever admitted to herself? The story of what happened in that alleyway behind the youth hostel in Marseille? She splayed her fingers on the worktop and looked at the short, bitten nails on the red raw hands that no manicure could get on top of. She had tried false nails, but had just gnawed them off.

Finally, she breathed in, looked Beattie straight in the eye and nearly spoke. But, at the last minute, she lost her nerve: 'I just wasn't any good at being on my own.'

'Was that it?' Beattie said, as if somehow she had expected something else, something more.

'Yes.' Kate dropped her eyes. By not telling the full truth, she was betraying Beattie's offer of understanding. She hated doing that – it was another of the reasons she had never countenanced therapy, despite having been in need of it all her adult life. 'I'd been travelling for a while. It was my first time totally alone – I was so young, remember – two years younger than you.'

347

'Three,' Beattie said.

'Three, then. And I had no idea how lonely I would be.' Speaking about it was bringing it all back to her – her vulnerability, the memory of how lost she had been after the attack. She noticed that her hands were shaking. 'When I arrived in a place I was scared even to go out in the morning and find myself some bread. And the evenings were hell. If I went out for something to eat, there was always some guy pestering me, not willing to give up, giving me grief.'

Beattie moved round the kitchen island and put her arms around Kate. 'Poor honey. I know it. It was the same for me. I had sore hands from slapping them off!'

Kate leaned her head on Beattie's shoulder, giving in to her embrace. 'But you could tell them where to go. I just didn't know how to say no firmly enough.'

'Ah, the great British sense of reserve.'

'I just think now, looking back, I was hopelessly wet behind the ears.'

'I never saw you as being like that.'

'Not a good condition to be in for travelling solo, really.'

'I really liked you.'

'A recipe for disaster.'

'I'm just sorry I was such an asshole back then,' Beattie said. 'All that Dangerous Game crapola. Just a load of BS from a girl who came from somewhere too comfortable, too boring. I should have handed in those wallets I found. And stealing from those Brit kids, that was so far out of order. Unforgivable. I guess I was just trying to impress you in some way.'

'We all made mistakes, Beattie. We were all idiots.'

'Nah.' Beattie put her hand on Kate's cheek and held her face up so that she couldn't avoid her gaze. Her green eyes seemed to bore into her, almost hypnotising her. 'You were fine. You *are* fine. We're nearly through all this. I'll get my passport and ticket, I'll go back and work hard to pay off what I owe you—'

'Oh, you don't have to do that.'

'I do, though. Claire McCormack don't take no pay-outs,' she said, smiling. 'And then we'll be free to live the rest of our lives in peace. No more Jake trouble for you or for me. It'll be like a new beginning for both of us.'

Kate touched Beattie's hand, then broke free, sliding off the stool to raise a blind and let the pale spring sunshine into the kitchen.

All the things she wasn't telling Beattie.

Kate was growing a whole new hell garden of secrets to keep to herself. To her it felt less like a new beginning and more like being slowly lowered into a boiling caldera.

'Look. First sun we've seen for ages,' she said, turning to Beattie and painting a smile on her face.

'Must be a sign,' Beattie said. The smile she returned was full, honest and alight. 'We're nearly there, hun! Now, how about eating a bit of this lunch I've made for us?'

As soon as she could, Kate retreated to her office, where she only had to lie to herself.

She sat there, checking her emails every five minutes for word from Patience. In between, she either looked out of the windows or tormented herself by clicking through the Martha's Wish website and reading about all the charity's good works, all the children she would be stealing from.

Finally, as the setting sun stained the city skyline a yellowish pink, the message she had been waiting for pinged into her inbox.

Eagerly, she opened the attachment and leaned towards the screen to read it.

But, as her eyes ran over the figures, any hope she had felt was washed away. She had imagined vast millions of pounds coming into the charity as a result of the photograph. Everyone had been saying how well they had been doing. Indeed, the provisional end-of-year figures showed that the rise in donations had been five-fold compared to their usual donated income. But five-fold from last year's four hundred thousand pounds was only two million.

Kate scrunched up her face and rubbed at her cheekbones with her thumbs. 'Only' two million.

She scribbled the maths down on the pad she kept at the side of her desk.

With contingencies, it cost twenty-five thousand pounds for Martha's Wish to build one simple school. Project development and field costs took up another ten thousand per project. So, even with the UK admin and staff costs taken into consideration – which were mostly covered by Mark and Kate's own yearly tax-saving fifty-thousand-pound donation – the rise in funds meant that, if Martha's Wish had the infrastructure – which Kate knew they didn't – a further fifty-five schools could be built on top of the thirty they had already managed. Which would result in around eleven thousand more girls having their futures changed through not only education, but also provision of clean water and latrines.

Or it could be just over a third of what Jake was demanding from her.

Quickly, she picked up the phone and congratulated Patience on getting the report done so quickly.

'It's not so hard with the software Mark had installed for us,' she said.

'It's all in the reserve account?' Kate said.

'Yes.'

'I'm going to move it over to an account Mark's set up so that he can then buy the shares.'

Just for one beat, Patience didn't say anything. In that moment, Kate's cheeks turned from pink to scarlet. She knew what she was doing was wrong: really, really wrong, but she had no choice. And it wasn't like she was stealing the money. She was only borrowing it until she and Mark could sell the art.

There were lives at stake.

'It'll have to wait till the morning,' Patience said. 'I'll need to authorise it in office hours.'

'Sure,' Kate said, trying to sound cool about the delay. 'You'll do it first thing?'

'Of course.'

'And it's two million, right?'

'Yes.'

'Thanks, Patience. I'll send you an email to let you know it's gone.'

Kate hung up.

Then, in a gesture that was becoming something of a habit, she put her head on her keyboard.

Where was she going to find the other three million?

A noise behind her made her sit bolt upright.

'Oh, sorry, honey,' Beattie said from the doorway 'Are you still working? I didn't want to make you jump. I've fixed us a little supper. Do you want to come down and join me?'

Fifteen

'I've put three million dollars in your account,' Kate told Jake the next morning, after she had done the deed. That was what the Martha's Wish money converted to in dollars.

'Why thank you,' Jake said, his face as immobile as ever behind his great beard.

There was something different about him – at first Kate thought it must be coming from within him – a result of finding his family again, perhaps. But then she noticed that it was because the football posters and pennants behind him had disappeared. Instead, his backdrop was now pale and bare except for a brown and cream abstract geometric print. How had he moved all his stuff around? She supposed he had a carer who would have helped him. But why?

'But that's not enough, is it, Emma?'

'It's all I can put my hands on.'

Jake took in air through his tube then let go of a laugh so low and horrible it made Kate's bones vibrate.

'All you can put your hands on?' he said. 'You sit there in your fancy house in your fancy clothes and you tell me you don't have the wit – THE WIT – to raise a measly four and a half million dollars. That's just a dot in the ocean of your vast wealth, Emma, don't bullshit me.'

'You've got it all wrong, we're not as rich as you think, Mark's business is in trouble, and— '

'Oh, again, my heart bleeds.'

Once more, Kate felt that kernel of anger flare up inside – the sharp anger only Jake seemed able to ignite in her. 'You don't understand, Jake. I just don't have the money.'

'Raise it, then,' he said. 'Sell stuff.'

'It's complicated . . .'

'Seems simple to me. Simpler than your confession going viral. Simpler than poor Tilly going AWOL in Greece.'

Kate jolted as if he had reached out through the tangle of worldwide servers between them and slapped her round the face.

'AWOL in Greece, our old Alma Mater. I wonder which island she's visiting first?'

'How do you—?'

He wheezed wearily. 'Oh fuck, Emma, how many times do I have to go through this? There is nothing you or your family do that I will not know about. I have all the cards and I hold them to my chest until I want to play them. This situation will continue for the rest of our lives until you pay up, so please, do me a favour and just get your little stupid head around the idea.'

'Oh God. Oh God oh God oh God,' Kate heard herself say. Her breathing had become shallow. Black spots floated in front of her eyes. The windows of her office with their spiny cactus fingers pressed in on her, bearing down on her. Just before she blacked out, she thought she heard Jake say, 'I give you one more day.'

Sixteen

The ceiling looked like a wheel, with wooden beams radiating from a central point to a circular support on which the turret roof rested. She had never noticed it before, but then again she had never lain on her office floor like that, flat on her back.

One day. What difference would that make? She could pawn some of her jewellery and hope that Mark wouldn't notice. But that would only scratch the surface. The risk outweighed the benefits in a big way.

Then she remembered the full horror: Jake knew that Tilly was in Greece.

She crawled to her desk, knelt up and logged on to Facebook, pulling up Tilly's home page. Her relief at seeing that she had posted just the night before, when she got on the boat, was tempered by the chilling suspicion that this was how Jake had kept tabs on her. Tilly had over fourteen hundred friends. She couldn't possibly know them all in person. So her journey, from Gatwick to Athens, and now the fact that she was headed to Ikaria, were visible to all those people.

Kate opened up Tilly's friends list. Of course, there was no one called Jake Mithras. She scrolled down, examining the photographs, until she came to one she recognised all too well. A boy called Stephen Smith had long, dark, curled hair, the most beautiful, full, cupid's bow mouth and extraordinary eyes, as blue as the Aegean. A boy called Stephen Smith was Jake Mithras in better days.

Days before the fall.

Kate sent a friend request to 'Stephen Smith', to let him know she knew what his game was.

She logged out of her own account and tried to break into Tilly's, with the aim of un-friending him. She tried all the possible passwords she could think of, changing letters, adding significant dates. She tried Snowball – the name of Tilly's hamster when she was little – *Gwel an Mor*, the house in Cornwall, which she knew Tilly loved. None of them worked. Then she tried variations on a Martha theme, still with no luck.

It seemed that, unlike her tormentor, she had no knack for hacking.

She tried to Skype Tilly, but she was offline.

Slapping the table in frustration, she logged back on to her own account and, in desperation, sent Tilly a private message:

Tills. I have to ask you to stop talking about what you are doing on Facebook. I've just read this article about two recent cases of young people from wealthy families travelling in Greece being tracked down and kidnapped because of what they post. You need also to go through your friends list and delete anyone you've never met in person. It's nothing to worry about, but better safe than sorry.

She hoped that didn't sound too neurotic. She could imagine Tilly reading it and thinking she was just going off on one again.

She stood, closed her arms around herself, and looked out of the window. The sweet smell of a cake in the oven crept up the stairs and again, absurdly, she felt hungry. Or was it fear? It was hard to tell the origin of the coldness gnawing at her insides.

Both, possibly.

But what on earth was Beattie doing down there, baking again? Kate and Mark hardly ever ate sweet things, so whatever she was making would probably go to waste, without Tilly there to eat it.

Tilly.

Kate hoped she was safely on the ferry to Ikaria. She'd looked up the schedules online – how much easier it was now that you didn't have to stumble around a dockside to unearth that sort of information – and noted that the total journey could be up to twelve hours, depending on stopping points – faster than in 1980, but only just. If Tilly had managed to get on the night boat, she would still be en route. Kate couldn't imagine that they had Wi-Fi on Greek boats, so that would be why she wasn't available on Skype. She was probably just lying in the sun on deck, reading a book, enjoying herself, relaxing.

Kate started looking at travel websites, checking how long it would take her to get on a plane, fly out there, find Tilly and bring her back. Then she imagined the reception Tilly would give her when she arrived, and instantly dismissed the idea.

But, thanks to Facebook, Jake now knew exactly where Tilly was.

Kate tried to calm herself down. She checked Ikaria's size. How many cyber criminals would there be on a place like that with its population of just eight thousand, four hundred and twenty-three people? Would they even have Internet access there? But of course they would: she had found the population figure on the island's website.

But, of course, if Jake wanted to get to Tilly, he would find a way. It seemed that anything was possible for him.

For one crazy moment, she considered calling the police. But she couldn't. To do so would mean the end of everything. All her secrets would be out, everything would fall to pieces, and Tilly's world would be devastated.

No. Surely there were other, less damaging ways out of this?

She just had to find the money.

In one day.

One day to keep Tilly out of harm's way.

The thought made her mouth feel cold and dry.

Seventeen

She shook her body into action, pulled herself to her feet and ran downstairs to her bedroom.

'Everything all right, Emma?' Beattie called up the stairs.

'Fine, thanks,' she replied.

Even though Beattie was very adept at switching from one to the other, Kate wished she would call her by her new name. And to yell like that. What if Mark or Tilly came in unexpectedly and heard her calling her Emma?

But of course, neither Mark nor Tilly would do that, would they? They were both away. It was just Kate and Claire now. Or Emma and Beattie. They could shout out their old names to their hearts' content.

Kate went to her walk-in wardrobe and pulled out the drawer that concealed a safe containing her most precious jewellery.

She punched in the code – Martha's birth date – extracted her jewellery box, carried it through to the bedroom and tipped the contents out onto the bed. There was the white gold and diamond neckpiece that Mark had given her for Tilly's birth. It was so valuable, she hardly ever wore it. She could just pawn it rather than sell it, and when Mark sold the artworks, she could just slip off and buy it back. It would just be like a loan, Mark unwittingly buying his daughter's safety, in the same way that, through the charity money, Martha was looking after her sister.

She put the necklace to one side, along with a solitaire diamond ring with a stone so large she almost thought it a little vulgar and which had been Mark's present to her for her fortieth birthday. She had worn it only twice, so it would be extremely unlikely that he would notice its temporary absence. She looked at the delicate platinum and opal bangle he had commissioned to celebrate the day of Martha's birth. It, too, was worth a lot of money and she never, ever wore it for fear of losing it. But she put it back in the box. To run the risk – however small – of forfeiting that particular piece to a moneylender was too nightmarish to contemplate.

Keeping her selected items out, she returned the box to the safe and put the drawer back in front of it.

Then, grabbing her handbag from her dressing table, she pulled out her wallet and threw her credit cards on the bed. She had three. One gold and two platinum, all with high credit limits. She could raise a quarter of a million that way and the jewellery would probably pull in another seven hundred and fifty thousand. That made one million pounds, one and a half million dollars. One third of what she had to raise.

She threw the whole lot down on the bed, slumped down onto the floor and laid her head on the duvet cover.

It was hopeless.

She got up, pulled out the drawer again, opened the safe and, retrieving the jewellery box, once more tipped its entire contents onto the bed. There were ten remaining pieces, probably worth about another two million pounds, which would just about do it. She ran her fingers over the flawless stones of a slim, yellow diamond necklace that Mark had bought for her thirtieth, slipped on the diamond eternity ring he had given her when she set up Martha's Wish. Every single piece had a meaning, and she was loath to part with them, but, she reminded herself, they were just stuff. Just a means to an end. And what was at stake here, she knew in her heart, was Tilly's safety – something more precious to Kate than all the fine gemstones in the world.

There was a gentle knock at her bedroom door.

'Emma? Can I come in? I've brought you a whoopie pie— oh, my!'

Without waiting for an answer, Beattie had opened the bedroom door, and she stood there with a tray laden with the fat fruits of her morning's labour, her mouth open wide at the display of riches on the bed.

Kate scrabbled the lot together and put them back in the box.

'Wow, aren't they pretty?' Beattie said, coming over and peering in before Kate could shut the lid. 'Are these real?' She pointed at the yellow diamond necklace.

'Yes,' Kate said, closing the lid.

'Oh, please can I see?' Beattie said, sitting next to Kate on her bed, and putting the tray down at her side. 'I just love diamonds.'

Reluctantly, Kate opened the box and handed the necklace to Beattie. She didn't want to appear mean. 'I was just taking a look through them. They all mean so much to me.' The last thing she wanted was for Beattie to know what she was planning to do. She just wanted to get it all out of the way quietly and quickly, so that only she and Jake knew about it.

Beattie held the diamonds up to the light. 'So pretty. Did Mark buy them for you?'

Kate nodded and gestured to the jewellery box. 'He bought all of these. Each one has its own story, its own memories.'

'Tell me.' Beattie reached in the box for the large solitaire. 'Do you mind?' she said, slipping it on her finger, where it sat tightly.

'Not at all.' Kate handed each piece to Beattie, telling her why Mark had bought it.

'You are so, so, lucky, Emma,' Beattie said, looking down at the glittering mound of precious metal and stones piled in her lap. She started to put it all on – every ring, bangle, bracelet and neckpiece. 'What a catch that man was. You couldn't have asked for anything more for your life, could you?'

'I've been very fortunate.'

'Have a whoopie pie, honey. Celebrate your lot in life!'

Kate took one and bit into it. 'Nice,' she said, forcing herself to swallow the mouthful of cake.

'They're my specialty. The girls would always get so antsy when I was baking them. Though, of course, I have no one left to make them for now.' Beattie twirled in front of Kate's full-length mirror admiring the jewellery. 'So pretty.'

It wasn't right to wear all the lovely things at once and jumble them up together like that. She looked like a little girl dressing up. Kate wanted to tell her to take it all off and give it right back to her. Seeing all those memories twisting and turning in front of her made her feel uneasy, as if everything might suddenly fall off and disappear down cracks. Beattie held her jewel-encrusted fingers out to the mirror as though offering them for a suitor to kiss. Then she dropped her hand and looked round at Kate.

'Oh poor Emma. You don't look like yourself at the moment. What's eating you? You worried about little Tilly?' She sat on the bed and put her arm around her.

'I'm fine,' Kate said, trying not to let her shoulders stiffen and forcing a bright smile onto her face. 'Tills is fine – she's on a boat at the moment.'

'It's probably just a release after all that Jake stress, honey. I'm feeling it myself. But it's safely in the past now and we can truly relax.' Smiling, Beattie began to take the jewellery off, handing each piece to Kate, who put them back in the velvet-lined box.

'Hey, weird picture,' she said, nodding at the Rothko when everything had been put away.

'Isn't it? It's Mark's really. All the artworks are his. I could happily live without any of them.'

'Thank God his taste in jewels is finer than his taste in pictures,' Beattie said, and, despite herself, Kate smiled.

'Where do you keep it all?' Beattie asked, taking one last look at Kate's glittering hoard before she closed the box. 'I mean, it must be worth millions.'

Kate showed Beattie the safe and made a show of putting the jewellery away as if she wasn't going to take it out and pawn it the minute her friend's back was turned.

Eighteen

It was impossible to shake Beattie off. After putting the jewellery in the safe, Kate tried telling her that she had to work. But Beattie insisted she needed a break because she looked so 'awful done in'. Unwilling to seem too desperate to get away, Kate let Beattie lead her downstairs to the kitchen, where there was another almighty mess which needed clearing up.

Kate felt obliged to help. In any case, Beattie's idea of clean would probably mean she'd only have to do it all again if she let her do it herself.

But all the while she was desperate to get away and deal with the jewellery and the credit cards. After all, she had a tight deadline. Beattie made coffee for herself and a cup of tea for Kate, then sat her in front of another damn whoopie pie.

When Beattie tottered outside to the terrace to have a cigarette, Kate slipped the plates and mugs into the dishwasher and primed herself to be firm and make her exit. When Beattie returned, the stink of cigarette smoke wafting in with her as she closed the door, Kate straightened up and steeled herself.

'I've got to go to work now. I really have. I need to write the blog post for this week, and I have to pick some stuff up

363

from the dry cleaners.' Lies, all lies, she knew that. But wasn't that her forte? Her own special skill? 'Will you be all right on your own for a couple of hours?'

'Oh sure, honey. I'll be fine. I was thinking of taking a little siesta myself. I've baked myself quite into exhaustion this morning.'

It turned out to be that easy to get rid of her.

Kate almost ran up to her bedroom. Yet again, she went through the whole rigmarole of pulling out the drawer, keying in the safe code and retrieving the box of jewellery. She scooped her credit cards up from the bed, grabbed her handbag and, clutching box and cards, climbed quickly up to her turret office.

Logging into the various credit cards, she paid the cash advance limit for each into Jake's fake Stephen Smith account, taking the precaution of leaving a ten-thousand-pound buffer on one, because at that moment she had no access to any cash whatsoever, and Mark might start asking questions if she couldn't afford to buy food.

Then, using Google, she quickly found Mayfair Advances, a company just off Bond Street who pawned valuable items and provided instant valuations and payment through direct bank transfer. Gathering her stuff, she tiptoed hurriedly down the stairs, passing the guest floor with extra caution for fear of waking Beattie. In the hallway she pulled on her coat then ran through the needling rain to the main road, where she hailed a cab.

The pawnbrokers looked like a jewellery shop from the outside. Kate paid the taxi driver and, with her box of valuables clasped to her chest, she ran inside the building.

As she burst through the door, the two men inside both looked up at her from behind a glass security screen. She sensed that, on her entry, the mood in the room had changed from relaxed to *en pointe*. She stood there blinking for a few seconds, her eyes acclimatising to the change from the gloom of a wet spring afternoon to an interior so brightly lit and crammed with shining surfaces and lustrous items that it hit her pupils like acid. The smell of burning tungsten, new carpets and money threatened to overwhelm her.

Then she realised what she must look like. What had she been thinking? In her rush to get out and do the deed, she had forgotten to prepare for this meeting. Her hair was unbrushed and she wore no make-up. Under her good cashmere coat, she still wore her tracksuit. It had actually been rather expensive, but, nevertheless, it wasn't an outfit she would ever be seen out and about in. And, to her horror, she realised that she still had her sheepskin slippers on – a daytime look perhaps Tilly could pull off, but not at all becoming on a woman of Kate's age.

She saw herself through the eyes of the two men and realised that they had every right to be on their guard.

She drew herself up to her full five feet and one inch, smiled with as much confidence as she could muster and looked levelly at them. She was, she told herself, the wife of Mark Barratt, wealthy hedge-fund manager. She was the Face of Kindness – not that she was recognisable as such in her current rain-bedraggled manifestation.

'Good afternoon,' she said. 'I have some items I would like to – um – lodge with you for a short while.'

Her inner pep talk must have worked, because one of the men leaned his elbows on the counter behind the glass screen and smiled. 'Welcome to Mayfair Advances.'

When Kate opened the jewellery box and he had sight of the contents, his entire body language changed from formal to fluid.

'Please,' he said, rising to unlock the door that allowed

access behind the security barriers. 'Come to our back room. It is far more comfortable.'

So on an unbelievably squishy white leather sofa and with a glass of mint tea, Kate sat sweating as the man – who had introduced himself as Ali – leaned over a desk peering at her beautiful jewellery through a jeweller's loupe.

At one point, Kate's phone beeped with a message. It was Jake. So he had her mobile number. Of course.

How's it going, Ems? You have 20 hrs.

She switched off the phone and put it at the bottom of her bag.

Ali logged each piece of jewellery on a computer and, when he was finished, sent the results to print.

'Here,' he said, handing her the printout. 'This is what we can advance you.'

Kate looked at the sheet of paper. Without her glasses, the figures were like ants crawling all over the page. She screwed her eyes up tight and looked again, holding it away from her so that she could read it.

'Oh,' she said when she saw how much they were willing to pay out for all of her beautiful things, all of her memories, part of her soul, if such a thing existed. 'Seven hundred and fifty thousand pounds?'

Ali smiled and nodded. 'Is very lovely jewellery.'

It was two million less than she had hoped. Two million less than she needed to keep her daughter safe.

'You can't advance more?'

Ali made an apologetic face and shrugged. Kate had never been good at haggling. Even now, even now, when the stakes were so high, she couldn't bring herself to argue. Without the time to shop around, she had no alternative other than to agree. She would think of something. On top of the money

366

from her credit cards, it meant that Jake could at least have another million pounds or one point five million dollars. That might put him off for a little longer while she worked something else out.

The disappointments continued to pile up: she had hoped that the payment could be made directly into Jake's bank, but Mayfair Advances' policy was only to pay into bank accounts where ID was available, so she had to direct it to her own. It was tempting fate, putting another mystery sum through her joint bank account with Mark, but she had no choice.

As soon as Ali had transferred the sum and given Kate printed confirmation, she ran out of the shop and hailed another cab to take her to her bank. She had pawned all her best jewellery and had three months to come up with the money to buy it back, plus another thirty-five thousand pounds interest. Perhaps she should have felt lighter because she was another million on the way to paying Jake off, but instead a weight sat on her chest as heavy as a coffin.

With the Mayfair Advances money transferred successfully into Jake's account – something that was, despite her dishevelled appearance, easy to achieve, because her bank already knew his account number and why she was paying into it – Kate stumbled out onto the wet, grey street.

The rain had been so persistent that the drains had backed up in the street outside and were pumping swelling lakes up onto the pavements. Some side streets looked more like rivers than roads. Kate stood there among all the water, empty, emptied out. It was four in the afternoon and she was as hungry as a wolf. Smelling chicken, she turned and spied a Nando's across the road.

She stumbled into the restaurant, asked to be seated near the back, facing out, and ordered a double chicken burger and chips and a bottle of the house red. She ate silently, hardly looking up from her meal. Halfway through – so much food took her a long time to eat, and needed a lot of washing down – she ordered another bottle of wine.

'Are you sure, honey?' her waitress asked, shaking her black, glossy curls like a schoolteacher. The term of endearment reminded Kate of Beattie, and she wondered briefly if she would be worrying where she had got to. The moment passed.

'I am completely sure,' she said, facing up to the waitress, trying not to slur.

The woman rolled her eyes and stalked off, her unfeasibly large and lifted rump straining against the polyester of her uniform.

The second bottle was placed at Kate's side without the flourish that had accompanied the first. Kate doubted that, had she been a man, she would have received the same cool-handed treatment.

Later, after downing a gooey caramel cheesecake, Kate wobbled out onto the street. It was the tail end of rush hour. Weary office workers – the ones that stayed on late – formed the dregs of a throng around the tube station. Drunk on wine, sugar and carbohydrates, Kate stumbled dangerously out into the road and hailed a cab.

Nineteen

She let herself into the house and ran up to the kitchen, her feet out of control due to the wine, her mouth still ringing from the extra hot dressing she had chosen for the burger, her stomach in rebellion against the largest amount of food it had ever seen.

Beattie was sitting on the sofa, very still, very upright. A bucket lay on its side on the shiny white floor in a pool of dirty water, its mop toppled over to one side. Even in her befuddled state, Kate registered that this looked odd.

'Hey, Beattie, sorry,' Kate said, trying to think up an excuse for having spent such an inordinately long time on a trip to the dry cleaners. 'I got delayed, there was this terrible accident on the bridge: a bus and a taxi, and—'

'I'm sorry, Kate,' Beattie said, cutting across her. Kate focused her blurry gaze on her face and saw that her eyes were red, her cheeks blotched. 'I'm so, so sorry,' Beattie went on.

Black dots shot through Kate's vision. 'Tilly?' she blurted, standing there swaying in the kitchen doorway. Her full stomach seemed to help her stay conscious through the shock, through the dreaded fact that, in her drunken state, she already knew to be true. 'Something's happened to Tilly, hasn't it?'

Beattie just cupped her hands in front of her mouth and shook her head slightly.

Kate couldn't work out whether this meant that it wasn't to do with Tilly, or that whatever had happened to her was so awful she couldn't bring herself to say what it was.

Then she noticed the suitcase, overcoat and briefcase sitting on the kitchen floor to her right.

'Mark's back?' she said, her mind reeling. 'But he should be in New York for another two days. Where is he?'

'Upstairs,' Beattie said, looking at the ceiling.

Her heart pounding, Kate tore up to the bedroom. 'Mark?' she cried. 'Mark? What's happened to Tilly?'

He wasn't there. But the bedroom appeared to have been ransacked – Kate's drawers were emptied, their contents strewn across the room; the mattress had been flung back from the bed and the safe stood open, displaying its emptiness to the room.

'Mark?' she cried, stumbling up the steps to the mezzanine yoga room. But he wasn't there, either.

She darted out onto the landing. 'Mark!' she screamed at the top of her lungs, breaking her voice, cracking her throat.

'I'm up here,' he said into the silence above her.

Kate grabbed the banister rail to steady herself. Otherwise she might have fallen down the stairs.

Mark was up in her office.

She scrabbled up the curving staircase and burst through the door. He was sitting at her computer with the financial aggregator application open in front of him. He swung round in the office chair and fixed his eyes on hers.

She hardly recognised him. The laughter lines had been wiped from his face. His expression was entirely cold and neutral. He looked at her as if she, too, were some sort of stranger.

A dark, fiery sensation roared somewhere deep inside her. For a disorienting second, she believed it to be overwhelming sexual desire. But then she realised it was terror. Sheer terror.

She had been found out.

But still a hopeful voice bleated inside her: *But by how much?*

'Where has all my money gone?' Mark said, his voice like ice.

'I – I moved it into the offshore account . . .'

He held up his hand. 'That's pathetic, Kate. Do you think I can't call our bank to find out that you sent it to someone called Stephen Smith? And the seven hundred and fifty thousand you sent the same way today? Which, I find out when I look in our safe, you must have raised from selling all my presents to you, all my tokens of love.'

'I – I set the account up in an assumed name.'

'Don't bullshit me, Kate. The money went out of our cash accounts before I even told you we were in trouble. And as for the money you've stolen from Martha's Wish . . .'

Kate gasped.

'Oh, didn't you know I knew about that? I'm sorry. You see, late last night UK time, Patience rang me. She wanted to double-check the ethical credentials of the "investment opportunity" I had apparently planned for the surplus. I don't know: perhaps she smelled a rat. You can imagine what a situation her phone call put me into – and all while I'm failing to sweet-talk Manhattan dickheads into letting me keep their money. I had to pretend I knew what she was talking about, spin some bullshit tale about how marvellously ethical this mythical fund is.'

Kate closed her eyes.

Mark was silent. Then he breathed in and spoke. The rhythm of it reminded her horribly of Jake.

'What the hell do you think you're playing at? Do you know what would happen if it got out that you've embezzled funds from Martha's Wish? Do you want to totally ruin me? CAN YOU IMAGINE WHAT YOU HAVE PUT ME THROUGH?'

'I – I –' Kate stood in the middle of her office, her mouth opening and closing like that of a fish pulled out of water.

She wanted to go to him and coax the old Mark back, to let him take her and comfort her so that she could cry onto his broad chest and be protected from the world.

He moved towards her, sniffing at her like a tiger might its prey. 'You stink of shit food and cheap wine.' He looked at her, one side of his upper lip raised in disgust. 'You're drunk, aren't you?'

'No,' Kate said, trying to keep the slackness out of her voice. Her ears were ringing so loudly with alarm and alcohol that she could hardly hear herself speak. 'I just had one glass.'

'More lies,' he said. 'And here's something.' In one swift movement, he grabbed her arm and pulled up the sleeve of her jumper, exposing her Triskelion tattoo. 'When I got in, Claire was cleaning the floor. Very nice of her to do that for you while you were out. She had her sleeves rolled up.'

He was hurting her arm, gripping it so tightly that she knew he would leave bruises.

'The money was puzzling enough. But this completely mystified me. Why would two school friends who allegedly haven't seen each other since they were seventeen have the same weird tattoo in the same place? And how strange that these two women should "just by chance" bump into each other just before all my money disappears from my bank accounts.'

Our money, Kate found the clarity in her whirling mind to think. *Our* bank accounts.

But she didn't dare correct him out loud.

'Shall I tell you what I think?' he said, moving so close that she could feel the heat of his breath. 'Shall I? I think you and Claire have a thing.'

'What?' Kate spluttered. The idea was so absurd that she nearly laughed.

'That's what I think. You were never at school together. I don't know and I don't care where you met, but what I think is that you're planning to leave me for her, but you thought that, just to add extra pain to my life, you'd clean me out before you disappeared.'

'But it's not true!'

'I nearly caught you at it the other day when I came in for that awful fried dinner she cooked, didn't I?'

'NO!'

Mark waved his hands in the air. '"Sorry, Mark. I was having a liddle moment and Kate was looking after me." I'll BET YOU WERE LOOKING AFTER HER.'

'This is crazy, Mark, I—'

Mark loomed over her, yelling now, the tendons standing out on his neck. 'Is it? Is it? Dear little Claire loves you so much she had a little tattoo done, just like yours, "Honey".'

Kate shook her head in frustration. The room spun around her as if she were on a roundabout in its centre.

'Well what, then? Why did you start moving money away before you knew I was in trouble? Why have you STOLEN from Martha's Wish? Desecrated our daughter's memory? Money that was safe from any threat of my business collapsing? Why have you sold the most precious things I gave you? Why have you both got the same tattoo?' He let go of her, grabbed a notebook from her desk and threw it on the floor between them. 'And what's this?' he said, pointing at the words in front of her.

She looked down. She didn't need to get any closer. There, in her own handwriting, was the list she had written the other night:

- *Plead with Jake*
- *Expose Jake*
- *Tell Mark*
- *Kill self*
- *Kill Jake*

'And do you know who I think Jake is? He's Claire's poor husband, isn't he? Oh, "Ed this" and "Ed that". It's all so much bullshit, isn't it?'

'This is all wrong!' Kate said, putting her hands over her ears and shaking her head so violently that she felt her brain move in her skull.

'Bloody right it is.'

'I can explain—' Kate reached out to touch his arm and he flinched as if she had burned him.

He closed his eyes and exhaled, as if trying to calm himself down. Then he moved back to her office chair, sat down and folded his arms. 'Go on, then.'

'What?'

'Explain. It had better be good.'

Kate put both her hands out, searching for walls to support herself. The circular room had none, and the windows were too far away and obstructed by sharp cacti. Could she explain? Could she? Where would she start? That the person she had presented to Mark all of their life together was a fiction?

Unable to think, unable to prop herself up, she sank to her knees, put her hands flat on her thighs and looked down, like a medieval penitent.

'I – I can't.'

Mark sat back in his chair. He was strangely calm now, as if his anger had been a storm that had swept right through him. 'You *won't*, you mean.'

'No,' she said, so quietly that she didn't know if he heard it.

'I don't understand you, Kate,' he said. 'I've given you everything. I've shared everything I earn with you. You haven't had to lift a finger to enjoy this very comfortable life I've allowed you. You've just sat there, looking all decorative with your expensive clothes and your fucking yoga and your delicate fucking sensibilities and your little hobby charity.'

'That's not fair!'

'NOT FAIR? NOT FAIR? I've put up with all your lunatic shit for far too long. All the agoraphobic, obsessive-compulsive cleaning, overprotective mothering, anorexic crap.'

'What?' Kate said, looking sharply up at him.

'Yeah. I called you out, didn't I? You don't like that, do you? I've let you get away with murder in the last ten or so years. That little-girl-lost act was beginning to wear a bit thin with me, if you must know.

'You are a monster, Kate. Monstrously selfish. Monstrously ungrateful. Have you looked at yourself recently? You're a complete fucking mess. But then I suppose you don't have to bother about how you look for old Claire, do you? I mean it's not like she's much of an oil painting, is she?'

'For God's sake, there's nothing going on between me and B— Claire.'

'You can age into a couple of unlovely old dykes together.'

'Listen to me,' she pleaded.

'I mean, let's face it, Kate, you've really been just going through the motions of being my wife, haven't you?'

'What do you mean?'

'You've never really enjoyed sex, have you?'

'But I love you!' From her kneeling position, she reached for his hands, but he jumped up and recoiled from her as if she had some infectious disease.

'You have a fine way of showing it,' he said.

'Please, Mark, please.' Kate put her forehead on the rug and wrapped her arms around her head. She could hear the floor creak as he paced up and down in front of the door. For one minute she thought about her journals, which were right underneath where she was kneeling. All she needed to do was lift the floorboard and show him the truth. But she couldn't. She didn't have the courage.

After what seemed like her whole lifetime, his pacing stopped. She lifted her head to find him watching her.

'I really don't know what your problem is, Kate,' he said. 'Perhaps you've had some sort of breakdown. Perhaps you've gone a little crazy. But do you know what? With all your bullshit, I find I don't really care. I've had enough of looking after you.

'Here's the thing. You're going to repay the money you owe the charity, and you will pay me back every single penny you have stolen from me. After that, I want nothing more to do with you. You and your – whatever she is – can go off and do whatever the fuck you want.'

'I can't pay back the money,' Kate said. She wanted the floor to rise up on either side of her and swallow her up. She wanted to disappear, to die.

'You haven't spent it already, have you?'

'I can't get the money back.'

Mark knelt in front of her and held her chin, forcing her to look him in the eye. 'You damn well will pay it back, or I'll expose you as the woman who stole from the charity she ran. I will publicly disown you and I will drag you and that – that – monster downstairs down with you. Who knows, you two might even end up having fun together in Prisoner Cell Block H.'

Kate tried desperately to assemble her options. She could still come clean, tell him the entire truth. But even though he had managed to spin an entirely improbable case out of a few random, devastating discoveries, she couldn't imagine he would buy the actual facts. She grasped at the only straw still available to her: the partial truth.

'I'm being blackmailed,' she said. 'If I don't pay this man Stephen Smith money, he's going to harm Tilly.'

'Dragging our daughter into it? How low can you go?' With a sneer of disgust, Mark pushed her down, so she tumbled to the floor. He jumped to his feet and moved away from her, knotting his fists together as if he were holding himself back from striking her. 'Tilly? Who posted a picture of herself on Facebook just two hours ago, looking relaxed, happy and tanned?'

'Did she?' Kate's heart leaped, relief strangely intruding into her torment. 'Oh, thank God.'

'Very good, Kate,' Mark said, folding his arms and looking at her. 'Good acting.'

She knelt back up to face him. 'He hasn't got to her yet, but he will if I don't pay up.'

'Oh, don't give me this, Kate. Why on earth would this "Stephen Smith" want to blackmail you?'

It was the question she couldn't answer. 'He knows how wealthy we are.'

'How wealthy I am, you mean.'

'You've always said we share everything.'

Mark squatted so that his eyes – these new, cold eyes full of hate and hurt – were level with hers. 'Not any more, we don't. And if your bullshit story were to stun us all and be the truth, then why did he come to you and not me? He'd know that you're just the little wifey, no real clout. Lots of men in my position don't allow their wives access to any of their money. I was a fool to have been so trusting with you.'

'It was the Face of Kindness . . .'

This was too much for him. He lunged forward and grabbed her face so hard that she tasted blood where her teeth cut into the insides of her cheeks.

'Now you're really clutching at straws, Kate. Face of Kindness? Face of Betrayal more like.' As if afraid of what he might do to her, he pushed her away again and moved towards the door. 'I give you one week to get the money back to me.'

She scrambled to her feet. 'Where are you going?'

He turned and looked at her. 'A hotel.'

'What?'

'A hotel. Right now, Kate, I can't bear the sight of you.'

And he left, slamming the office door behind him, leaving her ears ringing with the sound.

She stood in the middle of the room. For the second time in her life, her world was in tatters, everything drained away. And would Mark talk to Tilly? Would she lose her as well?

Tilly. He said she had posted on Facebook.

She fell across the floor to her desk and logged in to her computer account. Mark had been using guest access to look at their money, which meant that he hadn't been able to see the emails between her and Jake, the record of Skype calls, the YouTube link.

Perhaps it might have been better if he had, though. Things between them couldn't be any worse.

She opened Facebook. Noticing that she had no messages in reply to those she had sent to Tilly and to Jake's pseudonym, she clicked straight onto Tilly's wall. There, indeed, was a beautiful photograph of her, standing on the deck of a ferry. Mark was right. She looked entirely happy. Behind her was a long concrete harbour wall from which rose two gigantic soaring metal fretwork wings which, because of the angle of the photo, looked like they were attached to Tilly's shoulders. On the wall, painted large, was the word Ικαρία – Greek for Ikaria.

So she had arrived. Kate clasped her hands in front of her and prayed to a God she dare not believe in that her daughter would be safe.

Then the thought struck her.

Who the hell had taken that photograph?

Twenty

Eventually, Kate stepped wearily down the stairs to face Beattie, who was still sitting on the sofa. The smell of cigarettes hung heavily in the air, but Kate was beyond caring.

'Mark left,' Beattie said, gesturing to the empty space where his bags once stood. 'He didn't say a word to me, but he wasn't happy.'

Kate nodded and sat next to her. 'I owe you an explanation,' she said, and she told her about Jake's further demands, that he knew where Tilly was, and that she had pawned her jewellery and borrowed the money from the charity.

'But that's a terrible thing to do,' Beattie said, putting her hands over her mouth.

'You're not going to start judging me too, are you?' Kate said. 'You're the only person I've got left in the world and you're judging me.'

'Oh, I'm not, honey.' Beattie put her hand on Kate's knee. 'I know you've been under a lot of pressure. It just must have been hideous for you. I wish you would have told me what was going on.'

'I didn't want to scare you or upset you. You've been through so much.'

'Oh, but look at what you've had to do all on your own, when I could have supported you.' She ran her hand down Kate's hair. 'You've been so brave.'

Kate edged away from Beattie's touch. 'And Tilly's posted this photo on Facebook and I think one of Jake's "friends" may have taken it. What if he's got Tilly? I'm still two million down and don't have an idea what to do.'

Beattie looked around at the walls. 'Could you sell a couple of these god-awful pictures?'

'I can't rip Mark off any more. He'll go ballistic.'

'Sounded like he already has.'

'God, could you hear him from down here?'

Beattie nodded. 'And I could hear what he was accusing us of.'

The two women looked at each other and then, absurdly, they both started to laugh. They laughed until the tears rolled down their faces, until Kate thought she might be doing her heart some damage.

When it was all over, and they were lying, splayed at different angles across the sofa, Kate looked at Beattie. It was as if the hilarity had completely sobered her.

'I need to talk to Jake. Fast.'

Twenty-one

'But it's all I can manage,' Kate said, trying to chase the whine from her voice.

Jake sat immobile, his blue, blue eyes regarding her like a monitor lizard viewing its prey. Again, the wall behind him seemed to have changed. This time it was pale and there was a pair of long curtains in the middle, presumably masking some sort of French windows. He was moving himself and his equipment around an awful lot.

'Like I said, it's not enough,' he said, wheezing through his breathing machine. 'Poor little Tilly. She's so happy at the moment, I hear.'

'Please,' Kate said. She pressed her right fist into her other palm, grinding it around in the bones of her hand, half praying, half stabbing. 'Haven't you got enough to be going on with? Can't I have a bit longer?'

'No,' Jake said, and the screen went blank as he disconnected himself.

'The bastard,' Beattie said from the doorway, making Kate jump.

'I don't know what to do now,' Kate said, sitting back in

382

the chair, her eyebrows high on her forehead, her eyes round with disbelief. Could anything else go wrong?

'Are you *sure* he's got Tilly?' Beattie said, looking as agonised as Kate felt. The only good thing left in the world was that she was there to share her pain.

'I don't know. I don't know anything.'

'You've got to find out, honey. Perhaps he's just making idle threats.'

'He doesn't make idle threats. You of all people should know that.'

'Has she been in touch?'

'I'll check again.' Kate turned again to her computer and pulled up Facebook. Frowning, she typed and clicked, typed and clicked. 'What's going on?'

'What?' Beattie said, peering over her shoulder.

'She's not there. My Tilly Barratt isn't there any more.'

'No!'

'She'd never shut her profile down. Facebook is her lifeline.'

'You've got a message, look,' Beattie said, pointing at the screen.

Kate clicked on it. 'Stephen Smith' had accepted her friend request. He had also sent her a private message.

Dear 'Kate', it said.

Poor Tilly has dropped her iPad and it's all cracked and not working. I thought it better, in view of your concerns for her safety, that she removed her profile altogether. She didn't buy the line about kidnappers, though. She wondered what sort of mug you took her for, or words to that effect. Anyway, she is safe and well and in my good care and control, but she won't be any of those things by the end of the week unless

you give me my missing cash. Or items to the value of. Then
I can hand Tilly back to you, and all the nastiness can be
forgotten.

All my love

'Stephen'

Kate looked up at Beattie, who was still reading, her lips
moving as her eyes grazed over Jake's words.

'It sounds like he's out there,' she said at last when she had
finished.

'Where?'

'Ikaria.'

'But how can that be possible?' Kate thought about the
changing backgrounds of the rooms Jake had been in recently.
'He couldn't make that journey with all his breathing equipment
and big wheelchair and everything, could he?'

Beattie shrugged. 'He is a force of nature.'

'And how could he harm Tilly, the state he's in?' Kate went
on. 'I've got to go out there, haven't I? Buy my daughter back
from him, or whoever's got her out there. But how? I've got
nothing left.'

'How about that red and orange painting in your bedroom?'

'The Rothko?' Kate knew it was worth at least what Jake
wanted – if not more. And, on a purely practical level, it was
small enough to take on a plane.

'If that's what it is.'

It would, as she'd already told Beattie, send Mark ballistic.

But, actually, what did that matter now? She had lost him,
as far as she could see, completely and forever. So she might as
well be hung for a sheep as for a lamb. It could end up with her

being charged with theft and imprisoned, which would probably mean her full identity would be outed. But at least Tilly would be safe, and that was the most important thing in the world to Kate, more important than her reputation, her freedom, or her life.

She turned to her computer and typed a message to 'Stephen Smith': *I'm coming. Where do I find Tilly?*

The reply came almost instantly: *Use your brain, Emma. And come alone. Ditch the bitch.*

Twenty-two

In her desperation to get to Greece more quickly, Kate was through security at Gatwick two hours before her flight was due to leave. She spent the time in duty free, covering herself in perfume trials and availing herself of enough free tots of hideously sweetened and artificially vanilla-flavoured whisky-based drinks to give her Dutch courage, but not so many as to make her lose her head and mislay her small portfolio containing the Rothko and the old map of Ikaria, which she had retrieved from among her 1980 journals.

When she pulled the tattered volumes from their hiding place under her office floor, she had once again sat with them in her hands, bracing herself to open them. It would have been useful to reread the sections she had written while on the island, just to refresh her memory of the geography. But, once again, she couldn't face looking at the words of the girl who had landed her in all this. In any case, she told herself, there was no need to look it up: every detail was still laser-etched on her mind.

The hypnotist she had consulted to help with her fear of flying for Africa taught her a breathing trick to put herself to sleep for the dreaded take-off and landing. But, with her current state of mind, it failed to work, so she endured a gut-wrenching half-hour as the plane slowly taxied to its take-off point, and another ten minutes of hell as the plane rose steeply past the airport car parks and into the thick and bumpy English cloud. But then cabin service came round and, with the portfolio tucked safely underneath her feet, she ordered two little bottles of gin and one tonic. On top of the free flavoured whisky and a couple of pills it was enough. The plane sliced through the sky over the Thames Estuary, and, despite her high levels of stress, she managed to fall asleep in a Jo Malone-scented alcoholic cocoon. She only came back to her senses over the sand-fringed islands off the Croatian coast.

But by the time she had endured the landing at Athens airport, she was itching with it all again. She was desperate to get to Ikaria. She could have jumped in a taxi to Piraeus and taken the night boat. But if she waited for the plane that left the following day, she would arrive sooner. If things had been different, if she hadn't fucked everything up with Mark, if she had done it better and been honest with him, they might have arrived together and he would have chartered a small plane to get them out there immediately.

She pulled herself together. If she had been honest with Mark, she wouldn't be in this situation at all.

Over the long hours of the night before her flight, she tried to contact Mark four times, in an attempt to tell him – somehow – what she was doing. But she couldn't get through. Like Tilly's Facebook profile, his number was suddenly unavailable. She wasn't even able to text or leave a message.

'What's going on?' she had asked Beattie, holding her phone to her ear as they sat up into the small hours, emptying three bottles of wine.

'Perhaps he's blocked you?' Beattie said, shrugging.

So Kate was doing this whole thing on her own. Apart from Beattie, who was back in Battersea, manning the phones in case of emergencies, her meagre network of friends and contacts and support had evaporated completely.

She used her one remaining solvent credit card to pay for a room in the Sofitel, just a short, sweltering walk across the road from the airport. As she wove her way through murderously fast yellow taxis plying their trade outside arrivals, she registered the undeniably magnificent feel of the Greek sun on her face. The sparkling quality of the light, too, even in the aviation-fuelled atmosphere of the airport, was like nothing found in London.

To economise, once she had checked into her room and realised how much the mini-bar was going to cost, she went back to the airport to buy a cheap bottle of wine from a shop selling Greek specialities to departing tourists. She looked at a stall selling various dehydrated-looking sandwiches and decided against them. In any case, she was still full from the Nando's blowout the evening before.

The only thing she needed to concentrate on was the safety of her daughter.

She quickly drank the entire bottle of what turned out to be an astringent yet syrupy wine and, with the help of a couple more pills, managed to find two or three hours of restless sleep in her airless room with its locked-shut windows. So efficient was the soundproofing that, instead of jets landing and taking off on the runways outside, what distracted her all night was the empty, tinnitus silence in her post-flight ears.

She felt terrible the next morning in the domestic departures lounge. The heat haze over the runway just made her feel even dizzier, and her fellow travellers – who, from their neighbourly chattering, she took to be islanders returning home after visiting the mainland – made her feel all the more lonely and isolated. Only one other passenger sat alone like her – a youngish man with, she noticed, an American passport. Scruffy, slightly overweight and in dark glasses, but for the passport he could have passed for a Greek. Kate strongly suspected that he could be one of Jake's contacts, so she kept well away from him, while also holding him in her sights at all times. She clutched her portfolio as if it were her baby, which, in a way, it was.

There was a coffee counter at the gate from which her plane was due to depart. After debating with herself, Kate finally bought a Greek coffee. A *metrio* – she remembered the word – a medium. Powdery and sweet, it had the power to make her feel like she was eighteen again. But not in a good way.

It was only when the airport bus had transported her and her twenty fellow travellers to the far end of the airport, past all the 747s and jet-powered planes, that she realised that the aircraft flying them fifty minutes across to the eastern Aegean was, frighteningly, almost toy-like in its proportions.

The bus drew up beside the propeller-driven plane and Kate's knees nearly buckled as she and her fellow passengers were guided across the tarmac in a genial but lackadaisical fashion. The worst of it was that, when she took her seat, she discovered that it was right up against the delicate, whirring blades that somehow – she didn't like to dwell on the details – would be carrying her up into the blue, blue, blue sky. But this unnerving thought was far outweighed by the fact that, sitting directly across the aisle from her, was the scruffy young American.

As the plane headed out across the sea, she didn't feel as nervous as she had thought she might. Perhaps it was because they were flying so low that she could easily pick out the waves and fishing boats beneath her. More likely, though, it was because she was on the last stage of her journey to save her daughter. The sense of purpose fortified her, while at the same time the tangible danger and urgency of Tilly's situation put the threat of being involved in a highly unlikely, hypothetical air crash into stark proportion.

So she turned her worry towards the American, who, she thought, was staring at her when she wasn't looking. At any rate, she felt observed by him, and, she had to remind herself, it wouldn't be because he found a haggard fifty-year-old woman attractive.

As the plane rounded the north-east corner of the island, readying itself to approach a tiny runway, Kate illogically strained for a sight of Tilly, or at least the rock where she had left Jake for dead.

She couldn't see either, of course. Besides, squaring up the old map with what she could see out of the window, it seemed that the airport – which had been added since the map had been drawn – was at the opposite end of the long, thin island to the bluff from which she had pushed him.

Stumbling off the plane, glad to put her feet on the same ground as Tilly's, she hurried across the wind- and sun-scarred runway into the tiny arrivals hall, where she came up against a larger-than-life, carved olive-wood figure of Icarus, wings melted, caught in mid-fall. Not a great sculpture for an airport, perhaps, but as an expression of how Kate felt at that very moment, it was surprisingly apt.

A rotund black-clad woman rushed through into the arrivals hall and embraced the American, showering him with kisses. So he was a returning grandson, then, and not part of Jake's international dangerous geek squad. Kate exhaled in relief and allowed herself to sit and hug her portfolio while she endured what seemed like an interminable wait for the baggage handlers to move twenty suitcases thirty metres from the plane to the arrivals hall.

Amazingly, the car-hire guy she had contacted by email the evening before, who had asked for no deposit and no advance driving-licence details, was there, waiting for her, with a sign saying MRS KATE.

Kate was glad this sweet young man had no idea what she was going to get up to in his vehicle. She thought about the sharp Henckels kitchen knife she had tucked deep inside her hold baggage. She had wanted to take the biggest in her collection, but she hadn't been able to find it. So, instead, she had packed her razor-edged boning knife.

She had readied herself as much as she could. She was prepared for anything to happen, so long as Tilly was safe.

After a mercifully brief exchange of details – car-hire guy wanted no imprint of credit card, no passport, and only a driving-licence number – she set off, reminding herself repeatedly to drive on the right as she negotiated the empty, potholed road that led south from the airport.

The island had changed. In her memory it was small, undeveloped outside the port town, and swelteringly hot. Here, in April, it was windswept, crumbled and blasted. Great gaping holes had been gouged out of the hills, mined for stone to build the many half-completed houses she passed on the way to her destination.

And it was big, Ikaria. Far bigger than she remembered.

Twenty-three

Even though she had both windows open in the tiny Chevrolet Matiz, Kate could feel the sweat pooling in the small of her back as she drove. She should have packed something lighter to wear, but it was still cold back home and, sick with worry, she hadn't been thinking straight, so she still had her jeans and long-sleeved black T-shirt on. Finally, she had the presence of mind to unwind her black pashmina from her neck and, for a brief moment, felt the relief of rushing air where before there had been the blanketing of 100 per cent cashmere.

It was the end of the afternoon in the middle of April, but it was hotter than an August midday during an English heatwave.

Away from the airport, heading west, Kate thought that, apart from the incomplete buildings that blighted the roadside, the island looked a lot prettier than the picture she had in her mind from the past. But then, of course, the last time she had been there, it was arid, after a long hot summer. Now it was in full bloom: poppies, gorse-flower, mallow and large, nodding daisies smothered the verges.

The smell was what brought it all back to her, though: that herbal, Greek scent of salt and pine and oregano and something faintly cat-pissy, like chamomile. Objectively, it was lovely, but it was something she had hoped never to experience again; to her it was a sweet shell underneath which lurked the sour reek of death and guilt, like one of those lilies that stink of rotting corpses. And yet, here she was, right in the middle of it again, terrified.

The road seemed better than she remembered – a lot of it was brand new, although puzzling occasional stretches of dirt track recalled the pickup-truck ride the three of them had taken, and how afraid Jake had been, and how she had sought to reassure him. If only the truck *had* gone over the side back then and killed them all. Wouldn't that have been easier for everyone?

She passed a big blue sign that seemed to suggest that the new road had been funded by the EU. Symbolically, perhaps, it hadn't been well done – the cliff had eroded so much that in parts only one carriageway remained of the formerly pristine highway, the outer edge having crumbled down to the rocks below.

But the difficulties of the route were nothing compared to what lay at the end of her journey. She held the steering wheel tightly and prayed to Tilly.

Tell me where you are, Tills.

After ninety minutes driving along the winding coast, she found the point where the old van driver had marked the map. Below the road was the beach they had stayed on all those years ago. She edged along the decaying cliff top and peered over. Down below she could clearly see what remained of the slipway stones across the beach, and the ancient, rusty winch which had almost crumbled to nothing. The cave where they had slept was invisible from the top, but she knew exactly where it was, tucked down to the left. She briefly closed her eyes and recalled the way the light of the sea refracted inside the white of the cave, the sound of the waves as they echoed around her when she lay there in her fever. It would all still be there, and part of her ached to be down there, to crawl back inside to a point of innocence.

What was different though was that a whole chunk of the cliff edge had crumbled away, taking the path down with it. Chunks of black and red and white rock that had once been up near where she stood, now littered the sand below.

She took a step back – there could be an overhang, and she could be standing on it. She had to keep herself safe so that she could save Tilly. Using her brain, as Jake had urged her to, Kate had reckoned that this was where she'd find her. But there was no way anyone could get onto that beach now, not unless they had a boat, and although she knew her daughter was resourceful, she didn't think she'd stretch to that.

Unless someone else was with her.

Whimpering at the thought, Kate dashed back to her car and drove faster than she should up the steeply winding track – now a metalled road – that led to the village where they had eaten and bought their supplies.

She roared the little vehicle up into the village square, revving the puny engine to make the gradient. Then she jumped out onto the pavement, alert, ready for action. But her clamour and nerves were met by complete silence and stillness. Somewhere up the mountain, a cockerel crowed.

Despite the newly tarmacked road, the village looked less inhabited than it had in 1980. Shutters were drawn on most of the houses, and although there were now three shops on the square, only the supermarket where they had bought their supplies for the beach was open. The taverna where she had eaten with Beattie and Jake seemed to be doing business too – one elderly, dusty-jacketed man, the only sign of life in the place, sat smoking in the lengthening shade of an olive tree, two glasses – one containing water, the other she knew would have ouzo in it – at his side.

Coming up against this wall of nothingness defeated Kate. She had travelled all this way, and yet she didn't really know where to start to find Tilly. She sat at a table at the taverna and unfolded the old map. Might she be here, in this village?

She felt like standing up and shouting her daughter's name. But she couldn't bring herself to do so, to sully the silence, to shock the old man out of his quiet afternoon drink, to draw attention to herself.

Where to start, though, now that the beach was out of the question?

Twenty-four

She heard a slight gasp at her shoulder and looked up from the map to see a pair of brown eyes, their warmth still showing through an expression of surprise. Above the eyes, a thick shock of greying curly hair fell over a forehead that had not been so lined thirty-three years ago.

'It is you! The American girl. Emma.'

The boy from the taverna! She recognised him as instantly as he did her.

'Not so much a girl any more,' she said, holding out her hand, which he took and shook, warmly. 'And not at all American. *Anglida*. English. But you remember after all these years?'

'Of course!'

'And your English is good now.'

'I spent some time in New York, working for my cousin,' he said. 'But I have to come back here when my mother got sick.'

'I'm sorry,' Kate said, though she was hardly listening, so surreal was the situation. She was sitting in what she now realised was the exact same seat, having a conversation with the same waiter who, as a boy, had served her all those years ago and promised to bring her fish. Then suddenly, looking into those same eyes, his name came back. 'Giorgos, isn't it?'

'Ah,' he said, nodding, breaking into a wide, white smile. 'You remembered me! You have changed very little. I have been expecting you.'

Kate blinked. 'Really?'

'Your daughter was here. She has a hat, all I can see is her face. I'm shocked. I think first she is you. But of course, not. Excuse me, but she's too young to be you.'

'My daughter was here?' Kate jumped to her feet, her heart quickening in her chest, her throat tight. Hope returned. She rummaged in her bag for her wallet, and pulled out a photograph of Tilly. It was recent, taken for her passport, which she had to have renewed before she left for Greece. It was a good likeness.

'Yes.' Giorgos nodded. 'It is her. Is OK. Her uncle has found her.'

'Her uncle?'

'The big American. He has found her. Are you all right?'

Overtaken by dizziness, Kate had steadied herself by putting a hand on the table.

'Sit, sit.' Giorgos put a hand on her shoulders and eased her back into her chair. 'He left a note for you. One minute.'

He hurried inside, leaving Kate feeling as if there were a thousand ants crawling over her body. She tried to focus on the distant sea, which, in the late afternoon light, looked like a load of dots, a million tiny living things, moving in the wind, like migrating birds.

'Here,' Giorgos said, returning with a tray on which sat a shot of ouzo, a glass of water, a basket of bread and two earthenware dishes containing bread, olives and chunks of some sort of hot sausage. Tucked between the taverna items on the tray was a letter, which he handed to her.

She glanced at the envelope, which was addressed to *Kate and/or Emma*. Her first worry was that Jake had told Tilly about her past. But she instantly realised what a minor concern this now was, given that he had her daughter in his clutches. Or, rather, virtual clutches, because, thinking about her journey, surely there was no way someone with Jake's disabilities could make it out to this tiny island?

She didn't know if this was a comfort to her or not.

She ripped open the envelope.

Dear Emma,

the letter inside said. It was typed, printed out from a computer. Planned, then.

I'm glad you came, arriving on the 14.30 flight from Athens on Sunday 14 April. I knew you would. I know you so well, don't I? If only things had turned out differently, this charming girl I've had the pleasure of making my friend could have been our daughter.

So.

I guess you want to meet up?

So when did I ever let you down, Emma? Of course we can all meet up. There is a well-known beauty spot near the village. A high point with remarkable views over the ocean, with steep – some may even say dangerous – drops to the water below. It's even found its way into some guidebooks. Did you know that? Anyway, I plan to visit it with your daughter on Monday evening at six. It's a great place to watch the sun going down. Romantic, some say.

I trust you will join us.
Jake.

Kate put her hand to her chest and exhaled shakily. So the 'uncle' *was* Jake.

Jake was here, with Tilly.

But how?

'Is it OK?' Giorgos asked her, sitting at the chair by her side. Part of her wanted him to leave her alone, but mostly she wanted him to stay right where he was.

He looked at her expectantly while she tried to frame the words. How could she start to explain to this virtual stranger what was troubling her?

He took the glass of ouzo off the tray and held it out for her. 'You need this,' he said. 'It'll make you feel better.'

Shakily, Kate took a sip. The burning aniseed taste was yet another trigger to take her back to the start of the hell that had surrounded her for thirty-three years. Another reminder that all of this was her fault.

For one brief moment – when Beattie had told her Jake was alive – she had felt a reprieve. But it had been so short-lived. The situation she now found herself in was blacker than anything she had ever known. And it seemed to be getting darker and darker.

The kindness in Giorgos's eyes made her want to crumple into him, but she held back. She could feel him watching her, waiting for her to find the words to respond.

'Was he in a wheelchair, this uncle?' she said at last.

Giorgos tilted his head upwards and tutted, which Kate remembered meant no. 'He was a big man. He was walking,' he said.

What was this? What was happening?

'Do you know where he's staying? Or she?'

He repeated the gesture. 'Somewhere perhaps on the coast,' he said. 'There are many places. Perhaps back in Agios Kirikos.'

'Did my daughter look well?'

'Yes. She was laughing a lot.'

'Did they look like they were staying together?' Kate asked, shuddering at the thought.

Giorgos shrugged expansively. 'I think so. He is her uncle, after all.'

Unable to stop herself, desperate to have an ally, Kate leaned forward and grasped his hand. 'He is not her uncle, Giorgos. He is not her friend.'

Giorgos frowned. 'So you are not happy she is with him?'

Kate shook her head. 'He wants to meet me tomorrow. But if I could find them now . . .'

'I can make some calls, ask some people, try to find out where they are staying, if you want?'

'Could you?' The thought of them staying together in the same place was almost too much for Kate to bear. The thought of that bulky, blasted body anywhere near Tilly turned the aniseed of the ouzo in her throat into bile.

'You must eat,' Giorgos said, motioning to the food he had put at her table. 'I will be back in ten minutes.'

Dusk closed in, and all at once the street lights snapped on, casting a pale yellow glow over the taverna terrace. Kate broke a piece of bread and slowly ripped it into tiny pieces, wondering what on earth was going on. No wheelchair? So what had Jake been playing at all along? She pulled out her phone to call Beattie, but there was no reception – which was why Giorgos had to go inside to phone, of course, to use the landline.

Giorgos was on her side. She knew this, instinctively. She

had to tell him everything. He knew the area, he knew the language. Without him, her task would be far more difficult, if not impossible.

'Sorry,' he said, returning to join her. 'No one knows. They have seen them around all over the island, but no one knows where they are staying. But the word's out. They will call me when they find out.'

'Thank you,' she said.

He sat down next to her and absent-mindedly took a piece of sausage from the plate he had set down for her. He had strong arms, she couldn't help noticing. Strong, brown, sailor's arms.

'I think I owe you an explanation,' she said.

'Yes?' He looked at her.

'You remember when I was here last time? With the two Americans, the girl and the tall boy Jake?'

Giorgos nodded.

'The man who says he is my daughter's uncle is in fact Jake.'

Giorgos frowned. 'But that is impossible.'

'What do you mean?'

He looked at her for a long time. Then he appeared to make a decision.

'Come with me,' he said, standing. 'And I show you.'

He crossed the terrace to have a word with the old man under the olive tree, then ducked inside his taverna and came out twirling a set of car keys around his forefinger. Kate noticed that attached to his keys was a *mataki* – an evil eye like the one she threw overboard when she left the island all those years ago. It reminded her of her holey stone, and she prayed that Tilly had held on to it, despite thinking it a loony gift from her superstitious mother.

'Follow me, Emma,' Giorgos said.

'My name's Kate now.'

He shrugged, as if this were the most normal thing in the world. 'Follow me, Kate.'

He opened the passenger door to a big Mercedes taxi and Kate slipped inside.

'What's this about, Giorgos?'

'I show you. You need to see before I tell you.'

'Is the taxi driver OK with you taking his car?'

Giorgos smiled as he started the engine. 'I am the taxi driver.'

'Is my luggage safe in my car?' She was worried about the portfolio, which was locked in the boot of the Matiz.

He laughed. 'Yes. It is safe.'

They raced down to the coast and he turned right, onto a road Kate had never taken before – once she, Beattie and Jake had arrived on the beach, they had not really had the time to explore any further.

The sun had gone down behind the mountain now, and a full, fat moon was rising up above the sea in front of them.

They turned a corner and there, caught by moonlight, was a grassy plateau above the sea, surrounded by olive trees and enclosed by a rusting metal fence. Giorgos drew up on a roughly gravelled parking area and Kate caught sight of a cross, silhouetted against the shifting, silver sea.

'What a beautiful spot,' she said, and Giorgos nodded.

'Come.' He led her along a scrubby path to a gate that opened onto a graveyard. The tombs were a mixture of old and new – some boasted fresh flowers, others had decayed into gaping holes in the ground. Kate was glad of the darkness that prevented her from seeing what lay inside. Giorgos took her to the other side of the compound. In the far corner, overlooking the sea, a hand-made wooden cross stood sentinel over a mound of scrubby turf. In front of it, a bundle of bay leaves sat in a vase.

Giorgos stood at the grave and looked down, crossing himself. 'This is your friend. Jake.'

'No.' Kate almost stumbled with the blow of his words.

'I'm sorry, but yes.'

'But how can you be sure it's him?'

'I found him. I was fishing out there.' He gestured to the sea. 'I was looking for your beach, to bring you some *barbounia*. I saw him fall, I tried to get to him in time, but there was no hope for him. I pulled his body from the water.' He pointed to Kate's Triskelion. 'I knew it was him. I saw this on you all when you were at my place that night.'

'Did you see how he fell?' Kate asked in a small voice.

Giorgos briefly closed his eyes and, almost imperceptibly, nodded.

So the nightmare had come back, but a million times worse.

She *had* killed Jake.

Then who the hell had her daughter? Who had picked her life apart at the seams? And *why*?

Giorgos caught her by the elbow.

'Sit, Kate. Sit.' He guided her to the plinth of a more elaborate grave, lit a cigarette and passed it to her. Without hesitation she took it and drew the smoke deep into her lungs.

'I'm sorry for this news,' he said, lighting another for himself. 'I saw a fight. I saw an accident. He was an angry boy. I saw that. I know nothing else.' He shrugged. 'You did what you had to do. You were young. It is past.'

'But the police?'

Giorgos smiled. 'We did things our own way in Ikaria back then. There were no police here. Many times we find bodies washed up on our shore. The sea brings them from Turkey, from Africa. Who knows? We don't know who they are. And I didn't know who he was, your boy. Now there would be official this and official that, EU *malakies* and all that. But back then we just used to make sure they were buried, that's all. It's the honourable thing. So here he is. I buried him here, and I bring him laurel – Daphne – for Apollo, for Icarus, for the boy who fell.'

'Thank you, Giorgos. Thank you.'

They sat and finished their cigarettes in silence, as if they were holding a short vigil for dead Jake. Then Giorgos stood and turned to Kate.

'And now we have to get back, to listen for the phone, in case anyone finds your daughter. Come with me. I have rooms. You must stay.'

Kate took his proffered hand and stood to face him.

'Could I have a minute alone?' she said.

'Of course.' He headed back towards the car. Kate stepped carefully over the uneven ground towards Jake's grave. She knelt and put a hand where she supposed his heart had once been, and she tried to hold herself still inside.

'I'm sorry, Jake,' she said. 'I'm so, so sorry.'

There was no reply, of course. Only the constant hushing of the sea as it crept up and down the shore.

Twenty-five

Had it been a different time in her life, Kate would have enjoyed spending the evening with Giorgos. It was as if he embodied something she had long ago shut out of herself.

She had wanted to drive with him around the island, searching for Tilly. But he had argued that, since she could be anywhere, it was no use – they would be better placed listening out for the phone. So they sat up at the table outside his taverna drinking village wine and talking. The phone rang several times, pulling Giorgos indoors, and hope into Kate's heart. But there was never any news, only concerned friends calling to ask if he'd had any luck. In between, Kate spelled out her unedited story, about how she had killed off Emma almost as soon as she had murdered Jake. Apart from Beattie, Giorgos was the only person who now knew the truth.

He took her hand at this point and held it in his. 'It was not murder, Kate. It was an accident, a terrible accident.'

When he said this, she wept. She didn't quite believe him but, nevertheless, it was a relief to hear it from someone so wise and so warm. It was like receiving the absolution she had craved all her life. She went on to tell him everything else, about her marriage to Mark, about Martha's Wish, about how everything had turned sour the moment this bogus Jake had turned up demanding money.

'Do you have any idea who he is?' Giorgos asked.

Kate shook her head. 'No one else knew about Jake.'

'Did he have a family? A brother, perhaps?'

Kate shrugged. Jake had never mentioned a family, and she had always pushed the thought that he might have to the back of her mind. 'No one knew except me, Beattie and, I suppose, you. Unless Beattie told someone else some time. I've not mentioned it to a soul.'

'Call her,' Giorgos said, leading her indoors to the phone. 'Ask her now who else will know.'

He left her to dial the long string of digits of Beattie's phone number into the taverna phone.

As she waited for Beattie to pick up, Kate thought about her at home in the London house. When she had said she had to go to Ikaria alone, strangely, and counter to all expectations, Beattie put up no opposition. Perhaps she was too scared. But as duped as Kate had been by this fake Jake, she couldn't help feeling a flush of annoyance at her friend for also being so gullible. If it hadn't been for that first meeting in the New Oxford Street Starbucks, Tilly would have been safe, Kate's marriage to Mark would have been as strong as ever, everything would have been as it had always been behind her shield of lies.

But Beattie had been desperate for Kate's help. Who else in the world could she have turned to? And hadn't she, Kate, been equally taken in by the story? True, with the benefit of hindsight, it sounded incredibly far-fetched. But might not her own life story, if told to a stranger, also sound too odd to be true?

'There's no reply. I'm afraid I need to go to bed,' Kate said, joining Giorgos back out on the terrace. It was gone midnight and, even though Greece was two hours ahead of the UK, she was done in, a little drunk, and at the end of her wits.

'Of course,' he said. 'You need to be fresh for tomorrow.' He helped her fetch her bags from her car, then showed her inside.

They went through to the kitchen, which Giorgos said his mother Elpiniki, despite her advancing age, still cooked in every morning. It was as sparklingly clean and well kept as Kate remembered from when she had visited it thirty-three years ago. Everything in the room seemed to be hand-made, solid, ancient, telling of a permanence that seemed impossibly exotic to her. A hefty wooden dining table stood proud in the middle of the room and antique woven rugs lay on stone seats by a massive stove. Above this hung the Madonna icon and an old rifle that Kate remembered from before, although the colours on both the painting and the embroidered strap of the gun had faded with time – she remembered them as being quite startling when she first saw them.

Giorgos caught her looking at the weapon – she was wondering, in fact, if it were still in working order, if it could be of some use to her.

'It was my great-grandfather's,' he said. 'It has been used against Turks, pirates and Germans. A noble weapon.' He reached up and touched it as if it were the icon and not the picture beneath it. Then he turned and smiled almost apologetically at her. 'Although today it only gets used for hunting.'

He led her upstairs, unlocked the door to her room and stood to one side to let her in, bowing slightly and bidding her *kalinichta*. The chaste goodnight mildly surprised Kate after she had bared herself so completely, so uniquely to him. But she was relieved. Anything else would have been wrong, with

Tilly out there in danger somewhere, and the shock of knowing that Jake was, actually, in a grave.

She realised, too, that, at fifty, however well preserved she was, she wasn't a young girl out travelling on her own any more. She could actually just go about her business as she pleased, without having to waste any energy on the unwelcome attentions of men. More than anyone, she knew she should view this as liberating, but, after having spent so many years trying to hide away, a part of her resented now being so invisible.

And what about Tilly, who was young and alone?

Fighting the urge to run out to her car and search – and she accepted Giorgos's argument that this would be futile – she surveyed her simple, stone-walled room. It was on the upper floor and its shuttered windows looked out to sea. With better timing it would have been a romantic place to stay, although, she thought – before she remembered that this was no longer a relevant concern – it was hardly Mark's style.

She unzipped the portfolio and checked on the Rothko, which was still there, glowing vibrant red and orange into the dimly lit room. Reaching carefully into the inner pocket of her suitcase, she touched the hilt of the sharpened boning knife. She'd had this worry that it might have been removed by some psychic customs officer who would have somehow known that it wasn't intended for butterflying lamb.

She pulled out her nightdress and washbag, then stashed the case and portfolio in the bowels of a looming dark wood wardrobe. Finally, she flung open the shutters and lay on the bed. From there all she could see was the great watered satin of the Aegean.

Her brain burned. She had thought many times during the course of the evening that she should call the police – Giorgos had said that there were now three small stations on the island. But she also knew that to do so would open a can of worms – quite literally, in the case of the grave – not only for herself, but for Beattie and Giorgos too. And anyway, this 'Jake' was using Tilly as bait to get at her. It would be far safer for her daughter if she were to play by his rules and turn up as arranged.

With the windows open and the bedside light on, the room had started to fill with whining, droning mosquitos. Soon one landed on her arm and she squashed it just as it was tucking into her, leaving a burst bubble of her own blood where its body had been. She got up and turned on the ceiling fan. The bugs soon dispersed, but, not wanting to keep the fan going all night out of consideration for Giorgos's electricity bill, she had to toss up between lights or open windows. With the heat of the night upon her, the latter won. She had realised by that point that sleep was out of the question. So she spent the time in the dark, sitting on a chair, looking out towards the coast, wondering where Tilly might be staying with – or being held hostage by – the man who had pretended to be Jake. She watched like a cat, every small movement catching her eye, drawing her attention, making her sit up straight.

She thought that, somewhere down towards the sea, she could make out the shape of the bluff where she was to meet him the next day. She needed to make a plan. She would happily hand over the Rothko, but would that see an end to it? Would that guarantee Tilly's future safety?

She was prepared to do anything necessary in order to save her daughter.

After all, she had already killed once.

Twenty-six

Unable to sit still any longer, at first light Kate left a note for Giorgos and slipped out. She spent the morning driving around the twisting roads that lined the coast either side of the village, craning her sore, tired eyes for any sign of Tilly or her captor. She stopped at every deserted or closed-down building – and there were many on this Greek island in 2013, which was suffering austerity measures like everywhere else in the country. Decay was all over, added to by the fact that the island was not yet into its modest tourist season, so even going concerns were still boarded up for the winter.

She pulled up outside an idyllically positioned stone house perched on a promontory overlooking a small bay. Had she visited it with Mark in her old life – imagining that she had allowed herself to travel for pleasure and to Greece – she might have suggested that they buy it and do it up. But it would need a lot of work – half the roof was missing and the shutters swung broken and blind over missing windows. Graffiti, · scrawled over the wall facing the road, declared allegiance to KKE, which, Kate remembered, was the communist party of Greece.

Despite its dilapidation, the place held signs of life, so Kate thought it worthwhile to take a closer look. Someone had put a plastic container of water outside for the gaggle of stray cats that inhabited the overgrown garden to the side of the house. That was the kind of thing Tilly would do.

Cautiously, her hand on the boning knife nestling in her handbag, Kate edged into the door at the side of the house. It opened onto a room that looked like it was trying to be a kitchen. A half-eaten loaf of bread sat on the shabby Formica table, beside an empty cup. Kate picked up the cup and sniffed it – it had contained Greek coffee, and the bread was only partly stale, so someone had certainly been there recently. Her heart racing, she edged further inside, forging through the darkness behind the shuttered windows, into a small room beyond, which was bare except for one upright chair set beside a fireplace that smelled as if it had been used recently. A doorway in the far wall was obscured behind a curtain of plastic streamers.

Without warning, from behind those streamers, a black shape launched itself at her, batting at her with something hard and heavy. Flight won over fight. Forgetting about her knife, forgetting about Tilly, Kate turned and hared out of the house into the bright morning sunlight, scattering the cats, who shot away from their lazy haven, screeching and yowling. At her heels, the black shape, now screaming what sounded like a string of obscenities, chased her right off the perimeter of the garden.

As Kate pelted out onto the road, she turned briefly to see who – or what – her pursuer was. To her shock and utter amazement the fierce shadow that had sent her running was a tiny, wizened old woman who looked at least a hundred years old. She was now standing guard at the gate to her property, waving her dustpan-and-brush weapons in the air above her, formidably spitting and cursing. Behind her, tethered to the grass, was the goat Kate hadn't noticed before, and behind the goat was the vegetable patch, well tended among all the overgrowth of the other parts of the garden.

She just hadn't seen. She just hadn't looked.

'Sorry,' she said, not able to say it in Greek. 'I'm sorry, I'm just looking for my daughter, I—'

The woman, who clearly didn't understand – why on earth should she? – made a move as if to have another go at her. It did the trick: Kate threw herself into her car, jarred the tinny engine into action, and drove off.

She searched fruitlessly until three, when she knew that if she were to have her wits about her after her sleepless night, she needed to rest. So she went back up to Giorgos's, where he gave her a coffee and listened thoughtfully to her story of her useless, futile day.

Twenty-seven

It was time for her to go to the cliff top.

'I will come with you,' Giorgos said.

'Thank you, but I need to do this on my own.'

'But—'

'I've already tangled you up too much in the mess of my life, Giorgos. Thank you, but I need to do this on my own.'

'But he is seriously a big man, and if there's trouble . . .'

'I have what he wants, Giorgos. Enough, anyway, to make sure my daughter is safe for now.'

With the portfolio clasped so tightly to her that her fingers cramped, she set off down the hill on foot. She wasn't going to announce her arrival by driving there. Rather, she wanted to keep surprise on her side.

She liked to think that, with the Rothko, she had a plan of sorts. But the new knowledge that she owed this stranger pretending to be Jake nothing whatsoever made her very aware of the knife in her bag. Part of her felt murderous about what he had cost her, the wreckage he had made of her life.

But that grave overlooking the sea told her that, imposter

Jake or not, she deserved every inch of that damage. She worked at controlling her breathing as she walked. The sun was still hot. An onset of wavy vision made her wonder if she was going to do one of her collapses again, but then she realised it was just ripples of heat from the dusty ground.

She was going into a delicate, unforeseen situation, and the most important thing was to make sure Tilly was safe. She had to be careful. It wasn't as if she was an old hand at this sort of thing. Apart from pushing a boy off a cliff and murdering him, losing a child – oh, and being raped (she always tended to forget that part, always pushed that to the very darkest recesses of her mind) – she had led a very sheltered life.

As she worked her way down the rutted road towards the coast, careful to stay in the shade of trees to conserve her strength, she began to regret refusing Giorgos's offer of help. She might have been able to use a strong man on her side.

But she had to do this alone. His presence might provoke 'Jake', and anything that could endanger Tilly's safety was out of the question.

She reached the point where the village track joined the coastal road, which she crossed to meet the headland leading upwards to the cliff edge. It was, she remembered, quite a climb. But oddly, even with her thirty extra years, she found it a lot easier than she remembered. Of course she didn't smoke now – the cigarette with Giorgos the night before excepted. And, she reminded herself, the last time she made this journey she had been taking a lot of drugs and was recovering from a nasty illness. That still niggled. What *had* made her ill that night? Had something poisoned her? Neither Jake nor Beattie were sick . . .

Something began to turn in her brain. Cogs finally began to whirr.

She arrived at the brow of the headland and at once she saw

him. Big, lumbering, he was of such a size that she wondered how on earth he had made it up there.

More mystifying still was how she could have thought that the beautiful boy Jake, with his blue, blue, blue eyes, had turned out to be such an ugly monster? Her guilt, she supposed. Had he still been beautiful, it would have killed her there and then to know that she had so ruined a life.

Instantly, she wanted to rip her insides out for having such a shallow thought. She *had* ruined a life. Two lives: Jake's and her own. Three, if she included Beattie.

But, she reminded herself, Jake had only been beautiful on the outside. What he did to Beattie was the work of the worst, most ugly soul. That's why he had ended up over the cliff.

And there was still the unresolved case of The Australian, whose passport had turned up in Jake's rucksack. Perhaps the Jake imposter didn't know about that and that's why he denied it. Perhaps Jake *had* killed him back in Athens.

If so, then he *really* deserved it. Didn't he? This death penalty which she had doled out to him . . . Didn't he?

If she found out that this man facing her on the cliff had laid a finger on Tilly, she would – if she could – send him the same way as his predecessor. Without hesitation.

She scanned the landscape. There was no sign of Tilly.

'What have you done with my daughter?' she said, stopping ten feet away from him.

'She's here,' the big man said, spreading his hands.

'You're not Jake, are you?'

The man didn't move or say a thing. Just held his bare, tattoo-free arms out and looked at her with eyes that were not blue, but muddy brown.

'Contact lenses,' he said, noting her frown. 'And suggestion. You wanted Jake to be alive, so you saw him in my eyes.'

'Who are you, then?' she asked him. 'And why are you doing this to me?'

'Money,' the fat man said. 'Just money.'

'Where's Tilly? I need to see her.'

Then the man did something that completely flummoxed her. His shoulders dropping as if he were a puppet whose strings had been cut, he turned to the creeping oak – still the only tree on the bluff – and called out.

'I'm done. This is where I leave. This is too much, Luanne.'

Luanne?

He turned back, set his face beyond Kate, and lumbered straight past her, motioning to the tree with his eyes and shaking his head. He didn't look happy. Kate could read exactly what was on his face: the feeling she had woven into the very core of her own being, the feeling she had read and hated in the Tracey Emin drawing: self-disgust.

He continued on, moving away from her, until he had disappeared over the lip of the headland, towards the coastal road.

She turned to the oak, which was silhouetted behind a magnificent early evening sun. Tilly was here, he had said. *This is too much*, he had said.

But who was he talking to?

Luanne? Who the hell was Luanne?

She ran, tearing across the scrubby grass towards the tree.

But a movement from behind the trunk stopped her in her tracks so suddenly that she nearly toppled over.

It was Tilly.

She was squirming out from behind the tree, her hands behind her back and duct tape wound around her legs and body. Something – someone – shorter than her, hidden behind her, was holding something to her neck. Sunlight flashed off it,

416

making it hard for Kate to see at first what it was.

Shielding her eyes, she made out a knife. But not just any knife. It was the big Henckels that she hadn't been able to find in her Battersea kitchen. For a second she tried to work out what was going on – had she had too much sun as she scoured the area for Tilly? Had her blood sugar plummeted from not enough food? Was she hallucinating?

But the look of terror on her daughter's face was all too real.

'Please, Mum. She's really serious about this shit,' Tilly said, every tendon in her throat extended, tight and ready for the slip of the razor edge of the knife.

'Who?'

'Me,' an unmistakable, tobacco-gruff voice came from behind Tilly, and Beattie stepped out, still keeping the knife poised in its killing position.

It *was* Beattie, but Kate felt like she was looking in a fairground distorting mirror. She was wearing clothes identical to her own – bigger, but the same clothes – and the hair and make-up were exactly the same, too. She even had a handbag just like the one Kate had slung over her own shoulder. The only difference was that Kate's own bag still contained her knife, whereas Beattie's was at her daughter's throat.

'You!' she gasped. 'It was you!'

'Emma, honey. So you got it *at last*. My God, but you are the best gull in the business.'

Kate reeled, images from the past weeks turning in front of her eyes like the wheels of a macabre carnival machine. What was going on? What *had* been going on? Then, before she had time even to register what she was doing, she had thrown herself across the grass towards her daughter and her captor.

'Let go of her!' she roared.

'STOP RIGHT NOW!' Beattie yelled, and, at the sound of that familiar voice using a tone she had never heard before, Kate skidded to a halt, the momentum taking her to her knees. 'I *will* cut her throat,' Beattie said. 'Have no doubt about it, Emma. I will *happily* do that.'

'What do you want?' Kate said. She held out the portfolio, which trembled in her hands. 'I've got the Rothko. You can have it. Please give me back my girl.'

Beattie renewed her grip on Tilly, who whimpered as the knife nicked her throat. Kate gasped as she saw a bead of blood blossom on her daughter's neck.

'Do you really think it's just about money, Emma?' Beattie laughed. 'Or some stupid art shit? I've had enough dough off you now to pay off old fat Sam there – not that he deserves a penny now but it's the only way to keep him quiet – and to keep me going till I goddamn die.'

'Sam?'

'Goddamn wuss of an actor. All OK when it came to doing it to camera, but he just don't cut the mustard when it comes to live theatre. DO YOU, SAM, BOY?' she yelled, her voice reverberating up to the peak of the looming black mountain behind them. 'Fucking waste of space. Cost me thousands, too, bastard.' She spat into the rocky, dusty ground. 'Bring him over to London and he hires a white Mondeo to trail us around. White Mondeo. Couldn't he have found something a mite scarier?'

'What do you want, Beattie?' Kate said, her voice tiny, her eyes locked on Tilly's, trying to reassure her, though she had no idea what she could do to stop what was going on, except to give Beattie what she wanted, whatever that was.

'I want your life,' Beattie said. 'I want your goddamn life, you lucky, lucky bitch. Oh, you were all right, weren't you?

With your brilliant reinvention, your doting rich-boy husband, your lovely daughters. So sad one of them passed away, though. So sad for you. Poor us. Poor me. One little bad thing in our life.' Kate realised that Beattie's voice had taken on her own accent and tone; chillingly, she sounded exactly like her again, as she had in Athens all those years ago.

The distorting mirror had taken on sound.

But there was no time for Kate's horror and revulsion. The look in Tilly's eyes told her that she needed to act, quickly.

'What happened to you?' she asked Beattie, her voice as level as she could manage, in an attempt to keep things calm, to buy time, to stop the woman veering off into complete insanity.

'Me? Beattie, you mean?' she continued her impersonation of Kate. 'That woman you know as Beattie never got it right, not like we did, Emma. She was in and out of jail all her life. Poor white trash, as I think they refer to them over there. Never got anywhere. She was always making mistakes, you see. Or, as she would say,' and here Beattie continued in a caricature of her own accent, '"fucking up the whole Goddamn ball game". You see, she never met another one quite so gullible as us again. Never met one who was so easily taken in who, dare I say, almost fell in love with her?'

'What do you mean?'

'Did you really believe all that friendship shtick "Beattie" gave you back then? Did you not ever, just once, get it into your tiny freaking brain too full of books shit that what you saw wasn't exactly what you were getting?'

Kate shook her head, her mouth open, catching grit and dust.

'"I think Jake fancies me." "I wonder if I'm a little bit in love with Beattie." Whatever shit you wrote in your stupid diary.'

'You *read my diary*?'

'What the fuck do you think? Jesus. How we laughed at your silly little English schoolgirl whimpering.'

'We?'

'ME AND JAKE, ASSHOLE!' Beattie threw the bound Tilly to the ground, where she landed with a thump. She stood with her foot on the girl's neck, holding the knife up towards Kate, who had instinctively moved forward. Tilly closed her eyes. Her knees twitched.

'You come near me and I'll stamp on her neck,' Beattie said to Kate. 'I've done it before. It ain't pretty, but it's effective. So now. Where was I? Oh yes. Beattie and Jake,' she continued, in her Kate impersonation. 'Or shall we call them Bonnie and Clyde, or perhaps, let's be honest, Luanne and Jack, for, my dear, those were their real names. Oh, they were a true couple of lovebirds, made for each other, together since they were thirteen. And of course they didn't come from Manhattan and San Diego at all: they never even graduated from High School. They were no-good no-hopers from JEFFERSON CITY OHIO. Where's that, my dear, you may ask? It's THE MIDDLE OF FUCKING NOWHERE.'

'But—'

'But they were very good at one thing. Well, two things. Well, let's say Jake was good at the second thing. Man, he was good. Best I ever had. Sorry you never found that out, poor little raped girl.'

Tilly shot open her eyes and looked up at Kate from where she was trapped under Beattie's foot.

'It's OK, Tills, just think of home,' Kate said.

'Yes, baby, think of home, Tills, darling,' Beattie said, her voice indistinguishable from Kate's. 'But that Luanne was excellent at taking people in, performing. She should have been a goddamn actress. She *shoulda* been a drama student at Tisch doing the grand tour. But her mom never made enough money even to feed her properly in between drinks. You know? Sad old, same old, same old.'

'So how did you get to Athens, then?'

'I InterRailed in my year orf,' Beattie said, her voice almost royal in its Englishness.

'I mean,' Kate said, realising now that she had to play along, 'how did Luanne and Jack get to Athens?'

'How they got to Athens . . . well, now. Luanne had this job in JEFFERSON CITY OHIO as a care assistant for this old, old woman. She took the job and for a whole fucking month she lived in the old, old bitch's giant stinking house, cleaning up her shit, finding out where things were kept, all the jewellery and the bank statements and, Jesus, she found out the monster – and, believe me, this lady was nasty – was loaded. So she forged her signature and withdrew a load of money at the bank and stole the jewellery, and then the bitch got suspicious and started flinging all these accusations around and threatening to call the police and then, well, Luanne was in deep shit, so she had to make good and sure the old woman couldn't tell no one nothing no more.'

Kate gasped. 'You killed her!'

'D'uh.' Beattie's voice had taken on a new accent Kate hadn't heard before. It was rougher, harsher, but it sat more easily with her cigarette-roughened tones than anything else she had heard coming from her mouth. 'So Luanne and Jack knew when they were making their plan that they were going to have to disappear after, which was a good thing because they had always wanted to get out of FUCKING JEFFERSON CITY OHIO. So, never one to do things by halves, Luanne made this plan that after the deed they would go to Europe, somewhere they still have plumbing, but where there was little likelihood of some poky murder somewhere nowhere in America being any kind of an issue. They flew into Madrid – they had such great sex there in Spain, Emma, your mind would have popped – and moved real quick. By the time the cops worked out what happened to the old bat and who did it – Luanne wasn't the kind who'd work under her own name, after all – our two fugitives were in Greece, lost in a muddle of bad paperwork, with shiny new identities.'

'Jake and Beattie.'

'You got it. Beattie was just a temporary name-change, but Jake was official. He even had his new passport, though you really don't want to know how he came by that.'

'The Australian who gave me a black eye . . .'

'Nope, but similar. That Ozzie bastard just wound Jake up the wrong way, but the payback I doled out on him – oh yes, Jake was a fighter, but he was never a killer, the wimp – made a problem for us. We had to get out of Athens fast, so you were lucky there.'

'What do you mean?'

'Jesus, you are so dense, girl. I was going to be Emma James, of course. There was enough of a similarity. I could have gone anywhere as you. I have your voice just right, don't I? Bit more of a northern accent you had back then, though, eh?' Beattie's voice wove in and out of accents and identities so quickly that Kate felt quite dizzy.

'What were you going to do with me?'

'What do you think? You were lucky those Greek brats turned up on those rocks up by the Parthenon, and then, with that Australian, it all got too difficult to do the deed in Athens. So we decided to go along with your stupid island idea. It presented an opportunity. Do it out there, with no one to see, then fuck off back into the world as Emma James.'

'So why didn't you, then?' Kate asked. Her need to know the truth now outweighed everything, but she also knew that Beattie was enjoying the telling of the story, and by egging her on, she was buying time and space for Tilly – and, she was beginning to suspect, for herself.

But at this point Beattie tensed up, and Tilly squirmed as her foot tightened on her throat, just where her carotid artery pulsed under her skin. Kate slipped her hand in her bag and grasped the handle of her knife, ready to move.

'Goddamn Jack,' Beattie said, through clenched teeth. 'The cheating skunk, he fell for you with your little-girl-lost, waif-and-stray shtick. He couldn't take a strong woman like me no more, the weakling, the milksop, the *bastard*. The American Shit. Like that, Emma? Another shit for your shit collection. He begged me to save you and I realised he would get me if I tried to go ahead. We had quite a fight about it that last night. HE DID EVERYTHING I TOLD HIM UNTIL HE MET YOU, EMMA.

'So when I got hold of your diary and read about that horny little Frenchy giving you it in France, well, I knew what kind of story would upset you most about Jake.'

'No!' Kate said, something molten and rotten welling up inside her. 'You lied and lied. You got me up here and we tortured him and all he wanted to do was save me from you.'

'Yep. Oops.' Beattie put her little finger in her mouth and sucked it like an Orphan Annie. 'But don't you see? He had to die. He was no use to me at all.'

'But why did you let me go, though? Why didn't you kill me like you'd planned?'

'It was the look in your eyes after you did it.' Beattie pursed her lips. 'You know what, honey? I saw a tiny bit of myself in you at that moment and, well, I just couldn't bring myself to finish the job.'

Shaking, Kate narrowed her eyes at Beattie. 'I'm nothing like you. Nothing like you at all.'

'And besides,' Beattie went on, smiling broadly at her. 'What would be the point of assuming the identity of somebody who had become a murderer? Kind of defeats the point.'

Seeing Tilly's eyes register this information, Kate stopped thinking. Knife held high, she launched herself at Beattie, whose absorption in her own storytelling had put her off-guard. The speed of the attack pushed her away from Tilly, but she escaped the trajectory of Kate's knife, looping herself round, ready to act with her own weapon.

As Kate faced her warped doppelganger, Beattie started laughing.

'You'll never beat me at this, girl,' she said, again in her true Luanne voice. 'I been cutting people since I was twelve.'

'I murdered an innocent man,' Kate snarled back at her.

Tilly made a noise behind her, but Kate couldn't take her eyes off her foe.

'What did you want from me?' Kate asked.

'Oh, don't put it in the past tense yet, honey,' Beattie said. 'I ain't finished yet. I told you already. I want your life. I have your wardrobe, I have your daughter – although she'll be going the same way as you after I'm done – and I have most of your money. The one thing standing in my way is you. At last your time is up. You gotta go, honey.'

'You're crazy,' Kate said, launching herself at her. But, true to her word, Beattie caught her arm, knocked the knife from her hand, and pushed her backwards to the ground, falling heavily down on top of her, her full weight winding her, thumping into her bones.

'We never did get to do this, did we?' Beattie said, grinding her pelvis into Kate's. 'Ain't that nice, eh? Mmmm.'

If Kate had had any food in her stomach, she would have vomited. But she was empty, drained of everything. Caught. Powerless.

'So, no knives, honey,' Beattie went on, breathing her stale tobacco breath into Kate's face. 'I don't want your pretty, skinny body cut none. If they find you, which they won't, will they – we know that you don't get found if you go over the edge, don't we? We've done the trial run, after all – but if they *do* find you, I want it to look like an accident or perhaps even some tragic double suicide: poor mother and daughter throw themselves off of the cliff. Not that they'll ever find out who you are, even if they get to you before all them little nibbling fishies.'

'Giorgos knows who I am,' Kate said.

'He knows you're called Emma,' Beattie said, looking lovingly into her eyes. 'He doesn't know where you're from, what your "real" name is; he doesn't know about me.'

'He does, though,' a male voice said softly, behind them.

Beattie looked round sharply. Giorgos was standing about ten feet away, his great-grandfather's gun pointed directly at her.

'Get up,' he said.

Beattie made to move away from Kate, but instead grabbed her by the hair and yanked her up so that she stood in front of her, shielding her from the gun. Kate felt the knife cut into her throat and she thought for a second how that would spoil it for Beattie when her body was found. Through the corner of her eye, she saw Beattie's Triskelion tattoo on the arm that held the knife to her throat, distorted with tension.

She was not going to give in, though. This woman had twice

425

planned to kill her and, worse than that, she had turned her into a murderer. She wasn't going to allow her to get away with it. Remembering a move learned in the self-defence classes she had taken with Tilly, she suddenly looped her arm into Beattie's, pushing away the knife and forcing her to drop it. At the same time she jabbed the elbow of her other arm back into Beattie's ribs, winding her. Then she turned and thrust her backwards, up the slope towards the edge of the cliff. Beattie stuck her heel in and launched herself back at Kate, but the odds were stacked against her, because Kate fought now with the strength of a mother protecting her young, her anger further propelled by the weight of all the wrong Beattie had done to her, all her life. She charged at her and shoved, using the force of every tendon, every muscle, every fibre of her body.

Beattie tottered backwards, her arms windmilling in the air, her feet trying to stay on the edge of the cliff.

The momentum from Kate's ruthless bulldozing and the weight of her own body propelled her unstoppably backwards.

She reached behind her, as if searching out a surface to halt her trajectory. Finding nothing, she toppled flat into the open, thin air.

Kate had seen the same look of terror many years ago in this same place, on a different face.

But she had never before seen a pair of eyes so filled with rage.

And then, with an almost audible whoosh, and just like Jake before her, Beattie was gone.

Kate rushed up to the edge of the cliff and watched as that bulky body tumbled down onto the rocks some hundred feet below, bouncing, breaking, smashing. She watched as the waves licked at her, gently pulling her to them; Poseidon making love to his Medusa.

It was over.

The monster was slain.

Kate wondered if Beattie's last thoughts had been that she was going to join Jake at the bottom of the ocean. The thought made her smile. Of course, Beattie had no idea that Jake was on land, tucked safely into the hillside.

And then she came to her senses. She realised what she had done, and who had been watching. And listening.

She turned, appalled, to face Giorgos and Tilly.

PART FOUR

NOW

6 May 2013 (Easter Monday), 6 a.m. Ikaria. Giorgos's taverna.

I'm still up after the busiest night Giorgos and Elpiniki have ever had. The last revellers – Eirini and Ilias, aged ninety-four and ninety-eight respectively – have just tripped off to bed after a full night's dancing, drinking and eating. G. and I wondered as they went off hand in hand if they were going to her bed or his.

Oh, my poor feet ache from running around with plates, but it's good for the business, and it makes Giorgos happy. So the pain is sweet.

For the record: I'm trying not to take pills, I've stopped drinking and I'm really trying to eat.

But without my little helpers, even though I'm tired, I can't sleep.

Damned sobriety.

So here I am. I'm going to try my hand at a journal again. Now I can once more tell myself the truth.

I've got a strange ride ahead. It's like jumping off into the blue. I don't know where I'm going to land, but it feels surprisingly OK.

Giorgos is a great help. Who knows what the future holds? But he says I can stay here as long as I like. As long as I need. Which may well be for ever.

Before I move forward, though, I need to put down what has happened since I killed . . .

I killed . . .

Since Beattie went over the cliff.

Tilly called again yesterday. She says it's weird without me in the house, but Mark has calmed down 'a little'.

But that's not the right place to start. I need to go further back.

Two weeks ago we went into Agios Kirikos after putting Tilly and the Rothko on a plane for Athens. Sitting in a café eating souvlaki – bread and all – I found a Wi-Fi signal for my iPad. After long deliberation – I had no idea what Pandora's box I might be opening – I downloaded my email. With some relief, I saw that there was nothing from anyone. It was as if, away from this island, I had ceased to exist.

But that was a good thing. It was better I was forgotten. I felt awful about Mark, about the money, but, as far as I could see, there was nothing I could do about it. It had gone, and that was that. Giorgos – and Tilly, in fact – have convinced me that, as far as the money was concerned, I acted with the best possible motives.

Tilly was safe, and that was good enough for me.

I hoped her turning up on Mark's doorstep, with the Rothko, which would easily cover the money I took . . . Well, I hoped she might be able to explain it to him. At least he'd listen to her, and she was primed from six days of me and Giorgos trying to explain everything.

What it felt like for her to know the truth! To be free of the dread of her finding out . . .

Well, it's like stepping into the light after the longest, darkest night.

I was just about to put the iPad away and finish my souvlaki when an email arrived in my personal account.

When I saw the name of the sender, I blinked and shook my head.

It was from Jake Mithras.

I stabbed at the screen to open it.

Dear Emma, it said.

This is Sam here. Soon I'm going to shut down this email, and try to forget all about Jake Mithras. After that I will never contact you again, I promise. But I need to tell you how sorry I am. I am shamed by my actions. I thought it was only cash. You know, extortion . . .

Only extortion!

. . . I swear I had no idea what Luanne was really up to, that she wanted to wipe you and Tilly out. Obliterate you, she said. I only found that out when she joined us up on the cliff and we'd tied Tilly up.

I'd thought we were just going to leave you both up there, then take that painting and disappear . . .

I knew that, in fact. Tilly told me.

She'd met the man who'd told her he was called Jake when she was having breakfast in Agios Kirikos after getting off the boat. He sat down and started talking with her and they realised they both had a shared passion for theatre. She said she felt almost instantly that she could trust him. He reminded her of her Uncle Julian, in fact. She said she 'was almost a hundred per cent positive he was gay'.

When, after they had talked non-stop for two hours about Ibsen and Shaw and Sondheim, he'd offered to take her round in the jeep he had hired, she hadn't even hesitated. They had a great weekend, hiking along mountain tracks, visiting villages full of really old people. They stayed in a bed and breakfast near a beautiful beach called Nas, where a river pooled and met the sea by a temple of Artemis, he in one room, she in another. Not for one minute did she feel threatened by him in any way.

On the Monday evening, he'd taken her up to the cliff, supposedly to show her the sunset. When they reached the top, she had been shocked to find the woman she knew as Claire up there waiting for them. She hadn't believed it when this big gentle new friend of hers had turned on her and helped that woman – who was nothing like the kindly figure she had met in London – tie her up.

And then Beattie told this man – whom she called Sam – what she wanted him to do when I turned up.

Tilly had no idea, of course, that I was on the island. But the shock of that discovery was obliterated by the realisation that this woman wanted this Sam man to kill us both.

Then Sam started arguing with Beattie. He said he wanted no part of it. Beattie put the big knife to Tilly's throat and said she'd kill her outright if he didn't 'Goddamn shut up' and do as he was told. That was when he told Beattie he was quitting, and started walking away.

'If you hadn't turned up then, Mum,' Tilly said, 'I think she would have killed me.'

. . . I'm not violent.

Sam's email went on.

It was just like a really well-paid role-play gig. I'm just a broke actor with bills to pay . . .

He's not violent.

Beattie must have faked every single injury I ever saw on her. The real Jake hadn't attacked her back in 1980, poor boy: she'd done it to herself. His only crime was trying to warn me about her. There were no henchmen in San Francisco or London. In her grim determination to get at me, Beattie beat herself up. Several times, in the most grim horrible ways.

There was no husband, there were no daughters, just a life of bad luck, prison and meanness.

Of course, Sam had no idea of the extent of her madness.

None of us did.

She was fucking good, wasn't she?

Everything that happened back in Greece thirty-three years ago was set up by Beattie or Claire or Luanne or whoever the hell she was. It was like some sort of reality TV game, but for real, and twenty years ahead of *Big Brother*. I was duped, led, forced into pushing Jake off that cliff, unwittingly punishing him for the 'crime' of falling in love with me.

So does that mean I'm less responsible for what happened? What I did?

I don't know.

It doesn't feel like that at the moment. Perhaps it will later.

Sam's email went on to tell me his version of what happened before I turned up on the cliff – which was exactly the same as Tilly's. If he hadn't done such awful things, I think I'd quite like him. But then I'm a fine one to talk, aren't I, about doing awful things?

He liked Tilly:

> . . . Your daughter is the most charming girl. She is full of life and hope and optimism. She reminds me of myself when I was that age. She called me Uncle Jake. She made me feel protective toward her. There was absolutely nothing else in my feelings, I swear . . .

Then he took a few further steps towards redemption:

> . . . You thought I abandoned you both after I walked past

you on the cliff. But I was there, hiding, listening out, ready to jump in and save you from crazy Luanne.

I even stuck around when that waiter guy came stalking along the cliff edge – I had no idea whose side he was going to be on. All I saw was a man with a gun . . .

So, like Tilly and Giorgos, he was witness to everything. And when it was all over, and he knew Beattie was finished and we were safe, he evaporated away from the island.

. . . Your guy had that gun, after all, and I should imagine I wasn't your favourite dude at that moment . . .

Too right he wasn't. But then he signed off with this:

. . . I want you to know that whatever happened on that cliff – both recently and in the past – is safe with me. All I ask is your forgiveness for my part in all of this, all the grief I have caused you and your family. I'm sorry. I was greedy.

Now to my final business with you. I still have access to the money – Luanne gave me fake ID to open the Stephen Smith account. Now I know more about what she was capable of, I don't want to think exactly how she got hold of it. But it's useful just for a couple more days.

If you let me have your account details, I will pay the money back to you.

!!

So it turned out he wasn't such a bad guy, after all. My heart would have broken from gratitude, if it hadn't been too busy soaring with joy.

Two days after she got home, Tilly phoned to say that Mark had got all the money back, except for two hundred thousand pounds. Before he de-friended her, 'Stephen Smith' sent her a private message on Facebook, explaining that it was for his 'expenses'.

I said he wasn't such a bad guy. I didn't say he was an angel.

And Tilly told me yesterday that Mark has now invested the two million for Martha's Wish in a way that is quite helpful to his own fund, as well as offering a great deal for the charity.

And Patience is none the wiser.

All faces are saved.

At some point he'll have to explain my absence, but I'm sure he'll think of something.

When Tilly was here, I told her where my old diaries are hidden in the Battersea house. She's read them through now, and I've asked her to post them on to me, so that I can finally face them and start to figure it all out for myself.

'In a way, it's all The French Shit's fault,' she said to me when she called yesterday.

'What do you mean?'

'Well, although you were clearly anorexic right from the start, you were a driven and brilliant and adventurous girl — and I know from seeing it in so many girls at school that sometimes that goes hand in hand with eating disorders. But all of that good stuff was pushed out of you when he raped you, wasn't it, Mum? The French Shit put you in a box that you've never quite escaped from.'

That sort of took my breath away. I'd never thought of it like that. I'd always put everything that happened down as my own making.

Perhaps, then, that absolution of thinking of myself as a victim is still open to me?

* * *

Tills assures me she understands. She just needs time to absorb it all. And when she has, she will try to explain it to her father, although I have asked her not to tell him where I am.

Not yet.

He's still very upset, she says.

I feel so sorry for him, for all I put him through. All these years he thought he was looking after someone else, entirely. He was completely mistaken about the nature of the bird he kept in that gilded cage.

But what he had, in fact, was a girl caught in stasis, frozen in free-fall from everything that had happened — here in Ikaria, in Athens, and yes, Tilly's right, in Marseille.

But now Beattie's gone, out of the picture, dead, washing around in the currents somewhere out there — Giorgos checks daily and as yet there are no reports of any bodies washed up.

I feel I've landed, and the jolt has allowed the real Emma to wake up.

And this Emma can't believe that Kate allowed herself to live like that all those years.

I don't know if Mark would ever be able to bear the real Emma James, aged fifty.

We'll have to see what happens.

I'm just glad the money's back — especially the Martha's Wish money. Apart from Jake, that's the part out of all of this that I feel the worst about.

I don't feel bad about Beattie, though.

No.

I feel proud.